WAGTAIL

BRIGHT LIGHTS BOOK ONE

Ian Atkinson

Published in 2023 by Ian Atkinson

ISBN: 978-1-913898-80-9

A Catalogue record for this book is available from the British Library.

Front Cover image: 'Waggy' courtesy of Andrew Brown

Dedicated to Eric Atkinson

27/09/1929 – 03/08/2023

Contents

My heart leaps up when I behold
A rainbow in the sky:
So was it when my life began;
So it is now I am a man;
So be it when I shall grow old,
Or let me die!
The child is father of the man;
And I could wish my days to be
Bound each to each by natural piety.

William Wordsworth 'My Heart Leaps Up' (1802)

Little trotty wagtail he waded in the mud
And left his little footmarks trample where he would
He waded in the water-pudge and waggle went his tail
And chirrupt up his wings to dry upon the garden rail

John Clare From 'Little Trotty Wagtail'
Poems of the Epping Forest / Northampton Period (1849)

If you leave the Bright Lights and travel east on the bypass for about ten minutes, turn sharp right into 'the lanes' then drive on unmarked and unlit roads between tall hedgerows until you think you are lost, you'll see a small turning on the right, or maybe the left if you really were lost, with a cattle-grid across the entrance and a sandstone pillar at either side, one of them ivy-clad. You'll likely miss the turning first time and have to turn around, either up or down the road. Over the cattle-grid, on the right is a gatehouse, also made of sandstone.

The narrow track is tarmacked and cuts for half a mile through Hawksheads, a large area of mixed woodland said to be haunted by the mad monk, who prowls the woods at night and carries a lantern, and is also invisible and hurls breeze blocks a hundred feet into the air, according to a local jobbing-builder who drinks in the Black Cock.

In the centre of the wood stands Hawksheads House, a large, derelict property, with a cobbled courtyard and a maze of crumbling outbuildings, a risky playground for idle children.

A short way past the house the tarmac peters out and the lane becomes strangled by grass and brambles and is demoted to a mere footpath, which meanders on for a further mile, past the old sand quarry, under the railway bridge, and on into the village of Yelland.

PART ONE

Good Friday 12th of April 1968

The world was in turmoil. It had been eight days since the assassination of Martin Luther King Jnr. In eight days' time Enoch Powell would deliver his infamous 'Rivers of Blood' speech. A generation was in the grip of political fervour and was venting its anger at social and racial injustice. There were sit-in protests, sit-down protests, protest marches and protest songs. There were teach-ins and love-ins, there were anarchists and loyalists, ETA, the IRA, the UVF and the UDA, the Black Panthers, the Red Army Faction, Khmer Rouge and FARC.

There was lsd and marijuana, flowers in guns at the Pentagon. Manson had yet to burst the hippy bubble. There were civil rights and gay rights, black rights, black power, the peace movement, the feminist movement. In the land of the free, citizens were being routinely beaten and worse by those whose official function it was to protect them, and the Cold War continued to threaten global destruction.

None of which mattered to me, John Woods, as I jumped out of bed, dressed, brushed, swilled, spat, and thundered three at a time down the stairs of a cottage in Yelland, a small village nestled in a fold of the Upson Downs.

* * *

It was a glorious spring morning and there was no school for a week. Lenny and me were off to scour the district for birds' nests and had to get an early start so that Swifty and his gang wouldn't see us and follow. It makes me laugh now when I think about it. Oh, no! It's Swifty's gang!

Andrew Swift was a playground bully who wound up married, mortgaged and obese. He still lives on Railway Terrace and drinks Tuesday and Friday nights in the Black Cock with his daft builder mate.

They were still adding to their egg collections and they always took the whole clutch. Lenny and me shared a collection that we kept at my house, (a box of abortions, my father said), until we saw the light.

* * *

With the express aim of not exercising them, the RSPB had secured the shooting rights to an area of reedbed and lagoons a few miles away and had erected hides that had opened to the public a couple of years earlier.

Lenny and me became part of the furniture in the hides and were taken under the wing of the warden who took a shine to us and took us along as helpers on early morning netting and ringing expeditions.

We went mist-netting amongst the reeds for small birds and cannon-netting for waders on the coast. I once held a purple sandpiper in my hands at midnight on a wind-battered skeer and when it had been identified, measured and weighed, and its leg was ringed, I let it go and it wouldn't fly away. It just stood there and looked at me, and as the busy torch beams swept the shore, I noticed others; dunlin, turnstone, knot, sanderling, all standing around, fully processed, in the departure lounge, watching the goings-on around the dancing torchlights. Lenny and me had seen the light too, and when binoculars had appeared under the tree the previous Christmas the transformation was complete.

* * *

It took us all night to break fifty-three eggs and each gave as much in its destruction as it had in its discovery. We took it in turns, the smallest first, the wren's tiny speckled orb, transported home snugly and safely in its moss-lined shotgun cartridge, then carefully blown, squashed in an instant under a hesitant index finger.

As we worked our way to the largest, we reminisced and relived each find, the location, even the weather.

'It was pissing it down when we found that.'

'Yeah, remember, you sank in the swamp.'

'And you nearly fell out of that tree when that owl flew out of that hole and then that bull chased us.'

'That mistle thrush knocked my hat off and you fell in the river getting to that dipper's nest and only one side of your body got wet and I couldn't stop laughing.'

I remember Lenny rubbed his shoulder as we approached the sparrowhawks' blotched beauty, the shoulder he had broken doing his Tarzan act in the giant pine the sparrowhawks called home. When the time came to break the last egg, that of the mute swan – a huge cask of putrid fluid snatched from a defunct nest which had successfully produced the six cygnets which floated nearby as the angry cob surged towards us and mounted the bank and chased us from its territory – we dismantled it together. It gave the whole collection the smell of bleach and sulphur.

* * *

Mum was sitting at the kitchen table and as I made my entrance she jolted and slopped some of her coffee. She was in her dressing gown and her face was pale and her eyes red and puffy. She shushed me as she mopped the spill with her sleeve and pulled a face and rolled her eyes and brought the steaming mug to her lips and blew.

She watched as I grabbed my boots from under the stairs and took my jacket and binoculars from a hook on the back of the door and draped them over the chair. I dropped the boots to the floor and sat sideways at the table to put them on. When I'd finished, I shrugged into my jacket and hung the bin's in their case around my neck. I turned and put my hands on the table. The clock ticked loudly from the wall, drowning out the Bush radio that was singing like a goldcrest from its perch on the windowsill.

'Are you alright, Mum?' I said.

She smiled thinly and said yes. 'Yes, I'm fine,' she lied. 'I just couldn't sleep, that's all. Your father's having a well-earned lie-in this morning,' she said, but I knew they were his words, not hers. 'I'm fine, honestly,' she whispered, and we sat, like arm-wrestlers, me and my unhappy mother, while the Englishman whose castle this was had his well-earned lie-in, snoring deeply, his sour exhalations setting the tassels on the lampshade swinging, his hangover biding its time.

My father was an angry, short man with a shorter temper and a liking for drink. He suffered no fools and could see the fool in everyone. He'd spent his entire working life as a process worker in a detergents factory on an industrial estate a mile beyond the Bright Lights and to hear him talk you'd have thought that he was the linchpin of British industry.

'Where are you off to at this time anyway?' she brightened.

'No school, and up at seven o'clock?'

'I'm meeting Lenny,' I said, and I went on to tell her about the census. 'We're going to record the nests of all the birds in Britain,' I announced, and she managed a real smile.

'Who is? You and Lenny?'

* * *

I told her that the census was being organised by the British Trust for Ornithology and that every birdwatcher in the country was taking part and it was going to take five years. I took a brand-new notebook from the pocket of my jacket and opened it. On the inside cover was the word NESTS written diagonally from bottom left to top right and blocked out in solid black biro. The pages had all been neatly partitioned into sections of varying width, which, I explained, were for date, time, species, location, nest contents, and one for notes of special interest, headed NOSI.

As she leafed through the book I told her about the cards I'd collected from the chairman of the local birdwatching society, cards for recording all this data, one for each nest, and about the Ordnance Survey map I'd bought because the location of every nest had to be given as a grid reference.

I reached for the book and took it from her hand and said I had to get going and she watched and smiled as I slipped it into my top pocket. My hair was all over the place and she reached over and tried to tidy it with the flat of her hand. I pulled away and stood and walked around the table and gave her a hug.

'I've got to go Mum,' I said. She went to put the kettle on again and I paused in the doorway and looked back. 'You're not going to leave us are you Mum?' I asked.

'No. No of course I'm not,' she lied again. 'Now get yourself off. Lenny will be waiting.'

* * *

Marjory Woods watched her son leave and took her coffee and sat back at the table. John had always been fascinated by birds, loved to watch them, even the everyday things, *especially* the everyday things, and she would often catch him transfixed by a chaffinch or a sparrow. As a small child, at the zoo he would gaze disinterestedly at the caged parrots in all their finery, and though his child's eyes would widen at the sheer size of the vultures and eagles, he would soon lose interest, preferring to watch the ducks on the pond or the blue tits on the feeder outside the cafeteria.

More recently, however, she had begun to think his interest was becoming an obsession, like a cuckoo that was threatening to evict all other interests from his mind, becoming more demanding as it grew.

Last month he had landed home from school sporting a black eye and with a nasty cut to his top lip. He had been attacked by a fellow member of the football team for deserting his post to investigate some movement in the canopy of a nearby tree, allowing the opposition to score the winning goal. Marjory was horrified.

'That's still no reason to— ' she started, but he cut her off.

'Mum, I'm the goalie,' he said.

He had started to draw birds too, and Marjory had been surprised to see that, although he seemed to have problems with scale and some of the finer detail, the drawings were really rather good. She was reminded of the recent parents' evening, where, though the consensus was that John had a winning charm and was obviously a popular lad, when it came to his work, only the art teacher, Mr. Swan, had had anything positive to say about his future prospects.

This census seemed to have him all fired up. She'd never seen him so excited, or so enthusiastic. Or so organised. Maybe it would be the start of something. Maybe it would help with his schoolwork. Maybe it would help him to grow up.

* * *

Marjory Finch met Frank Woods at a dance in the Co-operative Hall in the Bright Lights. He was just back from doing his National Service. He'd been posted somewhere far-flung, he said. He had intense blue eyes and a square jaw, like Dan Dare, and he swept her off her feet, literally, throwing her around the dance-floor and strutting his stuff in his brogues and his drainpipes and his Slim Jim tie.

It was the night of the Queen's Coronation, and by the end of her first year on the throne, baby John would be getting ready to make his entry into the world. Frank and his 'slap and tickle.' She couldn't remember the last time there had been any tickle.

She imagined the intervening years had passed more quickly for the Queen. Or was she, too, just waiting for the kids to leave home so that she could follow them out of the door?

* * *

Heavy footsteps crossed the landing and a flock of birds took flight in her thorax. She was up early again today, driven from the room by relentless snoring and the stench of flatulence. He couldn't have just a couple of drinks, had to get 'steaming' or what was the point? And he was such an angry drunk. Truth be told he was an angry sober too, and although he often cursed, he was worse when he was drunk, louder, and even swore in front of John.

Marjory had made sure she was in bed by the time he got home and pretended to be asleep, but he woke her anyway. Someone had annoyed him in the pub again. 'Got on my fuckin' tits,' as he put it. This time it had been a young man with his hair in a ponytail and a gold sleeper in his ear.

'What's the world coming to?' he fumed. 'It's turning to fucking rat shit. I'm telling you. You can't tell the blokes from the birds. Worst thing they ever did, getting rid of National Service.'

Upstairs, a tap was running. She got up and relit the hob and put coffee in a cup. There was a prolonged breaking of wind. More tea, vicar? Did he still say that, she wondered, even when there was no one there to impress?

* * *

Frank Woods had a crushing hangover. The lad had woken him, again, slamming the back door on his way out.

He leaned on the sink and looked at the mirror. Fucking toothpaste everywhere. How can one person make so much mess?

He swilled his face and dragged his fingers through his hair. He thought about staying up, but Marjory always had plenty to be getting on with. He had nothing spoiling, so he'd have another hour in bed.

The next time he looked at the clock it was eleven. He swung his legs off the bed and got dressed and went to the bathroom. He stood and peed. The headache was still lurking and a cold sweat was prickling his brow, but it was nothing that wouldn't be cured by a fry-up and the hair of the dog.

* * *

'I don't know what you've been eating.' He sat across from Marjory and picked up his coffee. 'But that bedroom stinks.'

She didn't answer. From Dan Dare to Desperate Dan. She got up and lit the grill and took some bread from the bread bin.

'I suppose you'll want some breakfast.'

'Oh, come on, I'm only joking. Where's your sense of humour?'

'Will toast do?'

'I suppose so, at a push. Fry us a couple of eggs though, eh?'

Marjory put the frying pan on the hob. 'Are we doing anything today? It's Good Friday. I thought we might do something, you know, go somewhere nice. I did mention it.'

He lit a cigarette and drew the smoke deep. 'Well I wasn't planning on it,' he said. He blew the smoke floorward. 'I thought I'd go to the Cock for a couple of pints, but tell you what, I'll meet you halfway. You stay here and get the dinner on and meet me in the pub about half one.'

Marjory cracked a second egg into the pan. 'But it's Sunday hours today, they close at two o'clock.'

'I know, it's criminal. You'll have to get on to the government.'

Marjory buttered the toast and started basting the eggs. Frank opened the paper and cocked an ear to the radio.

'Hey, turn it up Marjory, it's our song.'

Marjory's heart sank. She turned the dial and Sam Cooke's 'Only Sixteen' filled the room. She put the eggs on the toast, poured the tea and sat at the table to wait for Frank to charm her again, as he always did, with his own horribly offensive take on the lyrics.

He didn't let her down, and as he sang through a wad of

half-chewed toast and egg, she was reminded of all the previous occasions; dances, weddings, christenings, when the song had come on and he'd felt obliged to give everyone his own very unique and sordid take on the history of their courtship.

* * *

Fred and Noreen Fields had managed the Yelland Post Office and shop for twenty years and had reached middle age before finally giving up any hope of a child of their own, and adopting Lenny. He 'got away with murder' and would stand contrite whilst being quietly told off and would re-offend the minute their backs were turned.

Postmaster Fred was a jolly little man who had a 'chimbley pot' on top of his house and almost crashed his car under an 'arctic' lorry. He said things were 'ridickerless' and thought anything that was an anti-climax was a 'damp squid'. His greying hair was slicked back with Brylcreem, giving it the appearance of plastic. He wore buttoned-up cardigans and razor sharp 'slacks' and appeared to be breaking in dentures for a giant.

Fred took pride in his ability to carry out any number of tasks simultaneously; pass the time of day and listen to his customers' problems, furrow his brow and purse his lips when appropriate, dispense advice, congratulations and condolences, and still do his job and keep the queue moving. He was a true people person. They both were. They were regular churchgoers and when not working in the Post Office Noreen arranged whist-drives and jumble sales and flowers for the parish church. She wore sensible shoes and pleated skirts and wore her hair up in a bun and was so thin that she was, according to Fred, 'like a skellington'.

Lenny was my best friend back then. Every child in the village knew every other but we had no other friends outside school. We were inseparable from about the age of four and we shared everything. One day we would even share a woman. Her name was April Meadows and she became a kind of catchphrase, a secret code word. 'I could go an April Meadows' we would say, or, more subtly, 'fancy an April frolic?'.

Joseph Leonard Fields. Now, when I hear it said in full, I expect to hear it followed by, 'you have been found guilty of ...'

* * *

Lenny was standing at the side of the Post Office with his back and the sole of a trainer against the wall. He had his binoculars around his neck and the case hanging at his side and his hair was covering one eye. He was lighting two cigarettes and keeping his free eye on the window in case a parent was watching. He couldn't wait, had to live dangerously, for both of us, even though we both knew that the worst that was going to befall Lenny if he got caught was the dreaded telling off.

My father caught me smoking and gave me a good hiding and made me smoke ten fags one after the other and I managed eight before I was sick.

Lenny stole sweets from the Post Office for our treks, sherbet flying saucers and swizzles, parma violets, squirrel horn mini midget gems, cherry lips. He passed me a cigarette and pulled a curly-wurly and a mixture of fruit salads and black jacks from his binoculars case and slipped them into mine. I cupped the cigarette in my palm until we were between the towering privet hedges of the ginnel that leads to the sand quarry and on to Hawksheads before bringing it to my mouth and Lenny took the piss.

My father believed you should never lie to a child; your own or anyone else's. I was left in no doubt from the off that Santa Claus did not exist and that the presents I opened on Christmas morning had been paid for by the sweat of his brow and that the parents of all the other kids were lying to them.

In the ploughed field adjacent to the quarry we had our first find, a lapwing nest with three eggs. After some discussion we put one stone on top of another, ten paces from the nest when facing a chosen tree or landmark in the distance, and logged it in the book. We sat on a five-bar gate and I ate my curly-wurly while Lenny had a Bar Six.

Likewise, the tooth fairy. He said that you may as well take those coins and use them to chisel the remaining teeth from the gape of every child in the country.

The birch wood provided the next three finds; a wren's nest, built but unlined amongst the hanging roots of a toppled tree, its footprint flooded with black, peaty water. On the grassy side of the roots, a robin's moss and grass structure with two mottled eggs, and a magpie's empty craze of sticks less than eight feet from the ground in a birch tree. We sat by the gate to Hawksheads and I wrote them in the book.

The walk through Hawksheads turned up a song thrush applying the finishing touches to the mud lining of its nest in a hole in a dry-stone wall. We flushed a pair of woodcock as we searched out a dry path through the peaty birch but there was no nest and we made our way up the lane to the sand quarry.

The quarry had been deserted for only five years and nature hadn't made much headway with the job of reclaiming the landscape. A small pool of water had settled in the quarry floor and some grass had taken hold, but that was about it.

We found a blackbird sitting on its nest on a shelf in the

weighbridge office. It flew to the windowsill and stood and agitated as we counted the eggs – five – and had returned to its nest before we closed the office door. Once outside we stood in front of the quarry face and I wrote up Mrs Blackbird's chart.

Lenny had scratched his hand getting to the magpies' nest and he kept on whingeing and wouldn't shut up about it, so we decided to call it a day and headed home for something to eat and so that poor Lenny could get a plaster and a magic kiss.

* * *

Sand martins began to colonise the sand cliffs as soon as the quarry ceased production, a few at first, growing to hundreds over the years, digging their burrows deep into the sharp sand. Soon they would be back from Africa, but for now the quarry was deserted; a puddle, lots of sand and an ugly pile of rotting steel girders and hoppers.

But, from a hawthorn thicket behind the quarry, ivy was already sending tendrils across thirty yards of sand, tendrils that would one day take hold of one steel stanchion, then another, and another, and would go on to smother the two large sand hoppers that were used to load the thousands of lorries that blazed a dusty trail to and from this isolated spot when the motorway came through and the quarry was a whorl of activity, and turn them into twin pillars of green rising from the sand.

The small pool of muddy water in the quarry bottom became established over the years and grew in breadth and depth. Marsh grasses and yellow and purple iris flourished and formed a verdant belt around its rim, completely hiding the pale-blue, 1948 Ford Anglia, abandoned there in the early sixties and with only its rusting roof visible today above the vegetation, and then only from the lip of the quarry.

Frogs and newts appeared and in their turn attracted herons. Moorhens turned up and built their nests amongst the reeds and, slowly but surely, were joined by some of their smaller cousins, reed buntings, yellowhammers and sedge warblers.

The land around the quarry came to life too. Skylarks and meadow pipits came to sing above their nests among the tussock grass, and the outlying stony ground was home to sand lizards and in summer was tinged with the pink of orchids. Spiky gorse took root against the hedge at the top of the slope and provided nurseries for linnets and chaffinch and long-tailed tits. Sadly, today there are no longer any martins; they have disappeared, along with the lizards and most of the newts.

* * *

By summer's end we had wandered for hundreds of miles up and down rivers and through fir woods, across farmland and limestone pavements and salt marsh and had filled out cards for more than two hundred nests covering over forty species. We learned the value of patient observation. We watched a whinchat for hours before the male bird let his guard down and led us to his beautifully well-hidden nest down a small tunnel in long grass amongst a thicket of furze.

We learned to tickle heavy undergrowth and bramble patches with a switch of elder and watch for the exit of a sitting blackcap, whitethroat or willow warbler.

We soon found that the biggest problem with relocating nests came in the country lanes, nests like those of the robin and the dunnock, low down in hedgerows and undergrowth and hidden by the sudden rush of growth during May and June, a total change in the landscape, and we sometimes had to give up. 'Ten paces from the coke can,' but where's the coke can?

We visited some nests four or five times, some less often, and we recorded their progress, good and bad. A nest empty but for a helping of feather scale meant the young had fared well, but the smell of dead flesh touched deep in a copper beech hedge lingered on the fingers for the rest of the day and meant that they had not.

One dunnock's nest, which had contained five deep blue gemstones on the first visit, was later found to contain only one egg; a large, off-white duck egg; Swifty and his gang had been around.

'A duckoo's egg,' Lenny said, and he drove me mad for hours with plays-on-words and rubbish poems using duck, cuckoo and dunnock.

* * *

During the autumn we went to the RSPB reserve on regular ringing missions with the warden, Jeff, and his assistant, Mike. There was an old two-berth caravan at the edge of the reserve and Lenny and me used to ride there on our bikes with our sleeping bags and stay overnight in the caravan to be ready for an early start.

At first light we set the mist nets in narrow ginnels cut through the reedbed, pushing the bamboo poles into the soft earth and unfurling the fine mesh traps, and then retreated to the hide to wait. Everything we needed for the job was already in the hide; scales, rings, pliers, drawstring cloth bags to carry the birds back to be ringed, and, of course, a large flask of coffee.

I can remember being given the choice of removing a tiny blue tit or a kestrel from the net and getting it into a bag. I took one look at the kestrel's fearsome beak and talons and saw the blue tit's tiny mandibles and decided there was no contest. I have never forgotten the blood-blisters that peppered my hands before I had the most fearsome creature alive in the bag, or Lenny's smug grin and stupid chuckling as he casually unrolled an apparently sleeping falcon and popped it in a bag.

To the experienced warden and his assistant most of the birds netted on these outings were the usual suspects. Some, like robins, dunnocks and wagtails, were residents. Of the migratory birds, most were species that were to be expected at that time of year.

Occasionally though, a bird turned up that had even the experts scratching their heads and reaching for their field guides. Such a bird appeared one windy morning in September.

It was a nondescript looking thing and hadn't been recognised as an early Titian or a lost Picasso as it was removed from the net, and it was bundled into a communal bag, as if it were just another bird, and taken back to the hide.

It was only when Jeff retrieved it and prepared to take its statistics that he began to get excited and opinions were exchanged between the two men concerning the different characteristics of two particular species of warbler.

I had no idea how complicated it could be. The warden was sure from the start that the bird in hand was a barred warbler, a rare vagrant from Asia and the first record in northern England for umpteen years, and so it proved to be. It was confirmed as a young bird by the colour of its eyes and its similarity to a garden warbler but with a marginally longer tail!

To be honest it was only their excitement that got us going. We still hadn't got over the novelty, the thrill of holding a wild bird in our hands, any wild bird, just common stuff like a blackbird or a robin. When I held a male redstart in my hand

I thought it was the most beautiful thing I had ever seen as it sat quietly and waited its turn.

The excitement in the hide that day was palpable and was contagious. Something had been ignited, and when the birds had all been released and the nets dismantled we sat and finished off the coffee, and Jeff and Mike reminisced about the great bird fall of 1964 when a town centre in Suffolk was brought to a standstill by millions of migrating birds forced by adverse weather conditions to come ashore and land, and how people in the street found themselves being used as perches by an array of rarities, resting on their shoulders and their heads, and we sat, transfixed, like small children being read Peter Pan or Alice in Wonderland at bedtime.

Back in the caravan we lay awake and went through my bird book, picking out birds we would like to see and looking at the maps to see where we could see them. We were birders now, no question. Although a barred warbler may not have looked like much, it sounded good to us.

* * *

We stayed in a lot that first winter. We went to the reserve a few times and saw some new species, but the days were short and the holidays few and far between at that time of year.

A solitary black-tailed godwit turned up, a real rarity back then, and birders came from all around to see it. You could go to the same place today and see hundreds, a thousand black-tailed godwits, carpeting the shallows, at rest with their beaks tucked beneath their wings, see them put to fright by a patrolling peregrine, hear them calling, a silver cloud wheeling against a pure blue sky, and not believe what a thrill it used to be to see just one.

We saw some new species a bit closer to home too, like the redwing and fieldfare that spread out in small flocks across the countryside, birds we'd seen before without giving them a name – they didn't nest here so we weren't interested before – and the waxwings that invaded the churchyard, all here to pillage the winter food supplies of resident birds like the mistle thrush, which defended their resources gallantly but were no match for the mob-handed Viking invaders.

A party of delicate snow buntings graced the saltmarshes for a few weeks, but mostly we stayed in. I liked to draw, birds mainly, and by the time we found the first nest of 1969, in mid-February; a mistle thrush with three eggs in a holly tree in the school grounds, all of my posters of bands and footballers had been torn down and replaced with my own drawings. A sparrowhawk's citrine eye stared down from the ceiling. An osprey carried what could be a fish, in what could be its feet, across the bedroom door. I could never draw the attachments, like the fish. Or the feet. But it was most definitely an osprey.

I took up painting; I took *to* it as well. I painted a kingfisher that I was particularly proud of. It was the archetypal kingfisher picture; a bird, with a fish, on a 'No Fishing' sign, by a river. I thought it was the best thing I'd done up until then. I put the finishing touches to it and put it on the wall and when Lenny saw it he said 'Wow, that kingfisher's brilliant.'

I wasn't used to receiving praise, from anyone really, well, maybe Mum and Mr. Swan, but anyway I managed something like cheers, glad you like it, and he went closer and admired the detail on the plumage and the depth of the colour.

'You've even got the water just right,' he said, 'it's flowing. It must've taken you ages.' He came back and sat on the bed and we were quiet for a minute or two, then he said,

'Why is it eating a clothes peg?'

* * *

We reached the two hundred mark again in the second year. The star find was a grasshopper warbler's nest with five eggs hidden in thick undergrowth on the birch-wood floor. We'd heard the high-pitched, ratchety song of the male and knew it was there, but we looked and could find nothing. In the end we found it by accident. I saw the bird slip away from the nest and scurry along the ground like a mouse. We'd caught one or two in the mist nets at the reserve, but it was a rare bird and we were super-chuffed to find its nest.

We went to check the nest's progress early the next Sunday morning. As I left the house a song thrush was tugging comically on a stubborn lobworm, stretching it to ridiculous proportions as it tried to prise it from its burrow in the lawn.

Lenny was waiting by the Post Office as arranged and we talked excitedly and headed for the birch wood, eager to have another look at our amazing find.

The sun had barely risen above the horizon and the low-lying birch wood was still wrapped in a blanket of ground mist. The tree canopy formed green islands in a sea of wispy-white and we retreated to the sand quarry to wait for the sun to burn off the mist.

A continuous stream of sand martins was coming and going to their nests, and a pair of pied wagtails had built a nest in the glove compartment of the old Ford Anglia and had four healthy, noisy chicks. The blackbirds had nested in the weighbridge office again and five tufty-headed chicks with bright yellow gapes called for food. We were sitting on the outside step of the weighbridge office completing the log when we heard voices. There was no mistaking Swifty's rat-a-tat laugh so we dashed to the back of the building, but it was too late. We'd been spotted, and within a minute Swifty and two of his gang were upon us.

The Crowe brothers, Andrew and David, were identical twins, almost impossible to tell apart.

I'd slipped the book into my back pocket and we started making small talk, but Swifty had already seen it.

'What's the book for?' he asked.

'Nothing,' I answered, weakly. One of the Crowes moved behind me and snatched the book from my pocket and threw it to Swifty. He opened it and looked inside. He looked at me and screwed up his face.

'Nests?' he mocked. 'What the fuck?'

I reached for the book.

'Give it back,' I said, and a Crowe grabbed me from behind and got me in a headlock. Lenny went to help me and was punched and thrown to the ground by the other twin who continued to stand over him with clenched fists. I tried to struggle free but my Crowe tightened his grip and I felt my face turn red and my eyes bulge as Swifty riffled through the book trying to make sense of what it contained.

'So,' he said. 'Let me get this right, you're finding nests and writing them in a book? Fucking knobheads. Fucking queers.' He turned the next page and read aloud. '30th of May.' He glanced up from the page. 'Hey, that's today lads.'

Lenny's guard turned his head.

'What's it say, Swifty?'

'There's a blackbird's nest in there somewhere lads,' he said, pointing at the office. I was released and thrown to the sand and the brothers ran into the building. The cock blackbird flew out through a broken window uttering his frantic alarm calls. Swifty continued leafing through the book as his henchmen's shouts and mock cooing noises echoed in the empty building.

The bird species were written clearly enough, but most of the nest locations were in code or were abbreviated and he had no chance of working out exactly where most of them were. Luckily, grasshopper warbler was too long to fit in its allocated space, so I had entered it as G. Warbler and had written no location. The nest was only a few yards from a distinctive fallen tree and for fine tuning I had stuck a well-chewed Bazooka Joe at eye level in a fork of the birch tree nearest to the nest. I had already decided what I would say, assuming he got that far and didn't lose interest and tear up the book. In the end he beat me to it.

'Where's the garden warbler?' he demanded.

'In the bramble patch by the gate to Hawksheads,' I said.

The twins came back laughing and one was carrying the blackbird's nest, complete with young. He walked towards the small pool in the quarry floor.

'I wonder if they like sailing,' he said. I jumped up and ran at him, and he turned and threw the nest over my head to his brother. He caught the nest, but the chicks had fallen out and they sat, cheeping desperately in the dust. 'Aw, bless them,' he said, and he crushed them underfoot, one at a time, in a sickening game of hopscotch.

I totally lost the plot. I turned and ran at the nest-thrower with my head down and I hit him in the solar plexus and we went sprawling into the pool. It was the first time in my life that I had known blind fury. I knelt on his shoulders and pummelled his head and face with both fists, swinging my arms like bolas. I was screaming bastard, bastard, bastard, and

I carried on punching until I was felled by a kick to the side of the head from the other twin that sent me toppling sideways into the water. A second kick came in and I caught his foot in my hands and twisted. He rolled through the air and landed hard on his back and lay winded in the shallow water.

The first twin had crawled to dry land and was standing with his back against the old Ford Anglia, which stood at the water's edge, like an animal at a waterhole. His face was a Jackson Pollock of mud, blood, and snot and I remember looking from one twin to the other and thinking, now I can tell you apart you pair of bastards. I was hyperventilating but I managed to stand. I started back towards the weighbridge as the bloodied twin walked unsteadily to his brother and helped him to his feet.

Lenny was in a foetal position on the ground and was trying to shield his face and his balls as Swifty kicked him repeatedly in the head and ribs. I let out a primal scream and ran at Swifty, but when I was a couple of yards from him he turned and stepped to one side and caught me full in the face with a haymaker that broke my nose and left me flat on my back. Swifty turned his attention back to Lenny, who was standing and nursing his ribs. I brought my knee to my chest and thrust the sole of my boot into the back of Swifty's knee and his leg buckled and he collapsed to the earth like he'd been hamstrung. Now it was Swifty's turn to cover up as Lenny went berserk, dancing around him, kicking frantically and howling like a shaman. I thought he might kill him and I stood and dragged him away.

'Come on Len,' I said. 'Let's go.'

Swifty sat on the ground looking dazed and didn't try to get up.

The nests book was lying open and face down on the weighbridge. My hands were shaking as I picked it up and checked the damage. The pages were coming away from the spine, but it wasn't too bad. At least it was still legible. The twins were still leaning on the car and I hoped they wouldn't notice the wagtails' nest.

As we trudged up the slope to the top of the quarry they started shouting; 'wait till we get you at school;' 'you cunts are dead,' stuff like that.

* * *

We hardly spoke a word on the way home. Lenny was limping and his face was a mess. He had two black eyes and his cheek bone was purple and swollen. His ear lobe had been torn from the side of his head and blood had run down his neck and under his collar.

I was soaked to the skin and my left ear was red hot and still ringing. My front tooth was loose and my mouth felt like Plug's from the Bash Street Kids. Worst of all, blood from my nose had stained the front of my shirt and my jeans. They were my brand-new brushed denim Sea Dogs and I hoped I'd be able to sneak into the house and upstairs without my father seeing them.

We walked through the ginnel into Yelland and as we approached the Post Office Lenny started singing Manfred Mann's 'Box on the Run'. He did it all the time. He knew it wound me up.

'It's fox,' I said, 'A fucking box can't run.'

* * *

I followed Lenny into the house. Noreen broke down crying when she saw the state of him. When he refused to tell her what had really happened – '*I fell over*' – she looked at me. 'I don't suppose there's any point asking you,' she said.

Fred clacked his dentures.

'You both fell over, did you?' he said, sarcastically.

Noreen cleaned us both up and I asked her if I could borrow a pair of Lenny's jeans and would she wash mine.

'These are my new ones,' I said. She ruffled my hair with her palm and gave Fred a knowing look and tut-tutted sympathetically and brought me a clean pair.

Fred said he'd take Lenny to Bright Lights General to have his ear sewn back on to his head. I decided to go with them in case my nose needed straightening and to put off explaining myself to my father.

As we left, Noreen asked if I was going to be alright. I knew she wasn't talking about my nose.

* * *

The Accident and Emergency department was quiet. The receptionist tightened her lips and shook her head as we approached the desk.

'Been in the wars,' she said. It was more an observation than a question, but Fred answered anyway.

'Aaa-ye,' he said, resignedly. 'Blummin lads eh?'

She took our details and told us doctor would be along in a minute but he was quicker than that. He took Fred and Lenny into a cubicle and swished the curtain. The receptionist looked over and smiled. I tried to smile back but my mouth was sore. Lenny yelped from behind the curtain and I heard Fred urge him to be brave. He wasn't, and he squealed like a piglet throughout. He had three stitches in his ear and then went off to have an x-ray on his knee.

After a painful examination the doctor decided my nose required no attention. I did however need a stitch in the corner of my mouth and left the hospital looking worse than I had when I got there. Lenny's knee was swollen but there were no bones broken.

On the journey home Lenny was in the front and I was sitting in the back behind Fred. No one was talking, even Fred, which was unusual for him. It was a warm day and he had his window down and his arm was getting the sun. In the wing mirror I could see the side of his face. He had his tongue behind his top set and had pushed them half an inch clear of his lips. Suddenly he clacked them back in. The exposure had dried his teeth and he couldn't slide his top lip over them. I could see him in the mirror, doing a Humphrey Bogart impression to free his lip. He eventually managed it with the help of a finger.

'So, come on,' he said. 'Now there's just us blokes here, what really happened?' When we didn't answer, he sneered. 'Fell over? Fell over what? A blummin cliff?' He caught my eye in the mirror and smiled at his wit. 'I'm assuming there was more than one of them,' he went on. We still didn't answer and he asked a few more questions, but Fred was easy to fob off and when he realised he wasn't going to get anywhere he gave up and we travelled quietly through the lanes for a while.

A buzzard was soaring on a thermal above Hawksheads and I craned my neck to prolong the view. Lenny sat and stared through the side window at the passing hedgerows. Fred was eyeing me in the rear-view mirror.

'I caught them Crowe lads stealing from the shop the other day,' he said, matter-of-factly. He kept his eyes on me. 'They're wrong'ns them two,' he went on. 'It was the way they went about it that struck me. They worked together. One tried to keep me talking while the other … well, you know. They slipped up though. They thought they were dealing with an ammercher.'

'What did you do?' Lenny asked. 'Did you call the police?'

'No, I just took the stuff off them. Well, I don't want to get a couple of young lads a criminal record over a few Black Jacks and a bar of Caramac.'

* * *

We'd gone out early that morning and it wasn't even one o'clock when I walked up our garden path. It seemed like a week since I'd watched the early bird struggling with its breakfast on the lawn. It was only a few hours.

I was hit by a wall of heat as I walked through the back door into the kitchen. I could smell a joint of beef roasting and saucepans were bubbling on the hobs. Mum was wearing a pinny and had her hair tied back and her sleeves rolled up. She had a pan lid in her left hand and was poking with a fork and peering through a cloud of steam.

'Leave the door open love,' she said, 'let some of this heat out.' I opened the door and next door's cat tried to come in. I made a barrier of my foot and Sooty turned laconically and sat outside like a shadow against the wall.

'Your Dad will be home soon and I've still got to—'

Mum freaked when she saw my face.

'Oh my God what happened to you?' She sat me down and cupped my face in her hands and examined my wounds. I told her we got in a fight with Swifty and his gang and I told her why. It wasn't telling tales. Fred and Noreen would have called Swifty's parents and the police and would only have made things worse. Mum might give them a Paddington hard stare in the street, but no more if I asked her not to. I told her that Lenny was worse off than me and smiled the best I could.

She calmed down and she asked me where my jeans were and I told her. She took my shirt and put some fluid on it from the cupboard and put it in the washing machine.

'Now go and get a clean one out of the airing cupboard. I'd better get cracking. He'll be home soon and I've still the gravy to make.'

* * *

It was quarter to three by the time he landed home and he was pissed. He swore at the cat as he came through the back door and swung his foot as an afterthought and lost his balance and had to steady himself on the door jamb. I was already at the table and Mum was plating vegetables she'd kept warm in the oven.

'They get my fucking back up,' he barked, as he took two awkward steps and slumped heavily into his chair across from me. At first I thought he meant cats.

'Fucking hippies,' he spat. 'Fucking druggies.'

The back door was still open and Mum stepped across and closed it. He hadn't noticed my face. He'd had an argument with Irish Bob and his wife, Ann, in the pub that had nearly come to blows at closing time.

Bob and Ann had no kids and he had his own plumbing business. Bob had long hair that he wore in a ponytail, and they dressed in all the hippy gear; collarless hemp shirts, paisley waistcoats, smock-tops and tie-dye harem pants, and they still went to all the festivals, but I know they never used anything stronger than weed, not anymore, anyway. In a year or two's time I would share the odd joint with them myself.

Mum put the plates on the table and sat down.

'And it's peace this, peace that, peace the other,' he moaned. 'Where's the Yorkshire pudding?' He held a slice of beef on the end of his fork and wagged it in front of Mum's face. 'Love and marriage. Roast beef and Yorkshire pudding,' he slurred. Mum was concentrating on her food. I watched as he struggled to hit his mouth with the meat. I could have stuck that fork under his ribs and done for him then and there.

The washing machine went onto the spin-cycle in the next room.

'Doing a wash on a Sunday?'

There was a fraught pause, but then his glassy eyes looked over the fork and he noticed my face.

'Hello,' he said, 'who's been doing my job? I'll have the union on 'em.' He laughed to himself. 'I hope you gave as good as you got.' Then it was back to *his* business. 'And then that fucking Archie Beech, the kitchen bloke, had to have his tuppence-worth,' he said, 'started sticking up for 'em. Fucking gobshite. He's as bad as his fucking brother, he is.' He was quiet for a few seconds, then went on. 'Lesley,' he said, in a mocking tone. 'What sort of name's that for a fucking bloke, eh? A fucking girl's name. I'm not surprised he couldn't hack the army.' His voice trailed off, he looked distant, deep in thought, then he changed tack. 'Anyway,' he said, 'I told that Archie, I said you're getting divorced so you're a right one to talk.'

Sometimes, in view of the way things turned out, I wonder if I'd have seen any reaction to this news in Mum's face had I been taking more notice.

We ate in silence for a minute, then, without raising her

eyes from her plate, Mum asked, 'how do you know he's getting divorced?'

He jerked his fork over his shoulder, spraying the fridge with gravy.

'Because he's in the pub telling anyone who'll listen, that's why.'

Mum looked up, surprised. 'What? He was telling the whole pub?'

'Well, not exactly, but he will eventually. It was my turn today. He came sidling onto the stool next to me and I had him in my ear for an hour or more. I don't go down the pub to listen to that shite. Besides, it's his private business.' He bundled another forkful into his mouth. 'I don't know,' he said, through a mouthful of sprouts, 'they have a few drinks and next you know they're crying on your fucking shoulder.'

'Well he probably thinks it's better out in the open,' Mum reasoned. 'You know, stop the gossips.' She got up and started to fill the kettle. 'Is he upset about it?'

'Upset? How would I know? Fucking fairy. He likely wasn't doing his bit in the bedroom.'

I felt a speck of gravy hit my eyelid. I mashed what was left of my dinner and scraped it into the smallest pile it would make.

'I've had enough,' I said.

* * *

As Neil Armstrong was making history with one giant leap for mankind, Lenny and me were being splattered with projectile shit and vomit from all directions as we rounded up the still-flightless young of a large colony of herring gulls for ringing.

We'd spent the night in the caravan and Jeff woke us at first light. After a quick coffee we jumped in the car and within an hour were standing on a remote shingle beach being buffeted by a warm easterly wind. Behind us were fifteen thousand breeding pairs of herring gulls.

Different bird species have different ways of protecting their nests from potential predators. As in everything in nature, there are extremes. A charging capercaillie is said to be a fearsome prospect, Scotland's equivalent of the mountain gorilla, and I know from experience how scary a protective mute swan can be. But they are the exceptions. At the other extreme some, like the moorhen, do absolutely nothing. When disturbed, a sitting moorhen will slip quietly from the nest and disappear underwater leaving barely a ripple, ensuring it lives to breed another day. It seems to be an effective strategy as I can't think of any permanent pond, canal or drainage dyke where they don't thrive.

Others, like the lapwing and the ringed plover, will swoop to usher you away or feign injury to divert your attention from nest or young. Most small birds rely on either camouflage, like the whinchat, or inaccessibility, like the woodpecker. In defence of its nest a mistle thrush may get in your face and a brooding mallard duck might extend her neck and angrily untie your shoelaces, but generally speaking, these are futile efforts.

Herring gulls are a different proposition altogether. The instant we climbed from the car we were harassed and harried by birds hitting us on the head and shoulders with their feet and their beaks. It was like being the victim of a frenzied kite attack.

On the beach Jeff and Mike got all the ringing gear out.

'Come on lads, let's get cracking,' Jeff said. He couldn't keep the smile from his face. 'We've about twenty thousand to get through.'

We believed him and looked at each other and at the scrarking craze of gulls in the air behind us.

The young were large, dowdy characters. They were standing around looking unconcerned and seemed as though they would easily be caught and picked up, which they were, but we didn't know about their secret weapons. They have two of them, one at each end. The instant it was caught, each young bird's first line of defence was to empty its stomach and bowel contents simultaneously on its captor as a swarm of adult birds did the same from above.

Jeff and Mike had known what was in store for us and thought it was hilarious, which it no doubt was to the casual observer, but the aerial assault from the huge adult birds was frightening. From a distance it must have looked comical, but on the front line it was carnage.

The job complete, as they packed away the ringing gear, we had a walk up the beach. Soon, the gulls began to thin out and we found ourselves in relative quiet. We crouched at the water's edge and let the ebb-tide spill over our toes and cleaned our boots and our hands and faces. We'd only had to catch a hundred or so but were covered in shit. We looked at each other's clothes and hair and we started laughing; 'imagine what we would have looked like if we *had* had to catch them all.' We ended up on our backs, kicking our legs in the air and struggling for breath when we thought about trying to find the last one, the only one without a ring on its leg.

* * *

We never saw much of Swifty for the rest of the summer, or any future summers come to that. He was a year older than us and had left school to start work as an apprentice plant-fitter at a local limestone quarry. Without Swifty, the twins had no interest in birds' nests and preferred to hang around town. They did leave one calling card though. The grasshopper warbler successfully raised its young, but only at the expense of a dunnocks' nest in the bramble patch by the gate to Hawksheads. We'd missed it during our search, and the next time we went that way we found a gaping hole in the brambles and the nest on a gate post where we were certain to find it.

* * *

I've never heard a scream like it before or since. The breeding season was over but we wanted to check the final outcome of a few nests. We'd just left the Post Office and were making for the ginnel when we heard it. It seemed to come from the direction of the school, and we turned back and legged it the hundred yards or so to the school gates.

In the goalmouth at the far end of the football field a group of people were standing over someone curled up and writhing on the grass. In the small crowd we could see one of the twins. They had given us a wide berth since the episode in the quarry. We moved closer to see what had happened.

As we approached, a woman with her hair in rollers ran from a nearby house and shouted that an ambulance was on its way. There was a lot of blood on the ground and we could see that the injured party was the other twin. He was in a foetal position and was whimpering like a beaten dog. He had both hands in his groin. A group of women were standing close by. One was on her haunches and had her hand on his head. A few yards away three men grimaced and shook their heads and tried not to look.

It was a few days before we found out the full horror of what had happened. The injured twin had shinned to the top of a goal post and was transferring his hands to the crossbar. The other twin decided it would be a good idea to pull on his legs. The climbing twin lost his grip and slid to the ground. The nets had been taken down at the start of the summer break, the retaining hooks, however, remained solidly in place, and it was these that had torn his scrotum from his body.

* * *

Early in 1970 Mum finally plucked up the courage to leave my father and went to stay with her sister in Oldham. He was at the pub when Aunty Mary and Uncle Brian came to pick her up, and when they saw Mum's bruises Uncle Brian said he wanted to go and give him what for but Mum said it would only make things worse.

She cried a lot and hugged me tight and I promised her that I'd be ok and we finally persuaded her to get in the car. Aunty Mary said I could go with them but Mum said what about school? I agreed with Mum but I was thinking about the census really – and the look on Uncle Brian's face.

In her absence my father began to drink even more than before and didn't let work get in the way of a drinking session. He became a fixture in the Black Cock every night of the week and at weekend lunchtimes.

I kept out of the way as much as possible. We wandered further afield than usual in search of nests and had a cracking year with over two hundred and fifty cards completed. One Saturday we found ourselves fifteen miles from home with darkness closing in. We set off back but after only a couple of miles we were knackered and decided to spend the night in a barn in the corner of a field by the Bright Lights canal.

The barn was a corrugated iron structure and the wind rattled the walls as we slept fitfully on a few bales of hay amid an assortment of farm machinery. At dawn I was woken by a brood of young swallows receiving breakfast from industrious parents. Lenny was nowhere to be seen. I counted the heads in the swallow's nest and wrote it in the book. They were well grown and would certainly have fledged by the time we came out this way again.

There were some outbuildings adjacent to the barn and I scoured them for nests. There was a robin's nest in an empty paint tin which was lying on its side on a windowsill. The nest was full of feather scale and I could hear the cheeping of the fledged young. I made a note of it and had a pee in the corner and went outside.

Lenny was thirty feet up a tree by the canal side and was looking into the stick structure of a carrion crow's nest. It had been taken over by a pair of kestrels and the unhappy male soared close by. I walked to the base of the tree and looked up, shielding my eyes from the early sun.

'There's five chicks,' he shouted. 'They're well-feathered. Hold your jacket out and I'll throw one down. We can keep it at your house.'

My neck was aching by the time I managed to convince Billy Casper that to take one would fly in the face of everything we were doing and he accepted grudgingly and made his way back to earth.

A few years earlier we had each taken a magpie chick from a brood of seven in Hawksheads. They made great pets. They were full of character and made a fuss of us when we got home from school, calling noisily and landing on our heads. Early the following year they both got the call of the wild and flew off. To this day, when I see a magpie in Hawksheads, I wonder if it's a descendent of Mickey or Maggie.

* * *

At school I was failing in every subject, except art, and was coming under pressure to find a job. One day, after a lunchtime gallon, my father rolled in from the pub and slapped the local rag down in front of me. He supported himself on the back of my chair and breathed fumes over me and belched loudly as he jabbed his finger at the situations vacant section and congratulated me on my choice of career.

An engineering company that made industrial laundry equipment in the Bright Lights was looking for school leavers to train as either welders or metal workers.

'That's more fucking choice than I ever had,' he said. 'So you can forget your fancy ideas about being a fucking poncy artist and learn a man's trade. You're not a fucking arse-bandit are you? Eh? A fucking shirt-lifter?'

'But I'm not a school leaver either,' I protested.

* * *

In the summer of 1970 Lenny and me were almost drowned on a visit to a seabird colony further up the coast. We were trying to navigate our way around the base of the towering sea-cliffs to a remote shingle beach that was nestled between the twin sandstone buttresses that made up the headland.

The easiest way to access the bay was by a cliff-top path, but we were fifteen and daft and we decided that, though it would be far quicker, the path would be laborious and no fun at all. Our way, not only would we get a great view of the seabird colony nesting on the cliffs, but there'd be lots of rock-pools to explore on the way.

But we were soon to discover that our plan had a major flaw.

We left the beach and started to negotiate the monolithic boulders that litter the slender shoreline; huge edifices bearing ornate carved signatures, some claiming to be centuries old.

Thirty feet from the cliff face the shore plummeted away and the sudden depth turned the sea a stunning cobalt-blue. As we jumped from boulder to boulder and squatted by rock pools blithely searching for fish and molluscs, the tide was steadily encroaching. The water had been gently lapping the rocks but was soon slapping them, and before long full-blown waves began to appear, pushed shoreward by vast rolling swells that stretched to the horizon and drew their power from much further out to sea.

We realised we were in the worst possible place at the worst possible time. Before we sensed the peril we were about half-way around and were left with a stark choice; forge on, or turn back. One look back the way we'd come was enough to convince us that carrying on and trying to reach the bay was our best chance, so we moved close to the base of the cliff and began to jump and claw our way around the first promontory.

For a while we could see neither the beach nor the bay. We struggled on and soon rounded the point, but any relief we might have felt was short-lived. The outlook was shocking. The tide was battering the shore, sending tons of surf spuming through gaps in the boulders and pounding the cliff face, sending mist and spray high into the air. The mocking calls of gulls sliced through the din, and I remember we stood, unspeaking, looking at each other, in a desperate Bonnie and Clyde moment.

We searched the rock-face for handholds, some way of reaching a vantage point where we could sit it out, but there was nothing, and we had no choice but to keep going. Somehow, incredibly, a frantic half-hour later, exhausted and bedraggled, bodies stinging from brine-washed barnacle scrapes, two humbled individuals stumbled the final few feet to the safety of the bay.

We walked back over the clifftop path and I remember we were full of bravado, reliving skirmishes with giant waves and celebrating moments of individual derring-do, but we had the legs of new-born foals and the silences, when they came, were fraught.

We'd gone there because, despite living by the coast, we'd never seen any birds of the auk family, or kittiwakes or fulmar. On the train home we joked that we were like Victorian explorers, risking our lives in the name of progress, but, unlike the Victorian explorers, we'd made no progress at all, and hadn't seen any of the birds we set out to see.

'Maybe,' Lenny said, 'but at least we didn't slaughter them all and turn them into hats.'

* * *

I sat no GCEs and left school before my sixteenth birthday to start my apprenticeship. After three months of being a dogsbody in the factory, in September I was sent to the engineering department at the Bright Lights College of Further Education. It was a one-year course in basic engineering and I attended for forty hours a week. It was here, along with another twenty apprentices, that I learned the basics of machining, electrics, metal work and welding.

It wasn't as bad as I had expected; I got every weekend off

and was looking forward to having some money of my own. I received the princely sum of three pounds and twelve shillings a week. My father immediately introduced me to the concept of paying for my 'board and lodgings'. He took two pounds and twelve shillings a week.

'You've had a free ride long enough.'

* * *

Despite the awful things he said about Mum when he was drunk, it turned out that my father had been phoning her constantly, begging her to come home. He was on the verge of losing his job, he said, and couldn't cope. Finding herself with the whip hand for once, Mum agreed, on condition that he changed his ways – stopped drinking, got his sorry arse to work, and never raised a hand to her or me again.

Mum moved back to Yelland in time for Christmas. I don't think I ever had a happier Christmas. On Christmas morning, under the tree, was an enormous box wrapped in shiny gold paper. Inside was a large selection of paints, an easel, palette, brushes, pencils, eraser, and a beginner's guide to painting with watercolours; in short, everything a budding artist could wish for. The gift tag read; to a wonderful son, with all my love from Dad xx. It was two presents in one.

Dad didn't touch a drop over Christmas. He even made the Christmas dinner. Mum and me watched as he donned his tissue-paper hat and got all emotional as he wished us both a happy Christmas. We wished him one back and we had a three-way hug over the steaming vegetables. He even shed a few tears.

'Damned onions,' he said.

We tried not to stare and looked away when his hands

dithered as he carved the turkey.

He still hadn't touched a drink by the New Year and when he returned to work he was up on time every day and even made his own sandwiches. He started working overtime and brought a bunch of flowers home for Mum every Friday.

Mum had a confidence I had never seen before. She started going out to the Bright Lights for a game of Bingo and a few drinks with a group of women from the village on a Friday night. One night Dad asked if it was ok if he went for a few pints at the Black Cock.

* * *

We were still only sixteen, but we had no trouble getting served in the Eagle and Child. The landlord knew we were underage but let us have a couple of pints and a game of darts, as long as we behaved ourselves. That's what it was like back then.

As a result, in the fourth year of the census we barely reached the hundred mark. I was doing well at college but was missing the long school holidays. Lenny had failed all of his GCEs and had left school and was helping out in the Post Office shop. Most of the time we never ventured much further afield than Hawksheads and the sand quarry.

A notable exception was one Saturday in May when we went to check out a remote area of moorland and a small tarn I'd found on the Ordnance Survey map. It was a few miles inland and Lenny was determined not to spend another night in a barn and insisted on taking his tent and his cassette player.

We made sandwiches the night before and set off at dawn and by midday we were sitting outside the tent in the shelter of a growth of rhododendrons that huddled close to the tarn. It was a beautiful calm day and we sat and looked across the water. The rhododendrons were in full flower and were reflected perfectly on the water's sheet-silver surface.

The place was buzzing with life. On small islands scattered around the tarn fifty or sixty pairs of noisy black-headed gulls had nests. On the tarn there were Canada geese, pochard and tufted ducks, mallards and grebes, all with families. A spotted flycatcher launched its aerial forays from the outer branches of a solitary oak nearby and a cuckoo called so close by that the volume took our breath away.

We made a rough count of the gulls and logged the broods of the water birds and spent the rest of the day roaming the moorland and a couple of small woods and copses. We were thrilled by some of the finds. We found a pied flycatcher's nest, inaccessible in a tree hole. Likewise, that of a lesser-spotted woodpecker. Twenty minutes quiet observation led to the discovery of a yellowhammer's nest and we found three meadow pipit nests, two of which contained cuckoos' eggs.

And, we saw our first nuthatch. We heard it first, it's repetitive and resonant twee-twee-twee song. It took a while to find, but we saw it in the end. We were well-chuffed. We'd seen plenty of pictures, but it's an unusual bird, and nothing can really prepare you for the sight of a bird walking head-first down the trunk of a tree.

By the time we got back to the tent the tarn was burnished like gun metal by the setting sun. We sat in front of the tent and ate the last of the sandwiches. Venus hung bright in a sky the colour of plums. A long-eared owl was hooting and a nightjar churred across the tarn. We'd look for the nest in the morning.

In the meantime I had a subject I needed to broach with

Lenny.

* * *

Some of the lads at college were into cannabis and I'd picked up a quarter of an ounce to try. I was almost certain he'd be up for it but it wasn't something we'd ever talked about. I'd bought some rizlas and some tobacco so I just started rolling a joint. I tried to stick three skins together and my first effort was a mess and I started to dismantle it.

'What the fuck are you doing?' Lenny laughed. 'Give it here you useless cunt.'

'Have you done it before?' I asked.

'No, but I watched Irish Bob roll one in the beer garden at the Eagle one night and it looked easy enough. And *he* was pissed.' He looked at the thing falling apart in my hands. 'Besides, I couldn't make a worse fucking job of it than that. It looks like a fucking candle.' He took it off me and within minutes he'd rolled the perfect joint. He lit it and we sat and smoked.

Tiny pipistrelle bats flew circuits and harried the last of the day's flying insects, a roding woodcock soared overhead on quivering wings, croaking like a huge frog, and the nightjar continued to churr his eerie song from across the tarn.

* * *

'It's not doing anything for me.' It was dark now and Lenny was flat on his back. For the past half-hour we'd been talking nonsense and pitching mad theories about life and the workings of the universe and laughing ourselves mute. In the morning we'd wish we'd written them down.

'No, me neither.'

We listened to the night creatures calling and rustling all around. Lenny got up and reached into the tent for the cassette player.

'I think we should have a bit of background music.'

A few seconds later the most peaceful place on earth was reverberating to the blare of Black Sabbath's War Pigs. It was a shock at first, but the incongruous mix of sound and vision, music and setting, was mesmerising and we sat cross-legged and gazed across the tarn and around the twinkling firmament till the final notes of the album had faded. The silence that followed was absolute. Nothing stirred. No creature called, no foliage was rustled by any breeze, and we just sat and marvelled at it all.

* * *

One of the lads at college had been taking the piss out of me about my taste in music. The only album I owned at the time was a T. Rex album, and he used to tell me I should go on Desert Island Disc.

He'd given me a compilation tape and we spent the rest of the night being introduced to the likes of Neil Young, Grateful Dead, Bob Dylan and Pink Floyd. After that we rarely went anywhere without any weed. In fact, weed inspired us to find new places to go.

Lenny dug out the fishing 'tattle' that Fred had given him years before and we went night fishing and camping by the river. We caught mainly eels, snigs as we called them, and we skinned them and cut them into small steaks and boiled them in river water in a baked bean can and ate them for supper. They were delicious.

* * *

At the end of the college year, it was decided between the tutors and the company that I had an aptitude for welding, and so my future was decided. For the next three years I would learn my trade in the factory, attending college for one full day and one evening per week. As a productive member of the workforce my pay rose dramatically. I didn't mention it and wasn't asked so I carried on paying Mum the two pounds and twelve shillings a week, soon to be two pounds and sixty new-pence.

Things were returning to normal at home, as in my father was becoming a regular at the Black Cock again and missing work. He was boorish and abusive again, but he hadn't hit Mum, not yet. And she still went to bingo. Wild horses couldn't have kept her from her bingo.

* * *

A couple of years into the breeding survey I'd joined the local birdwatching society and, as a member, I started to notify them of any unusual sightings, for inclusion in their annual report, which came out in early January each year.

This could be anything; a rare or vagrant bird, unusual behaviour by a particular species, or a notably early sighting of a summer visitor, a chiffchaff or willow warbler.

On the afternoon of the 9th of November 1971 I was on the Bright Lights promenade when I saw two house martins. It was an overcast and blustery day and the tiny birds, normally speedy flyers, were struggling to make progress against a gusting south-westerly wind.

For this reason, I got a very good, extended view, and there was no doubt that they were house martins. This was the latest I, maybe anyone, had ever seen house martins, which are usually on their way back to Africa in September, early October at the latest.

I made a mental note of the sighting and reported it on the Monday morning, pleased to make a contribution and looking forward to that contribution appearing in the annual report.

I picked up my copy in the January and turned straight to the bird calendar for the previous year, and there it was, in black and white, the last house martin of the year, a solitary bird seen at the RSPB reserve on Monday the eleventh of October by 'well-known local birder, and secretary of the Bright Lights and District Birdwatching Society, Alf Reed.'

I was dumbfounded. Crestfallen I think is the word. What the fuck? I looked again, in case I'd misread it somehow, or I was looking in the wrong place, but no, last house martin, RSPB reserve, 11th of October, Alf fucking fuck face Reed.

I'd met him a few times. It was Alf fucking cunty bollocks Reed I collected the blank recording cards from before each breeding season, Alf fucking smug twat Reed who I took the completed cards to at the end of the year, and Alf fucking smarmy bastard Reed who cooed 'well-done, son, sterling work, your efforts are much-appreciated,' as I handed them in.

I was going to go to the next monthly meeting and confront him, but I decided against it. So what? I thought. Fuck him. Anyway, he'd only have fed me some guff about my age and inexperience, how they have to be sure before they put anything in the official record, and I'd probably have gone off on one; '*they were fucking house martins, hanging at eye-level in front of me, like a mobile over a baby's fucking cot*'. No, I knew what I'd seen, and that was good enough for me.

* * *

Over the winter I learned to drive. I passed my test and bought myself a tidy 1964 Ford Cortina. It was the best decision I'd ever made. The car gave us freedom. Now we didn't need to rely on bikes or buses or overnight stays. We could go to the reserve any time and regularly stayed till dark and smoked a joint and watched the murmuration of starlings come in to roost. Life was good.

We were going to gigs at weekends but we liked to get off our faces so I left the car at home and we took a bus into the Bright Lights. Any gigs further afield and there was always a coach going.

With only sixty-one cards completed, in terms of numbers, the final year of the census was a wash out. We were getting to like a few beers and didn't get out birding quite as much, but, now that we were mobile, we could visit a lot of locations in a day, and so, in terms of variety, it was the best year of all.

We travelled to a dead end in the wilds of the Pennines and tramped across moors and up white-water rivers to a gullery about as far from the sea as it is possible to be in England. We heard the sweet, fluty song of a ring ouzel and located its nest hidden deep in a gulley. On the way home we stopped anywhere that looked interesting.

We watched snipe as they climbed and plummeted and drummed their tail-feathers in the sky over a far-flung corner of marshland. We trained our bin's on a lesser-spotted woodpecker, no bigger than a sparrow, and watched as it led us to its nest-hole excavated in the underside of a high branch.

And, closer to home, we tied up some loose ends; we finally found the woodcock's nest, a clutch of three beautifully well-camouflaged eggs amongst the leaf-litter in Hawksheads Wood.

The pied wagtails were there again, in the glove compartment of the abandoned car. They hadn't missed a year, though they hadn't always been successful.

A pair of garden warblers did nest in the bramble patch by the gate to Hawksheads. We saw the young birds, squat and tufty, being fattened up for their marathon first flight.

The sand martin colony had grown each year and in this final year we counted over a hundred active nests. After standing us up the previous year, the grasshopper warblers came back and raised two broods. But best of all, though they were common throughout the area, it was heartening to see a pair of blackbirds successfully raising a family again on the weigh-bridge shelf.

* * *

Though birds were always my first love, I had started to take more notice of the other life around the estate. I bought a book on butterflies and could soon name most of those I saw. Then I tried to match the caterpillar to the butterfly or moth. I learned that the simplest way to do this, or to narrow down the options at least, was to identify the host plant the caterpillars were feeding on, so I bought a field-guide on trees and plants and before long I knew that the dark, hairy caterpillars munching on the stinging nettles were those of the red admiral, and that the writhing mass of long, black caterpillars alongside them were those of the peacock.

The beautiful lime-green caterpillars with the unicorn horn that I found on the leaves of the willow trees around the sand quarry would become poplar hawk moth. In the hand, the tiny green caterpillars of the brown hairstreak and the common blue would be virtually impossible to tell apart, but the first is found on blackthorn, the latter on bird's foot trefoil. This improved my knowledge of the local flora too, and I was soon on first-name terms with many of the species on my patch.

Apart from birds, Lenny's only interest was fungi. He noticed them more and more, everywhere we went, and started talking about them all the time. They became an obsession. In the birch wood he found it miraculous that the huge growth of toadstools covering the base of a tree had appeared since yesterday, thought it incredible that you could scour a field for mushrooms, pick every one, and come back the next day and find just as many.

He was amazed by the variety of shapes and sizes and colours. He bought a book to identify them and underlined them as a trainspotter would. He started pointing them out and reeling off facts about each. He soon knew all those that were edible; the cep, the elf-cap, the jelly ear, the huge, tiered mass of the chicken of the woods hugging the oak tree; and most of those that were definitely not; the fool's funnel, the panther cap, the death cap and the superbly named destroying angel.

It was these deadly varieties that caught his imagination at first, the death cap in particular. It grew in large numbers in Hawksheads wood and I remember him touching them and holding his fingers to his nose, then wiping them frantically on his jeans, lest the toxins should leech through his skin.

Of course, Lenny being Lenny, it wasn't long before he turned his attention to the hallucinogenic varieties, the so-called 'magic mushrooms.' His field guide made no distinction between toxic and hallucinogenic and simply stated they were poisonous. We saw Irish Bob and Ann in the pub and Lenny asked if they knew anything about them. Bob grinned and looked at Ann.

'Do I know anything about magic mushrooms, love?'

Ann looked at Lenny and raised her eyebrows. She picked up her drink and settled back in her seat.

'How long have you got?'

Bob knew his stuff. He said there were a few different types. The most common was the liberty cap, but there was the wavy cap and a couple of others. He and Ann didn't take them anymore, but when they had, they preferred the liberty caps. They were common in the fields around the Hawksheads estate and you couldn't miss them, they were tiny and shaped like pixies' hats, hard to mistake for anything else. Bob told him they grew in groups, that when you found one, if you looked closer, you'd see there were lots more.

'Like a village,' he said, and looked at Ann. He'd taken on a dreamy, nostalgic expression. 'We used to shout to each other, do you remember, love? "*Wow! Come and look at this! I've found a city!*"'

Ann returned his dreamy look.

'Of course I remember, silly. "*Sorry, love, false alarm, it's only a villa*ge."' They both laughed. Bob tore the back from a beer-mat and drew a liberty cap mushroom, to scale, and told him exactly the fields to try.

Lenny hit the jackpot first time and turned up at our house mid-afternoon one day with a small bag of them that he'd dried and crushed to powder. I wasn't keen on taking them at first, but he talked me round. It was impossible to say how many were in the bag. I asked him and he reckoned there were about fifty, 'give or take.'

Bob had said twenty-five or so was 'a mellow trip', so we halved it and washed down the nutty-flavoured powder with a jet from the cold tap. As we soon found out, there were far more than fifty in the bag.

Neither of us knew what to expect so we set off for the sand quarry to avoid bumping into any other people; an hour later we were so glad that we had. The effects started before we got to the sand quarry, if we even got there, which has never been fully established; metallic-tasting gums, eyes that felt as though they might never blink again. We were grinning like idiots as we walked under the railway and then stood for who knows how long making noises, shouting, whispering, howling, and listening to the echoes.

We forgot we were going to the sand quarry, not that it mattered much, and somehow ended up at the birch-wood. We realised we were walking like marionettes and couldn't stop, as hard as we tried. We were in hysterics. Neither of us could get over the low fence we'd scissor-jumped a hundred times before. It was undulating and wouldn't keep still. Lenny finally managed to clamber over and landed heavily on his arse in the marsh grass, and we sat, one either side of the fence, helpless with laughter.

After that, nothing is clear. We agreed that we went to Hawksheads and performed a ceremony to invoke the ghost of the mad monk, we think, and that Lenny climbed a tree and I got scared, but other than that, nothing, until we were walking, wet-through and filthy, dry-mouthed, up the ginnel, jaws and rib-cages aching. I decided that night that I'd never take magic mushrooms again, and I never have.

* * *

At Christmas Fred and Noreen caught Lenny stealing from the Post Office shop. He'd been caught before but only small scale; chocolate, a packet of cigarettes once. This time he had his hand in the till, and it wasn't the first time. When the Post Office counter was closed, they'd been letting him run the shop on his own, trusting him with some responsibility.

The figures hadn't been adding up for a while but now it was starting to cause financial problems for the business. Fred and Noreen had known but couldn't bring themselves to believe it. Rather than confront him they decided to take away the opportunity and rearranged their own shifts so that there was always one of them there with him. It didn't do any good. One day Fred stood and watched as he slipped money into his pocket and pretended to put it in the till.

Confronted, Lenny went on the defensive. He claimed it was the first time. When Fred quietly mentioned the total sum that had gone missing Lenny called him a liar and started kicking off and stormed upstairs.

I knew he was thieving. He was always flush, always had handy money for concert tickets and weed. He was always first to the bar and was building a substantial album collection. You didn't get that kind of money for a few hours in a shop, even if the paymasters *were* your doting parents. Still, even I was surprised by the extent of his larceny. His position as trustee also included sorting out the change. Any feelings of guilt I might have felt about all the stolen sweets I'd eaten paled when he laughed and said he couldn't wait to see the look on Fred's face when he found that the change bags were thirty quid light too.

Fred and Noreen put their shared foot down and told Lenny to find a job. To my embarrassment whenever I went to call for Lenny, they cooed over me and held me up as an example.

'John's got a good job,' Noreen would say, and Fred would

concur.

'He'll always have work.'

It was a depressing thought.

* * *

I never knew Lenny to freeload until then, not off anyone, but he soon became a master of the art. He'd always had a way with him, a cheeky demeanour, and he tapped into it and used it to maximum effect. He came up with lines that he used to convince people they wanted to give him a cigarette or buy him a beer, that they would be the beneficiaries.

'I'm saving your life,' he'd say, looking into the eyes of someone whose cigarette packet was about to become a cigarette lighter. Nobody ever seemed to take offence or think any worse of him. One night, in the pub after a gig, a guy we'd only just met came back from the bar and raised his newly replenished glass, a 'cheers' gesture, and Lenny took it off him and took a huge swig.

'Cheers mate,' he said, to the now empty-handed guy. 'But you shouldn't have bothered. I don't like being in a round. I like to drink at my own pace.'

I'd have got a smack in the mouth for my cheek. Lenny got his pint and the bemused guy went back to the bar and bought another drink and came back and stood with us again.

Then, unexpectedly, he got a job. He started work at the Bright Lights Pleasure Park, taking the admissions money for the Hall of Mirrors. The following month he moved from Yelland and took a flat in the Bright Lights.

He blamed Fred and Noreen, said he couldn't live with them anymore. He'd turned all his guilt for what he'd done into hatred for them for having found him out, and he bad-mouthed them constantly, often in ugly imitations of their own voices.

I stayed at the flat some nights and we partied and pulled a few girls. I went to Hawksheads some nights and to the reserve at weekends. Lenny came with me sometimes but he was losing interest and I was becoming a solitary birder.

I bought a notebook and kept a year-round record of all the birds I saw and heard within the Hawksheads estate; the mixed wood, sand quarry, birch wood and surrounding fields and hedgerows. The book was soon full and was quickly followed by another. To complement my guides to butterflies and moths, trees and plants, I bought books to help identify mammals, insects, reptiles and amphibians. I carried on with my art too and did a series of small paintings of branches in bud that Mum has on her wall to this day.

* * *

I finished my apprenticeship in the summer of 1974. On becoming a tradesman my wage jumped to forty pounds a week, but I'd spent the past four years hearing about the huge wages to be had on construction sites around the country, and immediately went looking for the big money. I landed a job on a local power station that paid more than three times my previous wage.

The power station was on the other side of the Bright Lights and I was expected to work my share of night shifts so I moved in with Lenny to be closer to work and to pocket the travel expenses I still claimed, and so that Mum could leave that cunt.

He'd been performing again, fighting in the pub, taking it out on her when he got home. Mum was crying. She told me that she had somewhere to go and I said then she should, but she wouldn't leave me there with him.

Lenny had been promoted to his dream job and was spinning girls on the waltzers. Our working hours conflicted but we got on fine, as long as we avoided the subject of politics. As soon as he'd started work he talked as if he was the only person in the world who worked for a living. During the miners' strike we argued constantly and it seriously tested our friendship.

'Lazy cunts,' he'd say, 'they don't fucking want work. I'd sack the fucking lot of them if it was me.'

I couldn't just ignore him, I always had to bite.

'It's a good job it's not you then, isn't it. Anyway, what the fuck would you know about it? You take the fucking money at the hall of mirrors. I'd like to see you do twelve-hour shifts a mile underground.'

He was overtly racist, too, and often sang the praises of Enoch Powell, and the National Front. I knew he was parroting the people he worked with on the fairground, but that didn't make his outbursts any easier to take, and we nearly came to blows a few times.

Our taste in television programmes was another problem when we lived together. He didn't get Monty Python's Flying Circus, thought it was 'too fucking stupid to laugh at,' and I couldn't bear to watch Benny Hill and On the Buses, less still witness his embarrassing impressions of Fred Scuttle, when he stood, saluting, with his elbow at ninety-degrees to his head and with his tongue sticking down to his chin. He genuinely thought he was being funny and didn't realise people were laughing to humour him and were secretly rolling their eyes when he wasn't looking.

Having said that, maybe my Ministry of Silly Walks, and

Upper-class Twit of the Year impressions weren't as funny as I thought, and were just as embarrassing for him.

But, as long as we stuck to common ground, we got along ok. We both liked a drink and were enjoying the speed and hash that Lenny picked up regularly from a fellow girl-spinner.

We went to gigs and discos, too. I met my first real girlfriend, (someone you stay in with), Jennifer, at one of the discos. I was twenty. You didn't come across many girls at the sand quarry. Lenny on the other hand had been spinning his charms, or vice versa, for a year by this time, and brought home a procession of spun girls, but he rarely kept me awake at night, and when I was working nights he often stayed up all night so that we slept the same hours.

Jennifer started coming round on Saturdays and sometimes we went out, but her parents were strict and she was under a curfew. Her father kept an emergency five-pound note in a jacket that hung in the porch. This negated the 'I missed the last bus and couldn't afford a taxi' approach, so we made the best of a bad job and stopped going out, shagged till midnight, then I drove her home and she took full advantage of the pocket bonanza.

* * *

On the 5th of November Mum left that cunt and moved in with Archie. Mum made him breakfast and saw him off to work as normal and by the time he got home she was gone. Simple as that. It was a Tuesday. That night, she said, from the window of her new home, it seemed that the fireworks were for her.

I spent Christmas Day with Mum and Archie. I stayed over on Christmas Eve and, in the morning, Archie lit the fire and we exchanged presents. It was my first visit and I expected it to be awkward but it was fine. Archie was a good bloke. He'd been up early and stuffed the turkey and put it in the oven and when we got up me and Mum sat at the table and prepared the carrots and sprouts. Mum was nominated to make the gravy as we all agreed it should be edible. We followed it with Christmas pudding and washed it all down with a few drinks.

We could barely move afterwards and Archie suggested him and me wash up and let Mum put her feet up with Doctor Zhivago. He washed and I dried and I asked him how long he and Mum had been seeing each other. I don't know why I asked that. I didn't want to know. It was none of my business. There was an awkward moment as he tried to do some quick calculations. I put my hand on his arm.

'Forget I asked,' I said. 'Mum's due some love in her life.'

* * *

Lenny spent Christmas with Fred and Noreen. He hadn't been to see them for a while. It wasn't so bad, he said, but he hadn't been able to get away quickly enough and got Fred to drive him back to the Bright Lights early on Boxing Day morning. As he drove, Fred told Lenny that he'd seen that cunt in the pub. He was drunk and had been telling his problems to anyone who'd listen. They were Fred's exact words.

* * *

One rainy Friday night in February 1975 we were on a coach heading for the M6 and I was laughing at Lenny singing Lynyrd Skynyrd's *Sweet Home California*. Genesis were touring their new album and we had tickets to see them in Liverpool. Jennifer would have preferred to see the Bay City Rollers and had stayed at home.

We'd had some speed and a smoke before we got on at the Bright Lights bus station and weren't paying much attention when the coach stopped in the back of beyond to pick up a solitary reveller. Her shoulder length blonde hair hung loose and she was wearing faded jeans with red monkey boots, a shiny purple waistcoat and a turquoise silk shirt with a preposterously long collar.

April Meadows sauntered down the aisle and introduced herself to her fellow travellers. 'Hi, I'm April, Hi, Hiya, there. I'm April, what's your name?' She made her way to the back of the coach, saying hi all the way, then turned and came back to the empty seat in front of us. She knelt and put her face between the headrests. She had bright green eyes that shone through a pair of bat's wings painted across her face

'Hi, I'm April,' she beamed.

'No? Never?' Lenny took the piss.

'I saved you till last.'

'Hiya,' I said, and held out my hand. 'I'm John.'

She took my hand.

'Hiya John. And what about Mr. Grumpy? Does *he* have a first name?' Without waiting for an answer she went on. 'Anyway, don't worry about him. I'll soon cheer him up.'

She was good to her word. She'd had a tab of acid and before we got off the coach she produced another for me and Lenny to share. She split the tiny microdot expertly with her thumb nails. It was our first and to this day I'm glad I didn't have a full one. I still struggle to believe that such a tiny amount of anything can have such a staggering effect on the brain.

The gig was a mesmerising swirl of lights and visual effects and sleights of mind. At one point Peter Gabriel literally vanished from the stage and when he reappeared moments later he had changed costume yet again and there were two of him, one at either side of the stage … that's how I remember it anyway.

More by good luck than good management we caught the return bus and ended up at April's father's pile, at the back of beyond, close to where Lenny had found the kestrel brood. August Meadows owned a left-wing national Sunday newspaper. He was still up when we arrived, in the kitchen having a nightcap with his son, Gordon, April's brother. I was totally paranoid and didn't know what to do; sit down or leave. Lenny helped himself to a can and started talking to Gordon while I hovered nervously. August seemed to me to be the perfect father. He poured us a drink and April did the introductions in a florid and demonstrative way and he grinned and they had a hug. Simultaneously tripping and hugging your father is something I could never imagine. I stood staring around like an idiot while they had a laugh but, eventually, I managed to relax and we sat around the kitchen table and had a crack. Then August and Gordon said goodnight.

'Have fun,' he said, August, as they left the room.

* * *

That was the start of the April frolics, a memorable example of which happened on the night that Ray Reardon beat Alex Higgins in the final of the Embassy world snooker championships. We'd been to see a couple of local bands at Bright Lights College and had bumped into April in the bar during the interval. She was with a bloke and she saw us and waved. She stood on her tiptoes and said something into the bloke's ear and made her way through the crowd.

April was a changeling. She never looked the same twice and

always looked wonderful. Tonight she was looking wonderful in bright, skin-tight green leggings, bumper boots, and a crudely tailored black dustbin liner. Nothing else. The bin liner clung to her tits and barely reached her crotch and her fuzzy pubic copse was clearly visible through the shiny leggings. Her hair was bleached blonde and was spiked like a mace and she wore black lipstick and fluorescent green eyeshadow.

She snogged us both full on and I sneaked a peep across to the bar, but though he was watching, the bloke didn't seem to mind and even raised his hand in greeting. April saw me looking.

'It's my brother, Gordon,' she said. 'You met him out at the house that night. Well, sort of. You don't remember do you?' She laughed. Her pupils were the size of tiddlywinks and she was chiggling a piece of gum with her front teeth. Lenny looked at me and tipped an imaginary glass to his mouth and set off to the bar. April stopped chiggling and kissed me on the lips and slipped a wrap of speed into my shirt pocket. 'See you both later yeah?'

Back at the flat it was the well-honed three or four hours of sweat and toil, one at the front, one at the back, swap over, one at the top, one at the bottom, flip over and same again, full of speed and vodka, with Hurricane Higgins, no doubt full of much the same, twitching his way to defeat in the corner.

What made it a particularly memorable frolic was an off-the-table incident, so to speak. The music centre was between tracks, Pink Floyd tracks, probably, and we could hear the TV commentary, and in a conversational manner the commentator said, 'he has the choice of pink or brown here' and Lenny had a laughing fit while he was down at the 'balk end' and that set me off and April said she'd 'finish my fucking self off,' and took a good half-hour doing it while we smoked another joint and watched the end of the snooker.

* * *

One night I went with Jennifer to a brand-new nightclub in a converted country mansion. She didn't like weed but had tried speed once and loved it. We'd been drinking and snorting and were talking for England as usual, and she came up with the idea of an amnesty for secrets, a confessional. Of course, I agreed without hesitation. After all, the world was a wonderful place, full of beautiful people, and our love for each other was such a powerful thing that nothing could come between us.

The music was thrilling and the mood perfect. There she sat, the perfect woman, radiant and alluring in an ever-so-sexy little black number that showed off a swathe of smooth shoulder and a generous expanse of glorious cleavage. With her silken hair and her eyes spangling in the half-light she oozed confidence and love and human understanding. We were soul mates, my little Jenny wren and me.

I looked at her and wondered why I had cheated on her in the first place. She was the only woman for me, the only woman I wanted, would ever want, and here was my chance of a new start, a clean slate. The threesomes were definitely history. Her hand felt warm in mine, comfortable, a perfect fit.

Jenny would go first. She worked nights at a local mental hospital, as it was then called, and she said that staff members regularly had sex on the night shift and I asked who with and she said each other. She said that a doctor had been coming on to her recently. Giving her the eye, she said. A squeeze-by here, a saucy line there. She hadn't done anything, she said, but had felt flattered and had been tempted. I didn't get off to a good start when I laughed and asked if she was sure it was a doctor. She gave me a dead-arm and said I wasn't taking it seriously but I assured her that I was.

There was a break in the music and the lights had stilled. A couple were arguing at the table behind us and two meatheads were getting macho with one another at the bar.

The atmosphere had gone and had taken my nerve with it and I decided on a change of tack. I would confess to a marginally less serious transgression than that of regular, ongoing group sex, namely a grope with Jackie from the offices at work, in the car park at the Christmas do the previous year.

Then she said that, anyway, even if she had done it with the doctor, it wouldn't mean anything, that she thought any less of me, 'or anything like that,' or that she didn't love me, 'or anything like that.' The lights in the room had come on and two bouncers were manhandling one of the meatheads towards the exit.

'Anyway, go on,' she smiled, 'it's your turn.'

In the glare of the overhead lights she looked pasty. Her hair was lank and lifeless and she looked like a tart in that outfit.

'Lenny and me have been having a threesome with someone,' I said, just like that. 'For a few weeks now,' I added, conservatively, to cushion the blow, possibly, and she pulled her left hand from mine as she hurled her drink over me with her right.

She gave me a lot of abuse and called me a pervert and shouted, 'I bet you and that fucking Lenny shag each other as well don't you?,' which turned a few heads. She ranted for a bit, but, surprisingly, she never asked who the third party was, and then she grabbed her coat and took a taxi home.

I was still living in the Bright Lights with Lenny at the time and had no money left for a taxi. I had a back-door key for the cottage so I decided to walk the five or so miles back through the lanes to Yelland. That cunt wouldn't be happy if

I woke him, but so what? Fuck him.

It didn't seem to take long. I had owls and bats and lots of hedgerow rustlings for company, and as I walked I looked forward to the upcoming Knebworth Festival. The Stones were playing. Lynyrd Skynyrd, Hot Tuna and 10cc. We had three tickets, one each for Lenny, me and Jennifer. We had a four-man tent and all the drugs you could ask for.

I arrived at the cottage at the same time as the milkman, Alf Heath, better known locally as Dry Cornflakes, and I said good morning and he gave me what he thought was a knowing look as I turned the key carefully and crept inside.

I could hear him snoring away upstairs. There'd be no waking him so I made a cup of tea and took it and curled up in the back bedroom with a hand under the quilt and wondered if April Meadows liked camping.

* * *

April Meadows loved camping and threw herself into it with great gusto. We met her at Bright Lights station and she waved when she saw us and skipped over and threw her arms around us and swung herself around and nearly sent us all spinning off the platform. I had a rucksack on my back with my sleeping bag tied to the top and had a small holdall to carry spare clothes and drugs. Lenny also had a rucksack, the tent and his sleeping bag.

In contrast, April looked as though she had just nipped out for a couple of minutes. She was wearing five items of clothing, if you counted her sandals and hair band, and was carrying only a hessian shoulder bag.

'Where's your sleeping bag?' I asked.

'Who's sleeping?' she teased.

We went into the station buffet and bought a can of

dandelion and burdock and swallowed a speed bomb each. As soon as we were settled on the train April produced a half-bottle of vodka from her bag. We drained the dregs from the bottle before we got to Birmingham and April pestered for a tab of acid to take with her last mouthful and when I refused, she sulked and stomped her feet in an amusing fit of pique. I soon gave in and we took the acid, and by the time we boarded the shuttlebus in Stevenage for the final leg of the journey, to our fellow travellers we must have seemed like extras from One Flew Over the Cuckoo's Nest.

We arrived at Knebworth well before dark. The campsite was already busy and April sat on the grass and watched as we set to work. It took us about two hours to pitch the tent, to the unfettered amusement of our neighbours, and April had crawled inside before the guy lines had been tightened. Once inside she turned and knelt with her head protruding from the doorway. She looked like a huge green tortoise and her hand appeared and she crooked her finger and beckoned us both inside.

'Come see what April's found.'

* * *

'Who did you say was playing?' she asked. It was dark now and we were crashed out in a splendour of spent limbs. Lenny was trying to roll a joint on his chest in the dark – we had forgotten to bring a torch – and he started laughing.

'The Stones.' he said. 'The *Rolling* Stones?'

* * *

The final April frolic was a defining moment in my life. A watershed. It wasn't the threesome. That was just another marathon where we slaved all night over an insatiable April Meadows with hard-ons a cat couldn't scratch, sensitised and invigorated by copious amounts of amphetamines.

No, it was afterwards. We were in our flat and April had crashed out among the floor cushions. Lenny and me were lying on the bed propped on our elbows and we were naked. Lenny had some squidgy black resin and he rolled a joint and smoked quietly for a few minutes. As he passed the joint, he looked me up and down and smiled and nodded, in a 'look at us hedonists' sort of way, as he blew the smoke upwards from the corner of his mouth, like Popeye.

Lenny had red hair and was pale and skinny and was, consequently, all prick and ribs, and as I took the joint, he laid back and let his hand fall into his groin and started working his cock. He pushed down at the base and held it vertical.

As kids we always joked about his proportions, but we rarely had as adults. Impressive as it was, his size had proved the stumbling block for both of his previous long-term girlfriends, both relationships lasting for as long as Lenny's personality made up for the lack of pain-free sex; three months, and six weeks respectively. The second, Pamela Beck, was pissed one night and she told me that she didn't feel like a lover, more a victim.

April was an exception. She even let Lenny 'score a hat trick' once.

'Fucking hell! Did you see that?' he said to me when she'd gone, as though it was something I could have missed.

He admired his folly. 'What do you reckon?' he said.

'Yeah,' I joked. 'Make my eyes water and all that.'

But the truth was it had crossed my mind a few times. Well it's bound to, isn't it? Like when you stand too close to the edge of a cliff and wonder what it would be like to jump?

He had his eyes closed and I watched his toes start to splay. I was hard again myself and I wondered, after all we'd done together, not only with April, but things when we were younger, like the 'camping wanking race,' what difference it made who was doing what to who.

So, I jumped.

* * *

I've often wondered, in view of how things turned out, if I'd known what the consequences would be, for me, for Lenny, and for April, for all of our relationships to each other, would I still have done what I did next? And every time I come to the same conclusion; it makes no difference, it's pie in the sky, as they say, because I did it, and nothing can ever change that.

I knelt and worked my way across the bed. He was arching his back and I reached over and wrapped my free hand around the end of his cock. He seemed to be ok with it at first and within a few seconds he went rigid and came into my palm. I was coming too but didn't get the chance. He rolled off the bed and stood and jabbed his heel in my groin, catching me hard on the wrist. He punched me on the ear.

'What the fuck are you doing?' he screamed. He was furious and he reached into the ashtray and picked up the joint and struggled to find it with the lighter flame. I didn't know what to say. I was mortified. I'd gone from wired and horny to hollow and hung-over in a matter of seconds. I rubbed my ear and picked up one of Lenny's socks to wipe my hand. I started sorting my clothes from the assortment on the floor. Lenny paced the room and seethed.

'I'm sorry Len,' I said. 'It just seemed like the thing to do.

When you didn't stop me, I thought you were cool with it.'

'Cool with it! I was coming, you thick cunt, with or without your help.'

'Look, I'm sorry Len,' I said again. 'I got the wrong end of the stick, that's all'

'You bet your fucking life you did.'

April emerged from the cushions and stretched. 'What's going on?' she asked.

'What's going on? I'll tell you what's going on. My best mate's a fucking queer, that's what's going on.'

April started laughing. 'You could have fooled me,' she said.

'I'm not fucking joking. He thinks it's '*the thing to do*,' he mocked.

'It was just the heat of the moment,' I said, which it was, but it sounded unconvincing now. April knelt and took a cock in each hand.

'Well I agree with John,' she said. Lenny swung his hips away.

'Fuck off April. This isn't funny.'

April reached for him again and he pulled away so she goaded him.

'Oh, come on. What's the matter Lenny? I always assumed that you two got it on when I wasn't around anyway. Plee-ease,' she pouted, as if she was asking him to put the kettle on. 'Go on. For April.' She reached between her legs. 'Go on, plee-e-ease. Let me watch you suck each other off.'

Lenny gathered April's clothes from the floor and threw them at her.

'Fuck off. Go on, fuck off. You fucking slut. You fucking bike. And you can fuck off with her you fucking puff.' He stormed out. April got dressed in silence.

'I'm sorry April. He doesn't mean it.' She was crying and I went to give her a hug, but she pushed me away.

'Leave it John.' She grabbed her bag and I followed her downstairs to the front door. She left and I called after her but she didn't turn around and I watched her disappear around the corner. I listened until the sound of her heels had faded and died, then I wiped my eyes and went back inside.

* * *

Lenny hardly spoke to me after that. He made sure he was out when I was in, which wasn't hard to do with the hours we worked. When we did find ourselves alone in the flat together, he stayed in his room. Then he started inviting his fairground mates round, a motley assortment of speed freaks and smackheads, and their hangers-on. It was obvious that he'd told them everything, or, at least, his take on everything. They covered their balls and backsides with their hands when I walked in, or stood with their backs to the wall and pulled faces of mock fear. The nicknames became ever more imaginative; 'Fucking hell, it's Scott of the Arse-Antics,' they'd say, in reference to the Jeremy Thorpe scandal that was all over the news. 'The fucking pillow-biter.'

Lenny started taking speed every day at work and stopped eating and lost weight he could ill afford. He stopped caring whether I was in bed or not. The flat was a bombsite. I regularly got home from work, dayshift and nightshift, to find my bed occupied and was twice threatened at knifepoint when I tried to evict the squatters. I liked my drugs as much as anyone, still do, some drugs, sometimes, but it became impossible for me to share a flat with Lenny.

Things came to a head when I arrived back from work

one morning to find a couple of smackheads 'on the nods' in the living-room, and one of his fairground mates with my binoculars, looking out of the window. When I walked in, he turned them on me and started taking the piss; 'Oh look, a lesser-spotted tit, oh, hang on, no it's not, it's a greater-red-faced fucking shit-stabber.'

Lenny was in an amphetamine frenzy, barking like a dog and rampaging round the flat with the hoover. He followed me into my bedroom and kept running the hoover into my feet.

'Out of the way. You wanted it cleaned, I'm cleaning it, now fuck off out of the way you whinging cunt.' He spun the hoover around and put the handle through the side of the fish tank that sat on top of my bedside drawers. He didn't seem to notice and carried on regardless, hoovering up everything; glass, gravel, plants, even the fish.

* * *

I moved into my own place; a one-bed flat even closer to work. I started spending more time birding. Work commitments hadn't kept me from the reserve completely, but they had curtailed the ringing adventures. It had been four years since the last one, which proved to be just that. There had been big changes at the reserve. Jeff and Mike had gone and there were new people at the helm. They were managers or caretakers or the like; strangers. I felt abandoned. All the birds ringed and their work complete, I consoled myself, Jeff and Mike must have moved on to work their miracle on another fledgling utopia.

But they had taken some of my enthusiasm with them. Not for birds or birdwatching, nothing could do that, (I was watching a heron in the sand quarry only this morning as it tried to swallow an eel that had coiled itself around its bill), but for the reserve. I found that I was happier on my local patch, that seeing something there, it didn't have to be new or particularly rare; a nightjar hawking in the sand quarry or yellow wagtails feeding their young in the damp meadow at Hawksheads, was a far better buzz than watching mallard and pochard drift to a soundtrack of scrarking black-headed gulls and the territorial bickerings of coot for hours on the off-chance of glimpsing a passing rarity and ticking it off in a book.

And so, though I admit to having peered from the bus window from time to time in late summer for the unmistakeable silhouette of a perching osprey, its jizz, on the dead trees by the lagoon, I abandoned the reserve and poured all of my energies into my local patch. I spent all my spare time there, evenings all year round, all day at weekends and holidays.

* * *

jizz (dʒiz) *n* a term for the total combination of characteristics that serve to identify a particular species of bird or plant (CED 1998)

I've lost count of the times I've been asked by non-birders, 'How can you tell what that bird is from here?' and the answer is, by its jizz.

It was a word we learned from Jeff and Mike. We thought they were having us on at first but we began to hear it more and more and soon discovered it's a word all birders use and can often be the clincher when trying to identify birds in the field.

Its jizz can be a bird's shape, the way it moves, some characteristic, habit, or behaviour that may be unique to a particular species, or it can be its song or call, or can even take in the location and habitat.

Once I found out what jizz was, I realised that I'd always used this method of identifying birds. I'd always been able to tell a spotted flycatcher from a distance by its upright, almost vertical, posture, and its aerial forays from an exposed perch to catch its prey. I didn't need to see it up close or know what colour it was.

Likewise the squat, dumpy looking, dark-coloured bird bobbing up and down on a rock three-hundred yards away in the middle of a fast-flowing stream can only be a dipper.

Redstarts are shy and inobtrusive and are often overlooked, and when we do see them they are usually flying away from us. Luckily, as its name suggests, the redstart has a rufus-red tail and rump that does give you a start when you see it, and that's all we need to identify it.

Conversely, the garden warbler is most easily identified by its complete uniformity, its lack of identifiable features; the epitome of the lbj, the little brown job.

Identifying birds of prey has its own set of problems. Some are obvious enough; most people would recognise the hovering kestrel, or the stooping peregrine, but many birds of prey have very similar calls, and we often see them from beneath as they soar at altitude. This makes them difficult to identify, and for this reason most field guides have illustrations showing their underwings.

Then there's the bird's song, a sure-fire identification tool when you know what you're listening to.

When I was younger I read somewhere about the yellowhammer's song resembling the phrase 'a little bit of bread and no chee-eese.' There were a few pairs of yellowhammers around the estate and I often heard the singing males, but, although I got the last, extended note, it still didn't sound much like 'a little bit of bread and no chee-eese' to me, not at first, anyway. It took me a while to understand that it didn't have to actually sound like it was saying that, I just had to hear that sequence of notes and make the association.

Once I got this, I started to make my own associations to help me identify the songs and calls of different species.

I once read that the goldfinch's lovely jingling song is 'expressive of the joy of living,' and to this day that's what I think when I hear one.

When I hear the greenfinch's twining, one-note call, I always think of a rusty wheelbarrow.

The blackcap's frenetic song brings to mind a blackbird on speed.

A blackbird's song reminds me of the Clangers.

When I hear a willow warbler's beautiful cascade of notes I think of a waterfall. No, it doesn't sound like a waterfall, not in the slightest, any more than a blackbird sounds like a Clanger, but it's what I think when I hear it, and that's what matters.

Some birds are named after their calls, the most obvious being the cuckoo. Others are a little more tenuous, birds like the chiffchaff,

This was something that Lenny never got.

'Why's it called a chiffchaff?' he'd say. 'It sounds fuck all like chiffchaff. You have to have lips and teeth to say chiffchaff.'

'No,' I'd say, 'but you still hear it and know it's a chiffchaff, don't you. That's the point.'

'I don't give a fuck, it still doesn't sound like chiffchaff.'

And on it would go.

The song thrush is well known amongst birders for repeating every set of notes at least once, and Lenny looked at me like I'd lost the plot when I cupped my hand to my ear and said, 'what?' or 'pardon?' after the first set so that it sounded like the bird was replying to me. Little things please little minds, I suppose.

The more I got to know the different birds' songs and calls, the more I enjoyed my birding. I started leaving my bedroom window open to hear what was passing over during the night. It's amazing what flies over our towns and cities under cover of darkness. I bought recordings to help identify those I didn't know, like the redwing and fieldfare, ring ousel, golden plover, dotterel, and a bird that, despite plenty of stiff opposition, would one day become my favourite bird; the whimbrel.

Then there's the starling. For reasons best known to themselves, many people tend to dislike starlings. I've heard people complain about starlings taking the food from bird tables that's meant for 'the other birds'. I've seen people block the starling's nest hole during the winter so it can't gain access the following year. They have a bad reputation that's definitely not deserved. Even their Latin name; *sturnus vulgaris* suggests unpleasantness.

Well I love everything about starlings. I love their character, I love their stunning, iridescent plumage, I love listening to their chortling voices as they shelter from the morning rain under the gutter outside my bedroom window, I love the winter murmurations that create fabulous displays over reedbeds and cities across the country, but most of all I love their amazing talent for mimicry.

I've heard starlings imitate a dozen or more bird species; curlew, magpie, even an owl, and I've often thought I've heard a swift's screaming call only to realise that it's the middle of winter and it was just a starling having a laugh.

* * *

Thatcher had been in power for a year and work was already drying up. I'd finished building the power station and had got used to the money and, although I was working, I had no intention of spending the rest of my days grafting my arse off and burning my fucking eyes out welding a million five-bar gates a day for five quid an hour for the tin-pot dictator who owned that particular sweat shop, or any other.

To make matters worse I was on permanent night shift and was being deprived of sleep by the barking and baying of a Jack Russell terrier left alone all day in the flat below. It only stopped when its master saw fit to return every evening. I had it out with him once but I was wasting my time. He was more animal than the dog and threatened to punch my lights out and there was no doubt that he was both serious and capable. I tried chain smoking half a dozen joints for breakfast but still couldn't sleep and ended up with bronchitis, exhausted, and skint.

There were still contracting jobs to be had, down south mainly, but it meant packing a bag and staying away for at least a month at a time. I didn't mind the time away. Mum was happy with Archie. She'd been doing a course for three years and was excited about getting her qualification, the first of her life, and over the moon at the prospect of becoming Archie's bookkeeper. That cunt would never have allowed that.

'I'm the breadwinner. There's no wife of mine working for a living'.

I had no girlfriend at the time, and there was nothing keeping me in England, so if I had to work away from home, I reasoned, then I may as well see a bit of the world while I was at it.

Friday 17th of October 1980

There was no point paying rent on a flat I wasn't living in but I needed somewhere to store my stuff while I was out of the country so I moved back into the cottage with that cunt. I'd only have to put up with him for a couple of days every so often. Besides which I was a different person to the one he had bullied all those years.

I hadn't seen Lenny since I moved out and I was worried about him, so I decided to go and see how he was and maybe try to rebuild some bridges before I left.

And I was hoping that what I'd heard wasn't true.

I stepped off the bus into a chilly onshore breeze. It was coming on to rain and there was a strong smell of the sea. I avoided the promenade and the bustle of the crowd and the stalls and the hand-written signs that always pissed me off and still do, adverts for HOT DOG'S and TOFFEE APPLE'S. We walked down the promenade when we were stoned and asked the stallholders; Hot dog *is* what? *What* is toffee apple?

The illuminations had been switched on by some soap-actor or other so the prom would be awash with tourists eating candy floss and the roads brimming with carfuls of stressed-out parents and noisy wide-eyed children, inching painfully through the drizzle.

I made my way across town through back alleys and tree-lined streets and ginnels. Away from the prom the town was quiet and I got to Lenny's flat at about six and it was already dark. The main door was locked so I threw a clatter of chippings at the dimly lit window on the top floor. A burly guy opened the middle-floor window onto the gloomy street and growled 'What?' and I pointed randomly from the elbow and mumbled 'No … sorry … I was just,' and he told me to fuck off and closed the window.

I went to the phone box at the end of the street and rang Lenny's number. It seemed to ring for an age. My mouth was dry. A part of me was hoping he wouldn't pick up and I was ready to take the neighbour's advice when he answered. I was suddenly overcome with emotion and tears began to well and stung my eyes.

'Hiya Len. It's me,' I said. 'It's John.'

It had been over three years since the curtain came down on the April frolics. I was certain that time would have changed the way he felt, but I couldn't have been more wrong.

'What the fuck do *you* want?' he snapped.

I had no idea what to say.

'Well?' he demanded. 'What is it?'

I managed to compose myself. 'I'm going to Holland on Sunday, that's all, and I wanted to talk to you before I go, but it doesn't matter. Maybe I'll see you when I get back.'

I was about to hang up when he seemed to have a change of heart.

'You might as well come up now you're here. I'll come and let you in.' He came and opened the door and I stepped inside. The stairwell smelled of weed and piss. He was the thinnest I'd ever seen him. He had no hips and a filthy pair of jeans hung loosely from a leather belt pinched tightly around his waist, the loose end hanging to his thigh. His face was blotchy and he had the lids of a chameleon. We didn't hug and he turned and I followed him up the stairs to the flat.

The living-room smelled of body odour and sour milk. We sat at a pine table in the corner. Lenny laughed and pointed over my shoulder.

'I got some acid,' he said.

By the faltering light from a pair of candles I could see someone sitting on the floor with his back to an armchair in the corner of the room. He was wearing white jeans and shirt and he had the face of someone who belonged in a straitjacket. He was marbled with melted chocolate and in his hand a party-sized bar of dark chocolate had wilted and tumbled into his lap. The only place he'd managed to avoid was the area around his mouth, and his hair was spiked and brown. Two broad sweeps formed a huge X across his torso from shoulders to waistband and he stared at the wall and laughed to himself about nothing in particular.

A toilet flushed and a girl appeared in the doorway and dance-drifted slowly across the room, feeling her way as if through syrupy air. She was tall, with wild blonde hair, huge eyes and vivid red lips. She looked at the chocolate man as she sat at the table.

'You're a rotten bastard Lenny,' she drawled, and Lenny giggled.

'This is Clare, by the way,' he said. 'And that's Ibby, he added, pointing. Then he introduced me as John, 'someone I used to know.'

'Anyway, he deserved it coming to see me dressed like that.'

Clare stood and was on the move again. She turned with her arms entwined aloft and moved slowly towards Ibby who had tried to scrape the chocolate from his lap with his hands but had forgotten what he was doing and was now trying to roll a cigarette. Clare put her hands on her knees and flexed from the waist and started licking chocolate from his forehead.

'Do you fancy one?' Lenny was looking at me and dangling a strip of microdots encased in sellotape. It looked like toad spawn. I said I wouldn't bother. He freed a trip and put it on the end of his finger and held it out.

I looked at Ibby oblivious. 'Actually,' I said, 'I was hoping we could talk.'

'Take no notice of him,' he said. 'Fucking idiot double-dropped. Anyway, if I remember right this stuff makes you talk for England.' He laughed and tugged my sleeve. 'I gave him that chocolate two hours ago,' he said. 'For the crack. He doesn't even know what it is.'

Ibby looked up and grinned massively, looking like a child left unattended at the toilet.

I turned the acid down again so Lenny took it himself with a swig of beer. 'Suit yourself. Here,' he took a bag of weed from his pocket and pushed it across the table. 'Skin up then. Do you want a beer?'

Before I left home I knew what I wanted to say. I'd thought about it all the way there on the bus. About us having grown up together, just the two of us. About our friendship and how much it meant to me. About how, now that we weren't friends, we were both friendless.

After the reception I'd got and the state of affairs in the living-room I'd felt so uncomfortable up to that point that I just wanted to leave. But a beer was a start, and even though I knew that when the acid kicked in Lenny would be incoherent I couldn't bring myself to leave with nothing resolved, so I agreed to a beer and I started to skin up while Lenny went to the kitchen and brought two bottles back to the table.

Ibby and Clare were kneeling and were quietly playing a brand-new game, 'finger-twister,' on the arm of the chair. I put the roach in the joint and we smoked and the strong weed soon took hold. I took a long drink from the bottle. Lenny spluttered a laugh but didn't share and nobody asked and it was silent again. I decided it was now or never.

'Is it true Len? What I've heard?'

He drew on the joint and inhaled deeply.

'That depends. I'm not a junkie if that's what you've heard.'

Outside, a car hissed over wet tarmac.

'You sure about that, Len?'

'I swear on my mother's life,' he said, vehemently, and right then I knew that he was lying.

And he knew that I knew.

Swearing on his mother's life had earned him the benefit of the doubt so many times at school and got him out of so many scrapes. He said it with such utter conviction that the teachers, responsible adult or whoever it might be, instantly backed off, sometimes even ruffling his hair and consoling him, like he was the victim.

Everyone in the village knew Fred and Noreen. They were lovely people, well-respected pillars of the community. But it wasn't Noreen's life he was swearing on. Even Lenny would never do that. He was swearing on the life of his birth mother, the one he had never met, whose name he never knew, who had abandoned him as a baby and disappeared from his life.

The one he often said he hoped was dead.

I looked at him. He's never going to change, I thought.

'Ok,' I said. 'Whatever you say. Anyway, it wasn't just that.'

‘So, what then?’

‘I’ve heard that you’re robbing chemists’ shops.’

He said nothing, which told me everything.

‘It’s true then.’

‘What’s it to you if it is? Besides I’m only the alarm man. I’m long gone by the time they go in. It’s the perfect arrangement. I do the alarm and come home. They keep all the junk and I get a shed load of speed. I sell enough to keep me in beer and weed and that’s it. You can have some if you want some. I’ve got loads. Red and browns, green and clears. Black bombers. I’ve got some Nembutal for the come-down. You have to be careful with them though. It’s like having an elephant sit on your head.’

I couldn’t believe what I was hearing. ‘The Alarm Man? The fucking Alarm Man? How did you come to be the fucking Alarm Man?’

‘Because of the Post Office. Fred showed me. The alarm. I know all about them.’ He got up, pushed a cassette into the player, spun the volume knob as high as it would go and came and sat back at the table. ‘I knew it’d come in handy one day.’

There was the sudden, shocking stab of a stylus hitting vinyl, a long crackle of static that seemed to dislodge my ear wax, then Rory Gallagher’s battered Fender swarmed through the room, a swirl of sound that both thrilled and threatened. My discomfort had come back and redoubled. Then the drums and bass kicked in and thumped through me, rattling my frame and vibrating the teeth in my head. My tongue was sticking to the roof of my mouth and I took another long swallow from the bottle. Lenny was grinning at me from across the table. He reached out and clinked my bottle with his and he smiled a weird smile that I thought bore more than a little contempt.

'Touché,' he said.

* * *

At least, I thought that's what he said, but I couldn't be sure. I was starting to get very confused. The music slowed, quickened, came in gusts that made me shudder, like an entity passing through me. My gums tasted metallic and I had butterflies in my stomach. There was no mistaking the onset of an acid trip. I'd been spiked and there was nothing I could do about it now. It was definitely no time for a row. All I could do now was hold on.

The room began to breathe and the flickering candles cast shadows that danced across the walls and ceiling. I looked at Ibby and Clare curled together on the floor and they seemed to meld like some mutant and I couldn't tell where one ended and the other began. I hadn't a clue what was going on. I stood and stretched and searched the wall for the doorway and went to the bathroom to have a piss in a vain attempt to clear my head.

My cock had gone into torpor and didn't seem real, and my bladder wouldn't cooperate. The mirror above the sink was smeared with chocolate and I pictured Ibby trying to wipe it off the wrong face. I lowered the toilet lid and sat and the room throbbed and the acid coursed through me like a train. I closed my eyes and a firework display flashed through my head. I was now officially on another planet.

I've no idea how long I sat there, but eventually I heaved myself up and stood and leaned on the wall with my palms either side of the mirror. My skin flowed like lava and my pupils were hugely dilated. I turned out the light and made my way unsteadily, like a broken marionette, back to the living-room, leaving the mirror grinning stupidly in the dark.

I took my seat back at the table and Lenny handed me a joint, a pointless gesture, but I took it anyway and then I sat and let it go out.

And Rory sang…

Well I lost my job

And I was back out on the street

A sudden chill came over the room, a cold draught that seemed to distort the music. The candles died then flared. Suddenly there was another being in the room; it was in the doorway. An alien. It was short and broad and was dressed in pale denim and its shadow was too big for the room and was stooped between wall and ceiling. A mass of earrings cascaded silver down the side of its huge head and it looked at Ibby and Clare, entwined on the floor. Then it looked at me. It looked mean and angry and it strode forward and jabbed a fat paw that nearly touched my nose and it shouted something that I couldn't make out because of my head and the music and the fact that it had its own dialect.

I walk on hot coals; sleep on a bed of nails

Walk on thin ice, skate on razor blades

It moved like in a strobe around the table towards Lenny and grabbed the bag of weed and waved it in his face and then pocketed it and Lenny started to rise but the rampant invader grabbed him by the neck and slammed his face to the table and bellowed at the back of his head. It had a clock-face tattooed on the side of its neck and its spittle sprayed Lenny's hair. My visual and aural perceptions were way out but I stood anyway, uselessly, and was choked and beaten viciously back into my chair by something like a ham shank that stammered through the air like a rock-video effect. Lenny sat with his head tilted back against the wall to stem the bleeding from his shattered nose. There was a ringing in my ears that drowned out Rory, and the maniac was a blur of turbulence as it ransacked cupboards and shelves around the room.

I wanna cause no trouble, no fuss no fight
See this match; I might set this place alight

Clare had struggled to her feet and was helping Ibby to his and it took two strides and kicked Ibby full in the face sending him backwards over the chair in a spray of teeth and blood. Clare screamed and went for its face with her nails but it grabbed her by the shoulders and butted her in the mouth and threw her back into the chair. Ibby crawled on all fours to her side and knelt and held her hand and stared with a face that was a mess of blood and chocolate but wore an untroubled expression. Clare hugged him close and sobbed.

Now I'm back in your town

The beast reached to the top shelf and brought down a shoe box and threw the lid to the floor and pulled out a carrier bag. A glance at the contents, a pointing finger, a warning bellow, a slamming door. A sudden chill came over the room, a cold draught that seemed to distort the music. The candles flared then died.

In your town, in your town, in your town.

* * *

Nobody spoke. The smell of snuffed candles filled the room. Ibby and Clare were sitting against the chair staring straight ahead, Ibby cradling his salvaged teeth in his palm. Clare was huddled into Ibby. She was crying softly. Her beautiful lips were torn and her nose was bruised and flattened. Lenny still had his head tilted back and was cupping his nose in a blood-sodden tissue that was dripping into his lap.

We were all in shock. I was less than an hour into an eight-hour acid trip and the world was suddenly a very bad place. Where the walls had been breathing like a healthy set of lungs, now they were consumptive, wheezing, terminal. Spindly black fingers searched the room. Outside noises seemed amplified. A bottle breaking on the street, raised voices. Was someone coming up the stairs or was it the wind? Was there a wind? I got to my feet and stood and swayed. I wanted to ask Lenny what had just happened but no words would come and I left without speaking.

It had stopped raining but the tarmac was still wet. There was no other person in the street. The wind had grown and chip papers rolled past like cottonweed. I wandered aimlessly around town. It was aloof and eerie. Buildings huddled around the streets and took on character. Sloping roofs became lank hair. Windows turned to staring eyes and doors muttered low under their breaths as I passed. I was convinced the world had ended; the end had indeed been nigh, and here it was. Somewhere someone laughed long and loud. Every person, the doorway-drunk, the solitary sentinel at the bus stop, every approaching figure, was a survivor, a mutant, a potential assailant. I crossed the road, back and forth, to avoid them, and made my way toward the bypass.

The further I got from the town centre the more relaxed I became. The houses on Chestnut Avenue had a much more welcoming disposition than those in town. They wore faces of contentment and promised security within their wall-arms and their gate-hands. There were no madmen or junkies behind those nets.

I sat on the wall of one to roll a cigarette. I tried to concentrate my thoughts on the trip to Holland on Sunday but I couldn't shake off the events at Lenny's. Who was the lunatic? The shoe box was obviously Lenny's speed stash. Did Lenny know him or was he just an opportunist out to rob junkies and dealers? In spite of his denials Lenny was both. He was taking speed every day of the week when I moved out three years earlier and by the look of him he'd never stopped.

I rolled the first cigarette inside-out and tried to salvage the tobacco but the wind caught it and blew it to the ground. The second wasn't a bad effort all things considered and I lit it and set off walking. It was seven miles and I did it the hard way, over fences and through fields, avoiding the road where possible.

When I got to Hawksheads it was after midnight and the acid was at its peak. No lights were on in the gatehouse. I crossed the cattle-grid and stood and peed against the garden wall. Pulsating silence. Grotesques loomed from the dark, took flight on bats' wings and swirled overhead, their faces twisted in pain. They seemed to follow me into the woods and I kicked on, walking faster and faster. Sinister voices whispered in the blackness and the vast void ahead appeared choked with spiders' webs of deep red and purple. I let it get to me and took my hands from my pockets and started to run. I didn't stop until I'd left the wood far behind, then I stood, surrounded by fields, looking back the way I'd come. Behind the gate to my right cattle slept, a cluster of dark smudges on the grass. To the left the sand quarry was invisible in the gloom. My chest was heaving and my mouth was dry. I turned and started walking. I passed the lane to the sand quarry and walked under the railway bridge. They were having a lock-in at the Eagle and Child and cracks of light escaped from behind the curtains. To cap a perfect evening a cold wetness had spread around my nether regions and was now chilling my inner thighs. Finally reaching the cottage I snuck in and went to the bathroom to clean up. I put my soiled clothes in a bag ready to be thrown in the dustbin and went to bed. Thirty-six hours later I was sitting in a coffeeshop in Amsterdam having my first ever legal joint as I waited for a train to take me on to Eindhoven.

PART TWO

Saturday 18th of October 1980

Having finally managed to stem the bleeding from his nose Lenny got up from the table and threw the sodden tissues in the bin. Ibby and Clare were still sitting on the floor, propped up by the sofa, with bloodied faces and thousand-yard stares.

Shock had overcome the acid, for now at least, and Ibby's chocolate-smeared whites and hair didn't seem quite so funny now. Lenny went to the bathroom. There was chocolate on the mirror and he made a half-hearted attempt to wipe it off. He looked at the gash on his nose, poked it, and it started to bleed again. He washed his hands and face and returned to the living room. Ibby and Clare were standing and staring vacantly around the room.

'Your jackets are on the floor. Behind the sofa.'

Ibby navigated a route around the sofa and stooped and emerged with a jacket in each hand. Lenny picked up the shoebox as they made their way awkwardly towards the door.

'You've got to take her to the hospital mate. She needs stitches in that lip. Really, she does. You haven't got anything on you and they can't do you for being stoned.' Ibby looked down at his clothes and ran a hand through his hair. 'And they can't do you for your appearance.' The acid was threatening to take over again and Lenny almost burst out laughing. He composed himself and turned his attention to the shoe-box.

He looked vainly inside and his mood suddenly darkened as the enormity of his situation hit him. He stuffed the bag into the box and threw it at the sofa. He saw the lid, close-by on the floor, and took a step and stamped on it repeatedly. 'There was a grand's worth of gear in there. A grand's worth of someone else's fucking gear.' He kicked the lid into the skirting board. 'I'm fucked. I'm fucking dead.'

Ibby was holding the door open for Clare and rooting with a finger in the small front pocket of his jeans. He produced a nugget of resin and handed it to Lenny. Lenny's face lit up and he grabbed it and sat down at the table.

'You fucking beauty.' He pulled three rizlas from a torn packet and started to stick them together. He paused and looked at Ibby, still standing in the doorway.

'Shouldn't you be at the hospital?'

* * *

He put a cassette in the player and pressed repeat and sat and chain-smoked the resin until it was gone, hoping to dull the acid, but he wouldn't be getting to sleep anytime soon. He took his trainers off and curled up on the sofa. Maybe he could get a few hours' rest, at least.

He had a clamour in his head and the Olympic closing ceremony behind his eyelids. Whenever he did get totally relaxed, he'd realise that he needed to swallow, or he'd get an itch, or he'd suddenly become aware of his heartbeat. Then he'd notice that he wasn't relaxed at all, that he was tense and was clenching his fists.

Faces loomed, threatened, retreated, hundreds of faces, coming and going, in and out. Then just one face, the same face, again and again, over and over, the same face, flashing silver, then another, another version of the same face, then more, and more, all flashing silver and shouting silently. The faces suddenly exploded and were replaced by just one, a different face, a clock face, a blue clock face that came and went and told no time. He opened and closed his eyes hoping he could start again. And on it went.

It was gone twelve when he opened his eyes again. The phone was on incoming calls only so he went to the phone box and rang Russ Marsh and arranged to meet him in the Rose and Crown at two. He went back to the flat and did some tidying up. In the bathroom he looked at himself in the mirror. There was no way he could go into town in this state.

He leaned back in the shower and let the hot water wash the blood from his nose. He dried, found his other jeans and his Lou Reed tee-shirt, and got dressed. He hadn't eaten for a day and a half but he wasn't hungry so he sat back on the sofa and closed his eyes.

When he opened them again it was almost two. Fuck! Russ would be fuming. He really couldn't face going into town but he needed some smoke and he'd made arrangements. With Russ. If he stood him up, he'd never be able to show his face in town again. He'd never hear the last of it. He had work tomorrow and had been hoping to have a good feed and a night's sleep tonight, but he saw no choice. He got his emergency speed stash from his sock-drawer and sucked his finger to the knuckle and plunged it into the bag. He withdrew the finger and rubbed it around his gums and rinsed his mouth with water and swallowed and grimaced. He grabbed his tattered bomber jacket and left the flat and set off on foot for the Rose and Crown.

He hadn't seen Russ for a while. The last time was a couple

of months ago, the night a gang of pub regulars got back from a trip to Morocco, where Russ had managed to have the worst time of his life. Someone had told him that the locals who sold weed to tourists were then paid to point them out to the police, so he smuggled low-grade Moroccan resin back to Morocco and spent the whole week in and around the hotel.

'Twenty years, no food. That's what you get if you get caught. Your family have to come over and feed you or you fucking starve.'

Russ couldn't understand any meal that didn't end with … and chips, or … on toast. In the hotel he'd eyed his plate with mistrust and picked and poked and prodded, moving things around and eating very little. He tried an olive, barely puncturing its skin, and recoiled and spat like he'd been stung by a hornet. Sitting on a hotel balcony in the Moroccan sun with a joint in one hand and a cool beer in the other he'd start moaning about what the weather would probably be like for a possible camping trip to the Lake District later in the summer.

'It'll be pissing down. It always is up there.'

On the one occasion he did go out with the group he bought a kid-leather wallet from the market and put his money in it then had it picked from his pocket.

There was a sudden hail shower, a strafing from the blue that had people running for shelter. Lenny stood under a canopy on the outdoor market and pretended to browse the stall. He could feel the speed but the buzz wasn't what he'd hoped for. He'd wanted to be flying, on top of his game. Russ was going to give him shit.

The hail was short-lived and he walked the last hundred yards to the Rose and Crown. The large pub was quiet. Two meatheads were sitting at the far end of the bar and they looked him up and down and kept their eyes on him and carried on talking, one leaning into the other to hear what he was saying.

The barmaid looked like the Mona Lisa. She was barely five-feet tall and wore no make-up and her eyes were heavy-lidded. The skin at the corners of her mouth was dry and cracked, eczema or psoriasis or something. He couldn't take his eyes off her cleavage.

'A pint please, love.'

She'd been chewing a piece of gum but now her mouth hung open. She looked at the row of taps and pump-handles along the bar.

'Are you going to give me a clue?'

'What do you recommend?'

'I recommend you point to one of these on here and I'll pull you a pint.'

He looked at the two meatheads. 'I'll have a pint of what they're drinking.'

Russ was sitting in an alcove as far from humanity as possible and Lenny raised his hand. Russ glared back and tapped his wrist furiously.

Mona Lisa gripped the pump-handle, a bit suggestively he thought, and heaved on it the same way. He had his foot on the rail and his leg was shaking. The Bee Gees' How Deep is Your Love was playing and he sang it quietly to himself. She put the pint down in front of him.

'It's a summer breeze not a submarine.'

He didn't react. He was staring at her cleavage again.

'Do you want a photo?'

He held out a fiver. 'Aye, if you've got one.'

She pinched the note from his fingers, turned her back, and went to the till and came back with his change.

'Have you got his number?'

He picked up his pint. 'Whose number?'

'Whoever did that to you. I think I'd like him.'

'I'm sure you would. You'd make the perfect couple.'

He carried his drink over and sat across from Russ. He was in his usual denim suit and black Docs buffed to a mirror. He'd grown his hair to shoulder-length and hadn't washed it for months, since some space cadet convinced him it cleans itself.

'Alright Russ, how's it hanging?'

Russ tapped his knee under the table and Lenny took an eighth of resin from his hand and glanced at it and put it in his pocket.

'Moroccan, eh? Your favourite, Russ.'

'Fuck off.' He tapped Lenny's knee again. 'A tenner.'

Lenny pulled a tenner from his pocket and threw it on the table.

'Good to see you too, you miserable, robbing cunt.'

Russ grabbed the money and looked over at the bar to see if there'd been any witnesses.

'You fucking prick.'

'Chill out. Fucking hell. I don't know why you bother if it stresses you out so much. You can't make much selling eighths and 'teenths.'

'There's one thing for sure, I'll make fuck all if I let everyone have it at that price and I see as little of them as I do of you.'

'That's two things,' Lenny said.

Russ didn't break stride.

'Anyway,' he said, 'it's not the dealing that gets me stressed; it's the *people* I'm dealing with. Where the fuck have you been? We said two o'clock. *You* said two o'clock. I've been sitting here with that in my pocket for nearly a fucking hour.' He took a swig of his pint.

'I could have come to the house—'

'I don't want you at the fucking house—'

'You mean Anne doesn't want me at the house—'

'Neither of us wants you at the fucking house Lenny.'

'Fucking hell, steady on Russ.'

'No, I won't. You've taken up with a bunch of fucking nutters Lenny. Them fuckers off the fairground. You need to ditch them.'

They both took a drink. Russ watched as Lenny rooted his baccy and skins from his pocket and started to roll a cigarette.

'I'll never forgive you for bringing them fuckers to my house Lenny.'

Lenny didn't look up. 'I didn't bring them. They were looking for me, that's all—'

'So how did they know where to find you? And why did they bring beer? They just sat down, cracked a can, and skinned up, like they fucking lived there. *I* felt like the off-comer.'

'That's just how they are. They're up-front, a bit in-your-face.' Lenny's leg was shaking and it looked like the baccy would end up on the carpet. He put his heel to the floor and his leg stopped shaking. Russ watched.

'And look at the fucking state of you. You're a right one to be telling me to chill out. You need to leave that whizz alone.'

Lenny lit the cigarette.

'And what happened to your nose?'

He put his hand to his face. 'A misunderstanding.'

'Yeah, you seem to have a lot of them. What happened, did Mongo find out?'

Lenny scowled and shook his head. He blew a jet of smoke at the floor.

'How many times do I have to tell you. Nothing happened.'

'Well, that's not what you told me the next night. All over you, you said she was, like a rash, the minute he started snoring.' Russ laughed at the memory. 'We had a right old chin-wag that night. Well, you did.'

Lenny took another long drag on the roll-up.

'I was pissed and bragging. I lie when I'm drunk.'

'But you weren't drunk, were you? You were speeding your fucking tits off.'

'Ok, so I lie when I'm speeding.'

'In that case everything you've ever told me has been bollocks. Robbing them chemists. The twos-ups with that posh bird. You and your mate Woodsy.'

Lenny went to knock ash from the cigarette but his hand was unsteady and he stubbed it in the ashtray and winced as he shook an ember from his finger.

'He's not my mate, not anymore.'

Russ started to laugh. 'Well, he must have been your mate back then, I mean—'

'Ok Russ, ok, it was all bollocks, ok? I made it all up, everything, but I'm telling you now, nothing happened with Mongo's wife.'

'Whatever you say Lenny.'

Mona Lisa was looking over. Lenny took a swallow from his pint and held her gaze over the glass. She turned her back. Russ was watching.

'You've never changed, have you? You're like a fucking dog. What's that poor lass ever done to you?'

'Fuck off Russ, I wouldn't touch her with yours.'

Russ took another swig of his pint. 'Ok Lenny, whatever. Anyway, I'm having a break so I'd make that eighth last if I were you. Mind, that's never been a problem for you has it?' Lenny started to speak but Russ interrupted. 'And don't tell anyone where you got it from.'

'Jesus. Stop being so fucking paranoid.'

'I'm not paranoid. A fucking head-case paid my man a visit last night. This bloke's built like a brick shithouse, as wide as he is tall, face full of piercings, and he turns the place upside-down looking for my man's stash. Took the fucking lot.'

Lenny didn't react and Russ looked him in the eyes, looked again at his nose.

'Fucking hell. So, Lenny Fields, never short of gear, rings me, desperate for some smoke, and turns up late, wired, and looking like he's had a run-in with Marvin Hagler. Fucking hell, I've been a bit slow.'

Lenny avoided Russ's eyes, raised his glass and took a drink. 'I don't know what you're on about.'

Russ shook his head and stood. 'I haven't got time for this. You couldn't tell the truth if your fucking life depended on it. You couldn't lie straight in bed.' He fastened his jacket. 'Like I said, I'm having a break so don't bother ringing. I've got to go. Anne's going on a girl's night out so I'm cooking.'

'A tagine is it? With extra olives?'

'Ha-ha, funny guy. I'd rather fucking starve. Thieving bastards.'

Lenny knew it was a mistake as soon as he thought it, but he said it anyway. 'And not that old 'girls' night out' chestnut.'

Russ was a puritan, always happy to cast the first stone, and he went off on one.

'What's that supposed to mean? She's going on a girl's night out. That's it. She's earned it. She's a fucking diamond. We're not all like you, you know. We're not all fucking obsessed with sex on the brain twenty-four fucking seven.' He shook his head and patted his pockets. He finished his pint and put the empty glass on the table.

'And anyway, she knows I'd kill the fucking pair of them if I ever found out.' He looked over at Mona Lisa then down at the glass. 'If she's interested, she'll be over for that the minute I'm gone.' He made to leave then turned back. 'I see him in here now and again. Mongo. We have a couple of pints. A game of pool and a crack. I'll tell him you were asking after him.'

* * *

When they were at school, Mongo was captain of the football team. He was big then, he was huge now, the profile of a totem pole and a basketball-size frizz of orange hair that said, 'I dare you to stare.' He took to Lenny for some reason, adopted him as his pet softie, always sticking up for him, whether he needed it or not. He found Lenny funny, and Lenny found he could get away with saying things that would earn someone else a kicking. Things like actually calling him Mongo to his face.

'You cheeky little ginger cunt,' he'd say, and pretend to punch him, but he'd be laughing as he said it, and the huge fist would stop well short. Lenny doubted Mongo would be doing much laughing, but the fist would definitely be finding its target if he found out he'd shagged his wife, Janette, on the sofa while Mongo was comatose in the next room.

It was a Saturday night back in the summer and he'd been having what he thought was a crafty joint in the beer garden at the White Hart in town when Mongo came out and smelled it. He didn't say anything at the time, just sniffed the air and gave a knowing grunt. It was two hours later that he announced that the Mongos would be visiting, 'We're coming round to yours after the pub,' and that it would be in Lenny's interests to be in possession of some agreeable tunes, 'None of your hippy shit.'

Back at the flat he pestered Lenny to skin up, and as soon as he had Mongo took it off him and lit it. He wasn't a regular smoker. He was one of those blokes who only ever want a smoke after they've had a gallon and a half of Stella and he took a succession of huge draws that poker-ended the joint and his face turned grey before his back had hit the sofa. Lenny tried to take the joint off him but Mongo had his elbow on the arm of the sofa and his hand was up and down like a rev-counter. His elbow slipped into his lap and the joint fell from his fingers onto the carpet. He made no effort to move and Janette picked it up and handed it to Lenny. She looked at Mongo and back again and shrugged. She had the remains of a black eye, a yellow smudge on her lower lid.

Mongo was like a nodding-poodle and he suddenly opened his eyes and got up and tottered across the room, threatening to topple with every step, until he found the bedroom and disappeared inside. He closed the door loudly behind him and within minutes his snores were rattling the walls.

He had no idea how it happened. Mongo's wife. What the fuck was he thinking? Mongo's in the next room. Fucking hell, you'd have to be mad. He remembered the snoring and them looking at each other and then, she just straddled him and went for it. Instantly. That's how he remembered it, anyway. Afterwards they curled up together and slept soundly on the sofa.

In the morning when Mongo appeared Janette was still asleep and Lenny was behind the kitchen counter making two brews. Lenny turned and followed Mongo's gaze to Janette. It was obvious to Lenny that she'd been forced to sleep on half of the small sofa, was squashed into the back, with a gaping void in front of her that someone had obviously just vacated. Mongo didn't seem to notice. He seemed more concerned about finding his shoes, and the vomit on his shirt.

* * *

Mona Lisa didn't come for Russ's empty glass. Lenny sat cradling his in his lap. He could suddenly feel the come-down off everything he'd taken since Thursday; the dope, the speed, the acid, the beer. He was feeling more and more light-headed. He managed to lean forward and put the glass on the table and slumped back again and closed his eyes. He daren't get up. A sudden blood-rush now and he'd be having a full-on whitey. Retching yellow bile from an empty stomach in public. He knew how that went. That'd impress Mona Lisa and the meatheads. Good name for a band, he thought, and smiled weakly to himself. Images flashed through his mind; an empty shoe-box, fairground lights, angry faces. Ibby. Blood and chocolate. He saw April Meadows. She was crying. Clare too. He saw Swifty and the twins. Fred clacking his dentures. He saw a kingfisher. A kestrel soaring at eye-level, John, tiny on the ground. Hay bales. John in a football shirt, mouth bleeding, Mongo standing over him. He saw eggs; big eggs and small eggs, blue eggs, green eggs, blotched eggs, speckled eggs. Broken eggs. He saw a golden tarn. He saw John, he was laughing, they were laughing …

He began to resurface. The whitey had receded. He heard voices and opened his eyes. The empties had gone from the table. He looked around the room. The pub was busy. A middle-aged couple were asking are the other seats taken. He shook his head, no, and they sat and he stood and swayed and straightened his clothes. His palms were clammy. He took a deep breath and patted himself down and concentrated on getting to the door. He felt the stares but saw none and hit the blinding autumn sun like he was winning the hundred metres.

* * *

To avoid the town-centre and the tourists he walked home along the seaward side of the promenade. In a few hours the illuminations would come on and the Bright Lights would live up to its name, but it was quiet for now. He was due at work in less than eighteen hours, a twelve-hour shift spinning families on the waltzers, being cool, confident, chatting up the lasses, showing off his effortless balance and poise as the floor undulates. He hadn't slept for three days, hadn't eaten for two. His head was frazzled. He could barely string two-thoughts together, never mind two sentences. If that wasn't bad enough, he had to think of a way to explain to his workmates that he'd lost a grand's worth of their gear. He didn't think the truth would be good enough, even with the nose damage.

He sat on the railing and watched nature going about its business. The sun was mostly hidden behind an expanse of dark cloud, and the end of a stunted rainbow coloured a patch of sand that appeared to be just a short walk away. The tide was being chased back by an army of tiny waders that was skittering busily along its edge finding newly-revealed morsels. He found he could still identify most of them; sanderling, dunlin, turnstone; the cloud of knot displaying over the receding water, flashing silver, now you see them, now you don't. He noticed curlew were spread out across the sand, probing for lugworm and pulling them from deep in their burrows. An enormous black-backed gull landed on the railing a few feet away and turned towards him with its wings out and stooped forward and let go a series of raucous calls. It had a ring on its leg and he wondered if one of them had caught it once, him or John, if it had been ringed that day, by Jeff or Mike, when it was a dumpy, frumpy little shitting and vomiting machine.

He climbed off the railing and had a last look at the view. He had a few days to get the money, and one last chance. It wasn't something he was looking forward to, and it would mean taking tomorrow off work. He was already on a final warning so would probably lose his job, but he could see no other option.

* * *

November was still a couple of weeks away but it had been another clear and frosty night that had left a coating of white on the lawn and the privet hedge that enclosed the Post Office garden. Around the borders Fred's beloved dahlias were still putting on a wonderful show of reds and peach and mauve, but the foliage was beginning to blacken. It was time to cut them down and lift the tubers for the winter.

Fred had been up since six and cut all the flowers and bunched them. He took a large, mixed-bunch inside for Noreen and she split them into two vases. She left one on the kitchen table and took the other through to the shop and placed it on the end of the counter. Fred stood the rest in buckets on a long trestle-table on the pavement at the side of the Post Office, to raise much-needed funds for the church. He placed the honesty box front and centre. After church he'd dig up the tubers and hang them in the cellar to dry before storing them over the winter. He was standing back, having a last look at the flowers, when Noreen appeared at the gate.

'Fred, love, time's getting on, you need to be getting ready for church soon.'

'I'll be in in a minute love, we've plenty of time.'

She didn't respond and Fred saw she'd gone pale and had taken on a vacant look. She seemed shocked by the sight of him, as if he'd grown another head, then he realised that she wasn't looking at him, she was looking beyond him, at a point across the street. He turned and saw a figure standing at the entrance to the ginnel, a figure they hadn't seen for five years and had worried they'd never see again.

* * *

Lenny had caught the bus to the bypass and walked the rest of the way to Yelland. On the bus he'd started to have his doubts and almost got off before it left the Bright Lights. There was no way he could go through with it. He hadn't seen them for years, had no idea how it would go. His best hope was a joyful reunion and when they finally finished hugging, they'd sit and have a cup of tea and he'd tell them, tell them straight. As he walked through Hawksheads and on past the sand quarry he tried to imagine how the conversation might go.

'I owe money to some people.'

'We haven't got any money.'

'If I don't get it for them, they'll kill me.'

'How much do you need?'

'A grand.'

'Ok, there you go.'

'Thanks.'

He'd arrived in Yelland much sooner than he'd expected

and had been standing at the entrance to the ginnel for a good half-hour, hidden by the overgrown privet hedge, chain-smoking and watching as Fred came and went with flowers for the table, fussing and faffing, arranging and rearranging. Even from this distance Lenny could see he'd let himself go. The Brylcreem had gone and his hair was longer, hanging over his eyes, and was going grey. He seemed smaller, too, and not so sure on his feet.

The longer he stood and watched, the more convinced he became that the whole thing was a mistake. There was not a chance that Fred and Noreen had that kind of money, and there was even less chance that Fred would hand over money from the safe, money belonging to his precious customers. The till drawer will have been removed and the till left open so that potential burglars wouldn't bust it open. The drawer containing the daily float would be upstairs under their bed and would be less than a hundred quid anyway. He was about to turn and leave, when he heard Noreen's voice. He took one step out from behind the hedge for a better look, but it was a mistake, and he found himself looking straight into her eyes across the street.

* * *

He stood motionless, his arms at his sides, as Noreen hugged him and burst into tears. Fred glanced up and down the street and suggested they go inside and manoeuvred them towards the gate.

In the kitchen Alistair Cooke was delivering his Sunday morning letter from America. Noreen turned down the volume and went to the sink.

'You two sit down and I'll make us a nice pot of tea.'

Fred and Lenny sat across from each other at the table as Noreen filled the kettle and rinsed the teapot. She was on the verge of tears again.

'Do you want something to eat, Joseph love? You look famished, son. I can make you a sandwich if you like. We've got some nice crumbly Lancashire or there's some lovely roast ham, and I have some of your favourite crusty bread.'

Lenny shook his head. 'No, I'm ok thanks.'

'Are you sure? Because you look like you haven't eaten for a week.'

Fred was looking at Lenny's face, the gash on his nose, the glassy, bloodshot eyes. He shook his head and clacked his dentures.

'Eee, Lenny, Lenny, lad, look at the mess of you. What have you got yourself into now?'

'I owe some people some money.'

'Who?'

'It doesn't matter who. I borrowed some money and I have to pay it back by Friday. That's it.'

'So, what did you do with it?'

'I didn't do anything with it. I got robbed.'

'So, what did you need it for, then, that you had to borrow it in the first place?'

Lenny scoffed and shook his head.

Noreen sat beside Fred at the table. 'And they did that to you?'

'This was just a warning.'

'You need to tell the police, Joseph.'

'I can't do that.'

'Then we will. Fred, call the police.'

Fred ignored Noreen and opened his wallet and put two

ten-pound notes and a fiver in front of Lenny.

'That's all I've got. Take it.'

Lenny picked it up. 'Thanks, but it's not enough.' He leaned back in his seat and put the money in his pocket. 'I need a grand.'

Fred clacked his dentures. Noreen looked at Fred.

'He means a thousand pounds love. Anyway, a hundred, a thousand, it's irreverent, because we haven't got it.'

Noreen stifled a sob and got up and went to the sink and filled the kettle.

'We've already got a brew, Noreen, come and sit down, love.'

She ignored him. 'What did we do wrong, love?,' she asked.

She was talking to Lenny, but Fred answered.

'I don't know, love. Maybe I should have been more like Frank Woods, drinking and raising his hand to his family.' He looked back at Lenny. 'I saw John this morning. He came over for a natter. He was waiting for a taxi to the airport, going to start his new job. He's a smashing lad, and after all he's been through.'

'Maybe you should have adopted him instead.' He spat the words at Fred.

Noreen was horrified and paused filling the teapot.

'There's no need for that, Joseph. That's a terrible thing to say."

'Water off a duck's back, Noreen love.' Fred turned back to Lenny. 'He asked about you. John did. Mind you, he always does. Of course, I couldn't tell him anything.' He did a double clack of his dentures and Lenny shook his head and gave him a withering look. Fred went on. 'He said you're not really in touch with him anymore either. It's such a shame. The best friend you'll ever have. You don't get many friendships like that in your lifetime, I can tell you that.'

Noreen could see that Lenny was getting more agitated. She was worried he might storm out as he so often had when things weren't going his way. She picked up the teapot and strainer and started to refill his cup. Lenny dragged it away by the saucer and tea poured onto the tablecloth. Noreen went to the drainer and came back with a dishcloth and started to rub furiously at the tea stain. Fred took her wrist gently in his hand.

'Leave it, love, it'll wash.' He turned back to Lenny. 'It doesn't seem five minutes since you were out there, the pair of you, playing and bird-egging. What happened, son? Eh? What changed?' Fred seemed close to tears himself and he got up, cleared his throat, and took his cup to the sink, rinsed it under the tap and went and sat back at the table. He went on. 'I remember it like yesterday, you both came home looking like the walking wounded and I took you to the hospital. I never thought then that I'd be looking back and thinking them were the days.' He looked at Noreen standing back by the sink, sobbing gently. He looked back at Lenny. 'Do you think your mother deserves this? Do you? She's not had a decent night's sleep for I don't know how long. Neither of us has.'

Lenny had zoned out. He knew he shouldn't have come. He should have listened to himself on the bus, should have known how it would go. He couldn't stand it anymore and jumped out of his chair and stood and zipped up his jacket. Noreen walked to him and took him by the elbows.

'Don't leave son, please, not like this. Come to church with us. Things won't seem so bad then, I promise. You've lost yourself that's all, for now, but the Lord will help you find yourself again, Joseph, truly he will.'

Lenny shook his arms free and turned and seconds later was out of the door and half-way down the path to the gate. The church-bells were calling the faithful to prayer as Noreen went to the door and shouted after him.

'Why don't you come home Joseph? Your bedroom is just how you left it …' but it was too late, and she watched as he disappeared behind the privet hedge and down the ginnel.

* * *

Fred suggested they were cutting it fine and maybe they should give church a miss this week, considering, but Noreen would have none of it. She needed church today more than ever, she said, and so, at nine fifty-five, Fred closed the garden-gate behind them and they linked arms and hurried up the hill to church.

From behind the hedge Lenny watched them leave. He stayed hidden until they were out of sight then went round the back and let himself in with the key he still had. He put the kettle on and buttered some bread, took a slice of ham from a packet in the fridge and made himself a sandwich. He made a cup of tea and took the snack upstairs to his bedroom. The door was closed and he thought to leave it that way when he left.

Inside, nothing had changed. It was clean and tidy now, but everything else was as he remembered it. He put the cup and plate on the bedside table and stood and looked around the room. John's painting was still on the wall; the pied wagtail with chicks in the nest. On the book-shelf; A child's atlas, Dandy and Beano annuals, Beezer, Topper, the Hamlyn Guide to Birds of Europe, Mushroom Hunter's Field Guide, the dog-eared copy of Kes.

He went to Fred and Noreen's bedroom. He'd intended

to take the float but when he looked under the bed it wasn't there. He'd planned to take the change bags too, maybe empty Noreen's rainy-day tin, but he searched the whole place and nothing was where it used to be. He went through their bedside drawers and cabinets, the wardrobe, but found nothing.

He made sure he left everything exactly as he found it; clothes straight in drawers, wardrobe doors closed and locked, bedroom door slightly ajar, and went back to his bedroom. He took the field guide down and sat on the bed and leafed through it as he ate the sandwich. His name was written in large letters on the inside cover. He turned the pages, avoiding the text and trying to name the various fungi from the illustrations. He was impressed with his score.

He finished the sandwich and drank the last of the tea and stood and put the book back on the shelf. He scraped crumbs from the bed into his palm and tipped them back onto the plate and put the plate and cup on the bedside table. He straightened the bed-spread and made sure nothing was out of place.

Downstairs, he washed and dried the cup, the plate and butter-knife, and put them away. He scanned the kitchen, could see nothing untoward, and was set to leave when his gaze was drawn to the open door from the living-quarters to the Post Office and shop.

The door was wedged open; the alarm wasn't set, so he went in. He browsed the shelves and filled his pockets with packets of space dust, a double-decker, a liquorice wheel and a sherbet fountain, being careful to reposition the remaining sweets to hide any gaps, then he walked behind the counter and took a two-ounce tin of Golden Virginia and some cigarette papers.

He opened the cover to the safe and squatted on his haunches and looked at the dial. Unsurprisingly, he'd never been trusted with the combination, and he knew he had no chance of cracking it, but he thought he'd have a go anyway.

He noted the position of the dial then started to turn it, slowly, listening for the faintest of clicks, feeling for the slightest sign of give. He tried for a minute or so, but it was pointless, so he returned the dial to its original position, closed the cover, and put his hand on the floor to give himself a push up. He managed to get upright but felt suddenly light-headed and put his hand out to support himself on the counter. His hand hit something and he turned and saw it leaning, toppling, and there was a hideous crash that cut to his core, as the porcelain vase hit the slate floor.

His heart sank. He stepped out from behind the counter and eyed the damage. Like a Picasso still-life, the vase was in a hundred pieces but was still vaguely vase-shaped and was surrounded by a large arc of broken flowers and puddles of water. He leaned back and put his hands over his ears and screamed silently for a few seconds, until his frustrations boiled over and he gave voice to the scream and finally went on a rampage. He kicked and stamped all over the flowers and the remnants of the vase, sending debris to every corner. He moved from wall to wall, emptying shelves onto the floor and tipping over displays. He threw a bottle of dandelion and burdock at the chiller cabinet. There was a loud, dull thud as it hit, a crash as it broke, and a long, drawn-out tinkling as a thousand pieces of glass cascaded to the floor.

When he finally fell to his knees and began to weep the shop looked like a bomb had hit it. In the sudden silence he could hear the church bells ringing for end of service. Still weeping, he got up and let himself out the back door. He locked the door, walked down the path and closed the garden-gate behind him. As a parting-shot, he kicked the folding legs from under the end of the trestle table and Fred's morning's work slid to the ground. He crossed the road and headed for the bypass and could still feel the crunch of glass and porcelain fragments underfoot as he waited to catch the bus back to reality.

* * *

Stu and Tony Savage were brothers who'd grown up on their family's travelling fairground until the old man had died and it had closed down. They hadn't wanted to put down roots; an itinerant life was well-suited to what were, at the time, their most profitable enterprises; robbing chemists' shops, which netted large quantities of Class A drugs to be sold-on, and selling fiver and tenner bags of weed to kids across the country, never in the same place for more than a few days, hard to pin down. A lot of kids, a lot of bags. But travelling fairs were dying out and when permanent jobs came up at Bright Lights Pleasure Park, with their total knowledge of everything fairground, they started the next day.

Lenny had been at the fairground for a couple of years when they turned up. At first, he had nothing to do with them outside work. Then he overheard them talking one day, about a chemist's they were planning to break into, and that they needed an alarm-man.

How he wished now that he'd kept his fucking stupid bragging mouth shut. None of this shit would have happened. They only did a couple of chemists but it was too late then. Since they'd found out where he lived, they'd started showing up more often, usually to sort and weigh their gear. They knew he was a soft touch, and he knew that they knew it.

* * *

It was getting dark when he got home. He'd walked a good part of the way, getting caught between stops and missing two buses. Tony's car was parked across the street and Tony got out and met him at the door.

'Where the fuck have you been? I've been sitting there for ages.'

Lenny didn't want Tony to see his face and start asking questions so he kept his back to him as he unlocked the door and Tony followed him up the stairs.

'I had stuff to do today … family stuff … look, Tony, sorry mate, but I've had one fucking shit weekend, and I really need some kip, so what do you want?' He knew he'd sounded too aggressive.

'No need to get shirty you little cunt. I'm here because we need a word, and you weren't at work, again—'

'Well, like I said, family. Have I still got a job?'

'You have but it was fuck all to do with me. You can thank Stu when he gets here.' Lenny turned and Tony saw his face. 'What the fuck happened to you?'

Lenny wanted to come clean and get it over with, but he didn't know how.

'It doesn't matter, just a shit weekend, that's all. So, what's going on? Why's Stu coming?'

'We need a favour, and we reckon you owe us one. You being still gainfully employed and all that.'

'What sort of favour?'

'We've an old mate that's just out and needs somewhere to crash for a few nights. You've a spare room, so that's dropped nicely.'

Lenny heard voices on the landing and the door opened and Stu appeared with the old mate. Tony started to introduce him but Lenny had already seen the bulldog-build, the mass of silver earrings, the clock-face tattoo.

PART THREE

January 1984

When I woke we were on the living room floor in a nest we'd built in the small hours from quilts and pillows and we were spooned and I was still hard. I kissed Jan's shoulder and felt her heart flutter against my palm. I raised myself on an elbow and pulled the jumble of platinum hair from her face and kissed her neck and she nuzzled her pillow and made a sound like a basket of kittens, but when I manoeuvred myself into a favourable position, she flapped me away as you would a wasp.

I lowered myself, hands behind my head. The sun had found a crack in the curtains and cast a wafer of light that formed prisms in the chunky crystal ashtray on the hearth. A partially smoked spliff shone like some ancient artefact only revealed on this day of the year at … I looked at the clock on the video player … 8.43am. I reached with the hand that was closest but my shoulder threatened to dislocate so I sat up, picked up the joint and stretched for the lighter. Jan stiffened like she'd been electrocuted and reached blindly over her shoulder for the quilt edge.

'Cover my back up, John. It's freezing.'

I lit the joint and drew deeply, squinting smoke from my eyes as I hoisted the quilt and formed it around her.

'You said you wanted a baby.'

'I do, but not just now. I want a fried egg butty first. Made with toast. And I want a cup of tea. Then I want a baby.'

I stood and charted a path through the ashtrays, cans and bottles, to the kitchen. I balanced the joint on the windowsill and stood immobile and looked around the room as if for the first time. I spotted the frying pan upside down on the drainer, gripped the handle, spun it and clattered a crash of cutlery to the tiled floor.

I poured oil in the frying pan and found I had created Africa. Trying to add Madagascar I swamped Mozambique and Tanzania and as I retrieved the cutlery my thoughts turned to lemurs.

The hob lit with a whoosh under the pan and I knocked more cutlery to the floor. I relit the spliff and leaned on the windowsill with both hands and looked out on the garden just in time to see a face disappear from the upstairs window of next door's new extension. I quick-stepped to one side and took Jan's apron from the chair-back and put it on.

I loaded the toaster and took an egg from the fridge and cracked it into the pan, bursting the yolk and retrieving stray slivers of shell ineptly with what was left of the two halves.

The house had two gardens. At the back was a cambered lawn with a small border and a few plants. The front was a sloping rockery hotchpotch with a smattering of white rock and yellow primroses. There was a stone bird bath and I planted an array of plants, including sunflowers and teasel to attract seed-eating birds during the lean months. Songbirds taking a bath became a blur of wings and water on a canvas of rudbeckia and helianthus flowers; a charm of goldfinches, a frenzy of red and gold clustered around the spent flower heads. In winter I even managed to coax fieldfare and redwing into the garden with a few apples thrown by the hedge.

From his sterile enclosure the bloke next door sarcastically offered to lend me his strimmer and his lawn-mower. His name was Albert Ross, which still makes me laugh.

I had no garden when I lived in the Bright Lights; straight onto the pavement at the front, with a dank, communal yard at the back where the dustbins lived and the only plants that survived were mosses and lichens. The only birds I ever saw or heard were town pigeons with deformed feet and bills, and seagulls, especially on bin-eve. The rest of the week they survived on discarded pizza, chips, and vomit.

As the pan spluttered, I took a carrier bag to the living room and collected the empty cans and bottles and returned to the kitchen and put them next to the back door.

I jumped as the toaster and kettle completed their tasks and I hovered between the butter dish and the tea caddy before reaching for the tray slotted between the fridge and the cupboard.

I carried the loaded tray precariously through to the living room where Jan was dragging herself up and flattening an area of quilt. The crockery was restless so I put it down on the hearth, and as I squatted, Jan reached under the apron and squeezed my testicles firmly.

'Thanks bed-bunny.'

'You're welcome.'

* * *

Breakfast gave Jan all the energy she needed to curl up and go right back to sleep so I dressed, put on my jacket, rolled another spliff and tiptoed out of the room. I took my binoculars from behind the door, had a walk to the quarry and sat on the cliff edge and smoked.

I remembered the times we'd had there, the things we'd done. The nest-recording. The pied wagtails, the poor blackbird family. I looked beyond the sand-quarry to Hawksheads Wood. I wondered how many hours of our lives we'd spent in there, making bows and arrows and cutting the hollow stems of umbelliferous plants to make pea-shooters for firing hawthorn berries at each-other. I remembered Lenny' lips, inflamed and swollen from the sap, then mine getting even worse than his, and us laughing and laughing and laughing.

Nobody took any notice of a teenager with a six-inch sheath-knife on his belt back then. The most dangerous thing they were used for was a daft game of splits we played where you had to stretch with your foot for the knife just thrown by your opponent then reach for the knife and have your throw. There were near-misses. I remembered Lenny getting a punctured trainer, but no injuries. I might have had an injury or two if I'd gone home with ruined trainers.

* * *

I'd not seen or heard from Lenny since I got back from Holland and I went to see Fred and Noreen to find out how he was getting on, but it turned out they hadn't seen him either, not since the day I first left for Holland. It was obvious they didn't want to discuss it, and they turned the conversation around to my time in Holland.

I was there for almost three years. The work was a doddle. I hardly struck an arc manually the whole time I was there. I just loaded components into a jig and pressed a button and a robot-welder did the rest as I stood under the extractor-fan and had a smoke.

The agent supplied us all with wind-up-and-go scooters to get to and from work and I made the most of mine. The Dutch aren't into working overtime and the foreman looked at me like I'd gone mad when I said I wanted to work seven days a week. I had to settle for an extra hour a night from Monday to Thursday.

I often took my binoculars and rode out to one of the nature trails that are absolutely everywhere over there; lakes, scrub, pine woods, and canals, of course. I saw goshawks, found feeding sites with feathers strewn all around, saw hen harriers and honey buzzards. Crested tits were as common there as blue tits are in England. But, no matter what I saw, I'd still rather have been at home watching sand martins in the quarry.

* * *

I only went home four times in total; every Christmas and once in the summer. I phoned Mum and Archie regularly and that cunt the odd time to make sure he hadn't been pissed and burned the house down with my stuff in it.

Mum said she talked to Noreen in the shop. Lenny was still in the same flat, had the same phone number, anyway, but he had a lodger, from Scotland, Noreen thought, who always answered the phone when she rang; 'He's out, I'll tell him you called.'

For the first twelve months I shared a spacious house in the middle of nowhere, close to the Belgian border, with four other blokes; two English, one from Glasgow and one from Cowdenbeath, said I'd know it as Cowdenbeath nil.

I got on really well with three of them but the other one had some beef with the English stretching back to about the fifteenth century and he tried to take it out on me. A saltire flew over the house and he challenged me to put up a union flag. Why the fuck would I want to do that? Luckily, we were on different shifts and I didn't see much of him.

At the back of the house was a large orchard and beyond that nothing but corn fields and forests. I put up a bird-table and hung nuts from the trees. One or more of my housemates had bought an air rifle and I came back one Sunday and found a scattering of tiny carcasses on the orchard floor.

My housemates were all off their heads on mushrooms and were riding their scooters around the orchard and in and out of the house, upstairs and down. I went to a bar in the village and stayed late. The following day I phoned the agent and asked for a change of digs. A week later I came home to find they were being moved to a new factory twenty miles away. I don't know what happened there, but whatever, I was glad to see the back of them.

We'd always taken it in turns to go for the beer each week, according to what shifts we were on, and their last week it was my turn. The flag-shagger was less than chuffed when he got home at midnight on Friday and found he'd got a case of alcohol-free Amstel. I got a smack in the mouth for my trouble, but it was worth it.

* * *

Isouri was Surinamese and the most beautiful creature I ever clapped eyes on; the presence of an eagle, the grace of an egret. She'd been in Eindhoven for ten years, since she was fourteen, her family having left Suriname to escape the military regime. She worked in the local coffeeshop and the first time we met we had a good laugh at some cultural faux-pas on my part. Sometimes it pays to be an idiot.

Apart from both being bipeds we had little in common, but she was my equal in the idiot stakes and we spent most of our time together laughing. I'd never had any intention of trying it on with her; she was way out of my league and I knew it, but we'd had a drink one night and were getting on so well that I almost kissed her. She saw it coming and moved deftly to one side and left me puckering-up to thin air.

'I think Lucas would not be liking,' she said, with a broad smile.

Lucas was Isouri's long-term boyfriend, and he was an all-round good-egg. He worked offshore, a month on, a month off, and, like most Dutch people I met, he didn't smoke weed, which explained why I'd never met him.

With no overtime, and with personal expenses taken into account, I'd have been better off working in a Bright Lights sweat-shop. The hourly rate wasn't bad, but there weren't enough hours. In addition, I got five-hundred gilders a week for accommodation and living expenses; roughly a hundred and sixty quid. The digs took a hundred quid, and I skimped on the living expenses, but you have to live, and I was there to make money, not spend it.

I'd told Isouri all this, and she'd mentioned it to Lucas. He suggested I move into their spare room, at the top of a dizzying number of stairs in the centre of Eindhoven. They wanted just a hundred gilders a week, about thirty-five quid, and some money towards shopping, so I moved in straight away.

It was a longer journey to work than I would have liked, but I had my scooter and I quickly got used to the city and its cycle lanes with their own markings and traffic lights. I was amazed by the courtesy that bikes and scooters were shown by car drivers until I learned that in Dutch law, if you crash into a cyclist in a motor vehicle, you are always in the wrong.

* * *

Isouri said she'd have a word with the coffee shop owner and get me some extra work. I pictured myself behind the counter of a coffee shop. How cool was that?

That's what I'd imagined, anyway, but that's not how it panned-out. Back then I thought weed was legal in the Netherlands, but I was wrong. They had what's known as a front-door open, back-door closed, policy, meaning it's legal for the coffee shops to sell, and for people to consume, but it's illegal to grow, meaning that the growers who supply the coffee shops are breaking the law, and every time a coffee shop re-stocks, so are they.

The following Saturday I was picked up in a van that made another couple of stops to collect a motley assortment of other employees and we were driven into the wilds to a large house in its own grounds. We were shown inside and the smell hit me before I was through the door.

The rest were obviously regulars so I followed their lead. The job was basically to snip buds from stems and place them in a large, shallow container on wheels to be taken away for other, more trustworthy employees, to weigh and prepare for distribution.

We were given gloves and scissors and were kept supplied with spliffs and coffee, and great takeaway food appeared as if from nowhere, and it may well be the best job I ever had.

It was certainly the most beneficial.

* * *

Niels was in charge. Like many of the dutchmen I met, he was getting on for six and a half feet tall, and I was reminded of something Lenny had once said. We were stoned and were watching a tv programme about the tribes of South Sudan. The men had an average height of six-feet-four and the women six-feet, and Lenny reckoned he knew why.

'They grow to fit their environment,' he said.

I burst out laughing.

'I'm telling you. They live in the desert. They can see for miles in every direction and they grow accordingly.'

'Fuck off, you nutter—'

'So how do you explain the pygmies in Papua New Guinea?'

'How do I *explain* them?'

'Well, there's none of them over five-feet tall.'

'So?'

'So, they live in the rain-forest. They never see more than a few yards in any direction. You see what I'm getting at?'

'What a load of bollocks.'

'Is it? It makes perfect sense to me. If you won a goldfish at the fair—'

'How the fuck did we get onto goldfish—'

'—just fucking listen, will you. And you put it in a goldfish bowl on the kitchen table, you could have it for years and it wouldn't grow, because if it did, it'd outgrow its environment and end up with its head and tail sticking out of the bowl. But then, if you transferred it to your average garden pond, it'd start growing, maybe reach six or eight inches long, then it'd stop growing again, for the same reason. But, if you let it go in a river, or a lake, it could keep growing and would end up huge.'

'So, have the pygmies of the world got bigger since the rain-forests started to be cut down?'

'Evolution's notoriously slow, John. Give them time.'

* * *

Niels was as laid-back a bloke as you could ever wish to meet. I'd met him a few times in the coffee shop, had a beer and a spliff or two, but had no idea of his role. I thought he was a punter, not the king-pin of a huge drugs operation. He was a sound bloke and when I finished my shift we chatted and he offered me a lift back to Eindhoven, but first he gave me a tour of the whole operation; the propagating room, the growing and drying rooms.

The growing room was huge and humid, like the tropical-house at Chester zoo. There was row after row of plants, at different stages of growth, in long, narrow troughs under sodium lights, and the extraction-unit did a poor job of getting rid of the smell.

He explained that the staggered planting led to staggered harvests, meaning that there was a manageable crop ready every two weeks, rather than being inundated every twelve weeks if they were all planted at the same time.

He told me about germination and talked me through the different processes; sexing the plants, how males are discarded to avoid pollination and prevent the females from going to seed.

He showed me the mother plants and told me how every plant they'd ever grown had been cloned from them. I was fascinated.

For the next fifteen months I never touched my wages. I worked most weekends and the odd evening shift at the 'farm' and lived comfortably on that and my expenses for the rest of my time there. Meanwhile, my wages were building up in the bank back home.

Then, on the phone one night, Mum happened to mention that the Hawksheads estate was being sold off, and so, though

I'd not contemplated returning home, when I got the chance to buy the gatehouse, I knew it was time.

* * *

Mum and Archie said I could stay with them until the sale went through, but all my stuff was at the cottage, so I moved back in with that cunt. It wouldn't be for long, and I wasn't scared of him anymore.

I'd fancied Jan Berry for years and always suspected it was mutual. Then, on one of my visits home, we had a hot New Year's Eve clinch while her husband was having forty winks at the bar. I flew back to Amsterdam two days later and thought that was that, but when I moved back, we soon started meeting secretly.

Her husband was huge and when he found out about us I thought my time was up, but in a bizarre change of tack, rather than tearing me a new arsehole as promised, he reneged and instead he fled the marital home and moved in with Heidi, a barmaid from the Black Cock, a red-head of Himalayan proportions who made dream catchers and wore tie-dye tapestries and, I'm guessing, listened to Clannad.

They'd been having an affair for years as it turned out. Him and Jan had no kids and he cut his losses and signed the house over to her. She asked me to move in with her behind the church on Primrose Terrace. I was looking forward to getting away from that cunt, but I had plans, things to do. They'd only had the house a couple of years and there was still a hefty mortgage to pay. Jan had a couple of part-time cleaning jobs and was on benefits that she'd lose if I stayed more than three nights a week. I managed to convince her that I should stay with her at weekends and spend the other four nights at the gatehouse. She agreed on condition that I got the phone connected.

Though she loved my paintings, and was enthused about my plans to turn it into my studio and office, Jan would have been about as impressed by my other plans for the gatehouse as I'd been with her announcement that she wanted a baby.

* * *

I finished the spliff and stood and was ushered down the hill by a buzzard that soared huge circles on the early thermals. I was home by noon, on the bus by one, and by two o'clock I was sitting in the Estate Agent's office signing the paperwork for the gatehouse.

The previous occupant was a sculptor who looked like a feral Ken Russell, and he refused to budge. He'd paid a ludicrously low rent for over thirty years and was taken aback when he received the news that the ninety-nine-year lease that fixed the original rent had lapsed. He was given first option on buying the place and had said no.

He made me feel like I was evicting him, throwing him out in the street. I was the oil executive callously turfing the old, widowed beachcomber off his tiny piece of paradise. My nit-picking about contracts and ownership was of no interest to him, he said, with a broad sweep of his palm, and when I mentioned money having changed hands, he pooh-poohed and muttered 'money money money' through his jowls as he shut the door in my face.

I granted him a stay of execution and stayed with that cunt in Yelland for another week. I bought myself an old transit van and on the agreed day I arrived with my stuff, but still he refused to move. He told me to go away. From behind the door, he said that, yes, we *had* both agreed, but, unfortunately, not with each other.

'I was agreeing with myself,' he said. 'I do it all the time. How else are decisions to be made and adhered to?'

I could have done without it. I'd been pissed the night before and my head was banging like there would be permanent damage and, in the end, I agreed to give him another week. As I got in the van to drive away, he opened the door and stood bravely in the porch with his arms in the air and shouted something about the pogroms then darted back inside.

When I walked past the next morning he'd gone. After all that he just disappeared overnight. The decrepit old Mercedes had vanished. I never thought it actually worked and I was amazed he'd been able to free it from the tangle of brambles and ivy that had escaped from the garden and overrun the lean-to 'garage'.

* * *

The gatehouse was empty. There wasn't a stick of furniture in the place. He'd burned the lot. He'd burned the table and chairs. He'd even burned the cupboards. All of it, ash in the grate. There was a long-handled axe standing up against the wall in the kitchen, and deep scars and wood splinters all over the stone floor in front of the range. What he hadn't burned, he'd drunk. There were empties everywhere, the vast majority in a large sprawling heap that I fell over the first time I went out through the back door into the garden. I reckoned he drank two-parts whisky to one soda, by the ratio of the bottles, and smoked a five pack of castellas to the bottle of whisky. It was the good stuff too, Talisker mainly. Later I would discover a tiny kitchen swing-bin, lidless under the glass mountain.

The huge garden that surrounds the house was a tangle of chest-high brambles, nettles, thistles and grasses. Imprisoned in this thorny wilderness were a large number of sculpted granite demons inflicting all manner of agonies on cowering grotesques in a disturbing depiction of hell. I'd already planned what to do with it, had imagined it for years. It was going to be my piece of heaven.

* * *

I had no intention of getting a job, ever again if I had my way, but for that to be more than a pipe-dream I needed to be up and running as soon as possible. I had plenty of money saved but I knew that what I had planned wasn't going to be cheap. I didn't want to sign on either and spend half my time at the Jobcentre jumping through all their hoops, attending, and deliberately failing, interviews and trade tests, and have them snooping around, so I decided it would be money well spent to pay a landscaping company to help tame the garden and clear a few paths and do a few other jobs. It would take me months but wouldn't be a big deal for an expert with the right equipment.

When he first showed up, I didn't recognise the expert. I hadn't seen Andrew Swift for about ten years. He'd quit the quarry a couple of years ago and started his own business. We had a bit of a crack about years gone by, but it was laboured and the conversation soon dried up.

He'd grown a lot, outwards mainly, and lost most of his hair, and he stood with his pot-belly hanging over his belt and a liquorice-paper roll-up hanging from the corner of his mouth as I told him exactly what I wanted; what to leave, what to trim back and what to get rid of altogether.

He griped and shook his head when I said I wanted the

teasel and thistles, dogwood and berberis, and most of the longer grasses to stay, said it would be easier to just clear the lot, but I explained the reasons and he got it, in the end.

He scribbled a few figures on a pad and we went round the back and I described the pond. I told him I wanted a deep pool at one end, and he said it wouldn't be a problem.

I thought I'd have to wait a day or two for a quote but he did some more scribbling and twisted his mouth and tapped his front teeth with the pencil and two minutes later he gave what I thought was a good price, which included taking away all the waste. He turned up early the following Monday with a young lad and a mini JCB and they got stuck in.

While they were busy in the garden, I got busy inside. I swept out all the debris then went into the Bright Lights to have a look round the charity shops. I dropped lucky and got a sofa-bed (bottle-green emblazoned with scarlet macaws), a well-used kitchen table and two bench seats, and a pine bookshelf, to be delivered, and two pairs of heavy curtains and a desk and office chair that I loaded into the van. I did two trips to the garden centre and picked up half-a-dozen trough-planters and ordered a large quantity of perlite and potting compost.

By late Wednesday afternoon the garden was done. Swifty asked what I was going to do with the sculptures and when I said he could have them he couldn't get them on the wagon quick enough. On the Thursday morning, as Swifty dug the pond, the young lad cleared all the ivy and brambles from the lean-to. They'd finished by Friday night and I paid cash and slipped the lad an extra fiver and they were gone, leaving me free to crack on with the important work indoors.

* * *

Niels was a great teacher. I'd bought seeds in Holland, and I put them to germinate while I concentrated on getting the growing-room set up in the bedroom. First, I knocked a hole through the wall, high up, and put in an extractor and a vent-pipe to help get rid of the smell.

I'd ordered four forty-five litre tanks, sodium lights, relay-switches, timers and a lights and ballast system from a company that advertised in a copy of High Times that I'd bought in Holland.

I mixed the perlite and potting compost and filled the tanks and had the whole system set up in a couple of days. I hung the heavy curtains at the window and door to deter any snoopers and to limit the smell coming into the living-room.

Six four-hundred-watt sodium lights, burning for up to eighteen hours a day, use a lot of electricity, so to disguise my energy consumption I didn't buy a fridge, freezer, tv or washing machine.

* * *

When the first crop came up, I chose the best plant as the mother, and the rest I planted three to a tank, twelve in all, leaving plenty of room for more if all went well, and left them to do their stuff. All I had to do was make sure I watered them and raise the lights as the plants grew. The only electric appliances I did buy were a kettle, a radio, and a fan that moved from side to side and wafted across the plants to create as natural an environment as possible.

The extraction was working, too, and I checked that the smell wasn't detectable outside. It wasn't. The back garden had been full of nettles when I moved in, and I had Swifty leave a large patch in front of the window so as to keep anyone from getting too close. I told him it was for the peacock and red admiral caterpillars, which it was, sort of.

By early July the first crop was ready to be cut and dried. The plants were around four-feet tall and were a beautiful sight as they swayed gently in the breeze.

* * *

The plants each produced an average of four-and-a-half ounces of dried buds, about fifty-four ounces all told. I'd arranged to sell the whole crop, and all future crops, to Smudge, a pipe-fitter I'd worked with on the first power station. We'd kept in touch and he was back, working on the second phase. He had a good customer base back home in Cardiff, which meant I didn't have to deal with any of the local dealers and potheads. He was a sound bloke and I was sure I could rely on him to keep his mouth shut. He'd take the fifty ounces, the rest I'd keep for personal use. To keep him sweet I let him have it for sixty quid an ounce, netting me a very respectable three thousand quid. Four crops a year; twelve grand. With overheads deducted I'd still be making twice what I would have earned working for a local engineering firm.

It was a cool set-up. I'd been out of the country for three years and wasn't on the radar of the authorities. I never went out other than to the Eagle and Child now and again and I hadn't even told Jan what I was up to.

I told her that I had a job in the Bright Lights, and that's where she thought I was during the day. When I stayed at Jan's I got up in the morning and made sandwiches and set off for 'work'. I drove to the gatehouse and parked the van in the lean-to. I tended the plants and spent the rest of my time logging everything that lived on the estate.

I bought a box of A4 scrap books and kept detailed records of every species I found. I decorated the inside front and back covers with sketches and paintings of the subjects; birds, mammals, butterflies, moths, flowers, trees and shrubs. The inside pages I neatly partitioned into sections of varying width for date, time, species, location, and one for notes of special interest, headed NOSI.

* * *

I paid the occasional visit to the reserve and did a quick tour of the hides to see what was around, but I never stayed long. On one of the visits, I saw someone I recognised in one of the hides. I couldn't place him at first, but when I heard his voice it came to me. It was Jeff, the ex-warden and ringing expert.

I wasn't a kid anymore and he didn't recognise me, so I went over and introduced myself. We had a long chat and it turned out he was back for a year to run a ringing course. I told him about the different habitats on my patch and the records I was keeping and he said I should enrol. I asked him where and when and how much and where do I sign.

* * *

On the afternoon of Friday the 13th of July 1984 I got to Jan's to find her sitting at the kitchen table nursing a cup of coffee. She was upset. Before I could ask, she told me that Mum had phoned a few minutes earlier to say that my father had been rushed into hospital. He'd collapsed in the snug at the Black Cock and the landlord had called an ambulance.

I hadn't seen him for six months, not sober, anyway. I'd been to the cottage plenty of times, to pick up a few things, the notebooks from the survey, a couple of paintings and my brushes and easel, but he was usually in the pub, or snoring in the armchair. The couple of times he was awake we'd argued and I'd left before it came to blows.

I changed my clothes and jumped in the van and drove to Bright Lights General. I spoke to a nurse and she showed me to his ward. A doctor was standing at his bedside and, as I approached, he took me by the arm and led me back outside into the corridor. I asked how he was and he gave me it straight. He was still unconscious, he said, and the prognosis wasn't good. It seemed the drink had finally done for him.

I went and sat by his bedside. He was connected to a swollen bag of fluid that hung from a galvanised steel stand and he was gaunt and had dark circles around his eyes and folds in the papery skin of his face and hands. The small ward was quiet. It was outside visiting hours and the other two patients dozed to the sound of the news on a tv in the corner.

He looked feeble in his threadbare pyjamas, the least threatening I ever saw him. It seemed the ideal time to get some things off my chest. So that's what I did. First, I called him a bastard for all the things he'd done to Mum. Then I called him another bastard for all the things he'd done to me. The third bastard I called him for what he'd done to himself. I told him things I should have told him years ago.

He didn't like Jan. The last time I went to the cottage he had a right go about our lifestyle. 'I know you're no saint,' he said. 'You never were, nor was I come to that, but you're the worse for being with her, and that's all I'm going to say.'

But it wasn't, and he went on for another twenty minutes about rods for own backs and made beds you can lie in. He said he didn't know what I saw in her. I wanted to tell him the story of a weekend of speed and tequila that ended late one Sunday night in a noisy queue in a Bright Lights takeaway with Jan panting to a discreet crescendo in my ear with her crotch hard against my thigh.

A nurse came and smiled and passed pleasantries as she took his blood pressure and inserted a machine into his ear and pulled a trigger to take his temperature. I pictured Leatherface with his bolt gun.

She wrote her findings on his chart and turned to leave, swinging her hair over her shoulder with a toss of her head as she went, her left shoulder, like Carol Vorderman putting the numbers up. I sat for a minute more then stood and said I'd see him tomorrow.

* * *

But I didn't. He died that night and was buried in Yelland cemetery on Thursday the following week. He was fifty-four years old. The congregation was small but still larger than I'd expected, swollen as it was by gloaters and hypocrites and souls with more forgiveness than I could muster.

Mum cried softly throughout the short service as Archie sat stoically at her side. Nobody other than the vicar spoke, no family member stood to say a few words and reminisce about the good times or to wax lyrical about the saintly character of the dearly departed.

When it was over there was no reception, no buffet at the pub. Everyone went home or back to work. We went back to Jan's and we went to bed and she held me in her arms while I broke down and sobbed my heart out.

* * *

We'd been trying for a baby for six-months, or rather, Jan had. The thought of having a baby had never appealed to me, so they'd been six months of stoically shouldered disappointments for her, six months of silent celebrations for me, as the weeks rolled by without an embryo in sight.

I did what I could to lessen the chances, but there's only so much you can do. Once keen on the theory, now Jan was never going to fall for the old line about it being full of vital minerals and good for your skin. There was to be no waste, and she insisted there would be more chance of success if I planted the seeds rather than sowed them and would draw blood in her efforts to plant them as deep as possible. Miraculously, still no baby.

That night I accepted that, for the first time in my life, I was in love. Now, though the idea of having a baby still didn't exactly fill me with joy, the thought of losing Jan did fill me with despair.

* * *

The ringing course was one morning a week, mist-netting on the reserve. The training involved setting the nets, identifying the species, safely removing birds from the net, how to handle birds, how to select and attach the correct ring, how to weigh and measure the birds, and how to complete the paperwork.

My previous experience served me well and I flew through the course. I was deemed proficient and in August 1985 I was thrilled to receive my BTO ringing permit.

I'd already bought everything I needed; a three-metre mist net, bamboo poles, fixing-pegs, holding-bags, two pairs of notched pliers to cater for all leg-sizes, bird-weighing scales, callipers, and wing-rules. I got all the necessary paperwork from the BTO.

* * *

I decided to limit the mist netting sessions to autumn and

spring, when migrants were passing through; there would be less chance of recapturing the same birds, and maybe I'd find a few rarities. In spring and summer, I'd ring the young of the tits, and, with any luck, the redstarts and flycatchers, that I hoped would breed in the nest-boxes I was going to make and number and put up around the estate over the winter.

Friday 18th of October 1985

My first, practice, ringing session, was a disaster. I set the net in a small clearing in Hawksheads Wood close to the house and caught a cock pheasant, a grey squirrel and a woodpigeon, which between them damaged the net beyond repair. I ordered a replacement and identified two sites for future missions; the birch wood edge, and the reeds and gorse surrounding the pond in the sand quarry.

I fared much better on my second ringing session. I erected the net by the reeds in the sand quarry and caught and ringed two dozen birds, including a green sandpiper, a rare wader that looked out of place in the net alongside the pied wagtails and linnets.

The sun had been up for a couple of hours when I let the last of the ringed birds go and packed away the net and poles. I picked up my backpack and had a last look around to make sure I didn't leave anything behind then set off for home. The path under the railway bridge was flooded and I'd got my feet soaked on the way there so I walked back through the estate.

Two workmen were wielding huge rubber-headed mallets and sinking gateposts into the ground either side of the path to Hawksheads. There were wooden posts, large rolls of mesh fencing and barbed-wire leaning against the adjacent wall.

As I approached, the younger of the two leaned his mallet

against the gate-post and lit a cigarette. He was wearing a faded Bruce Springsteen tee-shirt and a James Dean sneer.

The older one wore a flat cap and a collarless shirt with sleeve-garters, and heavy tweed trousers with braces. His thick, silver moustache hid his mouth and was discoloured with nicotine. He rested the shaft of the mallet on his shoulder and took off his cap, looked inside and shook it and put it back on his head. He looked me up and down and his eyes settled on the bamboo poles.

'I don't know what thaz been up to young fella, but I'd enjoy it while tha can if I were thee, cos tha'll not be ebble to traipse round here for much longer.'

I was stunned. 'You're putting fences up? But I come up here all the time. It's a public footpath.'

'Thad best tek tharrup wit new owner. There's not just this'n either, we've three o' these to purrup, an 'undred yard o' fencin', all towd.'

I felt suddenly hollow. 'What new owner? I thought the council owned it.'

'That's right, they did, but nor anymore, they've sold it to yon businessman, young Rod as has all them garages.'

Before I could reply he looked at his young colleague and nodded and they both got back to work. The conversation was obviously over, so I made my way home. I was knackered. It was eleven o'clock and I'd been out since five. I put the bamboo poles in the lean-to and went inside and put the backpack and ringing tools in the kitchen and made a brew.

I was still reeling from what the workman had told me. A new owner. A hundred yards of fences. I'd have no access to any of it. I knew who the new owner was, knew of him, anyway, but had never seen him. No doubt some suited dickhead with an aura of Paco Rabanne, a poser in a Lamborghini.

I finished my brew and put the mug in the sink. I checked the plants, raised the lights a few inches and closed the bedroom door and locked it. I grabbed my jacket and wallet and jumped in the van and by half-twelve I was in Jan's kitchen giving her the bad news.

Saturday 19th of October 1985

At lunchtime me and Jan went to the Eagle with Mum and Archie. Mum had been renting the cottage out but the tenants were moving out and she asked me if I had a problem with it being sold. I said I hadn't, that me and Jan were happy where we were, so she said she'd put it on the market.

I'd never seen Mum so happy and I told her so when Archie went to the bar. She thought the world of Jan and Jan felt the same and they had a right old natter whenever they met. I sat across from Archie and while Mum and Jan chatted away, I told him about the estate being fenced-off. I got a bit animated and started slagging the new owner off. Thankfully, Mum had been listening and she interrupted.

'John, love, before you say any more, he's Archie's nephew.'

Jan threw me a surreptitious grin. I fumbled for an apology but Archie started laughing.

'Don't worry about it, son,' he said, 'it obviously means a lot to you.' He took a swallow of his beer. 'I know he's bought the land, but I don't know what he plans to do with it.'

I barely heard the last part. I was still on 'son'. I was used to 'lad,' or 'cheeky little fucker.' This was the first time anyone had called me son, well, apart from coppers, or the occasional barman when I tried to get served underage. But this sounded fatherly. No, this *was* fatherly.

At that moment I felt an enormous sense of love and admiration for my Mum. She'd had to wait until into her fifties to find a man who loved her, who really loved her, and who she could love back, and they were certainly in love, it was written all over them.

She'd given so much for so many years with so little in return, staying with a drunken brute for over twenty years to protect me. Her love was the only thing that got me through my childhood. Seeing her now, so happy with Archie, my eyes filled up and I almost burst into tears. Luckily it was my round so I collected the glasses and went to the bar and ordered the drinks and by the time I returned to the table I'd managed to compose myself. I sat and we got back to business.

His name was Rod Jay. He owned five garages in the area and was a millionaire. I asked Archie if he thought he could arrange for me to meet him. He said they didn't have much contact, other than Christmas cards and the occasional family function, but he'd give him a call and have a word.

* * *

We always had a long lie-in on a Sunday, and spent the afternoon on the sofa, watching all the detective shows and courtroom dramas that we enjoyed, and that Jan taped during the week while I was at the gatehouse. This Sunday was no different, except I couldn't concentrate. My head was all over the place, so I just sat and worried myself sick and let the programmes wash over me. Jan had to stop me phoning Archie a couple of times to gee him up.

We had dinner at tea-time and started a game of scrabble but there was no point, I still couldn't focus, so we curled up on the sofa and watched Saturday Night Fever and Jan's favourite cookery programme and we were in bed by ten.

On Monday I was up early, made sandwiches and set off for 'work'. I drove into the lean-to and had to brake suddenly when I saw the bamboo poles were lying on the ground and I was about to run over them. I distinctly remembered putting them away on Friday. I got out of the van and locked the door and picked up the poles and went to put them back on top of the ladder, but the ladder had gone. My first thought was that someone had stolen it, that's what I was hoping anyway. The alternative didn't bear thinking about.

I put the poles on the hangers and went into the house and put my sandwiches on the table. I was frantic. I went searching for the ladder but couldn't find it and was ready to write it off as stolen, but then I had a second look at the back of the house and saw two parallel scrapes down the wall, and the bottom of the ladder protruding from the nettles.

PART FOUR

Friday 18th of Oct 1985

Clocherty had claimed the main bedroom as soon as he moved in and a few nights had become a few years. His devastating visit on the night they were tripping, the drugs, the money, were never brought up, though it was mentioned on occasion by one or another of them that he still owed them a grand; 'Think on,' they'd say, and they'd all laugh.

Lenny did the shopping, the cooking and cleaning, and was confined to the box-bedroom. Anything they required, he'd be given the money and sent out to get it. They liked to belittle him, too, piss-taking and name-calling. His current nickname was 'Squatter', which he could live with. He'd been called worse.

What he couldn't live with was the constant threat of violence. He'd been a punch-bag numerous times. He'd considered leaving but didn't fancy telling Clocherty he was homeless, that *he* was about to become the squatter. And where could he go? He still had to work with Tony and Stu, so they'd soon find him and it would all start again. He was resigned to his lot and consoled himself with the fact that he had his own money and was never short of free gear, and that was worth more than the rent.

When they weren't at work, the Savages were an almost constant presence at the flat, only going back to their own place to sleep. They had long-since given up robbing chemists and now focused all their efforts on the street drug trade. By sheer thuggery the three of them had taken total control of all the drugs coming into the Bright Lights, and they ran the business from Lenny's flat.

The drugs were all weighed out and distributed from the flat. In the event of a raid, the tenancy was in his name, Clocherty was officially of no fixed abode, and the Savages had a place of their own and would, no doubt, be just visiting. Lenny knew that when that day came they'd hang him out to dry.

When they weren't working or taking care of business they were partying, and the flat was party central. They weren't really parties, as that would imply that there were invited guests. They never invited anyone else. They were more like competitive binges, where the three of them would vie for the title of world's maddest bastard. Whenever they had a couple of days off, they just went for it. Lenny used to brag he could keep up with anyone, but never before had he come across animals like these.

He'd seen them have 'play' fights, games of 'chicken,' when they took free swings at each other, busting noses and blacking eyes, laughing and joking afterwards as they cleaned themselves up in the bathroom. Clocherty would lift Tony's precious baccy tin and put it in the pocket of Stu's jacket, then watch the ensuing drama, emceeing from the sidelines and then commentating on the inevitable fight.

One night Clocherty had forced Lenny to fight Tony and Lenny had taken a beating. The next time they were all out for the day he'd fitted dead-bolts to his bedroom door. He felt much better knowing he had a safe room.

* * *

Most of the dealers that Clocherty had put out of business had quit dealing altogether. The rest now dealt only for the Savages and were too fearful of the consequences to even think about stepping out of line. None of them wanted another visit from Clocherty.

Some high-grade green had started appearing in the pubs in the Bright Lights and was affecting sales of their low-quality resin. The three of them had been out all morning trying to find where it was coming from before it became a major problem. Lenny pitied the poor fucker if they found him.

But anyway, it wasn't his problem. He was off for the weekend and it started here. It was Friday lunchtime and he had the flat to himself for once. He was making the most of it, sitting stoned in the living-room watching tv, when Clocherty and Stu came back. They weren't happy. They'd visited most of the dealers and come across nothing but their own supply.

Lenny didn't understand. 'Well, that's good, isn't it?'

Clocherty ignored him. 'Forget it for now,' he said. 'Seeing as there's no gear in the flat and yous are all off until Monday we'll have a session.' He turned to Stu. 'Take the van and get enough beer for the weekend. Get whisky, a couple of bottles of tequila. Nobody will be in a fit state to go out so get a loaf and … I don't know, some crisps or something.'

Stu did as he was told. Clocherty walked to the sofa and kicked Lenny's leg.

'We can make some noise, Squatter, eh? You go and get some trips off one of them soft-lads you used to knock about with. Get plenty, a couple of dozen, and get them laid on. You'll pay for them Monday.'

Lenny wished he'd stayed in his bedroom. There was no

way he could get any acid by tonight. He hadn't seen any of his old contacts for a couple of years at least.

'I wouldn't know where to get it anymore—'

Clocherty was about to speak when Tony came in and threw him a small bag of weed and shouted 'Bingo!'

Clocherty opened it and pulled out a bud, broke it open and smelled it. Lenny could smell it from across the room.

'It's definitely the same stuff, Clock. I went to see Smiffy. He's been shifting less and less gear, so I asked him for the names of anyone who'd stopped buying recently, figuring they must be getting it from somewhere else, you know. I paid a couple of them a visit and got that off some mouth-piece in the Rose and Crown. I asked where he got it from and if he knew where I could get a couple of ounces. Talkative he was. He got it from a Welsh geezer that works at the power station. I thought maybe contractors were bringing it from away and that we were fucked, but he couldn't stop talking this little fuck—'

'A bit like you, Tony, eh? For fuck's sake, get on with it.'

'Alright, alright, fucking hell. I'm telling you what he said. Anyway, he says not, says it's local grown, but comes into town from the power station. The grower probably thought they'd sell it back home and he'd be squeaky clean here, but they're selling it here and staying squeaky clean back home. I'll bet he didn't see that coming.'

Clocherty paced the room. 'And he won't see us coming, either. Anyway, get to the fucking point Tony; does he know who this grower is or not? Please tell me this chatty cunt gave you a name and address.'

Lenny sat, pretending to watch tv, but listening to every word.

'Not exactly, but he gave me a nickname, and he lives out Yelland way, in the Oak Head lodge or something, in the middle of nowhere, in all them narrow lanes. He said that's all he knows, and I believe him. Like I say, he couldn't stop talking. He'd have told me how his bird likes it if I'd asked.'

Clocherty put on a rictus-grin and feigned extreme patience. 'Tony. The name. What's, the fucking, name?'

'Well, that's the best bit Clock. That's why I was dragging it out, for dramatic effect, like. You see, apparently the geezer who grows it's an old mate of *yours*.'

Lenny was waiting for Clocherty to answer, but when he looked up, they were both looking at him. He felt his face flush.

'A mate of mine?' he said, weakly, and wished he could disappear.

'That's right Squatter. Woodsy. Remember him?'

John had always dreamed of buying the Hawksheads Gatehouse, and he knew John was home. He'd seen him, must be twelve months ago, probably more. He was in town, loading some furniture into the back of a van. He'd looked in Lenny's direction as he closed the rear doors and walked around the van and Lenny had ducked into a doorway and watched until he drove away. Could he really be the one flooding the town with green?

Tony started to laugh and turned to Clocherty.

'This fucker was Squatter's best mate. Isn't that right, Squatter? He was living here when me and Stu first came round.' Tony was getting into his rhythm. 'He watches birds, Clock.'

'Watches them do what?'

Nobody answered. Tony carried on. 'They fell out. Didn't you Squatter—'

'Is that right, Squatter? What did you fall out about?'

'Are you going to tell Clock why you fell out, Squatter, or should I?'

Lenny opened his mouth to speak but Tony couldn't wait.

'He tried to shag Squatter.'

Clocherty looked pained. 'He did what?!'

Tony was giggling now. 'He's a fucking bender, Clock. The fucking geezer tried to shag Squatter. Seriously. I don't know about you, Clock, but I'd never forget a bloke who tried to shag me.'

His fists balled, Clocherty continued to pace the room. 'No, or forgive him, either.'

'Do you know what I used to call him, Clock? I used to call him—'

'Shut the fuck up, Tony.' He turned to Lenny. 'Right, we're going round there first thing Monday and sorting this cunt out. You and me. We're going to shut him down, and you can have some fun. Teach him a proper fucking lesson. Sounds like you've waited too fucking long. A bit of closure, eh? I'll bet you can't wait after what the dirty cunt did to you.' Lenny didn't answer. His stomach churned and his mouth was dry. 'But that's for Monday. Until then, we're going to have that session. If you can't get any acid, go and pick some of them fucking mental mushrooms you used to get. And make sure you get plenty. Make one of your fucking mad stews, enough to keep the four of us going all weekend.'

* * *

When he first tried mushrooms Clocherty loved them and had Lenny out picking them whenever it crossed his mind and they were in season. He had an incredible tolerance to them.

It wasn't that they didn't affect him – he'd be absolutely off his face – but he had no boundaries, no limits, and became an insane person, manic and incoherent, laughing hysterically one second, threatening extreme violence the next.

Lenny wasn't looking forward to this weekend.

He put a handful of carrier bags in his backpack and caught a bus to the bypass. He didn't head straight for the sand quarry. Instead, he cut through the lanes and called at the gatehouse. He still couldn't believe it. What a fucking state of affairs. He had to warn John, give him all weekend to clear the place out and make himself scarce.

He approached the gatehouse and saw that all the ghoulish sculptures had gone. He remembered John hated them. So far, so bad. He'd fretted all the way there about meeting John, but there was no van in the lean-to and no sign of life.

He opened the gate and was stunned by the cloud of chattering birds that suddenly appeared over the garden and dispersed into the surrounding woodland, leaving thistledown and dandelion seeds floating like tiny parachutes in the rays of sunlight streaming through the tree canopy. A sparrowhawk called close-by. A squirrel ran along the wall and leapt to the trunk of a nearby oak and scampered out of sight.

At first glance, the garden looked as it always had; unkempt and overgrown, parts of it totally inaccessible, but he soon realised that it wasn't, not at all, that it was just the opposite. Yes, there were a lot of brambles, and tall weeds and grasses, but it was organised and had taken a lot of planning and hard work. There were brambles to the height of the wall and a metre deep but that's where they stopped. Unchecked they'd be over-running the rest of the garden and disappearing over the wall. These were obviously cut back regularly.

The adjacent wall had a thick coat of ivy, but this too was kept in check. The rest of the garden was a random patchwork of giant thistles, teasel, and a range of other plants that he recognised but couldn't identify. One thing he was sure of; they were all plants to attract wildlife, to feed birds and insects all year round. If he'd had any doubt before, he didn't now. This had to be John, there was no question.

He walked to the front door, hesitated, then knocked half-heartedly. He stood with his back to the door and looked again at the garden. A few well-hidden paths, all less than a foot wide, gave access to even the most wild-looking areas, and beyond that was the rich, mixed woodland of the Hawksheads estate, with its towering Scots pines, beech, oak and ash, the rowan and holly and hawthorn, and the thick undergrowth; ground elder, anemones and wild garlic. Lenny shook his head in wonder.

As he'd expected, there was no answer. He decided to have a nosey and walked to the first window. Through a gap in the curtains, it looked like someone had been camping in the living-room. There was a bed-settee with a sleeping-bag, half unzipped, and in the far corner was a busy desk and a crammed bookshelf. Nothing else. No tv, no ornaments.

In the kitchen-area there was no fridge or any other white goods that he could see. It was clear that nobody lived there, not on a permanent basis, and there was definitely no sign of it being a cannabis factory. Russ had got it wrong. It was obviously Russ that Tony had talked to in the Rose and Crown. Fucking gobshite.

He was about to leave but decided he may as well have a look around the back first. A flagged path led around the house and as he turned the first corner he disturbed yet more birds. A cock pheasant blundered through the undergrowth and clapped its wings and just about managed to clear the wall with its undercarriage intact and disappeared into the fields. Dunnocks, chaffinch, robins, bullfinch, nuthatch, scattered into the woods. In the left corner of the back-garden, where it met the fields of Hawksheads Farm, and obscured until now by the corner of the house, was an enormous bird-feeding station. There were bird-tables of different sizes and a variety of bird-feeders hung at various heights in trees along the woodland-edge. He heard a loud, harsh croak and rounded the wall to the back of the house in time to see a heron push off with its long legs and defy gravity to lift-off and find a gap in the trees and make its way across the fields on slow, rhythmic wingbeats.

Most of the back garden was now a large pond. It hadn't long been completed and didn't look very natural, but it soon would. Some iris had been planted along the far-shore and a few marsh-marigolds and water-lilies floated on the surface. Other water plants were propagating in troughs along the back wall ready to be transferred. Here and there, rocks had been positioned in the water to provide creatures with a landing-stage. In the middle of the pond was a small, grass-covered island, maybe two feet in diameter, and in the middle of the island was something metallic. He saw it shining and got closer and leaned across for a better look. He laughed out loud when he realised what it was, the laughter almost turning to tears as the memories came racing back; it was pale blue, with chrome trims; it was a Dinky cars model of a Ford Anglia.

* * *

He turned to the back of the house. There were two windows,

one either side of the porch. The first was frosted glass; the bathroom, so he turned his attention to the other window, probably the bedroom.

The path that he'd assumed went all the way around the house actually stopped when it cleared the back-porch, thwarted by a large, well-established patch of nettles that were even better-tended than the brambles and ivy. Here the stone flags had been removed and nettles had begun to grow right up to the wall of the house.

He made sure the legs of his jeans were covering his ankles, pulled his sleeves down over his hands and raised his arms in-front of his face as he walked carefully into the bed of nettles. He made slow progress but reached the window without getting stung. The curtains were drawn and he could see nothing; they were blackout curtains and when he put his hand to the glass to cut out the glare of the autumnal sun, he noticed the glass was warm to the touch. Too warm.

He slowly retraced his steps, backwards, until he was clear of the nettles, then stood back and scanned the wall of the house. Above the window, just below the gutter, was a plastic vent-pipe that protruded a few inches from the wall and was covered with a metal grill. The grill was still shiny and there was no lichen or algae on the mortar surrounding the pipe.

He went looking for something to stand on, a wheelie-bin or a box, something to get him closer to the vent. In the lean-to he saw a ladder hanging on the wall. There were some bamboo poles on top of it and he took them down and laid them on the floor. He took down the ladder and carried it to the back of the house. He leaned the top against the wall, as high as he could without the bottom of the ladder going into the nettles, and started to climb.

He smelled it before he reached the vent. So, it was true. John was The Man. He climbed another rung and got his nose to the grill, and stayed there for a minute, taking deep breaths until he felt light-headed. He started his descent, but there was a sudden scraping and he felt the ladder collapsing and the ground came up to meet him and he landed face-down in the nettles. He jumped up and got more stings as he flailed his way to safety. He walked quickly around the house and down the path and closed the gate behind him.

He picked dock leaves as he walked, rubbing them over his hands and wrists, neck and face, to alleviate the stinging. He sat on the wall at Hawksheads House and did the same to his ankles and shins. They were still stinging when he walked through the sand quarry and around to the fields that Irish Bob had told him about and that he'd visited many times since.

It was a good year for liberty caps. Every couple of paces he'd see a city and drop to his knees and raze it to the ground. The first bag was soon full; less than an hour and he reckoned he had at least a couple of thousand.

There wasn't a bus for an hour. He put the bag in the backpack and crossed the field and sat on top of the gate into Hawksheads. He rolled himself a cigarette and lit it and watched the blue smoke curl into the air.

What to do now. He could go back to the gatehouse to see if John was home. He had the time, but he knew there was no point. It was obvious nobody lived there. It must be just where he grows his weed.

And what if he did manage to warn John? What then? What difference would it make, really? Clocherty wasn't going to give up. John would probably think he could talk him round or do a deal with him.

He tried not to think about Monday, but what else was there to think about? He couldn't imagine a best-case scenario, but the worst-case scenarios came thick and fast and raced through his mind.

He knew there was a strong chance that John could be badly hurt.

Killed, even.

And so could Lenny.

He sat for ten-minutes more, smoking and thinking, but no matter which way he looked at it, he could see only one scenario, one outcome that would be best for all concerned.

Bile flooded his throat. He managed not to vomit. He rolled another cigarette and climbed down from the gate. He took another bag from the backpack and walked into the woods, over the highest point and down the other side, to the beech tree circle, and its beautiful fairy rings.

* * *

He got back to the flat to find Clocherty on the landing. He was just leaving and said he had to see a couple of people and wanted the stew ready when he got back.

'Don't fuck about drying them,' he said. 'Just get them in there.'

Lenny took off his boots and cleaned them thoroughly in the kitchen sink and went and put them by the side of his bed and put on his trainers. He went back to the kitchen and got the large aluminium stock-pot from the cupboard and put it on the hob. He liked to dry the mushrooms first, to lessen the bulk and hide their presence, but he'd never had any intention of drying them today.

He looked at the closed door.

'Ok, Clock. Whatever you say. Mate.'

He took two bags of mushrooms from the backpack and emptied them into the pot. He boiled the kettle twice and poured it over and brought the pot back to the boil then got a wooden spoon and crushed the mushrooms against the side of the pot. He remembered there was some veg in the cupboard under the sink. It had been there for weeks, but so what, it really wasn't going to matter.

His hands were shaking as he peeled and chopped a bag of dried-out onions and some blackened carrots and a mouldy half-cabbage and put them in with the mushrooms and threw in a large dose of salt and pepper and put on the lid and let it simmer, stirring it and crushing the solids with the spoon every few minutes until it was the consistency of broth.

He filled a large bowl from the bubbling pot then emptied it back in and put the dirty spoon and bowl on the drainer. He filled a cup with water and grabbed the backpack and took it to his bedroom. There was no window in the box-room and he turned on the bedside lamp.

If Clocherty suspected him of 'slacking' he'd force-feed him from the pot. He couldn't let that happen. He had to be seen to be completely off his face. He took out the small bag of liberty caps he'd picked for himself. There were roughly two hundred and he sat on the bed and ate the lot, washing each mouthful down with the water.

A thought occurred to him. He opened his sock-drawer and rummaged to the back, squeezing each rolled-up pair, feeling for the dried liberty caps he'd had for years. He found them – maybe fifty or so in a plastic change-bag. He closed the drawer and left the bag on the table where it wouldn't be missed when all this was over.

Then he laid on the bed, feeling the drum-band in his chest, and waited for the chaos to begin.

Friday 18th of October 5.37pm

They say that when you take hallucinogenic drugs, if it isn't to turn into a nightmare, there are two golden rules you should always observe; make sure you're in an environment where you feel safe, and take them with friends, people you can trust …

* * *

He'd only really eaten dried mushrooms before and didn't know how much stronger they were fresh than dried. He was still on the bed when he heard voices, and bottles being put in the fridge. He couldn't make out what was being said. The voices seemed distorted, cartoonish, not like people at all. He opened his eyes. The walls were melting and the carpet was a swirling kaleidoscope of colours. He raised himself on his elbows and tried to get up but his limbs hadn't got the message and he fell and landed hard on the floor and began to laugh dementedly.

The door suddenly flew open and Clocherty marched into the room.

'Started without us Squatter?'

Lenny looked up at the ridiculous blue giant with the silver head and cracked-up laughing again.

Clocherty grabbed him by the shirt-front and hoisted him upright.

'What did I say, Squatter. No private parties,' he growled, and dragged him from the room and slammed the door. The Savages were behind the kitchen counter. Tony had started to fill two bowls with the broth while Stu scooped it straight from the pot with a slice of dry bread.

Clocherty dragged Lenny across the room and threw him onto the sofa. Lenny picked up a Rubik's Cube from the coffee table and sat back and turned it in his hand, wide-eyed and slack-jawed, as if he'd found a Fabergé egg.

'He's started without us lads. Look at the state of the cunt.'

The Savages glanced up and there were murmurs of 'fucking hell Squatter' and 'bring it on' and they carried on eating.

Lenny's key was in the door. Clocherty locked it and put the key with his own in the front-pocket of his jeans.

'Nobody leaves until Monday morning.' He took a bowl from the counter and wolfed the broth in seconds and grabbed his beer and took a long swallow. He went to the stereo and put in a cassette. Clocherty knew that Lenny hated Black Flag and tortured him with their oppressive din every chance he got. He turned up the volume and seconds later their demented racket was reverberating through the flat. Lenny sank deeper and deeper into the cushions.

Clocherty dropped heavily onto the sofa and it rocked backwards precariously. He leaned over and punched Lenny hard on the arm, sending the Rubik's Cube cartwheeling across the carpet. Lenny's hand stayed where it was and he turned and stared vacantly at Clocherty.

'This is proper fucking music, Squatter.'

The thunderous noise was relentless. Lenny sat and hugged his legs and rested his chin on his knees.

'If I hear any of your fucking Leonard Cohen shit this weekend, I'll fucking batter you.'

Clocherty lit the joint and leapt up and started pogo-ing around the room. He hit the ceiling-light with the joint and Lenny watched a hundred rainbows cascade to the floor.

Friday 18th of October 10.50pm

The three of them had been dipping into the broth every time they passed the pot and were totally out of their heads. Lenny hadn't moved from the sofa. Clocherty took one of Lenny's Leonard Cohen vinyl albums and duct-taped it to Lenny's bedroom door and disappeared into his own bedroom. He came back holding a set of heavy-barrelled brass darts and they took it in turns to aim for the eye, the nose, the mouth, the hat, giggling insanely, but they soon got bored and it wasn't long before Clocherty heaved Lenny from the sofa and stood him in front of the door. Lenny had no idea what was going on. The first dart stuck in his shoulder. He didn't flinch and made no sound as he removed the dart and held it in front of his face.

The Savages had come to blows over whose throw it was next and were knocking lumps off each other. Clocherty was still doubled-up laughing and wasn't even looking when he threw the second dart but it hit Lenny in the centre of the forehead and hung with the flights resting on his nose. He pulled out the dart and had a moment of clarity. He dropped both darts to the floor and spun and turned the handle and was hit between the shoulder-blades with the third as he fled into the bedroom.

He had the top deadbolt in place and was on his haunches fumbling with the second when Clocherty's boot connected with the bottom of the door. There was a loud crack as the door threatened to give, but before he could kick again the bolt slid across and Lenny retreated to his bed.

He reached round and removed the dart and dropped it on the bedside table. He sat on the bed and cowered against the wall as the three of them beat on the door and bellowed for him to give the dart back. He turned off the lamp but he could see more with it off than on and quickly flicked the switch again.

They soon tired of hitting and kicking the door and found other distractions. Occasionally they remembered he was there and banged on the door and demanded he come out. Next, they'd tap gently and try to lure him out with cooed promises of all manner of delights, then burst out laughing and revert to door-banging, name-calling, and murderous threats.

Lenny didn't sleep, but he did come to find a place in his mind where there was peace, and he retreated there and hoped he would never have to return.

Saturday 19th of October 10.05am

After what could have been an entire human lifetime, his mind started to clear and he began his descent back into the real world. He didn't know how long he'd been away. He'd had no concept of time. He was still off his face but the hallucinations had stopped. The events of yesterday were coming back and the full horror of what he'd done was beginning to dawn on him. He was terrified, but his overwhelming feeling was still hatred. The bastards deserved it, he told himself. He felt for Stu, but there'd been nothing he could do about that. Collateral damage.

His hands were shaking. He took a deep breath and slid the deadbolts back. He looked back to see the bag of dried mushrooms was still on the bedside table, then he half-opened the door. The stench that hit him was vile. He retched and held his nose and ventured into the living-room. Clocherty was slumped back against the sofa with his chin on his chest. He looked to be dead. His eyes were closed and he had vomit from his belly to his shins. He was sitting in a pool of liquid shit that had soaked the top half of his jeans and run down his legs and onto his boots. There was a large bowl, still half-full of broth, on the floor by his elbow, with the spoon a couple of feet away by the armchair.

The Savages were in the bathroom. Stu was wearing only

his underpants and was kneeling in the bath with his forearms either side of the plughole and was staring into a pool of his own effluent. He was sweating profusely and shivering and was retching slowly, like a car with a run-down battery. Tony was on his side and was curled, clearly dead, around the base of the toilet.

He went back to the living-room and got a beer from the fridge and opened it with his teeth. The pot on the stove was more than two-thirds empty. He turned and his heart thumped against his ribcage. Clocherty was still alive. The collar of his denim jacket was dark with sweat. He still had his chin on his chest, and his eyes rolled upwards in their sockets to look at Lenny.

'You're a fucking coward, Squatter. A spineless, fucking coward.' His voice was a weak rasp. He twitched and clutched his stomach and a stream of blood and bile oozed from his mouth onto his chest. Lenny came out from behind the counter.

'Maybe I am, but it's you that's fucking yellow, you horrible cunt. I mean, really, you are proper fucking yellow. Even your fucking eyeballs are yellow. Oh, and you seem to have shit yourself. Did you follow through?'

'Fuck you.'

Lenny felt a rush of adrenaline and took three paces and kicked him full in the face. The sofa slid into the wall and the back of Clocherty's head hit the floor. 'That's for Ibby. Do you remember Ibby?' He took a step forward and stamped once on his face. 'And Clare? Eh? Beautiful Clare? Remember her?' He stood above him like a boxer over a felled opponent. 'A bit of fucking closure, eh? A bit of fun? That's what you said. Well, you were right, I *have* waited too fucking long.'

Clocherty had managed to drag himself back and lean his head against the sofa. He stared at Lenny.

'What was it? In the stew?' He was barely audible.

Lenny finished his beer and threw the bottle behind the kitchen counter. His hands were flexing and clenching, flexing and clenching. He went to get another beer.

'You really want to know?'

Clocherty nodded slowly. Lenny took his beer and turned the armchair to face him.

'Ok, if you think it'll help.' He opened the beer and sat down. 'There were about two-thousand magic mushrooms, as requested ... yeah, you know, thinking about it, you should still be tripping, so why aren't you laughing? You're not having a bad trip, are you? No, it doesn't matter, I don't care. So, then I decided to spice it up with a few more fruits of the forest. Death caps, to be precise. Amanita Phalloides to the experts. And I am. An expert. I found a couple of destroying angels too. They're rare around here. Great name, eh?'

Clocherty clutched his stomach again and retched more blood...

'Obviously I don't need to tell you the symptoms.'

... he let out an agonised groan.

'Oh, sorry, you want to know. Ok, well, you obviously already know about the abdominal cramps, the nausea, the vomiting, the bleeding diarrhoea, so all that's left really is the complete organ shutdown, and death. Is death a symptom? Never mind. Do you know how many it takes to kill someone? No? Half a mushroom. Half a fucking mushroom and that's you. Can you believe that?'

He took a long drink. 'That's what it says in the books, anyway, but people have recovered from eating just one or two.' He took another swig. 'Not that you need to worry about that. I didn't take any chances on that score.'

He got up and kicked Clocherty's foot to make sure he was still listening. 'Do you want to know how many you've had?'

Clocherty didn't speak, just glared. Lenny told him anyway.

'I put about forty in that stew, all told, so, looking at that pot, and knowing what a greedy cunt you are, I'd say you've had at least a dozen, probably more. They were big ones too. Turns out it's a good year for mushrooms.'

He went to the sideboard and shouted across the room as he scoured the cassettes. 'They take a long time to work, much longer than the magics, but you'll have noticed that.' He picked a tape and held it up. 'How about a bit of Leonard Cohen? Oh, no, sorry, I was forgetting, not your bag, is it. He laughed hysterically for a few seconds, then stopped abruptly. 'No, no, you're right, let's not kill the mood.' He threw the cassette down and picked another. 'Here we go, perfect, you'll love this.' He put the tape in the player and pressed play and walked back and stood over the hapless Clocherty. The sound of helicopter blades, Jim Morrison's voice. Lenny stared at Clocherty and sang …

'This is the end, beau-ti-ful friend'

He grinned. 'It's your apocalypse, now, Clocherty.'

And he sang …

'This is the end, my on-ly friend, the end'

Clocherty stared back, defiant …

'Of our elab-orate plans, the end'

…but his breathing was slowing down …

'Of every-thi-ing that stands, the end'

…his lights were dimming …

'No safe-ty o-or sur-prise, the end'

Lenny bent from the waist and glared into his jaundiced eyes …

'I'll ne-ver look into your eyes … again'

Clocherty's eyelids closed. Lenny stood upright, picked up his beer, leaned back, spread his arms, and at the top of his lungs, he sang …

'Can you pic-ture, what will be, so-o limit-less and free'

He tilted the bottle and drank …

'Desperate-ly in need of some strangers hand'

He walked to the window, pulled back a curtain …

'In a des-perate land'

He looked out onto the street …

'Lost in a Roman wilder-ness of pain'

He closed the curtain and knelt beside Clocherty and leaned forward …

'And all the chil-dren are in-sane'

… and Clocherty's eyes sprang open and like a cobra strike his hand gripped Lenny by the throat. Lenny dropped the bottle and grabbed the hand in both of his and tried to loosen its hold but it was locked solid as a hyena's bite …

All the children are insane.

* * *

He pulled Lenny to the floor and rolled himself over until he was on top and they were cruciform on the carpet. Lenny couldn't move and was choking. With his free hand Clocherty reached for the bowl by the sofa and dragged it closer. He stretched for the spoon and lifted both onto Lenny's chest. Lenny was about to lose consciousness when Clocherty relaxed his grip as he heaved himself onto his knees and sat across his midriff. He grabbed Lenny's cheeks and squeezed and his mouth opened and he thrust a spoonful of the lethal broth into his gape. Lenny pushed with his tongue and closed his gullet but Clocherty clamped his palm over his mouth and nose and Lenny had no choice but to swallow. Clocherty removed his hand as he refilled the spoon and Lenny drew his lips into his mouth and bit down, but Clocherty pushed the spoon into the crease and Lenny felt his teeth begin to break and he opened his mouth and swallowed another spoonful. He was exhausted and struggling for breath. He thought he might die. He went limp and opened his mouth wide and started to hyperventilate. Clocherty picked up the bowl and spoon and scraped the remaining poison straight in and clamped his hand over his mouth. He had broth coming out of his nose. He was suffocating. He looked into Clocherty's bloodshot yellow eyes, watched them fade, and his world went dark.

* * *

It could have been minutes, it could have been hours. He had no way of knowing. Clocherty was slumped forward with his rancid chest on Lenny's face. Lenny took him by the shoulders and pushed until the lifeless body fell backwards onto the floor. He crawled out from beneath the legs and went to the bathroom.

Stu was still on his knees but had toppled sideways and seemed to have stopped breathing. Lenny stood with his feet either side of Tony. The nerves in his teeth were raw and he winced with every breath. He thrust his fingers into his ravaged throat and retched violently, but nothing came out. He feared it may be too late. He rinsed the puke, the shit and congealed gunge from his face and swilled his mouth with cold water. The pain was excruciating.

He went to his room and changed his shirt and grabbed his bomber jacket and put it on and rushed to the door. The key had gone. He ransacked the bedrooms and searched the living-room. No key. All the exertion would be speeding the poison through his system, but he knew that any more than two hours and he could well be joining the three of them.

He needed to get to the hospital. He went to Clocherty's corpse and knelt and held his front pocket open with his index finger and pushed his other hand into the sodden pocket and found two keys. He took both and unlocked the door, stepped onto the landing and turned and relocked the door and leaped down the stairs a landing at a time and within seconds was on the street and heading for Bright Lights General.

PART FIVE

Monday 21st of Oct 1985

I retrieved the ladder and hung it back in the lean-to and did a thorough search, inside and out. Nothing else seemed to have been touched, but it was still a big worry. I had a crop that was only half-grown, but I'd be looking at a prison sentence if I was caught, so I cleared the place out.

I took a chance and left the plants in the tanks and put them against the wall behind the feeding station. I lifted the ivy from the wall and draped it over them; if I'd been rumbled, they'd be looking for a factory; surely they wouldn't bring dogs? Whatever, I decided I'd know before the weekend. If nothing came of it by then maybe I could salvage some of them.

I dismantled the set-up and gathered all the associated paraphernalia and put everything in bin-liners and taped the tops and hid them in a thicket in Hawksheads Wood. I disconnected the extractor hose and put it along with the canopy behind a tarpaulin in the lean-to. I used a full tin of air freshener in the bedroom and opened the front and back doors, took my easel outside and spent what was left of the day painting in the garden.

By Tuesday night I'd still heard nothing. I'd been out all day and was updating the log-books when the phone rang. I feared the worst, or thought I did, until Mum dropped her bombshell.

* * *

'Hiya love,' she said, 'are you ok.'

'A bit stressed Mum,' I replied. 'You know, all this stuff with the estate,' I added, conservatively.

There was a long pause. I was beginning to think she'd hung up, then she came back on.

'Have you seen the Gazette?' She asked.

'You know I don't read the papers Mum.'

There was another pause, shorter this time. 'Well, I've got some bad news, I'm afraid, love. I saw Noreen Fields this morning. She's in a right state. Lenny's in the hospital.'

An overdose, that was my first thought. At least she said hospital, not mortuary.

'How serious is it?' I asked.

'He's in intensive care. He's eaten some deadly mushroom or other.'

I thought I must have misheard. 'Mushrooms? Like, death caps or something, you mean? Are you sure, Mum?' I asked.

'Well, that's what Noreen said.'

My mind went into overdrive. How the fuck had Lenny come to eat poisonous mushrooms? It didn't make sense. He could identify just about any fungus, and he knew everything there was to know about them, especially the poisonous types. He used to be forever pointing them out and gleefully reeling out the symptoms. It would be his specialist subject on Mastermind, for fuck's sake. Something wasn't right.

Mum carried on. 'But it's worse than that, son.'

'Worse? How can it be worse?'

'There were four of them, love. Lenny's been the lucky one.'

I almost laughed. 'Doesn't sound very lucky—'

'It's serious, John. Two of them are dead, love, and the

other one's in a coma.'

I was stunned. Mum broke the silence. 'Lenny's in a very bad way, love.'

'I suppose I should go and see him—'

'He's not allowed visitors, well, Fred and Noreen, but that's all. Noreen said the police were there. They say it may have been deliberate. They're looking at the possibility that someone else was involved. They've been waiting for Lenny to come round so they can ask him what happened.'

'Lenny knows his mushrooms, Mum. He wouldn't have knowingly eaten them. It must have been an accident.'

'Well, I'm sure the police will get to the bottom of it.'

There was another fraught silence.

'Anyway,' she said, 'I do have a bit of *good* news. Archie phoned Rod and he says he'll meet you in the Eagle on Friday night, early on, half-past six, when it's quiet, if you can make it.'

Temporary elation. 'Tell Archie thanks and to tell Rod I'll be there. Thanks Mum.'

* * *

My head was battered. The ladder, all the estate stuff, and now this. What the fuck? Very few people die in England from eating poisonous mushrooms, and those that do are invariably people who've been foraging in the woods, or in their gardens, and picked the wrong ones. Accidents, all of them. Ok, the victims in this case were a world away from the middle-class couple with the orchard garden, unwittingly picking the wrong breakfast item, but there was still no reason to think that this was anything but an accident. I was certain of it. The police were wrong with their fifth person theory.

In my version of events, it was just a magic mushroom session gone horribly wrong. Nothing more. It was obvious what had happened. The other three had picked the mushrooms, and one or more of them had picked the lethal ones by mistake. Then, when they got home, they put them in a casserole, maybe dried them first, and Lenny never got a chance to see them. Case closed. Lenny can't have even been there, or he would have seen them and known what they were. That was the logical explanation.

But I still felt uneasy. When Lenny was involved, nothing was ever quite so straightforward.

I decided that if I knew when it happened, and where, and who these other three blokes were, I might get a better handle on what had gone on, so I rang Mum back.

Archie answered. He said he was sorry to hear about Lenny. I asked him if he had the Gazette handy and he went to get it.

'Does the article have the names of the other three?' It was quiet for a second or two. I heard the paper rustling.

'Yes … Anthony Charles Savage … and … Robert James Clocherty, they're the two unfortunates that are no longer with us … and … Stuart Savage is the one in a coma. A terrible thing.'

I wrote them down. 'Does it say where it happened?'

'It does … somewhere … aah … yes … Alfred Street.'

Lenny's place. 'Does it say when?'

'He was admitted on Saturday afternoon, that's all it says. Oh, and the other three weren't discovered until Sunday morning, apparently.'

'Thanks Archie, and thanks for talking to your nephew. It means a lot.'

'No problem, son. I hope it goes well. Give him my best.'

'Will do, thanks Archie.' I nearly said dad.

Anthony and Stuart. Tony and Stu. They didn't look like brothers, as far as I could remember, but it had to be them. That said, I hadn't been in touch with Lenny for five years. Who knew how far downhill he'd gone or who he had dossing in the flat?

I'd seen Russell Marsh, the denim dickhead, in town about twelve months earlier. He said he hadn't seen Lenny for a long time, not to talk to, anyway. The last time was in the Rose and Crown and Lenny was wasted and had a busted nose. Lenny had 'got pally with some fucking nutters off the fairground,' Russ said, so he'd given him a wide berth since then.

I reckoned that would be the same busted nose he got when I went round and he spiked my drink, the night the lunatic turned up. I doubted that pally was the word Russ was looking for.

I looked at the other name again. Clocherty. I remembered Mum telling me that whenever Noreen rang Lenny she never got to speak to him. It was always a Scottish accent that answered. His so-called mates off the fairground had started to make themselves at home in the flat while I was still living there. Maybe this Clocherty was another one.

I made a brew and sat at the desk and tried to focus on the meeting with Rod. He obviously had big plans for the estate that I had no chance of changing, but I had to do something. I just hoped I could convince him to give me access to whatever was left after he's finished butchering it. But why would he? I had to show him what was at stake. I had three days to prepare myself for what was, for me, the biggest interview of my life.

* * *

I finished the brew and went to bed, but I was tormented by the business with the ladder. The scrapes on the wall were either side of the vent-pipe; whoever had been snooping obviously knew what they were looking for, even if they hadn't managed to get to the vent to confirm it before the ladder collapsed.

I was missing something, something obvious. Smudge was the only other person who knew I was growing weed. I thought about our relationship. He'd always seemed like a sound bloke, but was he? How well did I know him, really? Was he as reliable as I thought? Had he told someone where he got his weed? Someone on the power station? Or had he broken our agreement and started selling locally? Maybe he'd shared a joint with somebody in town? But even if he had, Smudge didn't know where I lived. We'd always done the deal, a nervy couple of minutes, in a layby, miles from anywhere, and he sold it on in Cardiff.

Or so he said.

I wondered if he did much drinking in town, how drunk he got and who he spoke to. Had he had a drink with Russ, shared a spliff, possibly, or sold him some weed? Fucking Russ and his big mouth? That would make sense; Russ had bought some weed from Smudge, or they'd shared a joint, and Smudge had let my name slip. Maybe that was it. I couldn't remember telling Russ about buying the gatehouse, but it was around the time of the sale when I'd last spoken to him, so it's something that could have come up.

There were loads of possibilities, none of them good. Whatever had happened, it was too soon to get the business up and running again. Not only that, I had to forget about salvaging any of the current crop, and dispose of the plants completely.

I settled down again and was on the verge of sleep when it came to me. I normally spent all day Friday at the gatehouse and got to Jan's at around teatime, at five, or even six o'clock, so when I discovered the missing ladder on Monday morning, I assumed it had been moved over the weekend, on Saturday or Sunday. I hadn't even considered Lenny and his crew as suspects, as the fatal mushroom session had happened on Friday night. By Saturday morning they were all busy dying or getting comatose.

But last Friday was different. I'd just got the news about the estate being sold off and was at Jan's by lunch-time. The ladder could have been moved on Friday afternoon. The longer I thought about this, the more sense it made, and I eventually had to accept that I may have been ignoring the obvious, and that my first inclinations could be wrong.

My mind mulled over another hundred what-ifs before finally giving in to an erratic sleep, during which I had what I believe is known as a lucid dream. In fact, it didn't seem to be a dream at all. As weird and out-there as it was, it seemed completely real, like I was conscious the whole time, and could have opened my eyes, unzipped the sleeping-bag, and got up at any moment.

* * *

I was in a cathedral, huge and cavernous, arches and columns, stained-glass windows high in the walls. I was trying to reach a solitary figure seated on the high altar in the far-distance, fighting my way through a white-water torrent that was pouring from the vast central dome and crashing down the nave towards me.

In the pews, an anonymous congregation of blank,

featureless discs, looked on in silence as I battled the deluge. Above these, looming, a gallery of enormous faces.

There was Swifty, massively, cartoonishly, fat, and the Crowe twins, in manacles, two identical heads sprouting from the same prison-uniform. April Meadows, Jan, and Jennifer, my ex, were all there, together, laughing, crying, cheering me on. Fred and Noreen, too, Mum and Archie, my father, all whooping, clapping, whistling and crying, until I finally reached the towering cataract, and broke through, and stood in the silence of the quire beyond.

In the distance, on the high altar, the tiny figure still sat. Suddenly, the strains of Night Fever, and a giant mirror-ball, set high in the ceiling-dome, spinning, firing splinters of blinding white light flashing around the vast space. Beneath the ball, an image, two figures flickering on and off in the stroboscopic light. Dancing their way down the quire towards me, lieutenants Columbo and Kojak.

Then they were in front of me, up close, right knees flexed, right hands raised, index fingers pointing skyward. Columbo like a tramp; shabby raincoat, dirty white shirt, loose tie, trouser-legs concertina-ed from the knees down, shoes scuffed and turned up at the toes.

Kojak, smart as a dart; silver-grey suit-trousers and waistcoat, mauve shirt, plum tie, black patent leather shoes, mirrored sunglasses.

In my face, one then the other.

Kojak had a lollipop in his mouth. 'We got three stiffs, lieutenant,' he said, 'but we don't got no perp.'

Columbo sucked the stub of a cigar. 'But we do, Theo,' he said, 'we do got a perp.' He removed the cigar from his mouth and turned and pointed at the seated figure in the distance.

‘There’s our perp,’ he said.

Kojak grinned hugely and waggled the sucked end of the lollipop at Columbo. ‘Why, so it is,’ he beamed. ‘Who loves ya, baby?’

Columbo turned to walk away, then turned back. ‘Just one more thing, Theo.’

‘Tell me what I want to hear, sweetheart.’

‘My wife loves your programme.’

He sucked again on his cigar and the two lieutenants spun around, laughing, and danced away.

The music had stopped. There was just one single light, a spotlight that illuminated the distant high altar and the figure still seated there. I walked towards it, but the congregation reappeared, and grew, and grew, more and more heads appeared, and I got no closer.

I turned and tried again to see the faces of the congregation, but they had gone, and standing there in front of me was a pixie that bore a resemblance to a famous television chef. He held his hands full of mushrooms up to my face. They were all the colours of the rainbow and were multiplying and spewing from his hands to the floor.

‘He’s not a chef,’ he said. ‘He’s a gastronaut.’

‘Who is?’ I asked.

‘Him,’ he said, jerking his head over his shoulder, towards the seated figure.

‘Who is it? I asked

‘It’s the perp,’ he said. ‘Don’t you listen?’

Suddenly, I was there, on the high altar, and I could see plainly, now, that the seated figure was Lenny. He was in a black, padded leather office-chair, arms on the armrests, gripping them tightly. He avoided my eyes. I circled him, or he revolved around me, maybe both, I couldn’t tell, and behind him, barely visible in the shadows, were Smudge and Russ, huddled together, thick as thieves, conspiring.

Then a different music; drums, snare and bass, the sound of doom, of approaching menace.

A voice suddenly boomed from the void.

'And, so,' it said, *'after the specialist round ...'*

It was a voice I recognised. I looked towards the source.

'... and leading at the half-way stage ...' it continued.

But it wasn't who I thought it was, who it should have been.

'... with twenty-five points ...'

He was wearing a wig.

'... and no passes ...'

With a row of curls at the front.

'... tonight's winner is ...'

It was a Judge's wig.

'... Joseph Leonard Fields.'

The Judge held a square of black cloth in his hands.

'No!' I shouted. 'Not the death cap!'

I watched in horror as he placed the cloth on top of his head and rose to his feet.

I was pleading, now. 'Not the death cap! Please! You can't! Not yet! It's too soon. We haven't had the second round!'

Then Lenny was standing on the seat and was under a huge pine tree and had a noose around his neck. The top of the tree was invisible in the vastness of the vaulted ceiling, and the Judge stepped forward, kicked the chair from under him, and left him swinging like a pendulum.

'Please,' I sobbed. What about the second round? We haven't had the second round.'

He grabbed Lenny's legs and pulled.

'I've started so I'll finish,' he said, over and over. *'I've started so I'll finish, I've started so I'll finish, I've started so I'll finish...'*

Wednesday 23rd of October 1985

When I opened my eyes it was seven o'clock and the sleeping bag was drenched with sweat. I hadn't had a drink but I felt hungover. I had a headache and my tongue was stuck to the roof of my mouth. I got up, made a cup of coffee, and sat at the table.

I was glad Lenny wasn't allowed visitors. At least I didn't have to feel guilty about not going to see him. There was no way I was turning up at the hospital and getting dragged into this shit, but I needed to know what was going on. I'd go and see Fred and Noreen, but first I needed to finish cleaning the place out.

When it came to it I couldn't bring myself to throw all the immature buds away, so I kept them for personal use. I bagged them up and hid them in a tree-hole in Hawksheads Wood and buried what was left of the plants in the midden heap. The mother plant was too precious to throw away. It was quite small so I left it behind the curtain on the windowsill in the kitchen where it would survive for a good few days and would, hopefully, be overlooked by anyone looking for a large operation.

If my name came up and the police paid a visit, the empty tanks might arouse suspicion, so instead of cleaning them out, I filled them with ornamental plants and put them against the wall of the house, two on either side of the front-door. I spent the afternoon painting in the garden, had something to eat, then went into Yelland.

* * *

I got to the post office just before six. Fred showed me into the kitchen and closed the door behind us. He collected an assortment of used crockery; plates and mugs, cups and saucers, from the table and took it and put it on the drainer. He came back for the cutlery and condiments.

'I'm sorry it's a bit of a mess, lad. Noreen's not here. She's staying at the hospital.'

I went to the sink and started the tap.

'There's no need for that, lad,' he said.

'I'll do this while you make us a brew,' I said. 'Deal?'

Fred turned on the kettle and picked the last two mugs from the mug-tree and we worked in silence. When we'd finished, we took our drinks and went to opposite sides of the table.

'Mum saw Noreen,' I said, as we sat. 'What's happened?'

'We don't know much, really. He landed at the hospital on Saturday, about lunchtime, in a right state, he was. They pumped his stomach and then had him sedated until the early-hours of Sunday. That's when he told them…when he came round…about the…about the others…that's why they never…why they're…' his voice trailed off. He was close to tears. There was a prolonged silence, then he started to talk, and once he'd started, I thought he'd never stop. It all came out, all the problems with Lenny over the years, the things he'd got up to, the attitude, the thieving, the temper, and the toll it had taken on them, on Noreen in particular.

'Do you know the last time we saw him?' he asked. 'It was

the day we had a natter out the front here, me and you, the day you first went off to Europe.' He paused for a second. 'I was setting the flowers out.' He paused again, lost in thought. 'We hadn't seen him for five years then and we hadn't seen him for five more since,' he said. 'Until now.'

He sat and stared into the distance. He spoke quietly. 'He came to borrow money, that last time. Owed it to some thugs. It was probably these same people. Anyway, we didn't have it and he left empty-handed. But he came back while we were at church.' He looked at the door to the shop. 'Smashed this blummin place up proper he did. You've never seen anything like it. Completely smashed everything up.'

He was sobbing silently and a string of mucus had bridged the gap from nose to knuckles.

'Why would he do that, eh, John? Why would he do that? To us, lad? To his Mother?' He took a handkerchief from the pocket of his cardigan and wiped his hand and blew his nose. He looked at me and smiled the best he could, then he seemed to brighten. He reached across and took my forearm in his hand and shook it vigorously. It was a strange, sad gesture. 'Eee, you've made a smashing young man, John,' he said. 'And after all you've been through.' He sighed and the smile disappeared. 'Maybe I had it all wrong,' he said, resignedly. He retrieved the handkerchief and dragged it across his face and sat up and composed himself. 'I'm sorry lad,' he said, 'you'll have to forgive me. I don't mean to speak out of turn. It's been a real struddle has this lot.'

He looked drawn. His mug shook slightly as he picked it up and raised it to his mouth.

'Eee, John lad,' he said, 'what's he got himself into now?'

He didn't wait for me to answer.

'It'll be the end of her, this lot will … Noreen … God love her.'

There was an awful silence bar the loud ticking of the kitchen clock.

'I can't imagine what you and Noreen have been through,' I said, eventually. 'Has Lenny said anything yet? About how it happened?'

Fred pulled himself together.

'He's saying it was a slip-up. He says they'd been picking these blummin psychopathic mushrooms and somebody must have picked these others by mistake.'

'Who does he say picked them?'

'They did, he says, the other three. He says he had nothing to do with it. As usual,' he added, under his breath.

'Do you not believe him?'

'I'll be honest, lad, I don't know what to believe. There's more gone on than we'll ever know.' He drained his mug and put it on the table. 'You know what he's like. He told me umpteen times in the past that he wasn't robbing us blind. Anyway, it doesn't matter what I think. The police don't think it was an accident.'

At last, a way in. 'Why, what do they think happened?' I asked. 'Have they said?'

'No, they've not said much, really, just that maybe someone had a grudge and has done it deliberate. I don't think they have a blummin clue, really.'

He picked up his mug again and raised it to take a drink. He noticed it was empty and put it back on the table.

'He's in a terrible way, lad,' he said. 'Not just with the poison. His throat's all bruised, purple it is, and his front teeth have been smashed in, not knocked out, mind, but smashed in. He still has them, thankfully, but they're bad to see.'

So, Lenny had been beaten up, as well as poisoned. Smashed teeth and a bruised throat. An uncomfortable new scenario was beginning to form in my mind.

Fred had slumped in his chair and was close to tears again.

'But it wasn't just him that had been beaten up,' he said. 'They all had injuries, the police said, busted noses and bruises and such like.'

Lenny wasn't a fighter, never had been.

'All blaming each other, do you think?' I asked. 'Maybe there *was* someone else, a fifth person.'

I didn't believe this for a minute. There was no fifth person, I knew that now. But it was no accident either.

Fred seemed lost in thought and didn't answer. We sat in silence again, for a few seconds, then he carried on.

'He doesn't want to see you, by the way. No, he made a point of telling me. He said if I saw you I was to tell you he doesn't want you there and if you turn up, he won't speak to you. The best friend he ever had, best he'll ever have. What's got into him, John?'

Why would Lenny feel the need to say that, if not to protect me, to keep me out of it? I was more convinced than ever that Lenny had something to hide. Had he done it? Could he have spiked them all?

'The police took his clothes,' Fred went on. 'From the hospital. And they're coming here to look through his things.'

I didn't want to be there when they turned up. 'When are they coming? Today?'

'No, tomorrow or Friday, I'm not sure. Noreen knows.'

'But he hasn't lived here for years,' I said. 'What are they looking for, exactly?'

'I don't know. I don't think they do either. It's just something they have to do, I suppose.' He cleared his throat and sat up and looked at me. 'Do you know them? These other lads?' he asked, surreptitiously, like I might know more than I was saying, and that anything I might know would stay between the two of us.

'I don't recognise the surnames,' I said, 'but I think there was a Tony and Stu that used to come to the flat. They didn't look like brothers, but I don't suppose that means much. Did they work with him at the fairground do you know?'

'Aye, I think so.'

'That's probably them. If it is, I wouldn't put this past any of them.'

He looked at the clock and stood and picked up the empty mugs.

'I need to be getting to the hospital,' he said.

I told Fred that I needed the loo and I went upstairs and when I came back down he was waiting by the front door. On the doorstep I turned and he looked me in the eye.

'And what about our Leonard?' he said. 'Would you put it past him?'

This time he did want an answer. There was a short pause.

'Who knows, Fred. Who knows what any of us is capable of when we're desperate?'

* * *

That night I went over it all again in my mind and eventually came up with a whole new version of events. I couldn't believe how gullible I'd been. This was Lenny, for fuck's sake. I tried to find holes in this new theory, but it was no good. I had to face up to the awful reality.

In this new version, Smudge *wasn't* as reliable as I'd thought, and Russ *had* found out that I was growing. He'd then bumped into Lenny and, true to form, hadn't been able to keep his mouth shut. I could almost hear the wheedling little gobshite;

'Hey, what about your mate, Woodsy ...'

In this new version, the person who'd been snooping around the gatehouse, and the person who picked the mushrooms, were one and the same, and that had to be Lenny, because whoever it was, they knew about the plants, and had it been any of the others, they would have broken in.

In this new version, both incidents had happened on Friday afternoon. Lenny had been to pick the mushrooms, and on his way had called at the gatehouse, maybe to cadge some weed, he was cheeky enough, and finding the place empty had decided to check if what Russ had told him was true. Or, maybe he was using his newfound knowledge as a reason to pay me a visit. Maybe he wanted to rebuild a few bridges. Or maybe that was just wishful thinking on my part.

As for the poisonous mushrooms, the other three may have known a magic mushroom when they saw one, but that would have been the extent of their knowledge. Beyond that, they wouldn't know a puffball from a stinkhorn. But Lenny did, and he knew a death cap from a liberty cap. What's more, he knew where to find both, just a few hundred yards apart.

In this new version, I finally accepted the truth I'd been avoiding all along; liberty caps and death caps grow in very different habitats; one in the open fields around the sand quarry, the other in the mixed woods of the Hawkshead estate. It couldn't possibly have been a mistake.

Lenny had deliberately poisoned them all. I knew that now. But why? What had they done to make him take such extreme action? Was he being bullied and simply couldn't see any other way out? I was the main focus of their piss-taking when I was living there. Had Lenny become the new me? If so, he'd been taking it for years. How bad had it got? Bad enough for him to kill three people?

And then there was the bigger mystery; knowing his fungi like he did, why had he eaten them, too? Had he been so out of it that he'd actually forgotten what he'd done, and eaten some himself? Surely not? Nothing I came up with seemed feasible until, in the end, I was left with just the one, horrifying theory.

I imagined the scene. If the death caps had been added to a strong magic-mushroom casserole, and they kept digging into it, they wouldn't have known what was going on. They were probably laughing as they shit themselves. When they realised what was happening, and that Lenny was the only one not puking and shitting, had they force-fed him? I thought about the bruising on his throat, the broken teeth. If I was right, it must have been like a horror film.

PART SIX

Thursday 24th of October 1985

DI Jack Dawes was losing his patience. He pulled again, and again, yanking harder and harder, becoming more and more furious. Finally, he gave up, sat back and folded his arms.

'Fuck it!' he snapped. 'Fucking stupid law! Fucking nanny state. Come on, let's go.'

DS Dawn Starling stifled a snigger.

'It's trapped in the door, Sir.'

He opened his door a fraction, freed the belt and pulled it across himself. Starling noticed his hands had a slight tremor, and that he'd removed his wedding ring since yesterday. He smelled strongly of stale cigarettes.

She turned the key in the ignition.

'I'm guessing she hasn't changed her mind, then?' She checked the mirror and pulled away from the kerb.

'She changes it so fucking often I can't keep up, but no, no she hasn't.'

'Are you sure you're ok, Sir? Maybe you should have taken a bit more time?'

'Don't start again, Starling. We went through this yesterday. I'm fine. I was going spare at home. I'm better off at work, keeps my mind off … things. Anyway, enough about me. Let's go and hear what the mushroom murderer has to say for himself.'

Starling looked shocked. 'Sir? I thought you said yesterday—'

'I know what I said yesterday, Sergeant, and if you'd been here the day before yesterday, you'd know I said we were looking for someone else entirely.' He held up a folder bursting with paperwork. 'But that was before I'd had the pleasure of spending an entire fucking night going through this lot.'

'Is that the forensic report, Sir?'

'Yes, and this is only what's in so far.'

Starling glared at him.

'How long have you had that? You could have given me a chance to catch up, I was late enough to the case—'

'Alright, Sergeant, alright, keep your wig on. I only picked it up late last night, ok? I had fuck all better to do, obviously, so I stayed back and caught up on some paperwork. I saw Les Hedges from forensics and I pestered him for copies of what they have so far. The full report won't be in for a couple of days yet.'

Starling drove on, eyes fixed on the road.

Dawes cleared his throat.

'How was the holiday, anyway, Sergeant? I forgot to ask yesterday.'

Starling ignored the question.

'I didn't get to see the crime scene, either,' she said.

'Neither did I,' he replied. 'I was only given the case myself on Tuesday afternoon. The bodies had been long removed by then, and forensics had taken most of the evidence away. As far as anyone was concerned it was misadventure, nothing to do with homicide. When they found the others and realised there was more to this than they first thought, they took me off the night club stabbing and gave it to fucking Splinterdick.'

'Splinterdick?' Starling started to laugh. 'Who on earth's Splinterdick?'

'Jack Woodcock. I'd more or less wrapped it up. He'll finish the paperwork and get all the kudos.' He took a pack of cigarettes from his pocket and lit one. Starling wound down her window and leaned towards it.

Dawes carried on. 'Anyway, by all accounts we're lucky we didn't have to see it. The crime scene. Fucking awful, they say. A police photographer with twenty-odd years' service threw up, apparently. Never seen anything like it. They had to break the fucking door down to get in. Fields had locked it when he left, and guess what? Looks like he had the only key.'

'Unusual, only one key, Sir.'

'There's been no other key found. He locked the poor sods in to die.'

'So, you really think he's done it deliberately?'

'I know it, Starling. I thought his story was dubious from the start, to be honest. Reading the notes from his interview with the uniforms, you'd be forgiven for thinking it was a terrible tragedy; four mates, out for some fun, accidentally poison themselves. But that's a load of old bollocks. It was Fields who picked the mushrooms, and it was him that concocted that fucking witches' brew. He knew exactly what he was doing.'

'You're sure he isn't just as much a victim as the others, Sir? I mean, he's been lucky to pull through himself, by all accounts—'

'He's as guilty as the day is long, Starling. Trust me.'

'Can we prove it, Sir?'

He waved the folder in the air. 'I think so, Sergeant. You see, fortunately, unlike our suspect, forensics don't lie.'

'So, why would he do it, Sir?'

'That's what we need to find out. Once forensics get finished, it'll be up to us to piece together what's happened. We can save ourselves a lot of work if we can get Fields to talk.'

'We've still got Stuart Savage, Sir. There's a chance he'll come round.'

'A chance, yes, but we can't rely on it. He might be our trump card if we need him, but we have to work on Fields, get him to crack.'

Up ahead, an ageing couple stood, arm-in-arm, waiting for a break in the traffic. Starling slowed the car and held up her palm to let them cross. Dawes reached over and honked the horn, stopping them in their tracks.

'There's a fucking crossing up the road,' he muttered angrily.

Starling gave them an apologetic look and drove on. They made the rest of the journey in silence. Starling pulled into the hospital car park, found a space and turned off the engine.

Dawes removed his seat-belt and thrust the folder at her as he reached for his coat on the back seat. Loose papers fell between the seats and into the foot-well.

'There's some photographs of the flat in there,' he said. 'Fuck knows what was going on. Have a quick look,' he said. 'But hurry up, he's not well, bless his cotton socks. They won't let us question him for long, and we're already ten minutes later than was agreed.'

And whose fault is that, she thought.

'That's ok Sir, she said.' She pulled the lever and pushed her seat back. Her cheek brushed his thigh as she struggled to gather the papers from the foot-well. She sensed him about to speak, raised her head and gave him a stern look.

He dropped his coat on his lap and raised his palms.

'What?' he asked, with exaggerated innocence.

'You know what,' she replied. 'Don't you dare.'

'I wasn't going to say anything.'

'Well that'd be a first, then.'

She put the loose papers in the folder and handed it back.

'It's a bit late to go through all that, now,' she said, pointedly.

She relocated her seat and took the keys from the ignition. They got out of the car, closed the doors and faced one another across the roof.

'Do you fancy giving me the basics, Sir, as we walk?'

'You're up to speed on everything else? You've read the reports on the four of them?'

'Front to back, Sir, more than once. You're not the only one that had a late night. I could just do with a quick heads up on the forensics.'

She locked the car and they set off towards the hospital entrance.

'Ok, but we haven't much time, Sergeant, so I'll just ask you this. What do you think saved our Mr. Fields' useless, miserable, fucking life? Why did he come out of this in so much better shape than the others?'

Starling shrugged. 'He didn't ingest as much poison as the others?'

'Well, it seems he did have less than the others, yes, but according to forensics he still had more than enough to kill the average person several times over.'

Dawes held the hospital door open and Starling gave him a look of surprise as she walked through.

'Thank you. Been on a course, Sir?'

Dawes ignored her, let the door swing shut, and they stood in the foyer.

'Well, go on, Sergeant, any other ideas?'

'I don't know, Sir, maybe he has a stronger constitution, or a slower metabolic rate.'

Dawes was shaking his head emphatically.

'No, no. He's by far the smallest of the four. No, It's all about the timing, Sergeant. You'll see. Come on, showtime. Let's nail this fucker.'

They approached the reception desk. Starling looked at Dawes.

'So, what's the strategy, Sir?'

'Oh, I think our Mr. Fields will respond well to a bit of good cop, bad cop.'

'And which one will I be, Sir?'

'Don't push it, Starling, not today.'

* * *

Lenny could see the reception desk from his bed. He knew they were police as soon as he saw them, talking to the receptionist and showing her their ID. There were two of them again, a different pair today. Plain clothes this time. The Big Guns. Well, they were wasting their time. They had nothing. He just needed to stick to his story. Short answers, no need to get too elaborate. They picked the mushrooms, and they cooked them up.

The tall, thin one introduced himself as Detective Inspector Jack Dawes. He was pale and hirsute, with wiry black hairs protruding from his cuffs and collar. His hair was close-cropped and he hadn't shaved so his whole head had a five o'clock shadow. He looked dishevelled, like he'd slept in his suit. He carried a black raincoat over his arm and had a thick folder in his hand.

His partner dragged two chairs from the corner of the room and placed them by the bed. She was a foot shorter than him, with auburn hair, pulled back in a bun, and steely-looking eyes in a no-nonsense face.

She gave Dawes a hard-stare as they took their seats. 'And I'm Detective Sergeant Dawn Starling,' she said.

A drip hung from a metal stand beside the bed. She looked at the prone figure, the bruising, the cut lips, the sunken eyes and yellow pallor. Lenny stared at his hands folded in his lap. Dawes caught Starling's eye and raised his eyebrows. She cleared her throat and turned to Lenny.

'Looks like you've been a lucky lad, Joseph.'

Lenny snorted. 'Yeah, that's me. Born lucky I was. And it's Lenny.'

'OK, Lenny. How are you feeling?' She glanced towards the door and at the other, empty bed. 'Are they looking after you ok? A room to yourself, that's nice, anyway.'

Dawes sighed loudly. Starling ignored him and went on. 'Well, Lenny, we're just here to find out what happened, that's all. Do you feel up to answering a few questions?'

'I've already answered them all. I've nothing else to say.'

Dawes took a notebook from his inside pocket. Lenny thought he saw his hands shaking.

'Well, that's the thing, Joseph. You see, you didn't answer the questions, did you? Not all of them.' He leafed through the notebook. 'Hardly any of them, in fact. "I can't remember" is hardly an answer, is it?'

'Have you ever eaten two hundred magic mushrooms?'

Dawes ignored him and read from the notebook. 'Yesterday, you told our uniformed colleagues that you, and your … your *mates*, you called them, that you and your mates, had a session on hallucinogenic mushrooms and that the other three, these three poor sods who are unable to contradict your story, they picked the mushrooms. Is that correct?'

'Yeah.'

'All of them?'

'All of them, and it's not a story, it's the truth.'

'You're sure about that?'

'Positive. They fucked up. And by the way, they *are* my mates.'

Dawes pointed at his neck and mouth. 'So, what about the injuries? What was the fight about?' He looked again at his notebook. 'Clocherty … fractured jaw, two black eyes … both Savages cut around the eyes and lips.'

'We were just having a laugh. We often had play-fights when we were out of it.'

'Play-fights? Come on, son, give us *some* credit, at least. You can't be more than eight-stone wet through. You're telling me that you liked to play-fight with these three? Pull the other one, son.'

Lenny shrugged. 'Suit yourself.'

'Oh, I will, believe me. Ok, let's go back to last Friday, in the morning … back to a time that, presumably, you *can* remember … tell us, in detail, what you did on Friday?'

'I went through all this yesterday.'

'Humour us, son.'

'Like I said, I was in the flat all day. They were out all morning—'

'The three of them?'

'Yeah, they'd been sorting some business—'

'What sort of business?'

Lenny paused. 'I don't know, they didn't say.'

Dawes gave a cynical snort. 'So, you were in the flat. Doing what, exactly?'

'Watching telly.'

'All morning?'

'Yeah.'

'What were you watching?'

'I don't know. Cartoons, I think—'

'You think?'

'I can't remember, I was stoned—'

'First thing in the morning?'

'I'd had a couple of joints.'

Dawes sighed and shook his head. 'So, they'd been out all morning, sorting some … *business*, you say. Then what?'

'When they got back—'

'What time was that?'

'I don't know, about dinnertime I suppose. They were stressed-out about something, and Clocherty … Clock … he decided we were having a magic-mushroom session, cos we were all off work till Monday.'

'Clocherty didn't work, is that right?'

'No … yeah … but the rest of us did. And we all had the weekend off. It doesn't happen often—'

'You say Clocherty decided that you were all having a session…'

'Well, he suggested—'

'That's not what you said.' Dawes looked back through his notebook. 'Here we are, you said it in your interview yesterday, too, "Clocherty *decided* we were going to have a session." It sounds like Clocherty, sorry, that your mate, *Clock*, called all the shots.'

Lenny didn't answer.

Starling leaned forward in her chair. 'Lenny, the flat on Alfred Street. It's in your name, yes?'

'So what?'

'But Clocherty was living with you. Is that right?'

'Yeah, he needed somewhere to stay for a few nights and never left.'

Dawes glanced at Starling and took over.

'Why is that? Got on so well, did you, you and your mate, *Clock*?'

'We got on alright, yeah.'

'So well, in fact, that you moved into the box room and let him have the main bedroom.'

This threw Lenny. He felt himself start to blush. 'I never—'

'Nothing gets past us, son. And it's nothing to be embarrassed about. He was your mate, after all. That's right, isn't it?'

Lenny's face was burning. Dawes went back to his notebook.

'So, anyway, back to Friday … dinnertime … Clocherty … session … then what?'

'They went out to pick the mushrooms—'

'You've had these sessions before?'

'A couple.'

'And who usually picked the mushrooms?'

'Well, me, usually, I suppose, but—'

'You suppose? So why not this time? Why did you trust these townies to get the right mushrooms? You're the country boy, Lenny. You know what to pick and what not to pick, what's edible and what's not.'

'I know a magic mushroom, but—'

'So, on Friday, did they ask you to go with them?'

'No.'

'And you didn't offer?'

'No.'

'You see, DS Starling and myself, we don't think the other three would have a clue what they were looking for—'

'Well obviously somebody didn't … that's how we got where we are … look, if you're trying to say I did this on purpose, then I'd have to know what a death cap mushroom looks like and where to find them. And I don't. Yeah, I know what magic-mushrooms look like, but apart from that I don't know one from another—'

Starling began to speak but Dawes interrupted. Fields had made a schoolboy error.

'I noticed you said death cap there, Joseph. It seemed to fairly roll off the tongue. I'm asking myself how you know that.' He pointed at the folder in his lap. 'I know it because I've read the report. But how do you know? I'll bet even DS Starling here didn't know that.' He looked at Starling. 'Did you know that, Sergeant?'

'I didn't, Sir, no.'

Under normal circumstances this was where Lenny would get up and storm out. Dawes and Starling sat, waiting. He could hear people talking in the corridor.

'One of the nurses must have told me,' he said, too quickly, desperately, it seemed to him. He felt his face flush again, imagined himself scarlet, and was convinced he'd blown it.

Dawes shook his head and returned to his notebook. 'So, they've been out all afternoon picking mushrooms —'

'Yeah, and getting beers and stuff.'

'So, what were you doing while they were all out running around after you?'

'They weren't … it wasn't like that—'

'Where were you?'

'In my room.'

'You weren't watching television anymore?'

'No I was in my room all afternoon. I think I had a kip

but I can't remember to be honest.'

'Knackered, were you, after a hard morning smoking pot and watching cartoons?'

Lenny didn't answer and continued to stare at his hands. Dawes looked at his notes and continued.

'And you say the next thing you knew, Clocherty … *Clock*, was shouting you to get some stew?'

'Yeah.'

Dawes looked at Starling and gave her the slightest of nods and a half-smile.

'And what time would this be?'

'I don't know exactly. About tea-time. Sixish, maybe.'

'And you say you all ate at the same time.'

'Yeah, we did, but I only had one bowl. That's why—'

'At six o'clock?'

'Yeah, something like that, but they were at it all night. They made a huge pan and nearly ate the lot—'

'That's as may be, but you're saying that all four of you had your first … dose, I suppose we should call it … you all had the first bowl at the same time?'

'Yeah.'

Dawes tapped the folder in his lap.

'Well, the science would beg to differ. Six o'clock more or less tallies with what's in here—'

'Well, there you go, then.'

'—for the other three, give or take, but according to this report, you didn't ingest the poison for at least another ten hours, or thereabouts, possibly more, meaning that, if they *had* eaten the first at six on the Friday evening, then you can't have eaten any until four o'clock on Saturday morning, at the earliest. How do you explain that?'

More or less, if, thereabouts, give or take, possibly, at the earliest. Lenny knew these would come back and bite Dawes in the arse. The effects of amatoxins vary wildly from person to person. Lenny knew this. Years ago he'd spent hours in the library reading about them. It had been an obsession at the time. He couldn't get enough. While other teenagers were reading Pan horror anthologies, he was reading accounts of amanita poisoning. He read them over and over. No two cases were exactly the same. Some people were dead within hours, others lasted days, some even seemed to recover and returned home, only to have a sudden relapse and be dead shortly after. Lenny had taken no risks and had put a massive amount in the stew. They'd had nothing to eat beforehand and nothing else afterwards. A crisp sandwich, maybe. There was nothing else in. He'd made sure of that. Hydration played a big part too, but they'd drunk only alcohol. The worst thing you could do.

Lenny continued to gaze at his hands and shrugged.

'I can't explain it. The science must be wrong, that's all I can think.'

Dawes threw Starling a furtive glance and reached into his inside pocket. When Lenny saw the bank-bag dangling from Dawes' fingers his heart almost stopped.

'So, what about these, Joseph? Hmm?'

Starling glared at Dawes.

'Sir—' she started. Dawes raised his hand to silence her. He never took his eyes off Lenny.

Lenny felt his face turn crimson. So much had happened that he'd completely forgotten about putting the bag on the bedside table. Seeing Dawes produce it now he'd instinctively assumed it was bad news. But it wasn't, because now he remembered the reason he'd left it there.

'Well, Joseph?'

Lenny put the heel of his hand to his forehead. 'That's it,' he said. 'That's what happened. It's coming back, now. I didn't have a kip at all. No, I already had a few hundred dried mushrooms. That's it. There weren't enough for everyone. I'd already taken most of them.' He pointed at the bag still in Dawes' hand. There's hardly any left in there, so they went to pick their own.' He laughed. 'That's right. I didn't go because I was already wasted.' He laughed at the thought. 'I wouldn't have been much use—'

'So why did you eat the stuff you claim they made?'

'I've told you, I didn't see what they'd picked. I had no id—'

'I meant if you'd already had two hundred of the damned things, why did you need more?'

The redness had left Lenny's cheeks. He was back on safe territory.

'Never taken drugs, have you,' he laughed.

Dawes hesitated, momentarily. Starling looked up from her notes.

'Of course not,' he replied. 'We are in no way alike, you and I. Other than gender, we have nothing in common.'

'Whatever you say. Anyway, that answers your question. That's why I ate that shit so long after they did. It probably *was* the early hours of the morning, now I think about it.' He pointed again to the bag in Dawes' hand. 'I can't believe I forgot about them. What an idiot.'

Lenny stopped there. No need to over-egg it.

Dawes shook his head.

'The truth is, you picked these death caps, and cooked them up, and watched them eat them, *your mates*, and these…' he waved the bag in Lenny's face, 'these were your cover.'

'So why would I eat it myself?'

'You never intended to eat it yourself. When the others realised what you'd done...' He looked at the bruising on Lenny's lips and face. 'Well, I think we both know what happened there. I'd put money on it; two of them held you down while the other fed you like a baby.'

Lenny stared at his hands, counting the freckles on each. He didn't think he'd ever noticed them before.

'Well? Am I right or am I wrong?'

Lenny swallowed drily, raised his head and looked straight at Dawes.

'You're wrong,' he said. 'I swear on my mother's life.'

* * *

There was a sudden burst of activity outside the room. Nursing staff were coming and going, moving briskly up and down the corridor. A huddle were gathered by reception and one nurse broke away and came to the doorway and motioned to Dawes. He got up and left the room.

Starling looked at Lenny.

'On your mother's life, Lenny? Really?'

Lenny shrugged. 'Believe what you want. I don't know what more can I say.'

'You can tell me what really happened. We know that you did this. The gaffer's not bothered one way or the other. He'll see you sent down for murder. I think that would be a shame. I think you were driven to it. I think that these three targeted you, moved in on you, *with* you, in Clocherty's case, and you reached breaking-point, and if that's true, then it'll go much better for you if you come clean now. We know what sort of people these are.' She opened her notebook. 'Clocherty, a string of convictions for violence, sentenced to three-years for GBH in November seventy-seven. He could have been out after eighteen-months but chose to serve every day rather than apply for parole. Released from Barlinnie on sixteenth of October nineteen-eighty. Been on nobody's radar since. Until now.

'The Savages, well, we don't have much, but the more we learn, the worse it gets. If you stick to your story, and a jury finds you guilty, it'll be murder and a life sentence. Come clean and it'll be manslaughter, and I guarantee you'll be out in five years. So, tell me the truth, Lenny, while you can, what really happened?'

Lenny sat in silence and stared at his hands. He could feel the rhythm of his pulse. He desperately wanted to tell her everything, to shout it till it resonated loud and clear down the corridors into every ward and out the door and into the street and through the town into every house and pub and bar of the Bright Lights and into the ears of Mona Lisa and the Meatheads and fucking big mouth Russell Marsh and on down the bypass and through Hawksheads and into Yelland and the Eagle and Child and to the Post Office and to the entire population of the whole fucking world:

SAVAGES??! THEY WERE **ALL** FUCKING SAVAGES! I WAS CUCKOOED! A DOMESTIC SLAVE! FIVE FUCKING YEARS, TREATED LIKE CHATTEL! A DOORMAT! A FUCKING PUNCH-BAG, BULLIED, BEATEN, BUTTED, KICKED AND BRUTALISED, SPAT-ON, CONTROLLED, HUMILIATED, BLACKMAILED AND THREATENED, LIFE A FUCKING MISERY, DOING SOLITARY IN A FLAT TURNED INTO A FUCKING DRUG WHOLESALERS!

But for what? He knew how it would pan out in court, six months down the line, in the cold light of day with his injuries all healed. He'd poisoned and killed three people. Provocation would be no excuse. And, anyway, five years or fifteen, it made no difference to him. He wouldn't survive one year in prison.

He looked at Starling.

'It was an accident,' he said. 'They picked the wrong ones, that's it. I've got nothing else to say.'

Starling couldn't hide her disappointment. She had her bottom lip between her teeth and shook her head as she looked at Lenny. She looked to have tears in her eyes.

Dawes returned and took his seat by the bed.

'So, what have I missed, Sergeant?'

'Nothing, Sir. I've explained to Lenny that it would be better for him if he told us the truth now, rather than a jury decide it later, but he still says it was an accident.'

Dawes smiled broadly. 'Yes, well, you stick to your bullshit story, son, but we'll know the truth soon enough. It seems your mate Stuart's on the mend, so as soon as he's fit to answer a few questions, we'll have his version of events.'

This was the news Lenny had been dreading, and he panicked. 'Yeah, *his* version,' he said, without thinking, and instantly felt his gut tighten.

Dawes was on him straight away. 'Why would there be more than one version, Joseph? If it was an accident, why would poor old Stu say any different?'

Lenny's insides churned. He closed his eyes and wrung his hands together.

'He won't. You're confusing me. Have you any fucking idea what I've been through? I'm a fucking invalid. And they have me pumped full of drugs. I'm not thinking straight.'

'Pumped full of drugs and not thinking straight? Just another day in the life of Joseph Fields, isn't it?'

Lenny looked over his shoulder and grabbed the cord hanging by the bed and pulled it hard.

'Tell me,' Dawes went on. 'Why did you lock the door? The door to the flat? You were running for your life, but you still thought to lock the door.'

'Just habit, I suppose. You might be able to leave the door unlocked on Millionaire's Row or wherever the fuck it is you live—'

A nurse appeared in the doorway. 'Is everything ok?'

'I've had enough, nurse. I don't want to answer any more questions. I don't feel well.'

'That's enough for today, officers,' she said. 'He needs his rest. He's not out of the woods yet.'

The nurse left the room. Starling and Dawes got up and replaced the chairs. Dawes had his thumbs in his waistband and his chest out and was switching his weight from one foot to the other continually. He turned to Lenny, bent forward, leaned one hand on the bed.

'She's right, sunshine,' he said. 'You're not out of the woods yet. Not by a long way. This is your last chance to own up before your mate Stu drops you in it. You picked those mushrooms and you knew exactly what you were doing.' He brought the bag of dried mushrooms from his pocket and waved them in Lenny's face. 'And these. These were your cover, weren't they?'

Lenny didn't respond, just carried on staring at his hands.

Dawes stood and pocketed the mushrooms.

'Come on, Starling.'

They left the room and headed for the exit.

'Come with me, I just want to check something.'

Starling followed Dawes to reception. The receptionist looked up and smiled. 'Yes, can I help?'

'I was just wondering, is it common knowledge, amongst the hospital staff, the type of poison they ate? Fields and Savage?'

'Oh, yes,' she replied. 'They've talked about nothing else. Well it's so unusual, isn't it. They were *death cap* mushrooms.' She spoke the name as if that in itself was dangerous.

'Ok. Thanks for your time.'

They turned and walked through the exit and set off for the car park.

'Typical,' Dawes said. 'One door closes and another slams in your face.'

They reached the car. Starling unlocked the doors and they got in.

'Not to worry, Sir, at least we've got Stuart Savage now. How soon will we be able to speak to him?'

They fastened their seat belts and Starling started the engine.

'That depends, Sergeant.'

'On what, Sir?'

'On whether you know a decent clairvoyant.'

* * *

PART SEVEN

Thursday 24th of October 1985

I had an early night on Wednesday and enjoyed my best sleep for a week, but I was still awake and up well before first light. I'd planned to spend the day ringing in the sand quarry but decided I needed to get back to basics, enjoy some simple pleasures, away from the gatehouse, the estate and all the hassle.

I made a flask of coffee, grabbed my binoculars, jumped in the van and set off for the reserve. I called at the garage on the bypass to pick up a sandwich and some crisps, and arrived at the reserve just as the sun was peeking over the horizon.

I spent the first hour or so relaxing in the van, having my first coffee of the day, and watching the comings and goings at the feeding station in the car park.

It was buzzing with activity, a constant stream of small birds; coal, great, and blue tits, a marsh tit, a nuthatch, chaffinch and greenfinch, siskin, redpoll, jockeying for the best positions, sorting out the pecking-order. A pair of shy bullfinch waited quietly in a nearby tree for a chance to make a quick foray to the feeder before returning to the branch.

There were a few tree sparrows, too, a lovely little bird, unmistakeable with their chestnut crowns and little black cheek-spots. They were very common back then, but not today.

A greater spotted woodpecker arrived to feed on the half coconut shell full of fat, and the feeders were all left swinging as the smaller birds fled into the branches of nearby trees.

On the floor, cleaning up after the messy eaters, a pair of dunnock, a robin, a woodpigeon, a trio of hen pheasants and a pair of mallard.

This was how it all started for me, the very essence of my enjoyment of birds since I was a kid, and I felt a powerful nostalgia that had me close to tears.

I put away the flask, locked the van and made my way to the first hide. A hen harrier soared silent circles overhead, and bearded tits gave away their presence with their pinging calls. Having fed on insects all summer, they were busy gathering grit put out by reserve staff, transforming their tiny stomachs into seed-grinding mills to deal with their winter diet.

I took a seat in the hide and opened the viewing hatch. Everything had an orange tinge; the overcast sky, the lake, even the brown reed-stems were all bathed in the early sun's rays and looked to be on fire.

A spotted redshank was dashing around at breakneck speed in the shallow water, sweeping its pointed bill from side to side as it took on fuel for the next leg of its journey south.

I scanned the edge of the reeds and a bittern became visible as it stepped away from its reedbed camouflage and into open water to hunt for a breakfast snack.

I visited all of the reserve's half-dozen hides, and although I couldn't ignore the rarer species; a pair of little grebes, never on the surface long enough to allow a decent view, a great white egret stalking the shallows, a ruff and a greenshank, among others, I spent most of the day watching the more common birds, like the resident ducks; shoveler and gadwall, tufted duck and pochard, dabbling, upending and diving, and coots bickering and squabbling.

I watched a sleeping teal slip its moorings and drift with its head under its wing and collide with a non-plussed shoveler, which gave the startled teal a stern ticking off and an indignant prod with its outsized bill, before getting back to its meal.

In the evening a group of red deer made their way quietly to the water's edge to drink less than twenty feet from the hide, and a rare Cetti's warbler sang vociferously from the thick scrub.

I stayed late to see the starling murmuration, which was the biggest I'd seen it for years. I watched them, groups of differing sizes rolling in from all directions, all converging over the reedbeds and forming one huge flock, the murmuration, that wheeled and billowed as one organism, putting on the most spectacular show before disappearing into the reeds to roost.

I enjoyed the day as much as I'd enjoyed any in a long time, and it was getting on for eight o'clock when I got back to the gatehouse. I completed the day's log and turned in. I was knackered and I had a big day tomorrow.

I slept well again. Mum rang in the morning and invited me for dinner with her and Archie at five o'clock, which was great news. I was a nightmare when it came to drinking on an empty stomach. It only took a couple of pints and I was slurring my speech and talking shite, so it was good to know I'd have a decent meal before I went to meet Rod.

I tried to put all the other shit to the back of my mind and concentrated on the meeting. I selected what I thought were the best books, those I thought would impress him the most, and spent the rest of the day wandering around the estate, thinking through what I wanted to say.

* * *

Friday 25th of October 1985

'Fuck me,' he said.

Rod Jay wasn't at all what I was expecting. He'd been browsing the books, had them spread out on the table and on the seat next to him; nest records, ringing records, trees and shrubs, all decorated with sketches and small paintings of birds and flowers.

I hadn't been able to eat much at Mum's, my appetite had deserted me. I got to the Eagle half-an-hour early, almost fell through the door when it opened, and was half-way down my third pint when he walked in, an object-lesson in punctuality.

I recognised him right away. I'd seen him in town now and again. He was a good six-feet tall, and didn't look like a millionaire, in his faded jeans, trainers, baggy-necked pullover and tan bomber-jacket. His shoulder-length hair was untidy, his face jovial, with ruddy cheeks and John Lennon glasses.

He came and introduced himself, smiling all the while, and I half-stood and nearly knocked my pint over. He had a firm handshake and his hands were rough, with oil under the nails. He was obviously still very hands-on despite his success.

He pointed to my glass. 'Bitter?'

I nodded. 'Please.' I said, and downed what was left of my pint.

He took the empty glass, went to the bar and came back

with two pints. I'd rehearsed my speech over and over, but in the short silence after he sat, I went blank, so I'd played my trump card straight away.

He'd been leafing through the books for ten minutes or more, having the occasional sip of beer.

'You did all this?'

I nodded.

He picked a book randomly and looked inside the front cover. He glanced up at me.

'The artwork?'

I nodded again.

He put the book on the seat and picked up his pint and leaned back in his chair. He waved his free hand over the books spread about.

'We'll come back to these.' He took a drink and cradled the glass in his lap. 'Obviously I didn't agree to come tonight without knowing something of what it was about. What *you* were about. Uncle Archie said you were keen on nature and were worried about what my plans might be for the estate.' He looked again at the books. 'I get it now.'

I was half-pissed by this time. I told him I owned the gatehouse, that I spent all my time on the estate, that when I'd seen the blokes putting fences and gates up I thought I'd have no access to any of it anymore and when they said some businessman had bought it I imagined one of Thatcher's yuppies and, what, with all the business parks and truck-stops and motorway services springing up all over the place, it would all be concreted and tarmacked and built on anyway, and on and on I went. I was off on a proper rant when he reached and put his hand on my shoulder to stop me.

'You can relax, John. You don't need to worry. I'm a twitcher,' he said. 'I'm not long back from the Scillies. This time last week I was on St. Agnes looking at a red-eyed vireo.'

He saw my lack of reaction.

'It's American. Rare, even for the Scillies. Looks pretty much like any of our leaf warblers, but it isn't. It's a red-eyed vireo. From America.' He smiled and raised his glass and took a long drink.

'You'll be telling me next it has red eyes,' I said, hiccupping mid-sentence.

'It does, yes, and it has a white eye-stripe,' he replied.

'Like a shedge warbler?' I slurred, trying to sound knowledgeable by stating the obvious.

He grinned. 'Yes, like a sedge warbler.'

Then, to impress him further still, I said, 'I don't get twitching, you know, dropping everything and driving for hours at the drop of a hat in the hope of catching a glimpse of some little bird that will probably never find its way home and will die lonely, then driving all the way back to tick it off in a book.'

'Well, we won't go into that, John, not just now, eh? Anyway, I'm sure you'd like to see a red-eyed vireo on your home patch, maybe even catch it in your nets, whether it could get home or not.'

There was a quiet moment.

'So,' he continued, 'there *was* a big concern looking to develop it, as it happens, and they might have got it, too—'

'But you've got friends in high places?' I interrupted, hiccupping again, seemingly hell-bent on fucking the whole thing up.

'—had it not been for a forward-thinking council that took the long view.'

He stood and picked up his glass. It should have been my round, but I wasn't sure I could have navigated a straight line to the bar, or that another pint was even a good idea. I hiccupped again.

He could barely contain his amusement.

'Can I get you another drink, John? A fruit juice, maybe? A coke?'

I still had half a pint left. 'No, thanks, but I wouldn't mind a bag of crisps,' I said, between hiccups, 'Any flavour, I'm not bothered.'

He nodded, finished his beer, and went to the bar.

I had a word with myself. I needed to get a grip before I ruined everything. I'd begun to slouch. I put my soles to the floor and pushed to sit upright and my seat went onto two legs and I hiccupped again and came close to crashing backwards onto the floor. I threw myself forward and managed to prevent a disaster. I looked over my shoulder. Rod was still being served and was talking to the barman. I took a deep breath and held it; the best way to get rid of hiccups.

I was still holding my breath when he came back from the bar and handed me a bag of salt and vinegar crisps. I nodded my thanks, as he put his pint on the table and sat down. The hiccups had stopped, so I let the breath out slowly and opened the crisps. I seemed to be in the clear so I took a large crisp from the bag and put it in my mouth.

'So, anyway,' he said, 'I couldn't let them get their hands on it. The last thing we need is another retail park, right? They're destroying all the beautiful places.' He picked up his pint, had a sip, and put it back on the table. 'Joni was right.'

I hadn't a clue what he was talking about.

'Too right she was,' I replied, just as the hiccups returned and I sucked a mouthful of crisp shards into my airways and had a coughing-fit that had Rod scooping his glass from the table and me gasping for breath and with bubbles of snot ballooning from both nostrils.

I jumped out of my seat, muttered 'sorry' from behind my hand, and legged it to the toilets.

I grabbed some tissue and blew my nose and went to the sink to wash my hands. I looked in the mirror and saw my bloodshot eyes. I turned on the cold tap and rinsed my face. I dried myself and ran my hand through my hair and looked again in the mirror.

I stood and cursed myself. 'You fucking knob,' I muttered. 'You fucking wanker.' A toilet flushed and a bloke came out of the end cubicle. He gave his hands a quick rinse and me a wry grin and went back to the bar. I stayed another minute to give my reflection another rollocking before heading back to the table for a well-earned dose of embarrassment.

Back in the bar, Rod had moved the books to let a couple sit down at the table. They had their backs to me, but the long, grey ponytail and crimson, satin waistcoat were a giveaway. My heart missed a beat.

I approached the table and took a seat opposite Irish Bob and Ann. They were each looking at a book and Rod had the rest on his lap. I said a quiet 'hi' to them and turned to Rod.

'Sorry about that,' I said, as I sat. I could feel my face-burning up. 'I should know better than drink on an empty stomach. I've got form. I was a bit nervous, that's all.'

Rod gave a short laugh. 'Don't worry about it,' he said. 'We've all been there.'

'At least now I know how to get rid of hiccups,' I said, and he laughed again.

'Sorry,' he said, I haven't introduced you—'

'Oh, we know John,' Bob said. He turned to Ann. 'Don't we, love.'

'Course we do,' Ann replied. 'Are you alright love?'

'I'm ok, thanks,' I said. I felt myself cherry-ing up again. I was thinking, please don't say anything, please don't make tonight any worse.

Ann looked at me, then at the book, and back again.

'These are lovely, John,' she said, 'a proper labour of love. So much detail. I'd no idea you were so talented.'

'They're brilliant,' Bob agreed. 'I wondered why you spent so much time over in the woods,' he said. 'I often see you when I'm walking the dog.' Then his face took on a concerned look. 'How's your mate, by the way?' he asked.

'Oh, yes,' Ann said. 'We couldn't believe it when we read it in the paper, could we love?'

'We couldn't love, no. We were shocked.'

'What's happened there, love? Did he get careless?'

I was cringing. 'I don't really know,' I said. 'I've had nothing to do with him for years.'

Bob was shaking his head. 'I told you, if you remember. Do you remember? You have to be careful, I said.'

I wanted to disappear. I wondered what Rod must be thinking. That's it, I thought. Everything's fucked.

Then Bob turned to Rod.

'We had some great times, didn't we Rod?'

Rod nodded but didn't speak.

'But we always stuck to the liberty caps, didn't we, Rod?'

Rod picked up another book and started browsing.

'We did, Bob,' he replied, quietly.

Ann suddenly got very serious.

'We *did*, but only after we'd got a bit adventurous and tried them flippin wiggly caps.'

'They were wavy caps, love, not wiggly caps.'

'Wiggly caps, wavy caps. They were too much, whatever they were.'

'Far too much,' Bob concurred.

'No fun at all. I thought we'd never be right again. We never had anything but liberty caps after that,' Ann said.

'That's right,' Bob said. 'And we always made sure we'd picked them ourselves. Like I say, you can't be too careful.'

There was a short pause. Ann began to laugh.

'The flippin laughs we had, eh, Rod? I remember you,' she spluttered, 'at that festival, out on the moors, in the middle of nowhere. Do you remember?' She turned to me. 'You should have seen him, John. It poured down non-stop and we spent the whole weekend sheltering under sheets of plastic.' She turned back to Rod. 'Do you remember, Rod, and you thought there were little clowns running about everywhere, all over the inside of your plastic, and you were talking to them? Eee, I'll never forget that.'

I had a feeling Rod wished she would. He was nodding and had a grin fixed to his face, but he was definitely looking a bit flushed around the gills.

'That was all a very long time ago, Ann,' he said

Bob had closed the book and he reached over and put it on the pile in Rod's lap.

'They're great them, John. You've missed your calling.' He winked at Ann. 'Come on love,' he said. 'We're interrupting. These two were talking business. And anyway, I think we're embarrassing Rod.'

Ann got up and handed her book to Rod.

'He's not embarrassed, are you Rod?'

'No, of course I'm not, Ann. It's always lovely to see you both. We'll have a good catch-up soon.'

Rod got out of his chair and they had a group hug. Bob and Ann picked up their glasses and went to take up their regular positions at the bar. Rod sat down and looked sheepishly at me.

I could barely contain my amusement.

'Bob and Ann, eh?' he said. 'Got to love 'em.'

'Don't you just,' I grinned.

* * *

I'd completely relaxed now and was feeling loads better. Rod had finished his pint, and mine had been empty for a while, so I said it was my turn to get them in. Rod was in the car but he said he'd have another pint and get a taxi, so I went to the bar and came back with a pint of bitter for him, a pint of shandy for myself, and two bags of salted nuts.

'Oh, thanks,' he said. He had a sip of beer, opened the bag of nuts, then carried on exactly where he'd left off before my embarrassing episode.

'So, as I was saying, Joni was right, you know, about paving paradise—'

'Aah,' I said, 'I'm with you now.'

'Exactly, so I decided to go for it myself. You have to remember that I haven't always lived in the Bright Lights. I moved there twenty years ago when I opened my first garage, but I grew up here, in Yelland. I played in the quarry and the woods when I was a kid, just like you. It was me and my mates who put the Tarzan swing up in the beech tree circle in Hawksheads.'

'I've swung on that,' I said, pointlessly.

'I don't doubt it,' he replied, 'I think everyone in the village has at one time or another.'

He had another sip and threw a few nuts into his mouth and carried on.

'Now, I came here tonight to have a quick pint and to tell you not to worry, that you'll still have access to the estate and the quarry, and then I'd be on my way.'

I was well-chuffed. 'So, I'll be able to carry on as normal?'

'You will, now let me finish. To be brutally honest I'm not obliged to tell you anything, John, not really. When Uncle Archie rang me I could just as easily have told him to send you to the Town Hall. The plans have been available for the public to look at for three months now. I agreed to meet with you as a favour to him. Ok?'

I nodded.

'But, now I've met you, and listened to you,' he waved his hand over the pile of books, 'and seen all this, I understand the connection you obviously have to the place, so I don't mind telling you a bit about the enterprise, the bare bones, anyway.

'I'll tell you now, there'll be aspects of the plan that you don't like, but there's no point getting on your high horse. I spent a long time putting my pitch together, and I'm investing a lot of money. The plans are set in stone, so you need to listen without interrupting. Ok?'

I nodded.

'Ok? he said, more firmly.'

I nodded again

'Ok, first I'll be reinstating the original track that connects the lanes to Yelland —'

'But—'

He arched his eyebrows. I stopped talking and he carried on.

‘Vehicles will enter the track over the cattle-grid by the gatehouse, your place of residence, but will only be able to travel the half-mile to Hawksheads House. I’ll be widening this section by a yard or so on the left side – hopefully this won’t require the felling of any trees, but it’ll depend on the root-systems – and I’ll simply clear away some undergrowth and move the fence back. Immediately inside the archway will be crusher-run. The tarmac won’t start till we’re about level with the lean-to outside your place. To start with, at least. The wagons and equipment will need a place to park whilst the work’s being done.

‘I’ll also be putting in three equispaced passing places, a requirement of the fire and rescue service. Just past the house, where the lane currently becomes impassable, will be the first of three gates. Between here and Yelland, though I’ll be reinstating the lane to its original width, purely for access – sorry, but that will mean removing a substantial amount of brambles – it won’t be tarmacked and certainly won’t be suitable for regular cars, in particular the section after the sand quarry, and under the railway bridge.

‘The second gate, the one you saw being installed, will stop vehicles accessing the sand quarry should either of the other gates be left open for any reason, or if the council leave their access gate open, the service lane from the bypass. There’s been a lot of car thefts lately, seems to be all the rage. I might have my own tow-trucks, but I don’t need to be removing burned-out cars every other weekend.

‘The third gate will be at this end of the lane, just outside the pub here. They’re being put in on Monday, actually. All three of these gates will be padlocked, and only those with a key – that’ll be just myself and the estate manager – will be able to drive from the gatehouse all the way through to Yelland.'

He stopped talking, for a while, at least, and he took a swig of his pint and grinned and asked if I'd any questions so far.

'So, how will I get through?' I asked.

'Oh, sorry,' he said, 'I should have clarified. There'll be a public footpath all the way from Hawksheads House to Yelland. When you saw Cyril Bunting and his lad putting the gate up, if you'd looked a bit closer and not got so emotional, you'd have seen that they were also putting in a kissing gate. I think he was having you on, actually. He's a dry stick is Cyril.'

'That's not what I was calling him.'

Rod laughed, and we both had another drink.

'You're not just buying it for the fun of it, so how will this make you money?' I asked.

'You're right, it has to pay its way. There's no way I could afford to buy that land outright and leave it as it is. The garages have done ok for me, but I haven't got that kind of money.

'My business interests are in the buildings; the house, stables and so on. To save the rest of the estate, the buildings have to do the heavy lifting.

'Now, as you're aware, they're all derelict at present, but the house will eventually be three high-end apartments upstairs, business or holiday lets, we'll see, with private access and fire-escape to the rear.

'Downstairs will be kitchens, licensed tea-rooms and café-restaurant. The half of the courtyard closest to the house will be an outdoor piazza, you know, European style, rattan furniture, patio umbrellas, and all that. That's a project for my wife and daughter. I've been told.

'All the outhouses, the stables and adjacent buildings will be turned into shops and rented out to local businesses, selling artisan produce, you know, dried flowers, fudge and handmade biscuits, bespoke knitwear, outdoor clothing, that sort of thing. There's already half a dozen interested parties.'

Listening to him in full flow talking about something he was obviously passionate about was an education. He was composed, and very personable, but unwavering too, and persuasive, with the air of someone who brooked no argument. He had a relaxed, almost hypnotic manner, and his voice and phrasing had the restful tone of a blackbird's song.

I could understand why the council went for his pitch, could imagine them, entranced, signing the necessary paperwork, and I sat, like a kid in class, as he ate his nuts, drank his beer, and told me, in the most agreeable of terms, how it was going to be. I could have listened to him all night, and thought I might have to at one point.

When he did eventually finish, he looked at me. There was a silence.

'Well?' he said.'

I jumped in immediately.

'Where will they park?.'

He screwed up his face.

'That's the bit you're not going to like,' he said, 'but, as I say, it's an integral part of the business plan, and there's nothing that can be done about it.

'There'll be private parking at the back of the house for the apartments. The visitors' car park will be on the left, just before the house.'

'How much of the wood will you have to chop down?' I asked.

'Altogether, just over half an acre.'

He saw my baffled look.

'About fifty yards square,' he said

'Fifty square yards?' I replied, hopefully.

'I wish,' he said. 'No, fifty yards square.'

'That's … a thousand … and … that's a lot.'

'Two-thousand five hundred square yards, John, sounds a lot, I know, but it's less than one twelve-hundredth part of the wood. Most of it's for the car park, the rest for three parking places and the fire-escape at the back.

'There'll be a minimum of disturbance. The tree-felling's due to begin in November and work on the car parks will be done before the end of December. The lane needs doing between the cattle-grid and the house first. We'll be starting that in the next couple of weeks. That'll be the only tarmacking, the car parks will be slate-chippings or crusher run.'

'So much for not paving paradise,' I said.

'I'm not paving paradise, John, just decorating the entrance hall.'

I didn't reply.

'Do you remember the rest of the song? The bit where she says "You don't know what you've got till it's gone"? Well, appreciate what you've got, John, because if I hadn't bought it, it would be gone, the whole thing; the sand quarry, the birch wood, everything.'

* * *

We had another couple of drinks and talked more about his plans. I moaned a bit, played devil's advocate, but he was right. A few homeless swallows was a small price to pay to keep the woods more or less unscathed and stop the sand quarry becoming an industrial estate.

I woke up early on the Saturday morning with a banging

headache and a mouth like a bin. I thought back to the meeting. I could remember Rod looking again at the books, and then asking me more about my painting, but that's where my memory failed.

I tried a quick cuddle with Jan, but she had her usual negative reaction to being woken, so I left her in bed and got dressed. I winced when I saw the brim-full ashtray on the living-room table. I emptied it and did a quick tidy, and went to the kitchen. I managed some cereal and a brew and went for a walk to the sand quarry.

I found Rod's card in my pocket. It had his home phone number and 'Gatehouse Saturday 5pm (Art)' written on the back. He obviously hadn't thought he could rely on my memory. Just as well, really. I didn't remember making the arrangement or him giving me the card. How pissed had I been? I had a flashback to the hiccupping debacle and felt a rush of embarrassment.

I went home and took Jan breakfast in bed. She sat up and took one look at me and shook her head.

'Look at the clip of you. What are you like, eh?' she laughed, as she took the tray off me. 'It must have gone ok, anyway. You were a happy little bed bunny when you got in.' She winked. 'You should do it more often.'

'Really?' I said. 'Did we?'

'Did we? Are you kidding? You came in absolutely buzzing at about half-past nine, grabbed my hand and pulled me off the sofa and took me straight to bed. You got up again at about eleven and left me there, well-and-truly had. I think it was gone two o'clock when you came back to bed.'

She started eating her breakfast. I went back to the kitchen to get her cup of tea.

'If I'm not pregnant now,' she shouted after me, 'I doubt I ever will be.'

'Fingers crossed,' I shouted back, 'and if not, then we'll just have to keep trying.'

I swear I could feel her smile from the kitchen.

* * *

I went to the gatehouse early to make sure there was nothing untoward I might have missed. I rolled my sleeping bag up and moved the sofa-bed against the wall, closed the kitchen and bedroom doors, and leaned all the paintings against the wall around the living room.

I was sitting having a brew at five when Rod turned up in a car that sounded like a tank. I went to meet him at the door, but when I opened it he was still extricating his long legs from the footwell of a rainbow-coloured mini. It was done up for rallying, with wide-wheels, and a roll-cage inside, and had number forty-two painted on the doors and bonnet.

I smiled to myself. Must have left the Lamborghini at home, I thought.

He finally freed himself from the car and shut the door and walked up the path. He had an amused look on his face.

'You got home ok, then.'

I nodded. 'Apparently,' I said, and stepped aside to let him in. He glanced around the room and I realised just how primitive it looked. I nodded to the sofa-bed and sleeping bag.

'I only stay here through the week,' I said. 'I stay at my girlfriend's at the weekends.'

'That's none of my business,' he said.

He declined a brew, and we stood in the living room as he looked through some of the other log books.

‘I’d no idea there were more,’ he said.

‘A book for everything,’ I smiled.

He put them down and turned his attention to the paintings, lifting the smaller ones to look at the larger, and nodding his approval.

‘Do you work? he asked, out of the blue.

This was a question I wasn’t prepared for. I didn’t want to lie to him. If I said yes, he’d ask where, and he’d know people all over the Bright Lights.

‘Not at the moment, but I’ll have to get a job soon,’ I replied. ‘I’m not long back from Holland.’

I’d been back for more than two years, but he wasn’t to know that.

He carried on looking at the paintings. ‘What were you doing?’

‘Welding.’

‘How long?’

‘About three years, give or take.’

‘Whereabouts?

‘A village called Vessem at first, but I was in Eindhoven for most of the time.’

‘I’ve never been to the south. Did you get to ‘dam much?’

‘Not really. I had an overnight on the way home a couple of times.’

‘I love ‘dam,’ he said, in a tone heavy with nostalgia, and we had a few minutes’ crack about Dutch culture. He made no secret of his past dabblings but, maybe with Bob and Ann’s comments in mind, he made it clear that it was very much his past, and not his present.

For my part I nodded in agreement and laughed where appropriate, and, I hoped, gave him the impression that for me it was strictly a *when in Rome* thing.

He looked at the last of the paintings and put it back on the floor.

'They really are good,' he said.

He got his car keys from his pocket and we left the house. As we walked down the path he stopped and turned to me.

'We've set a provisional opening date of Easter eighty-seven for the Centre, so it's eighteen months away yet.'

'The centre?'

'Sorry, yes, The Hawksheads Centre for Arts and Crafts. Sounds very grand, don't you think? I think we should add something about the tea-rooms, but we'll see. Anyway, we'll be looking for some artworks to hang in the entrance hall and foyer. Aerial photographs were mentioned, you know, before and after shots, but that's a bit old-hat, so we decided some quality paintings by local artists, landscapes, birds, and the like. Maybe one of the house when it's done.'

He raised his palms and looked around.

'You couldn't be any more local, and your work certainly fits the bill, so we'd like to give you a commission. If you want it, that is.'

I was taken aback. 'What, and you'd pay me?'

'Well, of course we'd pay you. That's how it works. What do you think? Would you be up for that?'

'Definitely,' I said, 'just tell me how many, what of, what size, when you want them…'

I couldn't get the words out quick enough and he started to laugh.

'Ok, well Roz has taken ownership of that side of things, the décor and colour scheme. Roz is my wife, by the way. I'll introduce you and the two of you can talk it over. As I say, there's plenty of time.'

We went through the gate, and he turned and looked at the entrance to the lane and at the sandstone pillars.

'When I widen the lane, I think I'll move that pillar out too. What do you think?' he said, so quietly he could have been talking to himself.

'That's up to you,' I replied.

'It'll still only be wide enough for one vehicle, but it'll make turning in a lot easier, and it'll look better. I thought it'd be a bigger job, to be honest, but looking again, I'd only need to take a yard of wall out and move the pillar over...'

His voice trailed off and he turned and walked to the car.

'Yes, I think I'll do that,' he said, quietly, as he squeezed his large frame back into the car. He pulled his seat-belt across and wound the window down. 'Here,' he said, 'I nearly forgot.' He had a key in his hand and he held it out of the window. I walked to the car and took it off him.

'What's this for?' I asked.

'I know they're not all up yet, but it's for the gates. It'll fit all three. It must be hard work carrying all your nets and poles everywhere.'

'Thanks, Rod,' I said, for some reason showing him the key he'd just given me, before putting it in my pocket.

Two jays were screeching in a nearby yew tree. We both turned to look.

'That reminds me,' he laughed, 'I'll have to get off. I'm giving the kids a lift to the pictures.'

Monday 28th of October 1985

The angular bulk of the twin power stations dominated the skyline over Bright Lights Bay. I drove into the workers' car park and spotted Smudge's bright red three-litre Capri straight away. There was a free space next to it so I pulled in and waited.

In a few weeks' time Smudge would be ringing to arrange the next shipment and I'd have nothing for him. The routine had always been for him to ring me to arrange a social drink, code for 'when will it be ready', and I'd give him an exact date and time for the transaction, if I could, or I'd say, 'I can't make it this week, give us a ring next week' if it wasn't ready yet.

After all that had happened I had to speak to him before then, so he could let his customers know that the next crop would be delayed, indefinitely.

It was only a few minutes from the end of the early shift and it wasn't long until he appeared. I wound down my window and shouted and he came and got in the van beside me. He looked very sheepish, struggled to look me in the eye.

'Alright Woodsy, what're you doing here?'

'Alright Smudge. I need a word, that's all. What's up mate? You seem a bit on edge.'

'I heard about your mates, what the fuck—?'

'They weren't my mates, Smudge. Who told you they were?'

Seeing such a big, burly bloke so nervous freaked me out a

bit. It was like I was there to beat him up or something, and I realised that he didn't know me at all, not really. I'd worked with him years earlier, but that was it. Until I approached him with the proposition to buy all my produce, I hadn't seen him for over three years and I got the impression that he thought I was now this big-time drug grower and probably had some criminal gang behind me.

'I don't know,' he said. 'Someone said they were, someone at work.'

'They were fuck all to do with me. And relax, Smudge, I'm not here to threaten you. We're mates. I just need to know something.'

'What is it? I'll tell you if I know.'

'Last weekend, someone came snooping around my place, having a nosey, so I had to clear everything out, a whole crop binned. Now, nothing's come of it since, and I think I'm safe enough, but I need to know for sure before I even think about setting up again.'

'What do you want to know?'

'First, how much weed did you sell in the Bright Lights? And how often? And I want the truth, Smudge, it's important.'

'Ok, bottom line, cards on the table, about fifteen ounce mate, that's all, honest, and just the once.'

'That's all?! Fucking hell, Smudge, we had an agreement mate, it was the perfect arrangement. You weren't to sell any around here. Fifteen fucking ounces?'

'I know, I'm sorry mate, but the job was behind and they put the overtime on, so I couldn't go home. If I'd refused the overtime I'd have been first on the list when redundancies come round. You know what they're like.'

He was right. I knew exactly what they were like.

'Me and a couple of mates go thirds on the gear. One of them came up from Cardiff and took their shares, but I was left with the rest stinking my room out in the digs. I didn't want to leave it in the car in case the car got nicked—'

'You could have rung me, Smudge. I'd have kept hold of it for you.'

'I know, mate, I'm sorry, I didn't think—'

'No, obviously,' I said.

We sat quietly for a minute. The car park had almost emptied and was now filling up again as workers arrived for the back-shift.

'Ok,' I said. 'And did you sell it all to the same person?'

'Yeah, a guy I met in the pub. I had a pint with him. He seemed sound enough—'

'Do you know his name?'

'Ross, I think it was. Smallish bloke, long hair, denims, doc martens.'

'Ok, mate. Now, no bullshit, did you tell him my name?'

Smudge looked like he was going to shit himself.

'I did, yeah,' he said, eventually. 'I'm sorry Woodsy, but he said you were mates. I could fucking kick myself. I've always stayed in my digs. I hardly ever went out in town before, I'm here to make money, not spend it, you know the score, but I needed to shift the gear, and this fucking Ross – I've never met anyone so fucking paranoid in my life, by the way – he insists I meet him in the pub every few days to get the money for what he'd sold so far—'

'Tell me you didn't fucking lay it on him—'

'I had no choice. There was nearly a grand's worth of weed. Who's got that kind of money laying around? Anyway, so I end up in the pub to meet him every few days, well I can't go in a pub without having about eight pints, and he winkles your name out of me. I'm sorry mate. What can I say.'

'I hope he's fucking paid you for it.'

'Yeah, course he has. I know I fucked up mate, but I'm not that thick.'

Neither of us spoke for a few seconds.

'I'll have to go in a minute,' Smudge said. 'What's the crack? Are you going to be growing again?'

'You need to know this first, Smudge. That bloke you laid the fifteen ounces on, his name's not Ross, it's Russ, Russell Marsh, and we're definitely *not* mates, and he's definitely *not* to be trusted. After you told Russ where you got the weed, he went and told someone else, and that someone else came snooping around my place and I had to chuck three pounds of weed on the fucking compost heap.'

'Fucking hell I'm sorry mate. I'd no idea.'

'Forget it Smudge, it's gone.'

He was genuinely gutted by what he'd done. He apologised over and over. I ended up feeling sorry for him, He wasn't going to do anything like it again, and I wasn't too worried about Russ, so I made the decision.

'I told you when we started, Smudge, I'm a one-man operation,' I said. 'I always have been. I *am* going to start growing again, and I'll be growing twice as much as before, and I'll be doing it for one year, four crops, then I'm out. Will you still want the whole crop? I know it's a lot. If you can't handle that amount, just say, and I'll find somebody else for the rest.'

'No, defo,' he said. 'I'm in, and I'll go and tell that dickhead that you've packed in.'

I could have swung for him.

'No, Smudge!' I blurted. 'You don't *need* to tell Russ

anything at all! Don't even speak to Russ. He's a wanker, mate. Look, we both stand to make a lot of money over the next twelve months, but we both have a lot to lose, too, if we get caught. You said you never used to go to the pub?'

'No—'

'And Russ owes you nothing?'

'No—'

'Then he'll be easy enough to avoid. There's plenty of pubs in the Bright Lights, just stay out of the Rose and Crown. And if you *do* happen to see him, you haven't seen me, alright? At all. I fucked you off, and you haven't seen or heard from me since. Ok?'

'Ok.'

'And in future if you need me to hold the gear for a while, just say.'

'Ok, cheers Woodsy, and sorry again.'

'No worries, mate. It'll be a while, but I'll let you know when we're in business.'

* * *

Obviously I wasn't going to tell him, but Smudge was crucial to my whole operation. I'd wanted to get the growing-room up and running again, but it had to be a quick killing, and I had to have him on board. I couldn't take the risk of selling in dribs and drabs to local potheads. That had never been the plan. I wouldn't last five minutes, and I'd never find a new outlet for the whole crop, not the amounts I was planning to grow.

Having made the decision, I couldn't get started quick enough. As soon as I left Smudge I went home and took the mother plant from the kitchen windowsill. I just managed to get the clones I needed, and I put them in small pots under the growing-lamps; the mother plant was all used up, so I'd keep the best of the new crop as a replacement.

Then I drove to the garden centre for some fresh compost and perlite. Back home I emptied the tanks, cleaned them out and filled them with the new mixture.

A week later the young plants had all rooted well, so I transferred them to the four tanks, six to each this time, watered them, positioned them under the lamps, and set the timers.

That same day a team of blokes turned up to start work on widening the lane. It was the two I'd seen putting the gates up, Cyril Bunting and his son, and four others.

They got straight to it and by the Friday they'd taken out the fence, cleared all the undergrowth, including the three passing-places, without felling any trees at all, and the pillar was dismantled and the sandstone blocks stacked against the wall out of the way.

Before they left, there was a knock at the gatehouse door – the first since I'd moved in – and I opened the door to find Cyril standing there, and his son leaning on the gate at the end of the path.

'That's us done, young fella,' he said. 'The gaffer said he's decided to do away wit fence altogether, said there's no need for yan. They'll be startin' tarmackin' on Monday, just so as tha knows. Tha'll not be ebble to move for tar boilers an' steam rollers an' whatnot.'

I asked him how long it would take and he pointed his thumb over his shoulder.

'They'll be startin' at big 'ouse and workin' back to yon gateway. I know young Rod'll want it done sharpish, so I'd think they'll be done in a week, ten days at most.'

I decided to stay at Jan's for the duration of the work. I

didn't need much of an excuse to stay, to be honest, and Jan was never going to argue. We were well-happy and we spent most of the week together.

On the Monday night I called to see Fred and Noreen to ask how Lenny was getting on. Fred opened the door and kept me standing in the doorway. I could hear Noreen crying in the kitchen. Fred staved off his own tears long enough to tell me that Lenny had been charged with three counts of murder and had been remanded in custody until his trial, which was due to start on Monday 20th of January. It was shocking news. I put my hand lamely on Fred's shoulder for a second, and left without saying a word.

* * *

I loved showing Jan around the estate. She wanted to know everything there was to know about everything we saw. She was particularly taken with the old nests I pointed out, almost impossible to find when in use, but now exposed by the lack of foliage; the whitethroats' delicate cup of grass suspended from bramble stems, the goldfinches' woolly structure high up in the thin, outer-branches of a tree, the long-tailed tits' once magnificent domed creation, destroyed by a dozen or more fledging youngsters bursting from its confines, and now a splodge of feathers, grass and lichen, spread through the centre of a blackthorn thicket.

She remembered things I'd talked about and asked where they happened. I showed her the remnants of the pied wagtail nest in the glove compartment of the old Anglia, the dilapidated blackbird nest on the weighbridge shelf.

We sat in the shade with our backs against the weighbridge office wall. I told her about the fight with Swifty and the twins, the hospital, Lenny squealing and Fred's dentures stuck to his lip, the bloodstains on my brushed-denim seadogs, and about Sooty the neighbours' cat.

She asked what the fight was about and was horrified when I told her. I did a daft re-enactment of the whole thing, and she went through all the emotions, palms on her cheeks, eyes like saucers, her mouth a perfect O. She reminded me of a silent-movie actress, and we laughed until our sides ached and tears rolled down our faces.

I told her about my father, warts and all, his intolerance of anyone a bit different, his insistence that a couple of years in the army would whip everybody into shape and was the answer to all of society's ills. I told her about the only family holiday we'd ever had, when I was about eight years old, the little I could remember; sand in the food, him fully-clothed and asleep in a deckchair, me and Mum alone in the caravan, the arguments when he got back, the fights. We travelled there and back in the only car we ever had, a black Ford Prefect. When we got home he sold it and never got another.

'We've no need, I can get a lift to work.'

I told her about Mum and how she'd stayed with him for my sake. I told her about the lovely dress she bought once from a neighbour's catalogue, something to wear for a special night out, somewhere nice, an occasion that had never happened, and how she finally wore it and people had stared as she sat, overdressed, in the Black Cock.

'Where do you think we're going,' he'd said, as they left the house, 'the bloody Ritz?'

I told her how much I loved to see her now, so happy with Archie.

Jan told me about her family, too; the fly-by-night father

– the inveterate gambler she'd met once but couldn't really remember, the half-sister she was close to and had missed terribly since she married and emigrated, and who sends a card from Canada every Christmas and birthday, and the flaky mother who lives with her 'new bloke' in the Bright Lights, and who she rarely saw.

'Watch her come running when we have a baby.'

We sat and faced each other astride the trunk of a fallen oak in Hawksheads, so close we could each feel the other's warm breath on our faces, and we talked about everything; the riots in Brixton and Toxteth (it'll only get worse with this lot in charge); the impending mobile phone revolution (we wouldn't have one given, thanks very much); the end of the miners' strike (a sad day all round); the newly-discovered hole in the ozone layer (a looming catastrophe); the phasing out of red phone boxes (no! not the one we used to sneak a snog in at the end of Primrose Terrace!); compulsory seat-belts (stop moaning about your rights and put the fucking belt on); the Battle of the Beanfield (the end of the Stonehenge free festival that Jan had always enjoyed until she met her husband, and he put a stop to all that with his own, more subtle, brand of brutality); the first televised debate in the House of Lords (people falling asleep while watching other people fall asleep), and Live Aid (Queen for her, Bowie for me).

We sat quietly and held each other for a while, then the subject turned to the future, our future, and we made some firm plans. I couldn't believe that I was excited, really excited, to be making the sort of plans we talked about. First we agreed that we should have two kids. I was thirty-one, Jan would be twenty-eight in a few months, not very old, but we wanted to enjoy having kids, spend plenty of time with each, not have a mob and let them bring each other up, but we didn't want just one, either, so two seemed like a good plan.

Then we talked about our living arrangements. I didn't want to spend any more nights at the gatehouse than I had to, but Jan would be in trouble if she was caught with a lodger for more than three nights a week. So I made a big decision; big, but easy.

'I'll move in full-time.'

Jan looked stunned. She smiled but couldn't hold it at the edges and it broke and she looked like she might cry.

'Go legit? Are you sure? I thought—'

'We'll go legit. We'll be ok.'

She grabbed me and hugged me. I held her and leaned back and looked her in the eyes.

'Jan, there's something I need to tell you—'

She pulled me back in close and I leaned back again.

'Jan, I need to tell you this before you say "oh yes and another thing, we should never keep any secrets".'

She went limp then, and loosened her grip.

'What is it John? What secrets? Have you been seeing someone else?'

'No, don't be daft, it's nothing like that. Do you really think I'd be making all these plans—?'

'So what then?'

'It's about the gatehouse.'

'What about it?'

'It isn't only my studio.'

'So what is it then?'

I don't think I've ever been more nervous about anything.

'I converted the bedroom into a growing-room,' I said.

'Is that it?' she said.

'Well I—'

'I know you grow your own weed, John. I've known for ages. I can smell it on your clothes when I do the washing. I wouldn't think you'd get done much more for growing an odd plant than you would for possession.' She tousled my hair. 'What're you like, you worry too much.'

'So if you knew, how come you never mentioned it?'

'Because it didn't matter. Anyway, I didn't want to know, the less I know the better.'

That last statement really gave me a problem. I was about to just go for it, but she carried on.

'Besides, the amount we get through I knew your wages at Johnny Moor's would never cover it.'

Another dilemma. 'Look,' I said, 'Jan, I need to come clean. It's not just the odd plant, it's more a plantation, really, I suppose, you might even call it a business—'

'A *business*? Just how much do you *suppose* you've been growing John?'

'About three pounds—'

'Three pounds—'

'—in weight, obviously, about every three months. Apart from our personal, I've been selling the rest to a mate from away, a lad I worked with at the power station.'

She took a minute to get her head around this information. I started to plough on but she held her hand up to silence me.

'And just how long have you been doing it?'

'The sixth crop was half-grown when all this shit with Lenny blew up so I cleared out—'

'So you've stopped?'

'I did, yeah, but I started again. I have another crop just getting going now.'

'Fucking hell John. How much do you make on a crop?'

'Just over three grand before, but I've doubled up now, so it'll be over six grand—'

'Every three months?'

She was doing her best to subdue a grin. She failed.

'Thereabouts,' I said, 'but I'm only doing it for another year, four crops, should be about twenty-four grand, then I'm done. It got a little bit hairy—'

'That's a lot of money John. You don't really need a job at that rate.'

Her grin was contagious and I'd caught it. 'Ah, well, that's the other thing. I don't have one. I haven't had one since I came back from Holland.'

Just when it seemed she might never speak again, she said, 'So, hang on, when you've left here every Monday for the past two years, you've been the potheads' answer to Percy fucking Thrower? You have to water them and then what? What have you been doing the rest of the time?'

'Painting, recording stuff around the estate, and looking after the plants.'

'And that's it?'

'That's it.'

'You're not bullshitting me?'

'No, I promise. You should see all the paintings. I can't move for them.'

Now we both started laughing. She punched me playfully, hard on the upper arm.

'You fucking dark horse. Fucking unbelievable. I don't know why I'm laughing seeing as how you've been lying to me all this time.'

'I've not been lying, not really, I just couldn't tell you. I couldn't afford to let anyone know. Anyway, you said it yourself, the less you know. Fucking hell I've been paranoid enough. I wouldn't be telling you now if I didn't have to.'

As we walked home, a tiny male merlin came speeding along the woodland edge, flying so low we could see the blue of his back, and a flock of linnets showed us their pink rumps and twittered as they passed. Jan insisted on calling me Mister Escobar, and asked, if she promised to keep her mouth shut, would I spare her life?

I said that I was feeling generous, so not only would I let her live, I was prepared to pay for her silence.

'Name your price,' I said.

'I'll have a foreign holiday, and a pair of binoculars.'

Tuesday 19th of November 1985

I'd intended to go back to the gatehouse on Monday, but didn't leave Jan's until first light on Tuesday. I spent the morning in the birch wood and the sand quarry. I'd bought myself a decent camera and a couple of extra lenses, macro and zoom, and had been taking photographs of plants and fungi, tree bark and berries, trying out the different settings.

We'd had a great week and I'd promised Jan that I'd go back to hers for tea and stay over for one more night, but I needed to check on the plants first. As I got close to the gatehouse the new tarmac was still warm underfoot, and the noise of machinery got louder with each step. The tarmacking gang were just finishing off and the air was thick with fumes. I had a quick crack with one of the gang and he told me they were just cleaning up and would be gone within the hour.

The smell from the growing-room hit me as soon as I walked through the front door. The extraction obviously wasn't working properly. I needed to fix it but there was no rush, I'd got all day, and it's a smell I've always liked.

I removed the film from the camera and put it in an envelope to send away for developing. I made myself a brew, turned on the radio and sat at the desk to complete my diary.

I'd just finished that and was looking through my reference books and field guides – I'd found a fungus I hadn't seen before

– when my attention was grabbed by the news headlines.

'Hello, I'm Hazel Brooks, and this is the BLBC news at twelve o'clock. In our main story this lunchtime, the man at the centre of the magic-mushroom killings has his murder charges dropped.'

I punched the air, but it was a premature celebration.

'Joseph Fields, the man accused of the so-called magic-mushroom killings, has had his murder charges reduced to manslaughter. Fields was originally charged with three counts of murder for the deliberate poisoning of three other men.

'Robert James Clocherty, and brothers Anthony and Stuart Savage, were discovered in a flat in the town-centre last month. Two of the men were pronounced dead at the scene. The third, Stuart Savage, survived in a coma but died a week later.

'At a preliminary hearing yesterday, the judge, Lord Justice Hawthorn, ruled that there was insufficient evidence to proceed with the murder charges.

'Fields, also a victim of the poison, spent almost three weeks recovering in hospital before being charged and taken into custody. Our reporter, April Meadows, was in court. What more can you tell us, April?'

April Meadows? Really? The last I'd heard of April she was one half of a celebrity couple – the other half being the singer of an up-and-coming rock band – and was working as a journalist for her father's national newspaper. Now here she was, reporting for the local radio station. "What more can you tell us, April"? I smiled to myself; about Lenny Fields? More than you care to know.

The sound of her voice almost brought me to tears.

'Well, Hazel, a police spokesman said that the surprise decision was due to mitigating circumstances and was taken on the advice of the Crown Prosecution Service. I did manage to get a few

words from the man leading the investigation, Detective Inspector Jack Dawes, as he left court yesterday, but it was an ill-tempered exchange and unfortunately parts of his statement are not suitable for a daytime broadcast, so I will *need to paraphrase.*

'DI Dawes said that he was "very disappointed" *with the* "unfortunate" *decision made by* "the people" *at the Crown Prosecution Service, and that he had no doubt that* "the accused" *had picked, prepared, and administered the deadly mushrooms himself.*

'He went on to say that, and again I paraphrase, he believed that the "so-called" *mitigating circumstances were a* "load of nonsense", *and that he was still confident of finding the piece of evidence that would prove the* "premeditated nature" *of this crime, and would send this* "young man" *to prison for a very long time'.*

'The trial is due to commence on Monday 20th of January. April Meadows, for BLBC Radio News.'

'Thanks April. And now to the weather...'

I turned off the radio. Even with the lesser charges, Lenny was still in deep shit. I didn't know much about the different tariffs but if he was found guilty of three counts of manslaughter I reckoned he'd still be looking at ten years in jail.

I finished my brew, took the cup to the kitchen, and went into the growing-room. The plants were doing well so I raised the lights and reset the timer.

The extraction fan was labouring. I turned it off and checked the filter. I'd never changed it since I started and it was clogged with dust so I took it out and threw it in the bin. I closed the bedroom door behind me, and left the front door open to help get rid of the smell in the living room, while I went out to the lean-to for a new filter.

* * *

DS Dawn Starling liked the look of Chestnut Avenue; nice semis, big gardens at the front, the back, too, from what she could see. She imagined the twin rows of cherry trees looked lovely in the spring. She'd like to live somewhere quiet like this, and if Jeff's interview went well today …

She eased the seat back a couple of notches. The winter sun was dazzling so she lowered the sun-visor and was pleasantly relaxed, planning her dream future, when the car rocked suddenly and she was jolted back to reality.

Jack Dawes pulled the door shut and put on his seat-belt. He leaned back in his seat and gave Starling a broad, toothy grin.

'Morning, Starling.'

'Hardly, Sir, it's nearly lunchtime—'

'Turn of phrase, Sergeant. You found it alright then.'

'I did, Sir. Nice area. You seem to have landed on your feet, I must say. It's amazing the difference a couple of weeks can make. It doesn't seem five-minutes since you were locked out of your own house and turning up for work stinking like an ashtray and looking like you'd slept under a bridge. Now look at you. I hardly recognise you; clean-shaven, trousers creased, shoes polished, all smiles, a spring in your step—

'Ok, Starling, ok, I get the picture.'

'—lipstick on your cheek.'

He pulled down his sun-visor, looked in the mirror and wiped his face with his palm.

'Just drive, Sergeant.'

Dawes craned his neck to see the tall blonde woman in the dressing-gown, waving from a porch across the street. He caught and returned her blown kiss and relaxed back in his seat.

'You can try, Starling, but I defy anyone to sour my mood today.'

Starling smirked and looked at her watch. He may look and smell better, with his shirt and tie, his clean shave and his eau-de-cologne, but none of that could disguise the unsteady hands and the occasional break in his voice. The smugness probably stemmed from an early-morning shag and would prove to be temporary.

'Where to, Sir?'

'To the back of beyond, Starling, where the devil can't shit for nettles.'

'Oh, I know it well, Sir.' She pulled away from the kerb. 'I was surprised to get your message, actually, Sir. I thought we were done with Lenny Fields a fortnight ago, until trial, anyway.'

'Yes, sorry to drag you away from your new partner, Sergeant—'

'I'm actually on holiday, Sir, I put in a day's—'

'—but I'm sure they can do without you for an hour. Anyway, you're stuck with me, on this case, at least. There were unforeseen developments at yesterday's hearing, you must have heard, it's all over the news.'

'No, I haven't had a minute all morning, Sir. I didn't even turn the radio on,' she lied.

'The fucking CPS are shit-scared of losing this case, well, not just this case, any case, it seems, so in their infinite wisdom they've deemed there'll be a better chance of conviction if the charges are dropped to manslaughter. They're citing mitigating circumstances.'

'I don't see how that affects us, really, Sir. We've still got to put our case, and manslaughter will be easier to—'

'Yes, but the sentence for manslaughter can be anything, Starling, from a community order to a life sentence, you know that. It's at the discretion of the judge, and you know what these judges are like. He could end up spending his days sorting clothes in a fucking charity shop, or ... or out in the sun, mowing lawns and painting fences. The CPS are obviously hoping that he'll hold his hands up to the lesser charges, say he was bullied relentlessly, had reached the end of his fuse and that he did what he did to save himself.'

'Like I've said before, Sir, I believe that's what's happened.'

'I know you do, Sergeant, and you're entitled to your opinion, but I disagree.'

'Not the first time, Sir.'

'No, but probably the last, eh. Anyway, where was I, yes, he'll then throw himself at the mercy of the court in exchange for a reduced sentence. That way, they'll get their conviction, all the boxes are ticked, and everyone goes home happy.'

'Not quite everyone, though, Sir?

'You can read me like a book, Starling.'

They approached the town centre.

'Which way, Sir?'

'Turn right and head for the bypass.'

Starling indicated and turned.

'He doesn't seem the type to change his plea, Sir, to be honest.'

'He doesn't, Sergeant, you're right about that, at least. He's planned this from the start, with a view to avoiding any jail time whatsoever. Playing the poor little victim. He's stuck with his not guilty plea since day one. No, I agree. He's in too deep, he's not going to lose face now, he'll stick to his story to the bitter end and hope for an acquittal. But it's a dangerous tactic. If he does stick to his guns, *"I was at home, they picked the mushrooms, it was an accident, blah blah blah,"* and gets found guilty, he's for the high jump. But his brief will do all he can to convince him to change his plea, and they can be very persuasive, these legal types. If he succeeds, we have to be ready.'

'So, what's your plan, Sir?'

'He's killed three people, Sergeant. We need to make sure that when he's found guilty his sentence reflects the seriousness of his crimes. To do that, we need to rubbish these supposed mitigating circumstances, expose them for the nonsense that they are.'

He pointed up ahead. 'You want the eastbound slip-road.'

'Where are we going, exactly, Sir?'

'We're going to see a certain John Woods.'

'The childhood friend.'

'The very same.'

'What do we know about him, Sir?'

'Not much, thirty-one years old, manual-worker, welder or metalworker or some such—'

'And so we're on the same page, Sir, what do we want from him?'

'Firstly, Woods is going to confirm for us that Fields isn't some softie, some shrinking violet that can be picked on and bullied, that he is a grown man with a nasty streak of his own, who is perfectly capable of handling himself, and that these mitigating circumstances are bullshit.'

'And secondly, Sir?'

'Secondly, when we called at the Post Office, you heard Fields' mother. Him and Woods were inseparable, she said. Spent their every waking hour in the woods, the very woods where the mushrooms in question were picked, by the way.'

'They're not so inseparable any more though, Sir. According

to Fields' father they haven't spoken for years.'

'Exactly, and that animosity, Starling, will be our trump card.'

'I got the impression they just grew apart, Sir, like people do. I don't remember any mention of animosity—'

'It wasn't mentioned, no, but it was implicit. And it makes sense. They're inseparable, then they don't speak for years. No, something's definitely gone on.'

'So you're hoping Woods has an axe to grind?'

'Exactly, or at least that he won't hold back, won't have any qualms about stating, on the record, that Fields knows what a death cap mushroom looks like, and where to look for it.'

He settled back in his seat and folded his arms.

'You need to turn sharp right soon. I'll tell you when.'

'Is it Yelland we're going to, Sir?'

'Not quite, no. He lives in the Hawksheads Gatehouse.'

'Hasn't Rod Jay just bought the Hawksheads Estate, Sir?'

'Yes, I think I read something about it in the Gazette.'

'So does Woods rent the gatehouse from him?'

Dawes wasn't listening. He'd leaned back and closed his eyes.

'I'll have him one day,' he said. 'Rod Jay, I mean. Hurtling about in his fucking technicolour matchbox, like it's the fucking wacky races.'

'You going to get a job with traffic just for the day, Sir, to bring him down?'

Dawes ignored her and they travelled in silence for a few seconds.

'You said your bloke's got an interview today. Jim, isn't it?'

'Jeff, Sir, and yes, he has. He's just finished uni.'

'What did he study?'

'Pure and applied science.'

'God, that sounds boring. What's the interview for?'

'A job, Sir.'

'Don't be smart, Sergeant.'

'Sorry Sir. Research chemist.'

'What do *they* do, exactly?'

'They conduct research to create processes to see how different chemicals interact, Sir.'

Dawes puffed out his cheeks and let the air out slowly.

'Some electrifying pillow talk to look forward to, then.'

Starling looked at her watch again, reached forward and turned on the radio.

'…three weeks recovering in hospital before being charged and taken into custody. Our reporter, April Meadows, was in court. What more can you tell us Ap…'

Dawes leaned forward and turned the radio off, sat back and stared out of the window.

'Fucking shite,' he snapped. 'She's a fucking hack that one. She needs to make her mind up what she wants to do for a living. One day she's a *journalist f*or that fucking commie rag, the next she's loitering outside the Crown Court hurling loaded questions at over-worked peacekeepers for a fucking third-rate radio station.'

Starling grinned and looked again at her watch.

'Not bad, Sir, eight minutes.'

'Eight minutes, Sergeant? What's eight minutes … oh, oh, I see, very droll, Starling, very dry.'

Starling enjoyed winding him up. It was the only thing she was going to miss. He could be funny, sometimes, but most of the time he was just an arrogant prick. She braced herself.

'Anyway,' she said, 'I don't know about any of that, but her boyfriend's a hunk.'

'A hunk? That neanderthal? He looks like the missing link.'

'He could have any woman in the world, Sir.'

'Then God help the world. And what does that say about women, eh, Sergeant?'

There were tall hedges on both sides of the road. Starling braked.

'We must be near the turning by now, Sir.'

Dawes leaned both hands on the dashboard and looked out of each window in turn.

'You must have missed it, Starling.'

'*Me*, Sir?'

'Well, you're driving, Sergeant.' He sat back again. 'You'll have to turn around up the road somewhere.'

Starling drove on until she came to a T-junction, and did a three-point turn. She set off back up the narrow road and had to stop to let a lorry out of a small entrance on the left. There was a sandstone pillar at one side, and a pile of sandstone blocks stacked against the wall at the other. The lorry was turning towards the bypass. She waved the driver out and pulled in and parked on the left, immediately inside the entrance.

Dawes looked at the gatehouse.

'That must be it,' he said.

Starling turned off the engine and they got out of the car and closed the doors. She was still locking the car as Dawes opened the garden gate and walked up the path. Starling followed on behind as Dawes approached the front door. It was wide-open and he rested his hand on the jamb and leaned his head and torso inside.

'Anyone home?' he shouted.

There was no reply. He took a step inside, turned to Starling and screwed up his face.

'Bloody hell, it stinks in here, Sergeant.'

* * *

I gave the last of the workmen a wave as they left, and went to the lean-to. The filters weren't where I thought they were, and it took me a minute to find them. I got one from the box and closed it again and put it back on the shelf.

I left the lean-to and saw there was a car parked at the edge of the wood, opposite the garden gate. It was a newish BMW, dark grey. I suddenly remembered I'd left the front door open and upped my pace. I got to the gate and saw there was a woman standing in the doorway with her back to me. She was short, with a chestnut-coloured pony-tail. There was a taller figure inside. They were police. I knew it. My heart raced. If the smell in the living room wasn't bad enough, I couldn't remember closing the growing-room door.

'Hello,' I shouted. 'Can I help you?'

The woman turned. She had a pale complexion, with pointed features. She turned away again and said something to the other figure, and he stepped outside and they both stood and watched me walk down the path. He was tall and thin, well-dressed and clean-cut. He smiled and showed me a large mouthful of white teeth.

'We certainly hope so,' he said. 'I'm DI Dawes and this is DS Starling.'

He looked at the open door then back at me.

'There's an awful smell in there, son,' he said.

I was done for, nicked before I'd even got started. The plants were only seedlings, but there were twenty-five of them, a large criminal operation. On top of that, I had all the buds I'd salvaged from the previous crop drying around the edge of the tanks, over a pound in weight. See you there, Lenny, I thought, we're both well and truly screwed.

Dawes held his arm out towards the open doorway and smiled.

'After you,' he said.

Heart in mouth and knees turning to jelly, I was ready to throw myself on their mercy, come clean and take my punishment. I resigned myself to my fate and walked past them both and into the house.

'You see what I mean,' he said. 'You should have closed the door.'

I glanced to check the growing-room door before I realised that the room stunk of tarmac. I almost started dancing. I could have kissed him.

'What a berk,' I said, trying to hide my elation. I felt as high as I ever had in my life. Fucking beautiful tarmac fumes.

I glanced again to make sure the growing-room door was shut and went to put the filter on the table. It was in a brown paper wrapper and looked pretty much like a hoover bag.

I turned around to find Starling looking at the paintings and Dawes stooped at the desk eyeing the reference books and journals. I noticed the mushroom field guide still lying open on the desk.

'I haven't got long,' I said. It was true. He'd closed the front door and I had no excuse for opening it again. It wasn't going to be long before the weed fumes started to get the better of the tarmac, in fact there was already a faint smell. 'So what's this about?'

Dawes turned from the desk.

'Ok, I'll cut straight to the chase. Joseph Fields.'

I wondered what line they'd take, what they were after.

Dawes seemed arrogant. I'd heard the radio news a few minutes before. He was obviously pissed off about the murder charges being dropped. He'd probably had a monumental rollicking from his bosses. He'd be desperate to make the manslaughter charges stick.

I'd been thinking about the mitigating circumstances, wondering what they might be.

'What about him?'

'You'll have heard about his … his predicament, no doubt?'

'I have, yeah. I don't know what I can tell you.'

'Just a couple of loose ends to tie up, that's all.'

'Shouldn't take long, then.'

'Hopefully not, no, once we've got what we want.'

'I'll tell you now, I haven't seen him for years. I'm not bothered if I never see him again, to be honest.'

'No love lost, then?' He looked at Starling then back at me. 'So you won't mind answering a few questions.'

'I will if I can,' I said.

Dawes was still hanging around the desk. I sat at the table and motioned for them to join me. He took the invite and sat across from me. Starling continued to move around the room and look at the paintings.

'You and Fields grew up together,' he said, 'hung around the woods here a lot, is that correct?'

'Yes.'

'You're nature boys, the two of you?'

'I can only speak for myself. Yeah, I'm into it all; ornithology, dendrology, lepidoptery—'

'I'm impressed,' he said.

It was obvious that he wasn't.

'I'm just trying to answer your questions.'

Starling sat next to Dawes at the table. She looked at me.

'And mycology?' she said.

'Yes,' I said. 'And mycology.'

Dawes shook his head and harumphed.

'Maybe I should leave you two to it.'

'The study of fungi, Sir. John here mentioned birds, trees, butterflies—'

I was certain I could smell weed, but they didn't seem to have noticed it. Maybe I was being paranoid.

'I thought you were here to ask about Lenny Fields,' I said.

'Ok,' Starling said. 'What was he like, Lenny, as a kid?'

'In what way?'

Dawes took over.

'A bit of a hard nut, wasn't he? Bit of a handful?'

So, that's where this was going. They were trying to rubbish those mitigating circumstances. It had never occurred to me until then. Fucking hell, I thought, if I'm not careful they'll be calling me as a witness for the prosecution.

'You must be kidding,' I replied. 'Fred and Noreen spoiled him rotten. He's as soft as shit, typical only child, used to go crying to his mum if he grazed his knee.'

'You're sure about that, because that's not what we've been told. Total animal, we've heard.'

'Yeah, well, I don't know who you've been listening to, but they can't know him, not really. They're talking about the drink and drugs. Take it from me. Nobody knows him better than I do. Lenny's not a fighter. His mouth's the fastest thing about him.'

'But you said you hadn't seen him for years—'

'I haven't, but you don't just suddenly become a hard case, you either are or you're not. And he's not.'

They were getting nowhere. It was Starling's turn again.

'According to Noreen Fields, the two of you were inseparable for years, then, suddenly, you fell out. What was that about?'

'Never had to live with him, have you.'

'So, a lifestyle thing, then?'

'Yeah, and working different shifts. He was taking a lot of drugs, drinking. It just wasn't working out.'

'And what about his so-called friends? Were Robert Clocherty and the Savage brothers on the scene at the time? Did you meet them?'

'The Savages, yeah, briefly. I didn't hang about long when they turned up. I didn't know the other one.'

'So you moved out?'

'Yeah.'

'What was it about them you didn't like?'

'There was nothing to like. They were feral.'

'They sound like scary characters.'

'They were. They didn't know me from Adam, but that didn't stop them giving me plenty of verbals.'

Dawes took over again.

'Sounds to me like they were all as bad as each other, four of a kind.'

'No. Lenny wasn't wild like them.'

And that became the pattern; Dawes hoping to trip me up, asking leading questions and making assertions, trying to get me to say that Lenny was some champion bare-knuckle fighter, and Starling more interested in getting the dirt on Clocherty and the Savages. I got the impression they weren't on the same wavelength, like they hadn't got their act together at all.

It was easy for me. I couldn't go wrong as long as I didn't lie, and was careful with the truth.

'I don't know what you want me to say,' I said. 'Like I told you, I didn't stay long when the Savages turned up, but I saw enough of them to know what they were like. Could they have bullied him? Definitely. Did they push him around? I don't know, I wasn't there for the last five years, but I'd say it was a good bet. Lenny's a soft touch. They were the animals, not him.'

For the rest of the interview, Starling never spoke again. I thought I could see a trace of a smile behind her icy veneer. She got up from the table and walked to the bookshelves and browsed the spines of the books, her head at a slight angle. Close to her left hand, the mushroom field guide was still open on the desk.

Dawes, on the other hand, definitely wasn't getting what he wanted. He turned away from me and looked at Starling and when he turned back I thought I saw the last remnants of a scowl disappear from his face. He looked back at me.

'So,' he said. 'Let's go back to this idyllic childhood, tramping about in the woods, the two of you. You'll have learned a thing or two about nature and what's what.'

'Birds were our thing. We recorded nests for the BTO. There was a survey on so we helped out. We'd been egg-collectors so we were good at finding nests.'

'So it was just birds? Not plants, or—'

'Or mushrooms?' I said.

'How *was* your mushroom knowledge back then. Pretty good I'd guess.'

'Well you'd be wrong. I know them all, now, but I hadn't a clue back then.'

'And what about magic mushrooms? You used to take them back in the day?'

I almost lied, but I had nothing to hide.

'Only once,' I said, 'when we were about seventeen. I hated them, can hardly remember anything about it. I never took them again.'

'What about Fields?'

'Lenny liked them but he wouldn't take them on his own and as I say, I didn't like them.'

'But Fields would know where to get them and what they look like?'

'I didn't think that was ever in doubt,' I said.

'And what about these others, the death caps?'

Starling had moved from the bookshelves and was leaning with one hand on the desk. She closed the mushroom field guide, picked it up in her other hand, stood upright, and started to leaf through it. She looked at me and raised her eyebrows.

I was getting more and more agitated, and to make matters worse I could definitely smell weed now. It was getting stronger. Why couldn't they smell it? Was it just because I knew about it and they didn't?

'He wouldn't have a clue,' I said, my voice suddenly getting louder, as if that would mask the smell, 'but even if he did, knowledge isn't a crime as far as I know. If it is then you'd better arrest me, cos I could take you straight to them now.'

I knew I'd overdone it but I needed to be rid of them. My nerves were shredding. Dawes couldn't understand it.

'Whoa, whoa, calm down, son,' he said. 'What's got into you? Nobody's accusing you of anything.'

Starling was still looking at the guide. She closed it and held it in her hand like she was trying to guess its weight. I just about managed to hold myself together. I never took my eyes from Starling, nor she from me.

'Sorry,' I said, 'but I just don't understand why you can't accept it was an accident.'

'Too many inconsistencies, son. Too many loose ends.'

Starling compressed her lips into a half-smile, then she reached up and placed the book on the top shelf and came back and stood by the table. I almost gasped audibly.

'I haven't helped you tie them up, then?' I said, my breath catching in my throat as I tried to keep the quaver from my voice.

Dawes didn't answer.

'Well,' I said, 'I can't tell you that Lenny has what it takes to poison three people, then sit and watch them die, because I don't believe he has.'

He stood and sidled his way from between the table and the bench-seat. He opened the door and they both stepped outside and turned to face me.

'Maybe you don't know him as well as you think,' Dawes said, and turned away again. He said something else as he started down the path, but I didn't catch it. I'm not sure I was meant to.

Starling held out her hand and gave me a firm handshake.

'Thanks for your time,' she said. 'You've been very helpful. Keep your nose clean, ok?'

She set off after Dawes, who was waiting by the car.

I didn't think I'd survive the next couple of months without knowing.

'Sergeant,' I shouted, and she turned. 'Do you think I'll be called as a witness?'

She had a glint in her eyes and gave me a knowing smile.

'Oh, I doubt it. Not for the prosecution, anyway.'

Keep your nose clean. The phrase stayed with me all week. What did she mean, or was I reading too much into it? I went inside and fitted the new filter. I made sure everything was sorted, then got ready to go to Jan's. The smell of weed had still not gone away. It seemed to be everywhere, and followed me around. Then I realised why. I'd put a bud in the breast pocket of my shirt earlier to take to Jan's, and it had been right there, under my nose, the whole time.

* * *

'What the fuck was all that about?'

Starling unlocked the car and they got in.

'All what, Sir?'

'You know all what, Sergeant. You didn't say a word for the last ten minutes. If I didn't know better I'd say you want Fields to walk.'

Starling fastened her seat-belt and started the car. She found reverse and inched the vehicle backwards and over the cattle-grid. The road was clear and she set off towards the bypass.

'Would it be the end of the world, Sir?'

Dawes was livid. 'He made sure it was the end of theirs, Starling. Think about that.'

'Don't you think I have, Sir? I've thought about it a lot. I've been working a new case for the past two weeks, but I've thought more about this one if I'm honest.'

'And have you reached any conclusions, Sergeant?'

'I have, Sir—'

'And what are they?'

'I agree with you, Sir, that Lenny Fields did pick the mushrooms, and he did make the concoction—'

'Then we agree—'

'On that, Sir, yes, but not on much else—'

'What else is there, Sergeant?'

'There's justice, Sir. You talk a lot about it, but I'm not sure you—'

'He took three lives, Starling—'

'And he'll never get over it, Sir—'

'And they will?'

'Of course not, Sir—'

'They're fucking worm-food, Starling. Do them poor fuckers not deserve justice?'

'Of course they do, but so does Lenny Fields.'

Dawes snorted. 'I'd give him fucking justice—'

'I don't doubt it, Sir, but this isn't the bible, an eye for an eye—'

'So what is it—?'

'It's the jungle, Sir—'

'So we should enforce the laws of the jungle?'

'No, Sir, I'm saying that this whole sorry story is straight out of the jungle. You read the reports on Clocherty and the other two, Sir. Woods is right, they were animals and they lived in a jungle.'

'So what sort of justice does he deserve, Starling? Lenny Fields?'

'That'll be up to the judge, Sir.'

'Yes, well, I won't be holding my breath on that score—'

'That's why we call them judges, Sir, because that's what they do, they judge.'

'He'll walk, Sergeant, you mark my words.'

'The way I see it, Sir, we both believe that he's guilty of three counts of manslaughter. If it's proven then it's up to the judge, and they will decide the sentence. If they believe it was the calculated act of a cold and callous individual, then they'll sentence him accordingly. But if the judge decides he suffered such awful and sustained abuse that he could see no other course of action than the one he took, then I hope he does walk, and I hope he enjoys his time at the charity shop, maybe even makes a few friends, and I hope that he makes a tidy job of mowing those lawns and painting those fences, and that he gets a nice tan while he's at it, because he'll have to live with what he's done for the rest of his life. Sir.'

They travelled in silence for a few minutes. When they reached the bypass Starling turned towards the Bright Lights.

'Where do you want dropping, Sir?'

Dawes seemed chastened. 'You not going back to the station, Sergeant?'

'No, Sir, I can drop you off, but I need to get home. I put in a day's holiday for today so I could see Jeff off for his interview and be there for him when he gets home. You'd know that if you listened.'

The bypass was quiet, like the rest of the journey. It seemed to take an age to get to the Bright Lights police station.

'Tell me, Sir,' she said, as she pulled onto the car park. 'Was that even an official visit to John Woods just now? You never took any notes whatsoever. That's very unusual, Sir. If I looked at your diary for today, would I see any mention of it?'

Dawes ignored her questions.

'And that stunt you pulled with Fields? That day at the hospital, with the bag of mushrooms. I thought you'd played a blinder at first. He seemed to lose his cool when he first saw them. I thought you had him, but it turned out you gave him the perfect get-out. You could almost hear the penny-drop.'

'Thanks for that but I don't need reminding, Sergeant.'

She watched his hands dither as he undid his seat-belt.

'I'll see you at the trial, Starling,' he said, getting out of the car. He held the top of the door and poked his head back inside.

'He's a very fortunate man is your Jim. I hope he appreciates you.'

Wednesday 20th of November 1985

I didn't tell Jan about Dawes' and Starling's visit, not a good start to our new age of openness, I know, but it wouldn't have helped and would have seriously dented our immediate plans. And anyway, it would be a good story for the future.

I said we'd have the foreign holiday but it would have to wait a year, until the last crop was done. Jan had me promise and swear on my copy of Gilbert White's Natural History of Selbourne, not just about the holiday, but about it being the last crop, too.

The next morning we went to the shop on the reserve and after taking a half-dozen pairs of binoculars outside to try, Jan chose a nice pair of eight by thirties, and in the book section she picked up a Collins pocket guide.

Then we went to the Bright Lights builders' merchants and I bought a portable workbench, an assortment of tools; hand-drill, tenon saw, hole-saw, junior hacksaw, screwdriver and galvanised screws, and all the materials I needed to make twenty nest-boxes; five planks of untreated wood, fifteen millimetres thick, a hundred and fifty wide, and six metres long, small hasps and staples for fasteners, and a sheet of rubber three millimetres thick to use for hinges (I ran out and had to cut up an old pair of wellies I found in the lean-to). I got the bloke to cut the planks in half so they'd fit in the van and we took it all to the gatehouse.

It was Jan's first visit. I showed her inside first, gave her the tour, and we had a brew while she looked through all the paintings and log-books.

'Bloody-hell John, you *have* been a busy boy.'

She loved seeing the set-up in the growing-room; the lights, timers and extraction, and she loved that smell. She stood and pinched a sticky bud between her thumb and index finger, let go and was still holding them under her nose ten-minutes later when we were back in the living-room finishing our brews.

Jan had a look around the garden, at the feeding stations and the pond, while I unloaded the van. It was a fine but cold day and when I'd finished I offered to take her home, but she zipped up her jacket and with the binoculars around her neck, the book in her pocket, and a smile a mile wide, she set off down the lane.

'I think I'll go the long way and do the sand quarry and birch wood,' she shouted as she left.

I said I'd see her later, and watched her bouncing off down the lane with her ponytail swinging from side to side. I pinched myself to make sure I wasn't dreaming, then I fastened up my own jacket, set up the workbench outside, and got to work.

I'd already bought a standard bird box and taken it apart and I used the different sections; back, sides, base, roof, and floor as templates. I made a few improvements; a two millimetre gap between sides and floor for drainage and to allow air to pass through, a detachable front so I could clean each box out at the end of the season and get rid of any parasites, and I scratched a couple of grooves on the inside of the front panel below the entrance hole so that fledgelings could gain purchase when it came time for them to vacate the box.

In eight of the boxes I drilled entrance holes of twenty-five millimetres for the smaller birds, the blue, marsh and coal tits, and in another eight I drilled holes of thirty-two millimetres for the larger birds; great tits, possibly nuthatch, and, fingers-crossed, pied flycatchers.

A couple of weeks later I'd numbered and attached these sixteen boxes to trees in Hawksheads and the birch wood, at heights of between four and six feet from the ground, and facing roughly northeast to protect the young birds from direct sunlight. Hopefully some prospective house-hunters would come for a look over the winter ready for moving in in the spring.

The remaining four boxes I fitted with a low front hoping to attract what had become my favourite bird; the spotted flycatcher. They were common back then; full of character and very conspicuous as they made their darting forays, from high perches and low, to catch their prey. I positioned these boxes much higher than the others, at about twelve feet up in trees close to the woodland edge and with a heavy coating of ivy for cover. I saved the fourth for when the work had been completed on the house and outbuildings. I thought a box high on the wall would give visitors the opportunity to get to know these delightful birds and maybe they'd get the same buzz that I got when I watched them.

* * *

Jan declared my residency at the house and I went with her to her Building Society and we put my name on the mortgage and I set up the monthly payment to go from my bank.

I'd been unemployed since my return from Holland but had never signed on. I still had a couple of grand in the bank and had been paying my national insurance stamps to protect my pension.

I'd been living on cash from the weed, the rest of which (over fifteen grand) was in a locked metal box under the floor in the corner of the growing-room. Now I'd start taking cash from the box and paying it into my bank weekly, as if I was getting a wage. Most people were still paid in cash in those days, so it wouldn't arouse any suspicions.

As for the birdwatching, there was no stopping her. And, as with all birdwatchers, it became a full-time obsession. She started noticing them everywhere she went.

'What's this on next-door's chimney?' she'd shout. 'Hurry up you'll miss it.' 'I think I saw a willow warbler this morning.' 'Does a chaffinch have white stripes on its wings?' 'Is it a greenfinch that sounds like a rusty wheelbarrow?' 'Does a dunnock go…' and she'd do her hilarious best to reproduce the song.

So I wasn't at all surprised when she said she wanted to spend her upcoming twenty-eighth birthday birdwatching. She wanted to go somewhere she'd never been and I suggested the reserve, but she wasn't sure, it being so close to home. I'd told her once about the time Lenny and me almost drowned trying to get a look at the seabird colony a couple of hours' drive to the north, and she suggested we go there.

'I want to see a puffin,' she said.

I'd never been back and said we would at some point, but I thought we should leave it for a couple of weeks to make sure we went at the optimum time. In the end I managed to convince her that she'd see things at the reserve she'd not see anywhere else, and she agreed, as long as we went to the seabird colony later in the summer. I said we definitely would.

'Gilbert's honour?'

'Gilbert's honour.'

PART EIGHT

Sunday 9th of March 1986

If he closed his eyes, the clanging of doors, the turning of keys in locks, sounded just like the opening sequence of Porridge. Less so the sound of beatings, and the cries that went unanswered in the night.

He soon got used to the sounds. And the smells. The cell measured twelve feet by ten, and, as always, it stank of shit and body-odour. He listened to the guttural snores and quiet sobs of his respective cell-mates; thirty-eight year old Billy Thorn, three years into his latest stretch, nine years for aggravated assault; and seventeen-year old Jamie Roache, a fellow remand prisoner awaiting trial on a drugs possession charge, and spending only his third night in incarceration, maybe only his third night away from his mother.

It was early days for young Jamie. He'd stop crying eventually.

Lenny did.

'Don't let him hear you crying.' That was Lenny's first piece of advice to the young lad, in the dinner queue the day he'd arrived. Lenny had found that out the hard way, with a hand around his throat.

'Keep that up and I'll smother you with your own fucking pillow, you gutless little wretch.'

That was nearly three months ago. Lenny had quickly

discovered that there were two Billy Thorns.

There was hard-man Billy Thorn; moody and taciturn, completely unsociable, with no time for talk, small or otherwise, who would happily go all day without speaking a word, and would think nothing of suffocating you in your sleep.

And there was nice-guy Billy Thorn; chatty and approachable, a friendly face, always ready to listen and give sound advice to any new inmate daunted by the harsh realities of prison life.

Unfortunately, nice-guy Billy's appearances were few and far between, and were short-lived. The rest of the time, along with the guards, who initiated most of the brutality, and turned a blind eye to the rest, Billy Thorn *was* one of the harsh realities of prison life.

Until Jamie's arrival, Lenny had spent twenty-two hours of every day alone in the cell with Billy. As a remand prisoner, Lenny wasn't allowed to work, but Billy could have been out of his cell and working every day. He wasn't having any of that, and each time he'd been assigned to a work detail, he'd assaulted another inmate and was no longer eligible.

'They're getting no free labour from me. It's fucking slavery.'

Lenny became adept at avoiding eye-contact, and soon learned not to interrupt him, especially when he was reading the paper. Or trying to do a crossword. Or smoking. Or thinking.

The most dangerous time was when he was on the cusp of hard-man and nice-guy, the point where his wife's visiting-day reassurances were beginning to wear thin and his jealousy started to regain the upper hand.

When Lenny first arrived, Billy had had a visit from his wife two days previously, and when Lenny walked into the cell Billy made him welcome and asked where he was from, and what he was in for.

'Fucking hell,' he said, 'I've got the Bright Lights poisoner as my roomie.' He gave Lenny a playful punch on the upper arm that left it numb for hours, then he winked, and tapped his nose with his finger. 'The *innocent* Bright Lights poisoner, obviously.'

That night he told Lenny how it was in prison.

'It's us against them, mate,' he said. 'Fuck the screws. You'll be alright, don't worry. We look after each other in here.'

He put Lenny's mind at ease, so much so that he actually managed to get some sleep that first night. He thought he'd dropped in lucky, was sharing a cell with the real-life Norman Stanley Fletcher. He could be Godber, he was even called Lenny, it was perfect. He expected Warren or Lukewarm to walk in any minute, escorted by a Mackay, maybe even a Barrowclough.

The following morning, after they'd slopped out, they got their breakfasts and returned to the cell. They settled on their beds to eat.

'What are you in for Billy? Lenny asked.

Hard-man Billy hurled his plate at Lenny's head.

'Why don't you keep your fucking neb out and mind your own business you nosey little cunt,' he snarled, and he picked up his paper, didn't speak again all day, and that night was threatening to kill him.

When Lenny had been discharged from hospital and moved to prison, he'd hoped that he'd get on with his fellow prisoners, especially his cell-mates, but the penny dropped early on; you don't get to be mates with Billy Thorn.

* * *

He laid in the semi-dark, listening to Billy and Jamie. He worried for Jamie. Lenny had been hit by any number of flying objects, and been on the receiving end of a few backhanders, but he never retaliated, never rose to the bait, and Billy got bored and stopped picking on him. Jamie would be next. Fresh meat for the caged animal.

Lenny didn't feel like he'd slept at all, but he knew he had, because he'd been dreaming.

He dreamed about the copper from the hospital. Dawes. He had a metal-detector and he'd found the key Lenny had dropped down the drain outside the flat as he legged it to Bright Lights General. The key had his fingerprints on it, shiny, silver fingerprints, clearly visible to the naked eye. The coppers were in a massive huddle outside the flat on Alfred Street, all patting each other on the back, then they had Dawes on their shoulders. Then he woke up.

His trial had been adjourned once, and had been rescheduled to start tomorrow. He struggled to get back to sleep. He was too busy tormenting himself with all the nightmare scenarios that were likely to come up.

He winced when he thought about the day he'd picked the mushrooms, trying his backpack on his front and his jacket over the top to make himself look bigger, thicker-set, and sunglasses to hide his face, and his hood up, the awful attempt at a Scottish accent. The best he could hope for was that the bus driver told the police they should be looking for a fat Pakistani. He forced a smile that immediately crumpled at the edges.

They were going to hit him with all the forensics, and he tried to think how he'd explain them away, but he just tied himself in more and more knots until he eventually nodded off again.

And in the end, the worry had all been for nothing; he arrived at court to be told his case was adjourned, yet again, for another two months, until the 12th of May.

He was relieved to be rid of the immediate anxiety, but he wanted the trial over with. Even if he was found guilty, at least he could start to look to the future. Maybe he'd even get more respect once he was convicted. And he'd be able to work and have time out of his cell, wouldn't have to spend all day with Billy Thorn.

Which proved to be another pointless worry. When he got back to prison, he was told he'd been allocated a different cell, on a different wing of the prison. He was overjoyed to see the back of Billy Thorn, and got the shock of his life when he saw who was waiting for him in his new cell.

Monday 10th of March 1986

His new cell-mate was wearing a white vest and light-blue tracksuit bottoms. He was on the cell-floor between the two beds with his forearms on the ground, his torso vertical, knees bent and the soles of his feet resting on the top of his head. He leaned his head back and looked up at Lenny from beneath his toes.

'Scorpion,' he said.

Lenny's expression didn't change.

The cell-mate dropped his body so he was on all fours, then stood and started doing stretching exercises; backwards, forwards, hands down each side.

'Yoga,' he said.

Lenny knew it was one of the twins, but had no idea which one. Whichever one it was, he'd grown, a lot. He was getting on for six-feet tall, and had obviously spent every second since they last met working out. Lenny wouldn't fancy fighting him now.

'You don't recognise me, do you. It's Andy. Andy Crowe.'

'I knew it was one of you but I could never tell—'

'Nobody gets me mixed up with that little runt these days.'

The stretching over, he shook his arms vigorously and his huge biceps rolled from side to side, then he gave Lenny a high-five and got his head in the sweaty crook of his arm in a playful gesture that Lenny feared would crush his skull and that left him red-faced and seeing stars.

Andy let go, picked up a towel, and sat on his bed. He draped the towel round his huge shoulders. 'Fucking hell, I can't believe it,' he said. 'I never thought you'd end up in the nick, mate.'

'I'm hoping I haven't *ended-up* anywhere yet—'

'Still a smart-arse, eh?' he said, and before Lenny could answer, he carried on, about Yelland, about school, about the teachers, about all the girls in the different years, about all the detentions they'd done.

'Were you there when our Dave got his balls caught on the goalposts? That was a fucking laugh that was.'

Lenny wasn't sure Dave would agree, but at least he knew now which one it had been curled up on the field that day. He must remember to tell John, if he ever saw him again.

'No. I remember we heard the scream and saw all the folk standing about—'

'Fucking idiot,' he said, affectionately, like it was a fond memory, as if it had been Dave's fault that Andy had pulled on his legs.

He went on. 'We had some good times, didn't we, eh, some laughs?'

Lenny was struggling to think of any.

'Yeah, didn't we.'

'What happened to your mate, Woodsy? What's he doing?'

'No idea, haven't seen him for years.'

'Remember when we put that duck's egg in that hedge sparrow's nest?' He slapped his thigh and burst out laughing. 'That was Swifty's idea. I'd love to have seen your faces when you found that.'

So, it was all just a crack; wrecking birds' nests, smashing eggs, killing chicks, the fighting, all just a part of growing up. He wondered, did that mean that if Lenny and John hadn't been around to find their atrocities, to be appalled by them, they wouldn't have committed them?

Andy Crowe obviously held no animosity towards him, bore no grudges. He was actually nostalgic, saw them as ex-schoolfriends, all members of the same gang, mates with a wealth of shared memories.

Lenny was feeling more comfortable now, had relaxed a bit, and was beginning to feel more like himself.

'Speaking of your Dave, what wing's he on?' he asked, and smiled.

Andy grinned and pointed his finger at Lenny.

'Ha-ha, nice one,' he said, and took a drink of water. 'He's not. He's in Strangeways. They never put us in the same nick.'

'So, what are you in for?'

'Nicking cars, joyriding and that.'

'And that?'

'We nicked a transit van and drove around till we found some coppers and then we wound them up to get them to chase us. There was fucking coppers everywhere. We ended up going wrong way up the motorway and caused a git pile up. It was fucking mint.

'Our Dave was driving and he had some weed on him so he got two and a half. He's mad for his drugs our kid.' He held his arms away from his sides and looked down proudly at his muscular bulk. 'I don't do drugs, I don't even drink. Never have.' Lenny didn't say anything and he put his arms back down. 'Anyway, I only got eighteen months. I'll do nine.' He started laughing. 'They're fucking idiots them judges. They banned us both from driving, again, you wouldn't fucking believe how stupid they are.'

'I'm not with you—'

'Well, we've never had a license between us have we, so how can they take it off us? When we get out, we'll just do it again.'

'So how long have you got left?'

'I've only been here a couple of weeks. I'm due out bonfire night. What about you?'

'Remand. I was at court this morning but it was put off again till May. That's twice now.'

'What did you do?'

'They're saying I poisoned someone.'

'Poisoned? Fucking hell. What, arsenic or summat?'

Lenny had seen plenty of films, tv shows. The cell-mate turns up as a witness in court and the guy's fucked. Was it a coincidence that he'd been put in a cell with probably the only person in the whole prison that he knew? He was probably being paranoid, but he couldn't take the chance. He'd have loved to tell someone the truth, get it off his chest, even if it was a Crowe twin.

'They picked some mushrooms and we ate them and here I am.'

'Oh, fucking hell, yeah, I heard about that. Was that you?'

'Like I say, it was an accident.'

'Were they looking for breakfast or were they after magic mushies?'

'Magic mushies.'

'You were right into them weren't you, you and Woodsy—'

'No, were we fuck—'

'Yes you fucking were. We saw you once. Me and our kid followed you—'

'You followed us? Where was this?'

'We heard you shouting under the railway bridge. We were fucking around in the sand quarry and we could hear you from there. We thought you were just messing about, you know, making echoes and that. You'd gone by the time we got there, but then we saw you trying to get over the fence in that boggy bit in the bottom. You were sitting there laughing your heads off. Then you went into Hawksheads. We sneaked up and we watched you. You were dancing about and chanting like red Indians. I thought you must have been drinking but our Dave reckoned you'd had some magic mushies.'

Lenny was gobsmacked.

'So you were watching us—'

'You'd lost the fucking script mate, honest—'

He felt his face flush, then suddenly started laughing.

'Fucking hell. We've often wondered what happened that day,' he said. 'Neither of us has ever been able to remember. What happened then? Did you talk to us?'

'You're fucking kidding, did we fuck. You were mental.'

'So, what happened next?'

'Like I say, you were making all these daft noises and dancing about, like you were doing a rain dance or summat, and our Dave started making noises, you know, "whoo-oo-oo-ooo" …'

Now they were both laughing.

'… and you both nearly shat yourselves. We were laughing like fuck, me and our kid, it's a wonder you didn't hear us.'

'What did we do?'

Andy could barely get the words out. 'You'd climbed up a … up a git big tree and … and Woodsy was nearly bawling cos he … he wanted to go home … and …'

They were both in hysterics now, laughing so much they couldn't speak. They calmed down and caught their breath, sat quietly for a minute.

Lenny was still wiping tears from his eyes.

'Aye,' he said, 'that'd be John, he always was a soft twat.'

Tuesday 11th of March 1986

'So, do you think you'll get off with it?'

They were in the queue for breakfast.

'I will if there's any justice.'

Andy laughed. He collected his slop and dipped his cup in the tea-bucket.

'I wouldn't fucking hold your breath then.'

They set off back to the cell. Lenny turned to Andy.

'Who was the geezer two in front of you in the queue? Thick-set, sandy hair—'

'I don't know. I didn't notice him. Why?'

'He kept turning round and staring at me—'

'You sure he was staring at you?'

Lenny could tell Andy was hoping it was *him* the bloke had been staring at. He looked excited at the possibility.

'Positive. He was looking past you and straight at me.'

Andy visibly deflated. 'You didn't recognise him?'

'Never seen him before in my life.'

'Point him out next time and we'll find out what his fucking problem is.'

They got back to the cell, sat on their beds, and started to eat their breakfasts. Andy looked across at Lenny.

'Another fucking suicide last night eh,' he said. 'Some poor fucker on D wing. Kid called Rudd. Found him hanging by his trouser-leg in the showers. That's three this month, all remand prisoners.'

Lenny stopped eating. 'A few months ago that could have been me.'

'What? You could have topped yourself? Really? Fuck that.'

'What was he in for?'

'A gram of speed I heard.'

'One poxy gram?'

'That's it.'

'It's mad. There's loads like him in here. How the fuck do you not get bail for a gram of fucking whizz?'

'System's all to fuck Lenny. Nobody gets bail any more. This place is at double capacity; built for five-hundred, there's nearly a thousand in here now. Fucking magistrates can't be arsed, mate, it's like a cattle-market; remand, next, remand, next, remand, next—'

'I was hoping to get bail and I'm up for triple manslaughter.'

Andy burst out laughing. 'You were never going to get bail you daft cunt.'

Lenny finished his food and took a sip of tea. He put his cup on the table.

'Did you say D wing?'

'Yeah.'

'You sure his name was Rudd?'

'Positive, why?'

'Not Roache?'

'That's it, yeah, Roache. I knew it was a type of fish.'

* * *

The shower room was a hub for trouble, the settling of scores, so he went straight after breakfast, hoping it would be quiet.

They were always at one extreme or the other; scalding or freezing. Today they were scalding. The room was like a sauna and Lenny could barely see his hand in front of his face. He had to stand a yard from the jet and feel for it with his hands and transfer the water to his body. He eventually got sufficiently wet and managed to open the sachet of gel and was coated scalp to groin in suds when someone gripped the back of his neck and kicked his ankles apart. His forehead collided with the wall and the shower jet felt like it was stripping the skin from his back and buttocks.

His assailant was naked, too, and hadn't reckoned on the searing water. He let out a sustained groan as he tried to drag Lenny backwards from the showers but he couldn't get a grip of his soapy skin and his hands slipped again and again and Lenny tried to kick backwards with his heel but couldn't make contact. He sank to his knees to avoid the worst of the water and his attacker managed to grab a handful of hair and dragged him out of the showers. He kept hold of his hair and pulled him to his feet and spun him around, and through the steam Lenny just caught a glimpse of his face, the stocky bloke from the breakfast queue, before he gave Lenny a haymaker that sent him careering across the room and crashing into a toilet cubicle. He was face-down in the toilet bowl and he tried to get up but was grabbed again by the hair, and the bloke was kneeling on the backs of his legs, and he pulled Lenny's head back until he thought his neck might break. Then he could see the bloke's face upside down, and the bloke attempted a head butt, but he butted his own hand and some of Lenny's hair came out and his face smashed down again on the rim of the toilet bowl.

Lenny curled around the base of the toilet and braced himself, ready for the next onslaught. He waited a few seconds, but it never came. He could hear a gagging noise, like someone struggling for breath or having a panic-attack. Then a voice.

'Lenny? Lenny? You alright, mate?'

It was Andy. Lenny could still hear the gagging. He turned around and started to get up. Andy was naked and had the bloke at arm's length, pinned high up the cubicle wall by the throat. His feet were a foot off the ground and he was choking. He looked like he might die any second.

Andy gripped him tighter still. 'Why were you having a go at my mate?'

The bloke's face was purple. He spluttered something they couldn't make out.

'Come on, talk, you cunt.'

Lenny was getting worried. 'I don't think he *can* talk, Andy.'

Andy kept the bloke pinned, looked at Lenny.

'I think you're strangling him mate.'

'What? Oh, yeah, right.' He loosened his grip slightly and let the bloke slide down the wall until his feet reached the floor. He would have slid all the way down, but Andy held him up with his hand under his jaw.

'I said talk. Who are you? What's my mate done to you?'

He didn't answer. Andy gripped him again, tighter.

'Ok, ok,' he said. 'I'm Liam, Liam Savage.'

Andy looked at Lenny. 'Does that mean owt to you?'

Lenny was in shock. He looked at Liam. He looked nothing like Tony or Stu.

'It fucking should do,' Liam said.

Andy tightened his grip. 'I didn't fucking ask you. Lenny?'

'Yeah.' Lenny was still looking at Liam.

'You another brother?'

'Cousin.'

Andy was getting more wound up. 'Whose fucking cousin?'

Lenny looked at Andy. 'Two of the blokes that were poisoned.'

'Is that right? Well, mister dead cunts' cousin, my mate Lenny told me he didn't do it, and if he says he didn't do it, he didn't do it. That's good enough for me. They poisoned their fucking selves. Thick cunts. Now I'm warning you, stay away from my mate or I'll fuck you up big style. Get it?'

Liam nodded vigorously. 'Ok, but I couldn't just do nothing.'

Andy let go of his throat. 'That's ok, we get it, family honour and all that, well you've had a go, done your bit, now you can fuck off.'

Liam did as he was told.

Lenny stood and supported himself with a hand on the wall. His cheekbone was bruised and his lip and chin were cut. His back was stinging and he was still shaking.

'You ok?' Andy asked.

'Yeah.'

'Good. Now maybe I can get a fucking shower in peace. And you need to see a screw, get to the medical room. You fell in the showers. You know the score.'

'I do, and thanks mate. I owe you one.'

Andy looked at Lenny standing naked, and nodded at his crotch.

'Yeah? How about you lend me that for a week when I get out?'

Sunday 11th of May 1986

Andy pressed the button on the wall again. He was standing and leaning with one hand against the wall and had his legs crossed.

'Come on, come on.'

There were heavy footsteps on the landing and the spy-hole cover drew back. An eye appeared at the hole.

'Use the pot, Crowe.'

'Oh, come on you cunt—'

'The pot.'

The spy-hole closed and the footsteps retreated.

'Absolute bastards.' He pulled the pot from under the bed, dropped his bottoms and sat.

'Sorry mate. Not much of a parting gift.'

'No worries.' Lenny picked up a newspaper and pretended to read.

Andy spoke in a vain attempt to mask the sound of his ablutions.

'Don't know what I'm fussed about. It's not the first time, and anyway, it's a historic moment, I suppose. One you'll always remember. The last time you got to watch me have a shit. What will you do for entertainment when you're a free man? Eh? How will you get your kicks then?'

He finished and wiped, pulled up his tracksuit bottoms

and stood. He pushed the pot under the bed with his foot. He looked at Lenny.

'So?'

'So what?'

'So what will you do tomorrow when you're a free man?'

'Free man? Yeah, right, fat chance—'

Andy took two steps and clipped him firmly round the back of the head.

'What have I been telling you? Eh?'

Lenny didn't answer.

He clipped him again.

'Think positive—'

'Correct. Think positive. You didn't do it. Just remember that. They picked the mushrooms and *they* poisoned *you*, ok?'

They settled on their beds.

'Will you move back to the Post Office?'

'Maybe. If they'll have me.'

'Course they'll have you. They're your parents.'

Lenny propped himself on his elbow with his head on his knuckles.

'What's your story, Andy? Where are you from?'

'You know where I'm from. I'm from Yelland.'

'No, before that. I remember you in the juniors, but you weren't in the infants' classes. I don't even remember you being in the early junior classes.'

He seemed reluctant to answer. 'Ok,' he said, eventually. 'Not that it's any of your business, but we came from Preston.'

'See. I've known you for years, but I didn't even know that. That's a start. So go on then—'

'There's nothing else to know.'

'There must be—'

Andy let out a long, heavy sigh.

'OK, mother was a bitch, father was a cunt. Let's leave it there, ok?' He said father like it rhymed with gather.

Lenny kept pushing. 'Go on, what else?'

Andy was getting more agitated. 'Why do you want to know? Eh? What's it to you?'

'I just thought, you know—'

'No, I don't fucking know, so tell me.'

Lenny sensed that, for once in his life, he should take a hint and shut up. The last thing he wanted to do was upset Andy. They'd become good mates over the last couple of months. Apparently Andy thought they always had been, but now he felt the same way. Andy had saved his skin, too. He owed Andy. And he didn't want a battering the night before court. He settled on his back and put his hands behind his head.

'Sorry, Andy, you're right, it's none of my business. I didn't mean to wind you up. I know I can be annoying. I've been told plenty of times. You've made this shithole bearable for me mate, and I'll never forget that. I don't know what I'd have done without you, where I'd be now if I was still bunking with Billy Thorn. I'd probably be with Jamie Roache.'

They laid in silence for a few minutes. Lenny could hear steady breathing from the other bed. Then Andy started to talk, quietly and calmly, considering every word, every phrase, before speaking.

'My real father was jailed,' he said, 'when me and our Dave were kids. Seven, I think we were. No, I don't think. I know. We were seven—'

'Andy, you don't have to—'

'I know I don't have to, now shut the fuck up Lenny, and listen.'

'Sorry, mate—'

'He abused us all; physically and sexually, me, our kid, and my sister, all of us. We were fucking punch-bags me and our Dave. Karen was a lot older than us. Fuck knows how long she had to put up with it. She was thirteen when they found out she was pregnant. She was taken into care. I've never seen her since.

'He got ten years, ten measly fucking years for destroying three lives. After that my mother started drinking, well she always liked a drink, but now she meant it. She's the reason I don't drink. The only fucking favour she ever did me.

'Anyway, she started bringing a different low-life home every night. We were taken off her and put in care too. I've never known why it was called that, cos no fucker seemed to. Then we both got fostered, the two of us, by the same couple—'

'You lived up near the church didn't you?'

'Aye. It's rare, brothers kept together. Fucking hell, they couldn't even put us in the same orphanage. But they said it's both or neither.'

'I always thought they were your real parents.'

'No, but turns out they weren't much better—'

'Really?'

'Lenny, you don't know the fucking half of it mate. He was a fucking nut-job, dead handy with his fists, but he wasn't banking on us growing up, was he. He started on our Dave one night and I joined in and we gave him a fucking seeing-to.'

'Fucking hell, what happened?'

'Nothing. They didn't report it. It could have been a lot worse – I had to drag our Dave off him in the end. We moved out after that. We were seventeen. Got a flat in the Bright Lights. I felt a bit sorry for her. She was alright, really. Didn't deserve to get lumbered with me and our kid, anyway. We were too far gone, I suppose, by the time they took us in.'

'I'm sorry, Andy, I'd no idea—'

'Don't be sorry, Len. Not for me.' He propped himself on an elbow. 'How do you think your parents feel? Eh?'

'My parents—?'

'Never had one visiting order from their only son, in what? Six months? My fucking parents would have lit a fag with it, but yours? Fucking hell, they'll be gutted.'

Lenny knew he was right. They'd be beside themselves with worry.

Andy went on. 'I didn't tell you so you could feel sorry for me, Lenny. It's too late for that. I told you so that tomorrow, when you're free again, you can get back to Yelland, to the Post Office, to Fred and Doreen—'

'Noreen—'

'For fuck's sake, Lenny. Noreen, Doreen, Maureen, it doesn't fucking matter, all that matters is that you get back there and you do whatever the fuck it takes, anything, no matter what, to put things right, because I'm telling you now, Lenny, you don't know you're fucking born.'

There was a fraught silence. Lenny laid on his back.

'I'm sorry Lenny, but it needed saying. I wouldn't have said it if I didn't give a fuck.'

He laid down. From somewhere down the corridor there was a scream, the banging of a door, more screams, then somebody shouting.

'Listen to that, Lenny, and make sure you never have to listen to it again. Tomorrow, in court, tell them what you told me, all of it, exactly how you told me, and tomorrow night you'll be curled up in your own bed. I guarantee it.'

Andy turned over and settled down to sleep.

'I mean, fucking hell, you nearly had me convinced, so you'll have no trouble blagging them thick cunts.'

PART NINE

Tuesday 13th of May 1986

The morning of her birthday Jan insisted on being the one to get up and make breakfast. We'd had an early night and I'd gone back to sleep. She had been listening to the radio when the news came on and I was startled when she shouted up the stairs.

'Hurry up, love,' she shouted. 'The news is on. It's about Lenny.'

Originally scheduled to start on the 20th of January, Lenny's trial had been delayed twice; the first time until the 10th of March, and then again until the 12th of May; yesterday. No reason had been given on either occasion, not to the general public, anyway.

I leapt out of bed, threw on my bathrobe, and hurtled downstairs. Jan pushed a cup of coffee across the table and I sat and listened.

'... and resulted in recriminations amongst police officers involved with the case, and in-fighting inside the Crown Prosecution Service itself. Our reporter, April Meadows, was in court. April.'

Jan knew about the April frolics and she looked at me and rolled her eyes, jiggled her head like a dashboard dog, mimed 'la-di-da' and took a sip of her coffee.

'Thanks Hazel. Yes, until this morning's drama unfolded in

court number one, the trial of Joseph Fields was considered by many commentators to be almost over before it began.

'It's now believed that doubts began to emerge about the strength of the case against Fields as early as November last year, when the Crown Prosecutor ruled that the initial murder charges be dropped to manslaughter.

'This, he said at the time, was due to "mitigating circumstances", believed to be a reference to Fields having suffered psychological and physical abuse at the hands of the deceased men over a prolonged period.

'This morning, having already been granted two prior adjournments, the Detective in charge of the investigation, DI Jack Dawes, addressed the court for a third time.

'Unkempt, and appearing nervous and agitated, he said that the prosecution had still found no clear evidence that the defendant had had any part in preparing, or administering, the fatal cocktail on the 18th of October last year, or indeed had the necessary knowledge to have done so.

'When further pressed by the trial judge, Lord Justice Moss, DI Dawes said that he was *now prepared to concede, finally, that the whole episode had, in all probability, been a dreadful accident, and that Fields was, in fact, as much a victim as the three deceased men. The inquest into the deaths is now expected to record a verdict of misadventure.*

'Fields, who has consistently denied any wrongdoing, was supported by his family, and wept openly during the proceedings. Today, after six months on remand, he left court a free man.'

I jumped from my chair and punched the air and then we were hugging over the toast rack. A free man. I wanted to go and see him, to see Fred and Noreen, give them a kiss, and the news got even better.

'Now, Hazel, after the verdict I did try once again to get a statement from Detective Inspector Dawes, but was subjected to what I can only describe as an infantile barrage of abuse and ridicule. This is not the first time DI Dawes has abused this reporter; you may remember back in November I was on the receiving end of a similar tirade from the same police officer, during which I was verbally abused and was very nearly knocked to the ground.

'In some respects this morning's outburst was worse than the last, far more personal, taking aim as it did at my occupation, my gender, my choice of life-partner, even my accent and my hair-style. It really was beyond the pale and I'd like to put it on the record now, on air, that I will be seeking legal advice.'

I remembered Dawes' visit to the gatehouse and got so wound up I nearly dropped myself in it. I just managed to stop myself from saying something I'd regret.

'Yes!' I shouted. 'Good enough for the fucking arrogant twat. I hope he gets fucking struck off, or whatever happens to coppers—' I noticed Jan was looking and I stopped abruptly.

'Steady on John.' She said. 'Anyone would think you knew the bloke.'

'Well, no, course I don't, but you heard her, he sounds like a right arsehole.'

I buttered another slice of toast and changed the subject, and half an hour later we were pulling into the car park at the reserve. We went to the reception desk and showed our membership cards, got our hands stamped, and made our way to the first hide.

The first thing we heard as we made our way between the tall reedbeds was the boom of a male bittern. Jan's face was a picture. She looked at me wide-eyed, mouthed a silent 'what the fuck' and we stood for a few seconds to listen. After six or seven booms it stopped. She knew what it was from my demonstration in the pub one night.

'It's even louder than you blowing in your beer bottle.'

In the first hide a trio of dyed-in-the-wool birders had made themselves at home, with telescopes and long-lensed cameras set on tripods at the viewing hatches, and binoculars hanging around their necks. One had his eye to his telescope's eyepiece, keeping a lookout for anything interesting, while the three of them talked quietly about their birding exploits.

As I always do I asked if there was anything special to be seen and was told that a bittern had been showing well ten minutes earlier, and a pair of otters had been seen just after dawn but would probably not put in another appearance until dusk. One of them said he'd been there the day before and had seen an osprey that hadn't been seen again, and had probably just stopped over on its way back to its breeding grounds in Scotland or Scandinavia.

Jan had said before we set off that she wanted to try to identify everything for herself and I was only there in case of emergency. She got seated and opened the hatch and started looking at the different duck species; tufted duck, pochard, teal and shoveler, and comparing them to the images on the charts pinned to the wall of the hide. She had no problem until she spotted a plain-looking grey duck, feeding alongside an even more plain-looking brown duck. She was struggling but then she noticed the speculum, the coloured wing-bar that's a giveaway for identifying most ducks. She looked at the charts, then back at the ducks, and did a tiny air-punch.

'A pair of gadwall,' she announced, and let out a quiet cheer and gave me a hug. The bemused twitchers looked on.

Then she trained her binoculars on the colony of black-headed gulls nesting on the numerous islands that were dotted around the mere. They'd started nesting there a decade earlier and the colony had grown year on year until there wasn't an island, no matter how small, that wasn't occupied. I was at the far-end of the hide doing my habitual scan of the reedbed edge, hoping to spot the bittern.

'What type of gulls are they?' she asked.

One of the old-timers couldn't help himself and let out a quiet, derisory snort. The one at the telescope didn't say anything.

'They're black-heads, love,' replied the third.

'No, I can only see one black-headed gull. It's bigger than the rest, isn't it, with a black stripe on its beak, I'm on about all the others, the smaller ones with the brown heads, the ones making all the noise.'

'Only one?' mumbled the first

'Bigger than the rest?' mused the second.

'Black stripe?' muttered the third.

There was a sudden swishing of waxed jackets and a scraping of tripods as the penny dropped and the old twitchers did their best to hide their reddening faces behind their telescopes.

In the middle of that vast black-headed gull colony Jan had managed to pick out the one, very rare, Mediterranean gull.

I took the seat next to her, opened the hatch, and we shared a grin.

When they'd had a good look at the bird, taken photographs, and their faces had cooled sufficiently, the twitchers came up for air.

'Very well spotted, love,' gushed the first, tipping his cap.

'Aye, well done lass, we'd missed that,' admitted the second.

'Beginner's luck if you ask me,' griped the third.

We all got back to some silent birding for a while, then Jan piped up. 'Why do they call them black-headed gulls when their heads are brown?'

It was a fair question, and none of us had the answer.

* * *

If the Mediterranean gull was bird of the day, the undoubted highlight of the day was a pair of marsh harriers performing a 'food-pass' over the reedbed, the male rising to a height then dropping his catch to his mate, who turned onto her back beneath him and caught it in mid-air.

We visited every hide and saw some good stuff; the avocet and cattle egret had Jan wowing, and we stayed as late as we could, but Mum and Archie were treating us to a Chinese meal in the Bright Lights, so we left the reserve at five and went home to get changed.

They picked us up at seven and we got to the Bright Lights in good time. Archie parked the car round the corner from the restaurant, behind his kitchen showroom, and said he was leaving it there for the night and was treating us to a taxi home.

We sat one to each side of a large, square table, me facing Jan, with Archie on my right, and Mum on my left. Archie had told them when he booked the table that it was Jan's birthday, and that she'd never eaten in a Chinese restaurant before. The staff were great and made a big fuss of her. There were helium balloons and glitter on the table and a Happy Birthday banner on the wall behind Jan's chair, and when we came to order, the waitress explained the menu in great detail.

For her starter Mum ordered dim sum, her favourite, which the waitress explained were steamed dumplings with a variety of fillings, and translated literally as "touching heart".

Jan closed her menu. 'That sounds lovely, I'll have that, too.' She raised her palm at the side of her mouth as if to whisper me a secret. 'As long as I can have a taste of yours.'

Archie ordered soup and I went for the ribs. The dim sum came first, then my ribs. The waitress put a bowl on the table between me and Archie, and disappeared again. Jan looked at the bowl of steaming, clear liquid, then she looked at me and pulled a face. Then she looked at Archie. I knew exactly what was coming.

'Your soup looks a bit bland, Archie,' she said. 'Is it that consommay or whatever it's called?'

'No, it's John's finger bowl, love,' he said, as the waiter returned with his soup. 'For when he's finished his ribs,' and the four of us doubled-up laughing, Jan most of all.

We shared a bottle of wine with the meal, and while Mum and Jan had a good catch up, Archie asked me how Rod was getting on with the work on the estate. I told him the car parks were finished and the fire escape installed, that the stables had been gutted and the place was awash with plasterers, electricians and plumbers.

I told him I was meeting Roz next week to talk about doing some paintings for the house.

'A commission,' I said. It sounded great.

Archie said he was pleased things had worked out, and we went on to talk about this and that, and we eventually got back to a four-way conversation. I told the story of the three twitchers from that morning, and Jan flapped her hand in mock modesty.

'Oh, it was nothing, really,' she said, 'but feel free to disagree.'

When we'd all finished eating, Archie motioned to the waitress and she brought out an ice-bucket, a bottle of fizz and four flutes.

Archie did the honours and we all clinked glasses over the centre of the table.

'To Jan, many happy returns, love,' he said.

'And to the future,' I added, winking at Jan, and there was another bout of clinking and we drank the toast.

I stood and leaned across the table and Jan leaned forward and we just managed to reach to have a quick kiss.

'Happy Birthday, darling.'

'You too,' Jan said, 'well, I know it's not yours … you know what I mean.'

There was a bout of laughter, then a moment's pause.

'Good news about your friend, Lenny, too,' Archie said.

'Oh, yes, I forgot to mention it,' Mum said. 'I saw them yesterday, love. Only for a minute. They were just back from the court. Noreen and Lenny went straight inside so I only caught a glimpse of Lenny, but he didn't look well. There looked to be nothing to him. Anyway, I managed to get a word with Fred. They're happy with the result, obviously, but they don't want any visitors just yet. He said it'll be hard enough opening the Post Office. He's going to run it until Noreen's ready to see people again. It's affected her terribly, the court case. And Lenny, too, of course. As I say, he looked drawn. I gave Fred your number, love. For Lenny, you know, when he's feeling a bit better. I didn't think you'd mind.'

'No, I'm glad you did. Maybe he'll surprise me.'

'I meant to ask you about that, love,' Mum said. 'Fred seemed to think you'd fallen out about something. You and Lenny. I said I didn't think so—'

I'd told Jan all about the final April frolic, and she looked at me and gave me her 'oops' look.

'No,' I said. 'I just moved out when he started knocking about with the fairground lot, that's all.' I picked up my drink. 'So,' I said. 'A double celebration,' and we all clinked glasses yet again.

'To Lenny,' we chorused and drained our glasses.

Archie picked up the champagne bottle and shared what was left between the four glasses. He picked up his own and pushed one towards Mum.

'Well, love,' he said. 'It's your turn.'

I don't know the last time I saw Mum blush, but she cherried-up now. She picked up her glass and looked at me, then at Jan.

'It's a triple celebration, actually,' she beamed.

I wondered what it could be, and for a weird instant I thought she was going to say she was pregnant.

'Jan, love,' she said, 'I hope you don't think I'm trying to steal your spotlight, I don't mean to, but …' she turned to me, '… yesterday, love, Archie asked me to be Mrs. Archibald Beech, and I've said yes. We've set the date for the 5th of November. We'll have been together exactly ten years.'

I'm prepared to stick my neck out and say that at that moment in time, I was one of the four happiest people on the planet, and not only that, in a remarkable coincidence, I happened to be sitting at the very same table as the other three. If you could have harnessed the warmth radiating from the smiles around that table, you could have powered a small town for a year.

Mum and Jan were both in tears and hugging across the corner of the table, I couldn't get near Mum so I leaned the other way and hugged Archie, then Jan let go of Mum and got out of her chair to give me a look-in and she gave me a hug as she passed and then I was hugging Mum and Jan was hugging Archie.

The restaurant staff must have thought we went a bit overboard with the twenty-eighth birthday celebrations in our family, and by the time we finished the hug-in and were back in our seats we had a small audience of staff members who were clapping, and they'd been joined in the applause by those diners who'd had a view of the goings-on. Mum hid her blushes behind her hand and I had to quickly draw my legs in as she slumped down in her chair and felt for Archie's feet with hers under the table.

There wasn't a dry eye in the house, as they say.

At the end of the night the restaurant owner approached the table and asked if we'd like a traditional Chinese toast for Jan's birthday. Mum moved closer to Jan to make room and I grabbed a chair from a neighbouring table and put it between myself and Mum.

The owner went to the bar and returned with a stone jar and five tiny glass goblets. She put them on the table as she sat down next to Mum, and Mum introduced us all by name. She was beaming. I'd never seen her having such a good time.

The owner spoke perfect English and introduced herself as Yu Yen. She explained that the jar contained baijiu, a very strong, grain-based liqueur, that's drunk extensively in China, mainly for toasts but for serious drinking sessions too.

She removed the wax plug from the neck of the jar and there was a strong, pleasant aroma as she filled each of the goblets with the baijiu and handed them around. Before the toast, she told us a little about baijiu and how to drink a toast in China.

Baijiu is made by a distillation process that involves no yeast, but a fermenting agent called qu, pronounced 'chew', and can be made from a variety of different grains. This particular brand was made from sticky rice, and was more than sixty percent alcohol.

When drinking a toast in China, small groups will clink glasses, as we do, but larger groups won't reach across each other to try and clink with everyone, instead they tap the base of their glass on the table, and in place of cheers, they say 'gan bei', pronounced 'gon bay', which translates as 'dry cup', a reference to the fact that you are expected to drain your glass in one go.

Once you've got the baijiu in your mouth, you don't swallow straight away, you allow it to wash over the gums and palate, and savour it first. Then, to prove that your cup is dry, you have to show everyone the empty glass.

On Yu Yen's cue, we tapped our goblets on the table

'Gon bay,' we all shouted, and took in the pungent liquid. We followed Yu Yen's lead and showed our empty vessels as proof.

Yu Yen sat, quietly savouring the drink.

Jan either forgot, or she didn't fancy keeping it in her mouth, and swallowed hers straight away, then sat, unable to speak, with a red face and eyes squinted and watering.

Mum got into the spirit of things, swishing hers around like listerine before swallowing it and putting the back of her hand across her mouth and starting to cough.

As always, Archie was as cool as they come, and he sat and gently rolled the sweet liquid around in his mouth before swallowing. Yu Yen finally swallowed hers and pointed.

'Yes, Archie's got it.'

I let the baijiu touch my palate for a nanosecond, then downed it like it was sambuca. I've never been keen on drinking neat spirits, and it was just as vile as I'd expected.

I asked Yu Yen if it was used in cocktails, like whisky and vodka here, but she said that it's considered bad form in China to water down any spirits.

She went on to tell us a bit about the culture of drinking in China. Being able to drink heavily and remain sober is seen as a very macho trait, whereas being drunk and making a fool of yourself is a no-no, news which gave me a twinge of rekindled embarrassment as I remembered some of my antics over the years, most recently my meeting with Rod.

In a country where making a complete tool of yourself in drink is frowned upon, it seemed strange to hear next that drinking games and competitions are common, and stranger still to learn that to turn down a drinking challenge is socially unacceptable.

Worse still, these challenges can come from anywhere; an adjacent table in a bar or restaurant, even at business lunches, where you can find yourself knocking back the baijiu and trying to stay drink-for-drink with a company's 'nominated drinker'.

I made a mental note not to emigrate to China, then I drifted off into a world of my own as they all chatted on.

I thought about how far we'd come, how much had changed.

I looked at Jan, saw how, when she smiled, she smiled with her whole face, every feature. Even with her hand over her mouth, hers was as radiant a smile as I'd ever seen. I loved her more than I would have believed possible, and just the thought of losing her, of not being with her, made me feel sick to my stomach.

I looked at her, having a laugh with Archie, and I hoped she was carrying our baby, wished that after Mum's announcement Jan had surprised us with a fourth toast, to little Jan or John Junior.

I looked at Mum, more contented than she'd been in her life, casting the occasional smile in Archie's direction as she listened intently to Yu Yen speak about her earlier life in China, saw her put her hand on Yu Yen's waist and admire her ivory-coloured, silk dress.

'It's beautiful. I love the style, with the high neck, the split in the side. Very elegant.'

'Thank you, it's qipao, traditional Manchu dress.'

Then Yu Yen returning the compliment, telling Mum how she loved the bright colours and floral design on hers.

I looked at Archie. He's always reminded me of a movie star, not like today's – unpredictable and fiery, a Christopher Walken or Robert DeNiro – more like someone from the golden age of Hollywood, a Gary Cooper or Gregory Peck; the strong, silent type. I remembered him at my father's funeral, being a rock for Mum when she needed it, and I looked at him now, talking and listening to Jan, but seeming to know exactly when to glance away to catch the smiles from the love of his life.

I don't think my father ever took Mum out for a meal, any meal, other than the odd bar snack when he wanted to carry on drinking. I remember his stock answer whenever Mum suggested it.

'I bought you a stove, didn't I?'

As for me, I was buzzing. I had Jan, I had my first commission, Mum would soon be Mrs. Marjorie Beech, and my best mate had just been cleared of triple manslaughter. On top of all that, I had plenty of money put aside, with still more to come over the next few months. Life was sweet.

Monday 19th of May 1986

I loaded some of my better paintings into the van and drove to Hawksheads House. I parked on the car park and looked for the umpteenth time at the work that had been done.

I didn't like it when I first saw it, thought it all looked a bit industrial, but now that spring had arrived, and the surrounding ground cover and tree foliage was returning, plugging some of the gaps with greenery, I realised that had been the problem, and now it looked great. Hardly any trees had needed to be removed, and the slate-chippings Rod had chosen for the car park's surface blended beautifully with the landscape.

As I walked alongside the perimeter wall and through the main entrance into the courtyard, I heard a song I recognised straight away. I turned and retraced my steps, trying to pinpoint the singer. My heart leapt when I found it – a nuthatch, noisily calling as it foraged for grubs on the rotten branch of a sycamore tree less than twenty-feet above me.

The last one I'd seen was also my first, exactly fifteen years ago, on our camping trip to the tarn. They'd been slowly expanding their range ever since and now here they were on my home patch. I can't even begin to describe how good that felt.

We'd arranged to meet at two o'clock and it was only quarter to, but they were already there when I arrived.

A woman was standing on the top step, looking out onto the courtyard with her back to the large front-door. She wore ice-blue jeans and a baggy, scarlet blouse, with a pair of sunglasses, and a baseball cap with a short black ponytail protruding from the back.

I assumed this was Roz. She'd seen me and was shouting to Rod, who was talking to one of the builders, and she was struggling to make herself heard over the cement-mixer that was rumbling away in the corner of the courtyard. I caught Rod's eye and raised my hand and he put his thumb up to the builder and came to greet me.

'All go,' he shouted, and smiled, and we walked over to Roz.

'Roz, this is John.'

She walked down the steps, took off the glasses and reached out her hand.

'Hi, John. Thought you must be him.' She smiled. 'I'm Roz. Rod's told me a lot about you.'

'Only the good bits, I hope,' I said, trying to think what they might be.

'Of course,' she replied.

We shook hands and made our way to the car park. I opened the back doors of the van and climbed in. I'd taken about fifteen paintings and I moved them to where she could reach them, blocking my exit in the process, and I had to climb into the front to let myself out.

When I re-joined her, Roz was hiding a smile and flipping through the paintings, hardly pausing for more than a couple of seconds at each before moving on to the next. She was halfway through the first stack already. She looked up.

'Oh, they're all lovely,' she said, 'but I'm not looking for bird portraits. I've nothing against them.' She nodded backwards towards the house. 'He'd never have married me. No, I'm mainly looking for colours, to be honest, the overall effect.'

She came to a painting that piqued her interest and she pulled it out and leaned it against the rest. It was a watercolour of a flower meadow, splashes of red, blue and pink, with a yellow wagtail in the bottom-right, poised to launch an attack on any one of a dozen mayflies strewn across the rest of the picture.

She stepped back for a better view.

'This is the kind of thing. A collage of colour, hazy, indistinct. I like that. It comes into focus when you take a step back. That's going to be important in such a large space.'

She stood the painting on the floor against the van's back wheel and continued to browse until she came to my own favourite, another watercolour, this time of the gatehouse garden in autumn; a blurry, pastel patchwork of grasses, and purple berberis leaves, verbena flowers, and berries; black, red and orange, dogwood, cotoneaster, and firethorn, with the dead stems of teasel on the left-side, and a trio of goldfinches hovering over the spent flower heads.

She held it at arm's length and nodded. She picked up the other and held them both next to each other.

'I love the Impressionists,' she said. 'These are very Monet-esque, don't you think?'

I showed her a face that I'm sure was very Philistine-esque, and she smiled.

'Come on,' she said, 'I'll show you what I want.'

She set off towards the house with the two paintings and I followed her into the courtyard and up the steps.

In the entrance, two teenagers, maybe fifteen and sixteen, a boy and a girl, were arguing about something. They stopped the second they saw Roz.

'Is this still the same argument?' Roz asked. Neither of them answered, just stood and looked embarrassed. 'Well if you intend to continue, then take it outside, please,' she said, with a calm authority. 'Some of us are busy.' They disappeared outside. 'This is John, by the way,' she shouted after them. She turned to me and shook her head. 'Rod Junior, and Alice. I was about to say you'll have to excuse them, but please don't. If they get under your feet, feel free to give them short-shrift.'

In the foyer there were three large blank areas of wall, one at either side, and a third straight ahead facing the main door. She leaned the paintings side by side against the facing wall and stood in the middle of the foyer. She pointed to the sidewalls.

'I'm in discussions with a number of other local artists regarding these two walls.' She turned and looked at the other. 'And this wall is yours.'

It was a massive area, at least twenty-feet high and twelve feet across. 'That's huge,' I said. 'How many will you be wanting? Those two and a couple more?'

'Oh, no, no. The reception desk will be here,' she said, indicating the base of the wall, 'and I just want the one painting above. I think eight feet square. This will be the first thing visitors see as they walk in the door, and they'll be looking at it all the way to the desk, so it's very important.'

She picked up "the gatehouse garden" and held it up to the wall.

'Something in this vein. A larger *version* of this, if you like, it's up to you.' She nodded at "the flower meadow" at her feet. 'Or that one. They're both so light and colourful, really lovely.' She put the painting down. 'As for the birds, I know what you're like, you twitchers, but if you must put a bird in every painting, if it's your trademark, I don't want it front and centre. I'd rather I had to look for it, like Thompson with his mouse-furniture. I don't want an Audubon, if you know what I mean.'

I knew what she meant, if not who she was talking about.

'Anyway,' she continued, 'shouldn't be difficult to hide a small bird or two on such a large canvas.'

I was still trying to imagine doing a painting eight feet square. She saw me staring at the wall.

'Are you sure you're up for it? Not too daunting?'

'No, I can't wait to get started.'

'Don't you want to talk about payment?'

'I can't afford much,' I replied, 'I'm not working.'

It was a weak joke that got the response it deserved.

'How long have I got?' I asked.

'Well, we're not opening until Easter, mid-April, but Rod says you prefer to paint 'live', as it were, rather than from a photo or from memory, so, as we can't summon the seasons as and when we want them, I thought the end of January? How does that sound? That'll give us plenty of time for framing.'

Rod came in then, closely followed by the two children.

'All sorted, then?'

'I think so.' I said.

'All systems go,' said Roz.

'Good,' he said. He handed a set of car keys to Alice. 'You two go and get in the car. I just need a word with the builders.' He turned to Roz. 'I'll drop these two off and come back for you.'

'No need, we're done.' She handed me a business card. 'I'll pay for all the materials, brushes etcetera, and if you need a bigger easel … just let me have the receipts.' She smiled. 'We'll talk about your fee next time.'

'Thanks Roz, Rod, see you later,' said the professional artist, and left.

* * *

Since the start of our dealings, I'd always weighed the weed into fifty separate ounces for Smudge. It was a lot of work for me, but I didn't mind. I had the space and privacy to do it, and I understood that he sold it on in ounces and that to have to start cutting it up himself at home might cause a bit of friction with his wife. For all I knew, she hadn't a clue what he was up to.

For the final four crops he made life a lot easier for me by asking for two separate kilos, and a third that he wanted cut into thirty-five one-ounce-bags. I did the sums and agreed to let him have the three kilos for six grand, giving him an extra five ounces or so for free, and I'd still have at least three ounces for myself.

We'd agreed to do all four of the deals on the day he was going home, whenever and whatever time of day that happened to be, and each one in a different location. The first we'd done on a Friday teatime in a layby just outside the Bright Lights, the second we did yesterday, at half-past midnight when he'd finished a back-shift, in a picnic area in a local beauty spot.

When Smudge set off for Wales, I went straight to the gatehouse and put the money with the rest in a metal box under the floor in the corner of the growing-room. I knew exactly how much was there, but I counted it again anyway. I put the excess in my pocket and left twenty-three thousand quid in the box and replaced the floor-panel.

I still had two more crops to go, then I could relax, and adapt the growing-room for a new venture I had in mind.

Monday 2nd of June 1986

Today was the day I was finally going to see the cliff-nesting birds that we'd failed to see, sixteen years ago, when me and Lenny were almost drowned, smashed on the rocks and our corpses washed into the Irish Sea. But this time I was going with Jan, and we'd be accessing the viewing points by way of the cliff-top path, not via the suicidal route that me and Lenny had taken all those years ago.

We were both excited about today's outing. We were visiting a unique habitat, the only sea-cliff nesting site on the west coast of England, and we'd be seeing quite a few species that neither of us had seen before. Jan had been birding for about six-months by now, and often had a walk through the woods and the sand quarry, but this was the day that she really got it, the whole thing, not just the buzz of seeing a new species, but how difficult it can be to differentiate between some species, and the weirdly conflicting feelings of excitement and frustration you get when you can't identify a bird, something you convince yourself was a rare sighting, but will always remain a mystery.

Jan was already up and packed by the time I got downstairs. We called at a garage on the bypass to fuel up and get some sweets, and we were on our way.

There's no better company on a long journey than Jan.

Until I met her I'd always treated driving as a necessary evil, but she changed all that. She is without doubt the best person you could ever have 'riding shotgun' as she called it. I still hate driving long distances on my own, but with her in the passenger seat, it's a different prospect.

We'd no sooner got on the bypass than she took out her field guide, and a pad and pen.

'Right,' she said. 'Let's draw up a target list of birds you think we'll see.'

'All day, or just when we get there?'

'When we get there.'

'Ok.'

Pen poised at the ready, she opened the book at the first image.

'Red-throated diver?'

'No, no divers. Keep going.'

She turned the page.

'Grebes?'

'No'

She turned the page.

'Albatrosses?' She started to turn the page.

'Whoa, whoa—'

'What? We won't see an albatross, don't take the mickey—'

'We'll see a fulmar. It's a type of albatross.'

She turned another page and found the fulmar.

'It says here it's a petrel—'

'Yeah, but they're all just little albatrosses.'

She wrote it in the pad, beneath puffin, which she'd already written at the top of the page and asterisked as her number one target.

'What about shearwaters?'

'No.'

'Gannet?'

'No.'

'Booby,' she said, and gave an exaggerated snigger.

'No,' I said, trying not to give her any encouragement.

'Oh, you never know,' she said. 'You might see a *pair* if it's quiet.'

She turned another page.

'Pelican? Probably not, eh?' She turned to the next page.

'Shag?' she burst out laughing.

I tried not to join in. 'I don't think so.'

'Correct,' she said. 'It'll have to be *very* quiet.'

She worked her way through the entire book, and didn't miss out one family of birds; herons, egrets, ibises, ducks, swans and geese, even sandpipers.

'You do know we're going to see cliff-nesting birds?'

'Well *I* don't know where they all nest.'

She never stopped, and had me in stitches all the way there, conjuring images of cliff-nesting flamingos, ocean-going orioles, and flocks of woodpeckers following in the wake of fishing boats.

'Well I don't know, do I, you're the expert.'

The long drive flew by. Singled out for particular hilarity were the bustards, great and little, and the red-knobbed coot, and we were laughed out long before we got to the twite and the yellow-bellied sapsucker.

When she closed the book, she had a list of thirty-two species, including raven, peregrine, and some of the smaller birds, rock and meadow pipits, warblers and chats, that I'd guessed would be nesting in the gorse, brambles and long grass at the top of the cliffs.

I parked on the beach-front car park and we made sure we had all our provisions. We'd been right to leave it a couple of weeks. When we got there things were in full swing, and as we made our way up the first incline the air was filled with hundreds of sand martins, flying in and out of their nests in the sand cliffs at the beginning of the path.

We reached the top and walked along the first of the two headlands and were treated to a lingering, eye-level encounter with a fulmar, soaring close by on rigid wings. Jan watched it through her binoculars for a few seconds until it tilted ever-so-slightly and disappeared over the lip of the cliff, then out came the pad for the first tick of the day.

'Wow,' she said, 'what a start, we've seen an albatross already.'

It was a still, sultry day and the smell of guano was wafting up on thermals from the cliffs below. Close to the sun, a skylark, Wordsworth's 'ethereal minstrel', sang his heart out, a mere speck in the sky. Jan shielded her eyes and I tried to point it out; 'there, just dropped from the blue to the edge of the cloud, on the cloud now, no, now against the blue, back on the cloud, no, lost it myself now, there, there, no, no, I've lost it again.' She tried for a minute or so, but gave up. She got the book out.

'What are you doing?' I said.

'I'm ticking it off.'

'You can't tick it off, you haven't seen it yet.'

The lark was now so high its song was barely reaching our ears. I managed to locate it by eye, but lost it again when I raised my binoculars. Then the singing stopped and I saw it start to fall like a stone from the heavens. Jan saw it too, and we watched as it hurtled towards the earth until it seemed it would crash, then spread its wings like a parachute to slow its descent, and come to land on a fence post less than twenty yards away. It raised its crest, twittered for a few seconds, then lifted off and began another ascent. Jan produced the pad and made a great show of ticking it off.

The views from the cliff-tops are spectacular. Across the sea, the Isle of Man and the sprawl of Dumfries and Galloway were clearly visible, a purple smudge on the azure sky. Ahead, a continuous line of yellow gorse stretched for as far as we could see. Linnets passed overhead twittering quietly, meadow pipits, like amateur skylarks, launched themselves from fence-posts to perform their short song-flights, and a pair of ravens climbed into the blue and tumbled haphazardly into the void.

The sea was dead-calm. Barely visible, rafts of auks were clustered offshore, and we stood a while to take it all in, until a tiny, belligerent stonechat puffed out his russet chest, flicked his tail, and launched himself from a growth of furze, tack-tacking loudly, and bullied us off his patch.

From here we headed down the path and into the gulley that opens onto the bay between the two headlands. Human traffic here is sparse, and the only person we saw was a bloke throwing stones at an irate fulmar that was relentlessly dive-bombing his dog.

About a hundred yards long, the narrow shingle beach is walled-in on three sides by a huge expanse of rock, and on the other by the sea; a real Shangri-La. Rock pipits were feeding amongst the pebbles and the plants that managed to survive in the narrow sandstone cracks and crevices. Jan wanted to know the difference between them and their cousins, the meadow pipits, we'd seen along the cliff-top path. I'd done my homework the night before, but she preferred to find out for herself. She looked in her field-guide and discovered that there are a few differences, the main one being the colour of their legs; dark for rock pipits, pale for meadow.

We walked the length of the beach and had a brew and a sandwich on top of a flat sandstone giant that protruded from the shingle.

Jan put her arm around me and rested her head on my shoulder.

'We should call this 'Salvation Point'?

I smiled and kissed her head.

'Yes,' I replied. 'I like that.'

We sat quietly for a half-hour. The sun had reached its zenith and a heat-haze blurred the terracotta cliff-face. The ebb-tide was becalmed, a sleeping behemoth licking timidly at the shore. Fulmars patrolled the air with majestic ease, and cormorant chicks called gruffly from above as their ungainly parents approached at speed and used their feet for brakes. A solitary black guillemot drifted idly, very much at home close to the point where, sixteen years ago, having survived the deluge, a pair of callow youths dropped to their knees and laughed until they cried.

* * *

We made our way back down the beach to the gulley and climbed the second headland. The best views of the cliff-nesting birds are on this stretch, and at the first vantage point the air was full of noisy kittiwakes and gulls. The cliff-face was white with guano and crammed with birds raising families on the narrow ledges. Hundreds more were coming and going, ferrying food to their hungry young, and fending off the attentions of herring gulls and black-backs, opportunists looking for an easy meal.

Suddenly there was drama as a raven swaggered into the auk colony and plundered the solitary egg from beneath a sitting guillemot, causing pandemonium on an already overcrowded ledge.

Two kittiwakes grabbed each other's tails and rolled through the air, a scraggy ball of noise that plummeted into the abyss and parted less than a yard from the sea's teal-green surface.

We spent a long time looking for the elusive puffin but, with only a few pairs breeding there in any given year, it was a lost cause and we gave up. One unexpected surprise was a splendid, regal-looking, thoroughbred Rock Dove, perched on the tip of a jutting sandstone slab. Now uncommon, the true Rock Dove is the original pigeon, ancestor to every feral pigeon. But, in stark contrast to the sad army of threadbare individuals that limp around the Bright Lights town centre today, this dapper-looking bird, with its iridescent headdress and black-barred, slate wings, was absolutely stunning.

Rather than retracing our steps, we walked inland and back to the town along narrow lanes with tall hedgerows. This added leg of the journey meant we saw birds that I hadn't expected; redpoll, willow warbler, chiffchaff, blackcap, and yellowhammer, and a couple more that were first-sightings; a lesser whitethroat, singing from the top of a hawthorn thicket, and the sighting of the day for me; a corn bunting, perched on an overhead wire, quivering its wings and stretching its beak wide open, like a feathered-Pavarotti, to produce just a few tiny, tinkling notes.

Back at the van we went through the list. Of the thirty-two species we'd hoped to see, we'd missed three; the peregrine, the whinchat, and, much to Jan's chagrin, the puffin. I reminded her that I'd never seen one either, and we promised ourselves a trip to the Farne Islands where we could see thousands.

On the plus side, we'd seen nine species that were not on the list, and a total of ten that I'd never seen before. A great day's birding. If only we could have been sure the large bird flying close to the surface, far out to sea, had been a gannet, and the pair of game birds that showed themselves all too briefly as they took off with a clapping of wings and disappeared over the hedgerow had been red-legged partridge, it would have been a round dozen. But that's the beauty of birding; we'd save them for another day.

* * *

Our trip up the coast heralded a long spell of glorious weather that showed the gatehouse garden at its stunning best. The back garden, from the pond all the way to the edge of the wood where the feeders were, I'd turned into a flower meadow – a striking mix of burnet, red and white campion, wild strawberries and knapweed, yellow rattle, pinks, thistles and teasel, bird's-foot trefoil, bloody cranesbill, dog-daisies, yellow and red poppies, purple loosestrife and corncockle – so I spent a lot of time over the next few weeks working on the commission.

The house on Primrose Terrace had no driveway, and the van wasn't the prettiest, so at Jan's insistence I'd started leaving it at the gatehouse and walking there when needs be, past the Post Office, down the ginnel and through the Hawksheads Estate.

I hadn't talked to Lenny since he was freed, but I'd seen him most days – his profile was a permanent fixture in his bedroom window, like Norman Bates's mother.

He was sitting on the windowsill, always facing the other way, with his left side to me, looking towards the gable end, so he never saw me.

A couple of times I spotted wisps of smoke drifting from the open window – there'd never been much he couldn't get away with, but he'd never been allowed to smoke in his bedroom – so at first I assumed he was just sitting there to have a crafty one, but then one day when I walked past I noticed a house martin flying into a nest a few feet from his window, and him craning his neck for a better view. Then he looked down and appeared to be writing something.

Surely not, I thought. After all the ribbing he'd given me over the years, all the piss-taking. No way. No, I was wrong, had to be.

It must have been early July before I saw him outdoors for the first time. Fred was cutting some flowers and Lenny was watering the garden. I went over to try and have a talk with him, but by the time I reached the hedge Fred was standing alone with half-a-dozen dahlias in one hand, and a pair of secateurs and the hosepipe held awkwardly in the other. He came to the hedge.

'He'll come round,' he said. 'Just give him time.'

* * *

The rest of the summer Jan and me went birding every chance we got. There were still construction vehicles coming and going so we mostly avoided the estate. I introduced her to the joys of sea-watching from the Bright Lights promenade on an overcast and blustery day.

We saw lots of dark shapes, ducks and grebes, a couple of petrels or shearwaters skimming the waves, and what I thought may have been a scoter, bobbing up and down far-out on the swell, but it wasn't her favourite type of birding, and, though I go at least once every autumn, Jan is always 'too busy'.

We travelled to a few out of the way places, too. We walked the edge of a salt-marsh, along rivers and over moors. I showed her the tarn where me and Lenny had camped. We were buzzed by a nightjar hawking low over the heath, saw a young cuckoo with its surrogate parent, a tiny wren, standing on its back and cramming a large moth into its voluminous orange gape, and laughed as a buzzard tried in vain to shake the coils out of a grass snake, swapping it from foot to foot, and back again, on the path fifty yards away.

I went on a solo visit to the reserve one morning in August and was greeted by the sight of five spoonbills – before then I'd seen a grand total of one in my life – at rest on an island in the lagoon.

I watched them for a good two hours and for the entire time they stood like sentinels, on one leg, bills beneath their wings and facing what little breeze there was that day. Not one of them saw fit to treat me to even a glimpse of that fabulous, prehistoric appendage.

I eventually got fed up of waiting so I did a tour of the reserve – saw a greenshank, a ruff, a hobby speeding over the reedbed – then returned, hoping the spoonbills had got bored themselves, but they were still exactly as they were.

'Are they real?' I joked to a fellow birder who'd been in the hide when I was there since early morning.

'I was beginning to wonder myself,' he laughed.

I thought he was serious. He saw my look.

'No,' he went on. 'Only joking. They were active when I got here first thing.' He nodded towards the five white stanchions. 'But they've been like that for hours now.'

I went home and told Jan. We had some dinner and I drove us back to the reserve. When we got there it was a completely different story. The five giants had come alive and were on the move, operating as a loose gang, striding speedily around the lagoon in water knee-deep, their feet almost clearing the surface with each step and their bills sweeping broad semicircles in search of fish and molluscs.

They were a hundred yards away to start with but in the time it took to remove the camera's lens cap they'd made their way, like speed-skaters, to the stretch of water in front of us, and we watched them, paddling backwards and forwards, bills snapping up their prey, until the evening sun had dipped below the horizon and the first bats appeared against the pinkness of the sky.

PART TEN

Monday 12th of May 1986

'We knew you were innocent all along, Joseph. We never doubted you for a minute, did we Fred. It was obvious that detective, that … that Dawson, he had it in for you from the start. He's a nasty piece of work he is. Putting you through all that. Putting *us* through all that. I don't understand … I don't know … how the judge could have let it go on for so long. Three times, and he had no evidence after all that. We should … we could … I mean, to even suggest that you were capable of such things … to think that you're anything like those others … it makes me ill just to … well it doesn't bear thinking about.'

Noreen hadn't stopped talking since they left the Bright Lights. She'd hardly taken a breath; seven months of stress and nervous energy finally released. Lenny sat behind her in the back and wondered who she bought her speed from and if she had any spare.

'That reporter from the radio seems nice,' she continued. 'She was definitely on your side. I wouldn't think they're supposed to pick sides, but she seemed to have a soft spot for you, the way she was looking at you. She kept giving you a little smile, did you see, Joseph? Well, no, you won't have been able to see her from where you were, probably, but she was definitely pleased with how it turned out … with the verdict, you could tell.'

She finally stopped to draw breath, and dabbed at her eyes with a tissue. Fred drove in silence and kept his eyes firmly on the road. He turned off the bypass and drove slowly through the narrow lanes. There was a sudden whoosh of air as he wound down his window and the smell of mayflowers filled the car. Lenny leaned back in his seat, closed his eyes, and took a deep breath. A gust of honeysuckle came and went, fleeting hints of yarrow and marigold.

He heard a crow's harsh call, a magpie's machine-gun cackle, the distant buzz of farm machinery. He got a faint waft of slurry and an image of Andy Crowe came to mind. He opened his eyes.

Noreen sensed his tension, reached between the front seats and took his hand in hers. He pulled it free and folded his arms. She tried to hold back her tears, dabbed her eyes again.

'We're nearly home, love,' she said. 'It's over now.'

'It'll be like a freakshow,' he said. 'I'll be an exhibit.'

'People have been very supportive, Joseph—'

'Of you, maybe—'

'Of us all, love … people care. Everyone's been asking after you, love.'

'They were just being nosey. I hope you didn't tell them anything.'

Noreen gave up and they travelled in silence. Fred pulled up outside the Post Office and Lenny got out of the car and set off up the path. Noreen followed a few steps behind. Fred got out and locked the car. Marjory Woods was standing across the road, and she raised her hand in greeting. Fred leaned on the car roof as she approached.

'Hiya Fred, love,' she said. She watched as the Post Office door closed behind Noreen and Lenny. 'He's home, then.'

'Aye. After all that, they'd no evidence.'

'That's wonderful, you must be so relieved. How is he?'

'Oh, you know, feeling sorry for himself.'

'Well, that's understandable, I suppose—'

'Aye, well. He'll be fine. Noreen's my main concern if I'm honest. Been through the mill, she has.'

'I can imagine.' There was a brief silence. 'Do you think Lenny would want to see our John? I know John would like to see him.'

'I wish he would. It'd do him the world of good. Do you have his number? Maybe if I ask him … he says he doesn't want to see anybody, but …'

Marjory opened her bag and rummaged for a pen. Fred opened the car, leaned inside and took a pad and pen from the glove-box. He handed them to Marjory.

'You're well-organised,' she said.

'Aye, well, you know, a place for everything and all that.'

Marjory rested the paper on the car roof and started to write.

'How is John, anyway? he asked. 'Is he doing ok?'

'He seems to be doing well, Fred. I don't know where he gets all his money from, I really don't. He paid cash for that gatehouse and just uses it as a studio now that he's moved in with Jan.' She rolled her eyes. 'He's determined he's going to be an artist. He's had his mind set on it for as long as I can remember. I offered him some of the money I got from the cottage, you know, till he gets on his feet. He'll be getting it anyway, one day, but he wouldn't hear of it.'

'He'll have made big money in Holland, I dare say.'

'He must have. Mind you, he says he worked every hour god sends over there, lots of overtime, hardly had any time off.' She laughed, shook her head. 'He's certainly made up for it lately, I have to say. Anyway, him and Jan are happy, that's the main thing. It's her birthday tomorrow. They're going off for the day birdwatching somewhere and we're all going for a Chinese meal later on.'

'That's grand. I'm ever so pleased. He's a smashing lad. They seem like a good match, what little I've seen.'

'She's a card is Jan, I'll tell you. There'll never be a dull moment in their house, that's for sure.'

She handed back the pad and pen. Fred looked at her. 'Do you know what it was happened between them,' he said.

'I'm not sure I know what you mean—'

'There was something went on, I'm sure of it. They were best friends, couldn't be separated'

'Oh, I don't know, Fred. I think they just took their own paths, you know, when our John went abroad. John's never said anything and he's always been open with me.'

'Oh well, maybe I'm wrong.'

Fred looked at the pad, then at Marjory.

'The top one's the house number,' she said. 'The other's for the gatehouse. He's usually at the house these days.'

Fred folded the paper and put it in his pocket. 'Ok, love, I'll see what I can do.'

'I think it'd do them both good to have a catch-up. Give Lenny our best and tell Noreen we're all thinking of her.'

'I will, thanks love. She'll be a while before she can face people. Apart from church, of course. She'll be spending a lot of time up there I imagine.' He put the pen and paper back in the glove-box and closed the door. He looked at Marjory. 'I don't know as she'll ever be right again, love, not really.'

Marjory put her hand on his arm. 'Things will soon be back to normal, love,' she said.

Fred sighed and shook his head. 'I'm not so sure what normal is any more, Marjory.'

Saturday 17th of May 1986

Noreen watched as Lenny moved soggy cornflakes around in his bowl. He hadn't eaten the solids, just kept pressing the bottom of his spoon into the sodden mass and watching as milk spilled over the edge, then sucking it up, and repeat, but at least he'd stayed downstairs today. That was a start.

Every night she'd been woken by his nocturnal shouts, his footsteps up and down the stairs. He tried to be quiet, she knew, but Noreen was the lightest of sleepers these days, woke at the slightest sound, and then had trouble getting off again.

She didn't like to badger him, but he needed to put it all behind him and make a fresh start. He was beginning to smell, too. His bed needed changing, but it was awkward, with him spending all his time in his room. And she hated the smell of stale cigarette smoke. It wasn't only his bedroom and the landing anymore. It was beginning to spread through the rest of the house, even into the shop. It was costing a fortune in air-freshener. Fred had wanted to raise the subject, but she said it would only cause an argument, and that they should count their blessings. At least he wasn't taking drugs anymore. The one good thing to come from all of this. Maybe he'd stop smoking as well, given time.

She looked as he stared into his bowl.

'Your dad's got a lot to do in the garden this afternoon,' she said, matter-of-factly. 'When he's finished in the Post Office.'

Lenny didn't respond. He'd hardly spoken a word to either of them since he got home, nothing civil, anyway, but he obviously needed to talk to *someone*; she'd heard him speaking quietly to himself in his bedroom when she'd been cleaning upstairs, nothing she could make out, even with her ear pressed to the door.

Noreen carried on. 'He's rushed off his feet he is. Maybe you could give him a hand. It's a good forecast and you could do with some fresh air. You want nothing being cooped up in your bedroom all day. You could at least get dressed. All your shirts and pants are clean and ironed, and you've plenty of clean 'jamas in the airing cupboard.'

Lenny had made a heap of the remaining cornflakes in the centre of the bowl and now had the spoon suspended from his index finger and thumb and was swinging it like a wrecking-ball and demolishing his previous work.

Noreen pretended not to notice and went on. 'He's out in the greenhouse now, actually,' she said, 'getting some flowers ready for me to take up this afternoon. It's Pentecost tomorrow. Whitsunday. It's a time for new beginnings, Joseph, for rebirth. I do wish you'd come with us, son. It would be a good way to draw a line, don't you think?'

Lenny dropped the spoon in the bowl, got up from the table, and went upstairs. He sat on the bed and picked up the piece of paper and looked at it again, at the two phone numbers. He stared at it for a minute, then put it back on the bedside table and went and sat on the windowsill.

His first day at home he'd noticed an industrious pair of house martins, busy renovating an old nest under the eaves just a few feet along from his bedroom window. Even with the sash-window fully opened, they didn't seem to mind him being there, and he'd been watching them at close-quarters for most of every day since, coming and going, fetching mud from the sand quarry, applying the finishing touches to what looked like a tiny wattle and daub igloo.

A couple of days ago he'd heard the two birds twittering away to each other outside the window, and when he looked out they were both clinging to the outside of the nest and one of them was holding a single white feather in its beak. It seemed the renovation was complete, and work on the inside furnishings had begun. He waited for her to go inside – he assumed it was her - but she didn't take it in straight away. First they spent a good minute-and-a-half, chittering away to each other, before he flew off and she took the feather inside.

He wondered what they'd been talking about.

He sat and watched them all day, flying backwards and forwards, bringing feather after feather, and as he watched, he wondered how they came about them, whether they landed to pick them up, or caught them in mid-air. After a while, he noticed something else, something that he was at a loss to explain; he realised that every one of the feathers they brought was white. What were the chances of that? he wondered.

He thought maybe they were chicken feathers from some small-holding, but he soon abandoned that theory; surely there'd be a mix of colours. The feathers they brought were uniformly brilliant-white. They had no other markings. He thought at one point that she must have been telling him the colour scheme she wanted – 'I want white' - but then it came to him; she must have found a swan's grooming platform by the banks of the canal, and had been telling him where to find it. That was it, he had no doubt; and anyway, whatever the truth of it, he liked this theory.

But things had quietened off since then, and this morning there'd been no activity at all. He was disappointed. He thought they might have abandoned the project for some reason. He started to worry that maybe something had happened to one of them. He sat for another hour or so, and was fearing the worst, when a tiny face appeared in the nest's entrance and one of the birds dropped out of the hole and her white rump receded into the distance.

It had to be *her*, because there was an egg in the nest. He was sure of it. That's why it had gone so quiet. He watched for another half-hour but neither bird came to the nest. That must be it for today, he thought. He reckoned she'd lay one egg a day, and wouldn't start to incubate until there was a full clutch, so that they'd all hatch together. She would probably lay four or five eggs, meaning the clutch would be complete on Wednesday or Thursday.

He'd been sitting in the window-frame with his knees up for a couple of hours and his leg had gone numb. He swung himself round and stood up and limped across the room. He found an old notebook and a pen in the drawer and sat on the bed. On the first unused sheet he wrote ***House Martin*** at the top, and beneath this, at the left-hand side, he wrote:

Saturday May 17th – Egg 1

He used the paper with the phone numbers to mark the page, then closed the notebook and put it on the bedside table.

Fucking hell, he thought, I'm getting as bad as John. He smiled to himself. No, John would have given them names by now; Dean and Millicent, or, more likely, Scorcese and Luther-King. Chuzzlewit, maybe.

He got off the bed and went to the wardrobe. He opened the doors. The smell of fresh laundry, jeans and shirts on hangers, all equally spaced along the rail. He took them out, a hanger at a time, and tried them on. Some of the jeans and tee shirts were new. Noreen had obviously believed he'd be coming home, that her prayers would be answered. The rest had been there since he first moved out twelve years ago, and he was shocked to find that everything still fit, in fact it was all too big; the shirts only fit where they touched, and the jeans and trousers needed a belt to hold them up.

Behind the last hanger he found his binoculars in their case hanging from the rail. He took them out, put the strap around his neck, and went to the window. The hinges and thumbwheel were a bit stiff and he worked them a few times to loosen them, then sat back on the sill and looked out on the garden.

Fred had shut the shop and was busy planting out his dahlias. He'd sunk wooden stakes into the soil, a couple of dozen in all, and strung twine at varying heights between them to support the young plants. He'd started to dig the holes ready for planting and was now standing with his hands on his hips, leaning backwards to stretch his back muscles.

Through the open window Lenny could hear him talking.

'You'll have to wait a minute, mate,' he said.

Lenny wondered who he was talking to. He raised the binoculars and scanned the garden.

Fred went on. 'I'm not as young as I was.'

Lenny couldn't see or hear anyone. He thought maybe a neighbour was talking to him from behind the hedge, but there was nobody there. He focused back on Fred. He'd stopped stretching and was wiping his shirt-sleeve across his forehead. He tucked his shirt tail back into his waistband and reached for the spade that was leaning on the hedge.

'Come on then,' he said, as he started to dig. 'Let's see what we can find.'

Lenny decided he must be talking to himself - not unusual for Fred - but then he saw it, standing in the border a few feet from where he was digging, a blackbird, flicking its wings and tail impatiently, an opportunist waiting for worms and grubs.

Fred levered a spadeful of soil from the ground and dropped it next to the hole. He split it two or three times with the edge of the spade.

'There you go, mate, fill yer boots.'

The blackbird jumped forward and began to rummage through the freshly-turned earth. A song thrush had been watching from the hedge-top and it dropped to the border and joined the feast. The blackbird made a half-hearted attempt to scare it away, but it took no notice, and Fred soldiered on with the digging and the two birds shared the bonanza, carrying tasty morsels away to their nests, the blackbird in the privet hedge, the thrush somewhere further afield.

Lenny watched as Fred dug the last of the holes and leaned the spade against the hedge. The thrush seemed to know when the food supply was about to dry up and had made itself scarce, but the blackbird was still standing expectantly a yard or two away. Fred turned his attention to the numerous small pots lined up along the path behind him.

'That's it mate, sorry,' he said. 'I've done digging for now.' He knelt and took hold of the first pot. The blackbird remained where it was and cocked its head to one side. 'These are dahlias,' he went on. He inspected the young plant. 'This is a single, but there's some pompoms to go in, too.' He turned the pot over and the plant came loose into his free hand. He dropped it into the hole and uncovered a worm as he replaced the soil.

He leaned back and pointed. 'There you go,' he said, 'you've missed one.' The blackbird didn't move so Fred picked up the worm and dropped it a bit closer. He watched as the bird took it and flew off. 'Oh, it's ok,' he said, with mock-sarcasm. 'No need to thank me. Not a problem.' He turned to look at the long line of pots, picked up the one nearest, then threw a quick glance up at Lenny's bedroom window. 'Don't you go worrying about it,' he said. 'I've a mountain of work to climb, but I'll manage. I always do.'

Friday 4th of July

Lenny had finished his breakfast – a large bowl of cereal followed by a full English, with double egg and fried bread - and was hurriedly mopping ketchup and egg-yolk from his plate with a third slice of bread and butter and washing it down with gulps of tea.

Noreen looked across the table at Fred and they both smiled.

'Someone's got his appetite back,' she said.

'And a bit of blummin colour in his face, too,' Fred replied.

Lenny pushed back his chair and stood up. He picked up the teapot and refilled his mug. 'Yeah, whatever,' he said. 'There's something I need to do,' and he disappeared upstairs.

'He's certainly on the mend,' Fred said. He reached across the table and took Noreen's hands in his. 'What a difference, eh, love, when you think how he was a few weeks ago.'

'I knew when he started to let me clean his room and change his bed … I could have swung for you when you brought it up and put him on the spot, but you were right, love, it couldn't go on … anyway, I knew then that he was getting better.'

'I could see you were at the end of your tether, love, so I had to say something, and I'd rather it was me he fell out with.'

Noreen squeezed his hands and got up. She went to the sink and filled the kettle.

'That was nice,' she said. 'The other night. I can't even

remember the last time we sat down as a family and watched television together.'

'Aye, it's a long time ago.'

'I imagine it must have been Watch with Mother or something like that, or maybe Bill and Ben,' she said, and she giggled, just like she used to, Fred thought, and he felt better than he had in a long time.

Noreen refilled the teapot and sat back at the table. 'I think he might have stopped smoking too, Fred,' she said. 'Or nearly, at any rate. There's still a smell in his room, but it lingers doesn't it, and there's hardly any on the landing anymore, and his ashtray's not been used since I cleaned it last week.'

'I know he hasn't stopped altogether, love. I've been finding a few dog-ends on the path under his window, not many, mind, but one or two.'

'That would explain it then. I think he's started to get interested in birds again,' she said. 'His binoculars have taken up residence on the windowsill.' She lowered her voice. 'I have a little nosey while I'm in there,' she said. 'He must have had that packet of tobacco for a month or more now, and there's still some left. It's tinder-dry, too.'

She poured them both a fresh cup of tea.

* * *

Back in his room he took a drink of tea and put the mug between his legs on the windowsill. Since the first egg was laid he'd been watching the nest every day.

He couldn't be sure he hadn't missed anything – he couldn't keep his eyes on the nest all the time - so he wasn't a hundred percent sure of the size of the clutch, but based on the first time he saw one of the birds taking food to the nest - meaning incubation had started – and the fact that the weather had been fine, he thought there may have been as many as six eggs.

He soon found out that the adults took turns at incubating the eggs – he'd witnessed the shift changeovers - and as the male and female are identical, he had no idea which of the birds was which.

There was just one nervy spell during incubation, when it rained continuously and the adults stopped bringing food – it would have been hard to come by in such weather - and stayed in the nest. He thought all would be lost; surely they'd all starve, he thought, but it only lasted for a couple of days, then the parents redoubled their efforts and were soon back on track.

He looked up at the row of tiny heads protruding from the nest's entrance-hole, saw their dark caps and their white chins. Their constant jockeying for position had displaced some of the mortar-work and made the hole bigger, but there was still only room for three heads. However, there had definitely been signs they were operating a rota system to allow more to be fed, so he stuck with his original estimate of six and completed his records accordingly:

House Martin

Saturday May 17th – Egg 1

Sunday May 18th – Egg 2

Monday May 19th – Egg 3

Tuesday May 20th – Egg 4

Wednesday May 21st – Egg 5

Thursday May 22nd – Egg 6

Saturday June 7th – First egg/s hatched –
adults removing shells
Sunday June 8th – more egg/s hatched and shells removed
Monday June 9th -15th – one adult fetching food?
Sunday June 16th – adults fetching food and
getting rid of shit sacks
Tuesday June 18th – heavy rain – no feeding – birds all in nest
Wednesday June 19th – same again – oh no!
Thursday June 20th – feeding again – phew!
Thursday June 26th – first head appears in entrance
Saturday June 28th – more heads – how many???
Thursday July 3rd – Fledging soon!!?

* * *

He watched the nest for the rest of the day, but none of the chicks seemed inclined to make that final move. By late afternoon both parents had taken up positions on the gutter and begun twittering their encouragement when, suddenly, one of the chicks that had been in the rear of the nest suddenly squirmed its way between those in the entrance and seemed to be fired from the nest. The youngster took to the air and one of the adults took off and followed it around the end of the building and out of sight.

Lenny was overjoyed and was almost filling up, but there was no time, as a sudden flurry of young birds took the pioneer's lead and vacated the nest en masse. Lenny counted four, making five in total. He waited a few more minutes, but there was no sign of any more. Just five then, he thought.

He opened the window fully, knelt on the windowsill and craned his neck to see if he could get a look at his newly-fledged babies but, though he could hear their busy twitterings close-by, he couldn't see them at all.

He picked up the notebook and completed his records:

Friday July 4th – 17.20 pm – 5 FLEDGLINGS –
INDEPENDENCE DAY!!!

Saturday 5th of July

Fred had closed the shop at lunchtime and was pottering around doing a few jobs in the garden. He was kneeling on a cushion on the path, weeding the border when he sensed a presence. He straightened up and shaded his eyes with his hand.

Lenny was standing at the side of the house. It was the first time he'd set foot outside since he got home. He'd changed into a pair of jeans and a tee-shirt, and had brushed his hair. He was staring at the gable-end of the house, at the row of young birds lined up on the telephone wire, chittering busily. Fred stood up and walked to Lenny's side.

'They nest here every year,' he said, 'the swallows.'

'They're not swallows, they're house martins.'

'Same thing, isn't it?'

Lenny harumphed. He pointed at a red dahlia flower, then at a purple cosmos.

'And they're the same as them, are they?'

'No, course not.' He looked at the birds again on the wire. 'So what did you say they are?'

'House martins.'

'Eee, you learn summat every day.' He went back and kneeled on his cushion. Lenny followed him.

'Is there anything I can do?' he asked.

Fred was taken aback. 'There's always plenty to do, son,' he said. He stood up again. 'What's brought this on?'

Lenny spun on his heels. 'Ok, I won't bother if you don't want me to—'

'No, no, of course I want you to. It's not that, it's just … well … it's a first, that's all.'

'I'm going stir crazy up there.'

Fred looked at the sky. 'It was looking like rain before,' he said, 'but it's clearing up. You can do some watering if you like.'

'Whatever.'

Fred went to the shed and came back reeling out the hose-pipe behind him. He handed the business-end to Lenny and started to show him how it worked. Lenny took it from him.

'You must think I'm thick.'

He turned the hose on and walked to the corner of the house where he got the best view of the newly-fledged chicks being fed.

'I'll start here,' he said.

Fred returned to his cushion and carried on with the weeding. Lenny moved slowly around the border, rarely taking his eyes from the martin chicks. Fred looked up occasionally to see how he was getting on, glad that dahlias were such thirsty plants. Any other plant would have been drowned by now, he thought, and smiled to himself.

The weeding finished, Fred took them to the midden and returned with the secateurs to cut a bunch of dahlias for Noreen. He'd cut a half-dozen or so when Lenny suddenly appeared at his side.

'Here,' he said. 'I'm going in,' and he forced the hose into Fred's hand and disappeared indoors.

Fred started to call after him, but it was too late. He was wondering what had come over him when he looked and saw John coming across the street.

* * *

Upstairs he took his Hamlyn Guide from the shelf and reclined on the bed. He opened it at the first page.

John never got tired of watching birds. He could sit and watch the same bird species over and over and still find them captivating. Lenny had never been like that. He'd always seen birdwatching as being akin to trainspotting, where you underlined each species in the book as you saw it, and that was that.

The first one underlined was the great-crested grebe. They'd seen plenty of those at the reserve. He remembered the grebe species; some of the easiest birds to identify in summer, but almost impossible to tell apart in winter, when they'd lost their flamboyant breeding plumage. Then, to him, they all seemed to be in monochrome.

Not for John. He was a whizz at identifying grebes in winter. Even on a blustery day when they were bobbing up and down and diving under the waves a hundred yards off the Bright Lights promenade, he could tell the most difficult species apart by the colour of their eyes, the size of their beaks, the length of a bird's neck and its angle in relation to their bodies, even the steepness of the forehead.

'Can you see … hang-on, wait till it comes up again … there, see how the pale cheek-patches almost meet at the back of the neck?' he'd say.

Lenny laughed to himself. 'No, can I fuck,' he said.

He had to turn quite a few more pages before he came to the next species he'd underlined, the cormorant. They'd seen plenty of those, too, at the reserve, half-submerged, like an overloaded barge, all the air squeezed from their feathers, diving sleekly beneath the water's surface. He remembered trying to guess where they'd resurface, being amazed by how far they travelled underwater. He could still picture them, afterwards, bellies full, standing in a line with their wings open, like a paper-chain drying in the breeze.

He came to the bittern, remembered seeing one, almost invisible against the reeds, and the heron, then the spoonbill. He recalled their excitement when they'd seen that weird-looking specimen, the most improbable-looking bird he'd ever seen, especially in flight, with its spatulate bill, and its neck and legs stretched straight out front and back.

And on he went, past the swans and the geese, to the ducks, the birds of prey, the waders. He tried to bring to mind the occasion they'd seen the rarer species, like the garganey and the scaup. He pictured the hobby catching dragonflies over the reedbeds, the peregrine cutting through the murmuration, like a barracuda through a shoal of sardines, a drop of detergent dripped on an oil-slick.

He looked at the pictures of turnstone and sanderling, dunlin and knot, and remembered the day - almost six years ago - when he'd sat on the railings on the Bright Lights prom and watched those tiny birds hurrying around feeding along the edge of the receding tide. He felt a chill and a shudder went through him as he remembered the chaos he'd brought to the post office the next day. He thought about Fred and Noreen, downstairs, always there for him, no matter what, and Andy Crowe's words came back to him.

'*Never had one visiting order from their only son … they'll be gutted … my parents would have lit a fag with it … do whatever the fuck it takes …* '

'You're right, Andy, I don't know I'm fucking born,' he said.

He lifted the top of the counterpane and wiped his eyes

and face. He left the book open, face down on the bed, and went back to the windowsill.

The sash-window was still down. A squadron of swifts hurtled past, screaming as they went. He could hear the steady hum of traffic on the bypass, and in the distance an evening heat haze shimmered the swathe of yellow gorse that seemed to hang above the sand quarry.

To his right he could see a large area of Hawksheads Wood. He turned and put his cheek to the window and could just make out the line of ash trees at the edge of the wood, and the Scots pine he fell from, twenty years ago, trying to get to the sparrowhawks' nest. John couldn't climb to save his life so they'd had to wait another year to add that egg to their collection.

He thought about their first mushroom session, imagined the Crowe twins watching their shenanigans, dancing around and chanting like lunatics, and felt his face flush.

'You'll be ok, Andy,' he said.

He envied him his resilience.

He swung his legs off the sill and went and sat back on the bed. He picked up the bird book and carried on where he'd left off. He skimmed past the gulls and the terns, and froze when he came to the auks; the puffin, guillemot and razorbill. He cast his mind back to the crashing waves and the sheer sandstone cliffs, pictured him and John, stumbling, falling onto the shingle beach. God, they'd been lucky that day. That was once the closest he'd ever come to death, but not any more.

He flicked through a few more pages, past the pigeons, the doves and the parrots. He put down the book, closed his eyes, and became lost in a warm nostalgia. He remembered things he'd long forgotten; camping at the tarn; the cuckoo's deafening call; the nightjar churring away across the water;

John's hilarious attempt to skin up; Black Sabbath blaring out, the silence that followed; the brooding tawny owl that brushed his face with its wings and left him hanging from a high branch by the crooks of his knees like a trapeze artist; the mistle thrush that caught John's woolly hat with its toes and carried it off; the bull chasing them across the field.

It seemed to him now that these adventures had all happened on the same day, a wonderful, halcyon day, a day long gone, when the sun was shining and the sky was a clear, azure blue, when the woodlands and hedgerows were in full bloom and the world smelled fresh, when it seemed there were no rules, no limits to how far they could go, nobody to tell them what they could and couldn't do.

His reverie was broken by the sound of a knock on the door - a light tap - and Noreen's voice. Fred had gone to get fish and chips for tea and would be back soon.

He picked up the book and carried on, and by the time he reached the reed bunting, the last species to be underlined, he was beginning to think that one day, if only to tie up a loose end, maybe he'd like to finish what he'd started.

PART ELEVEN

Wednesday 5th of November 1986

When I first met him, I thought Les Beech was the most obnoxious man I'd ever met. It was Mum and Archie's wedding day and we were on the car park outside the Bright Lights Registry Office. I'd travelled with Archie and we were there in good time, so he went to take his seat inside, and I was having a quick smoke before Mum and Jan arrived with Aunty Mary and Uncle Brian.

Rod and Roz were already there and Rod came over and we were having a laugh about something when a large, silver-coloured car turned into the car park. I saw Rod's face cloud over, and he looked at me, took a deep breath, and exhaled like a weightlifter.

'Brace yourself,' he said, his voice laced with dread. 'It's *the big I am*. Archie's honoured he's seen fit to leave his Island paradise.'

Crammed in behind the steering-wheel, *the big I am* had a row of rear-view mirrors that stretched the full width of the windscreen, and he reversed the car into a space without turning his head. He opened the door, looked at the markings on the ground, closed the door, pulled forward, and reversed again, three more times, to make sure the car was exactly in the centre of the parking space. He opened the door again and grunted his satisfaction, then he reached up a fat paw and took hold of the roof's rain gutter and hauled his bulk from the car.

'Island paradise?' I said.

'The Isle of Man. Been there fifteen years or more. Master of the Lodge and all that. Owns half of the Bright Lights, and doesn't see why he should pay tax.'

Rod went to greet him and I followed a couple of paces behind. *The big I am* turned to Rod as we approached and pointed to a tiny stain that looked like bird-shit on the car's front wing.

'Kids today,' he griped. 'I asked the lad next door to clean the motor the other day, said I'd pay him, obviously, but he didn't want to know. I said you're going nowhere in this life, son. You could have got your haircut finished, but anyway, don't you worry, someone else will be glad of the fifty-pence.'

He was about sixty, with the brows of a shih tzu on the face of a bulldog, and had a thick, grey moustache that didn't fill his top lip and looked like it was clipped into his nostrils. He was as tall as Archie but twice as far around. He wore an ill-fitting suit, with two-inches of cuff showing, the trousers at half-mast, and had one solitary medal pinned to his chest.

They shook hands.

'And how are you Rodney? Business thriving?' He didn't wait for an answer. He pointed at the car again. 'It's due a service. Not until next month, but we may as well get it done while I'm here. I'm going back on Saturday so I'll bring it in tomorrow.' He winked at Rod. 'It'll need no work done, and you can post-date the paperwork. No point having a mechanic in the family if you can't make the most of him now and then, eh?'

He turned to me, looked me up and down, like a slave-owner at market. I half-expected him to squeeze my haunches and peel back my lips to inspect my teeth.

'And you are?'

'Oh, sorry,' Rod said. 'This is John, Marjory's son. John, this is Uncle Les. Archie's brother.'

'The best man, son, never doubt it.'

Archie had never mentioned a best man, and for a second I thought he was joking, that he was a 'character', as they say. I was about to laugh, but Rod caught my eye and shook his head discreetly.

I offered my hand and he took it in his and proceeded to crush it, until I squeezed back and he released his grip. He put his hand in his trouser pocket and I could see the movement as he got the blood flowing again.

'So, Marjory's your mother.'

'That's right,' I said.

'So that would make you Frank Woods' son, then?'

'It would.' Fucking hell, I thought, not much gets past you.

He opened his mouth to say something, but thought better of it, and there was an uncomfortable silence, then he muttered something I didn't catch, something about being under instructions.

'Well,' he said, finally. 'Better get inside, see if the condemned man has any last requests.'

* * *

And the day had got off to such a good start.

Mum wanted me to give her away, and not wanting Jan to feel left out she asked her to be Matron of Honour.

'It's only going to be a small ceremony. There'll be no bridesmaids to organise or anything like that, but me and you'll sort out the flowers, the reception, and all that, and on the day, if you can just make sure everyone's where they're supposed to be, Jan, love, that'd be great.'

Jan got a lot of mileage out of that last instruction.

There were only two cars going from Yelland. In the first there was Archie and myself, and Archie's shop manager, Evelyn, and her husband, Sid.

In the second there was Aunty Mary and Uncle Brian in the front, with Mum and Jan in the back.

Jan referred to the cars as Car One and Car Two.

'John, Archie, you two are in Car One. Sid, Evelyn, you two are in Car One, too. Mary, Brian, you two are in Car Two with us two.

She had Mum laughing all day. She thought Jan was the funniest person she'd ever met.

'Give over Jan, you daft apeth, you'll have my mascara running.'

* * *

The ceremony went smoothly, and we went back to the Eagle and Child for the reception. There was no all-day opening back then, and we had the place to ourselves until seven o'clock. We got there at about one, and the buffet was already laid out. Quite a few friends and neighbours had turned up and the room was busy. I thought I might see Fred and Noreen, but they'd called in earlier and dropped off a card.

At the registry office Les hadn't been best-pleased when told I'd been charged with looking after the rings, and he seemed less than impressed when he saw that the reception was an informal affair with no 'top table'. Archie had a word in his ear and seemed to smooth it over, and Les got himself a plate, piled it high with food, and went and sat sideways on a stool in the corner of the bar.

The afternoon was just what the happy couple had planned; a delicious buffet, plenty of laughs, a good few drinks quaffed, and a stream of fifties and sixties hits on the stereo. At one point Evelyn and Sid succumbed to calls for them to show off their eye-catching dance moves as the rest of the room stood on the side-lines and whooped their encouragement and appreciation.

I knew it was going to be a long day, so I made sure I got tucked into the food straight away.

Les didn't move from his seat at all, just sat there, drinking whiskies, speaking only when spoken to, and then but briefly. I noticed he had a piece of paper in his hand that he kept opening and browsing then folding again.

When the remains of the buffet had been cleared away, he called Archie over and they had a few words. Les was getting a bit het up. Archie looked around and saw that nobody else had noticed. Mum and Jan were playing pool and having a right laugh, and he took Les by the elbow and led him out through the door and into the foyer. I went and pretended to play the fruit-machine by the open doorway so I could see and hear what was going on.

'A wedding without a best man?' Les said. 'Who's ever heard the likes?'

'I told you on the phone—'

'Well, I know you did, but what about tradition, Archie? Eh?' He waved the piece of paper. 'I made some notes. It'll only take a few minutes, and it'll give it the feel of a proper wedding.'

Archie laughed sardonically. 'A proper wedding, eh?

'I don't mean it like that, I just—'

'Look, Les, the day's not about you, not this time, so put

your notes away. I've sat through one of your best man speeches before, remember.'

'That was a long time ago—'

'Seems like yesterday to me—'

'It was a funny speech—'

'Funny how?'

'People were laughing.'

'They were embarrassed, Les.'

'Nonsense—'

'The speech certainly was. It was all lies, fantasies—'

'That's a bit strong, Archie. I admit I may have embellished the truth a bit—'

'You made it sound like we had the stag night in ancient Rome.'

'Now you're being ridiculous—'

'Maybe I am, but you know what I mean. Joyce was never sure, not a hundred percent—'

'I had to say *something*. How many blokes have their stag night in their local pub—'

'That's what I wanted—'

'There were six of us—'

'And I'm still in touch with the other four—'

'You were in bed by midnight.'

'Like I was every night before and have been every night since … look, Les, let's be honest, if you'd had your way I'd never have made it to my wedding. I'd have been dumped naked on the M6 or chained to the Isle of Man ferry.'

'Yes, well, it'd maybe have been for the best—'

'You know nothing about it. Me and Joyce had twenty good years, let me tell you. Who knows, if the grandchildren weren't on the other side of the world … well, like I say, who knows.'

There was a short silence. He looked at the piece of paper in Les's hand.

'Let me guess,' he said, 'some barbed comments about Joyce, about me being on wife number two, something about how no woman has ever managed to tie you down. Am I close? And I'll bet you couldn't resist a dig at you-know-who, could you?'

Les looked sheepishly back at Archie. 'I have to admit, I was tempted, but no, not a word, I promise. And as for no woman ever tying me down, it's true—'

'I don't remember any of them trying very hard—'

Les's face turned scarlet. 'Well,' he spluttered, 'I'm shocked, really I am. That was below the belt.'

They stood, Les red-faced and staring at the floor, Archie with his hands on his hips, facing the front door like he was hoping Les would use it. Then Archie must have decided there was no point leaving things unsaid, that one big clearing of the air was preferable to letting things fester until next time.

'I've never forgotten that speech, bigging yourself up, putting me down. The budding tycoon with the property portfolio, the little brother, pencil behind his ear and a sink-plunger in his hand.'

Les said something I didn't hear, and Archie waved his hand dismissively, and carried on.

'I'd barely been married an hour,' he said, 'and you turned to my new bride, do you remember? "Don't worry, love", you said. "When he hits hard times I'll always throw some work his way. I'll bail him out".'

'And I always have—'

'Bail me out? You've never bailed me out. I've turned down paying work to do jobs for you.'

'What do you mean, paying work? You've made a fortune

out of me over the years.'

'I've made precisely nothing. You won't spend. I have to lower my standards every time I do a job for you. And my prices. If anything, it's me that's bailed you out. You're a ten-bob millionaire Les, no better than a slum landlord. Rachman would have balked—'

Les finally blew. 'That's enough, Archie. I won't listen to any more of this. If you'd like me to leave, just say so.'

There was a stunned silence. Archie let out a resigned sigh and put his hand on Les's shoulder.

'Look, I'm sorry, Les, ok? I went too far and I'm sorry. We've all had a bit to drink, so let's leave it. And no, no I don't want you to go. I just want you to be a bloke who's a guest at his brother's wedding, and not make the day all about you.'

Mum and Jan were still playing pool and Mum was laughing. Archie smiled.

'You hear that? That's who today's all about, Les. Not you. Not me.'

Les had returned to his normal colour.

'You really love her, don't you?'

'I do that, Les.' he said.

Les gripped Archie's arm at the elbow.

'I'm pleased for you,' he said, 'and I don't plan on falling out with my only brother, not on his wedding day, best man or no best man, so I'll consider myself told, we'll call a truce, and you'll let me buy you a drink.' Les pulled Archie in close and they stood and hugged. They seemed to be out of practice, and I was wondering how long it had been since they'd last shared a hug, when Mum appeared at my side, merrily drunk, with a pool cue in her hand. She put her free hand on my shoulder.

'Aww, look,' she said. 'I'd no idea they were so close.'

Then Jan turned up. 'Come on Marjory, this isn't where you're supposed to be,' she said, and they gave me a kiss sandwich and disappeared back to the pool table.

I put twenty-pence in the fruit-machine and pressed the button. I watched Archie and Les walk back into the bar. As Les went to put the paper in his side pocket I could see his hand dithering and when they'd passed I saw he'd missed, and the speech was laying there on the carpet.

* * *

I picked it up and went into the foyer. Two leather armchairs sat at right-angles to each other on either side of a low coffee table. I sat and opened the paper.

It wasn't a speech as such, just a series of prompts. Two sheets of A4, stapled together, full of abbreviations. Most meant nothing to me. Some were too cryptic, others just scribbles that I couldn't decipher, but some were clear enough; – *dynamic, good looking, solvent, a great catch / anyway enough about me – women chased me but caught Archie – first stag – 6 of us, couldn't do worse – proved me wrong – didn't have one – Archie makes kitchens, I make money – he must love the taste of marzipan –* most of it just recycled, infantile stuff – *Honeymoon / going to Bangor for a fortnight – best man like body at funeral / the less he says the better* – a reference to Archie's first wife – *allergic to almond paste.* Then, on the last sheet, at the very end of the notes, he'd written:

Me and Archie – unlucky – missed war – National Service – proud to serve blah blah (SHOW MEDAL). * ~~*FW got a national dis service medal? moving quickly on*~~ * TOASTS

I put the notes in my pocket and went back inside. Archie and Les were drinking at the bar and they seemed fine. Archie finished his drink and left him to it and went and joined Mum. Les spent the rest of the afternoon back on his stool at the bar, like a trapdoor spider, roping in unsuspecting punters, buying them malt whiskies, whether they liked it or not, getting more and more pissed, no doubt sharing with them the hard-learned lessons life had taught him.

On the pool table it was winner-stays-on and Jan was having a great time. She was a demon at pool and was taking on all-comers.

'You should play with a handicap,' I said.

'Come on then,' she laughed. 'We're playing doubles, you can be mine.'

She was right, too. I've never been any good at pool and got us knocked off in our first game. There were no more challengers so Jan got a group together for a game of Killer and I got another pint and went and sat with Rod and Roz, and Aunty Mary and Uncle Brian, at a table close to where Les was still sitting at the bar. I raised my glass and took a drink. They all picked up theirs and returned the toast.

Rod had a business contact in Oldham and knew the town, and Brian was into his motorbikes, so they had plenty to talk about, and Aunty Mary and Roz were chatting away.

'I think I can smell petrol,' I said, nodding towards Rod and Brian.

'Boys and their toys,' Roz said.

Mary was looking at Archie and Mum, having a quiet minute together in the far corner, laughing and smiling.

'I've never seen our Marjory so happy,' she said. 'They're so in love.' She took out a tissue and wiped her eyes. 'He's the best thing that's ever happened to her.'

There was a grunt from the direction of the bar, and we all

looked round. Les was facing our table with his eyes half-shut and was nodding drunkenly.

'Aye,' he said. 'Aye, you're right there.' He put his finger to his lips and shook his head. 'Shhh, shhh,' he said, and turned away and picked up his drink.

There was a long silence. The five of us exchanged glances.

'How's that painting coming along?' Roz asked, finally.

'Nearly done,' I replied.

'Ooh, what's the painting of, John, love?' Mary asked.

'A pair of golden eagles, Mary, fighting.'

'I'd love to see that—'

Roz laughed. 'Take no notice of him, Mary. He's having you on.'

'No, it's of a garden, Mary, full of flowers.'

'Well, it sounds lovely, anyway, John,' she said. 'He's a good artist, you know, Roz.'

'Oh, I know that Mary. That's why we gave him the commission.'

Mary's eyes widened and she puckered her lips. She looked at me.

'Ooh,' she said. 'A commission. Get you.'

I barely knew Aunty Mary and Uncle Brian and had no idea what a double-act they were. I hadn't seen them for about fifteen years, since they'd come to take Mum to stay with them in Oldham. I hadn't seen my cousins, Derek and Beryl, for much longer, since the days when we had a car.

'How are Derek and Beryl?' I asked.

'They're grand,' she said. 'Derek has a decent job at the bank, but he still lives with us. We hardly ever see him. We see more of our Beryl. Derek sits away in his bedroom. We think he might be a bit …' she gave me a Larry Grayson flap of the wrist and mouthed the word silently, '*gay* … don't we Brian?'

'What's that, love?'

'Our Derek. We think he might be a bit …' and she did it again.

Brian puffed out his cheeks. 'Bloody hell aye, just a bit.'

'Not that we mind. We don't, do we Brian?'

'Mind? Christ, no. We've enough bloody grandkids.' He turned to me. 'Hey, he didn't, you know, did he? When you used to top-and-tail with him at our house—'

Mary picked up a beer mat and threw it at him like a frisbee, but it spun away and hit Rod in the chest. 'I'm sorry, Rod, it was meant for that horrible sod.' She glared at Brian. 'They were bloody six years old—'

'I know, bloody hell, I was only joking—'

'I'll give you bloody joking.'

Rod was laughing behind his hand. Brian carried on where he'd left off.

'So, Rod, as I was saying, I have an old Triumph Tiger Cub, and a 750 Kwaka,' he said.

'Not the widow-maker?'

'Not so loud, Rod, eh.' He glanced at Mary.

'I heard,' she said. 'I couldn't care less. I might even buy you another in case yours breaks down.' She turned her attention back to our end of the table.

'I don't know what I ever saw in him. Anyway, yes, so, that's Derek, and as for our Beryl, she's only happy when she's changing nappies. Like the proverbial pig in shit she is.'

'How many kids has she got?' I asked.

'Five and counting,' she said. 'Her sixth is due in February.'

'A bloody volleyball team,' Brian chipped in. 'It'll be a bloody football team by the time she's finished.'

'Well, they can afford it. He's got a good job has Warren—'

Brian started laughing. 'Aye, Warren, eh, bloody hell, you couldn't make it up, could you? They're *like* bloody rabbits.'

Mary ignored him. 'She landed on her feet there, did Beryl.'

'What does he do?'

'I don't know, exactly. He did say, but it went over my head.' She looked at Brian. 'What is it he does, Brian?'

'Who, love?'

'Our Brenda's Warren.'

'Oh, Christ, you've got me now. He's something to do with leisure centres, travels about a lot.'

'That's it, aye, leisure centres, swimming baths. Very sporty he is. Patience of a saint, too. Mind you, just as well.'

We had another couple of drinks, and people came and went to the table. Mary and Brian kept us all entertained, and the next thing I knew it was time to go. Mary stood and took her coat from the back of her seat and started to put it on. She looked at Brian, still deep in conversation with Rod. Brian looked up.

'Where are you going?'

'Not me, us.'

'We're not going yet are we?'

'Yes, we are, so sup up you big lummox.'

'Me and Rod are having a crack here—'

'You can carry it on back at the house, that's if Rod hasn't had enough of you yet.'

The barman came to clear the empties from our table.

'Come on, Brian,' Mary said. 'The staff have to get the place cleaned up. The pub opens in half an hour. The regulars don't want to see your ugly mug.'

I got up and was surprised to see that, apart from the five at our table, there was only Jan left. She had her coat on and was ready to leave. I asked her where Mum and Archie had gone.

'They've gone to get the house warmed up.'

'And Les?'

She screwed up her face. 'He's not coming back to the house, thank god. He's staying at the Bright Lights Grand. He's outside waiting for his taxi.'

I still had half a pint left so I told her to go with the rest.

'Are you ok?' she asked. 'You seem a bit … you don't seem right.'

'I'm fine,' I said. I held up my glass. 'I'll put a quid in the bandit and finish this, and I'll see you all back at the house.'

* * *

Outside the registry office that morning, when he'd felt duty bound to swallow whatever it was he'd wanted to say, I made a mental note to confront Les Beech when I got the chance. He obviously had an opinion about my father and had been told to keep it to himself.

I knew it wasn't the best idea I'd ever had. It was Mum's wedding day and we'd be having a lot to drink, and as the day went on I gradually talked myself out of it. Why should I be bothered what Les Beech thought. So, his opinion of my father was the same as everyone else's. So what. That was no surprise. I had no rose-tinted glasses as far as that went.

Even after I'd heard their conversation, and read the notes, I still managed to put it to the back of my mind and enjoy myself.

But then, true to form, the more I had to drink, the more I started to obsess.

'I'll bet you couldn't resist a dig at you-know-who'

You know who.

'wondered if FW got a national dis-service medal'

National *dis* service …

It wasn't just a dig at Archie's predecessor. Les obviously disliked my father, and it seemed to go back a long way. I had to know.

I left the bar and walked into the foyer. I looked at the front-door. I was as close to it as I was to him. I could have just left. I could have walked straight past him and out the door. I'd managed to drink for about five hours solid without fucking anything up. Now, here I was, about to risk it all.

I looked at his huge frame, like late-career Orson Welles, filling one of the armchairs. I walked over and sat in the other chair. His eyes were almost closed and he looked like he might be nodding off. Then they sprang open and he seemed surprised by where he found himself. He looked at me and strained to focus.

'Young mister Woods,' he said, finally. 'What can I do for you?'

He was still pissed, bleary-eyed and slurring. I took the dog-eared papers from my pocket and held them up for him to see. He looked confused at first, then had a moment of recognition and checked both of his side pockets. He held out his hand and snapped his fingers.

I kept hold of the papers. 'You can tell me what it was you were itching to say to me this morning. About my father.'

'It was nothing. I never particularly liked him, that's all.'

'Nobody did. So what?'

I thought he was going to ignore me, then he turned, with a great effort, and amid much creaking of wood and squeaking of leather, until he was facing me head-on.

'None of this will help anyone—'

'It'll help me.'

'It'll just cause ructions—'

'For who?'

'Me and Archie, Archie and you, you and your mother—'

'Nothing you could tell me would surprise me—'

'I'd hate to prove you wrong, son. Anyway, I gave my word—'

'Who to?'

'To Archie—'

'Why did Archie think you'd mention my father in your speech?'

'There was never going to be a speech.' He nodded at the papers in my hand. 'I thought I may be able to talk him into it, so I came prepared. Archie told me I wasn't to bring Frank Woods up at all, even in conversation—'

'Why would you, anyway? I don't understand. This was their day, so why bring him up at all? And why did he make you give your word?'

'On the rare occasions that we spoke, Archie always referred to your mother by her maiden name, as Marjory Finch, so I'd never made the connection. It was only when we spoke on the phone the other day that he mentioned who her previous husband had been, and I told him—'

'But why was that such a big deal to you?'

'I never liked the man—'

'Neither did I—'

'Then let it go, son, think of your mother—'

'You told him what?'

'I beg your pardon?'

'You said you told Archie, told him what?'

'Forget about it son, you don't want to know—'

'Yes I do.' I showed him the papers again. 'I could just go home now and show them this, say that you've told me everything, the minute you got me alone, that you couldn't wait. It'll come out, then, whatever it is—'

'You need to think long and hard before you do anything—'

I opened the papers. 'So just tell me. What does that mean? A national *dis*-service medal?'

He stared at the middle distance, seemed to be weighing his options.

'Just tell me what you told Archie,' I said. 'I'm assuming Mum doesn't know either?'

'Certainly not, and she mustn't find out.'

'I won't tell her—'

'If she thinks for a minute that Archie knew all along, she'll never forgive him. Or him me. And neither of them will forgive you. Think about that.'

'Ok,' I said. I'll go and tell them we had a chat—'

A bloke in his shirtsleeves came in from outside.

'Taxi for Beech?'

'I'll be with you in a few minutes, lad, when I'm finished here.'

He gave Les the thumbs-up. 'I've another fare—'

'You'll be there on time, or I'll make it good. You'll not be down.' Les waved him away in the manner of a Roman emperor. The driver left, and Les started to get up but the chair seemed to be pulling him back down. He held out his hand. 'Help me out of this damned thing, will you.'

He took my hand and I managed to heave him out of the chair, and we stood, eye to eye, locked in a handshake. With his free hand, he lifted the medal pinned to his chest.

'You see this, son?'

I nodded.

'Have you ever seen one before?'

'I don't think so.'

'It's a National Service Medal. Everyone got one who completed their national service.'

'There must have been one in the house somewh—'

He was shaking his head. 'No, son, your father didn't have one.'

'But he did national service—'

He started to nod. 'He was conscripted, yes, early in nineteen forty-nine, and he did spend a short time at Oswestry, where a great many of us did our basic training.'

We were still joined at the fist, and he nodded at the armchair.

'You better sit down, lad.'

I did as I was told, and he perched one buttock on the broad arm of the chair. I had no idea what was coming. I braced myself.

'Your father didn't finish his eighteen-months, son. He was there for less than two weeks, actually. I know this, because I was there.'

'That can't be right,' I said.

I tried to free my hand from his, but he gripped it tighter.

'Did he ever talk about it? His national service?'

I was certain that he had. 'Of course he did,' I said.

He raised his eyebrows. I tried to remember any instances, any stories or anecdotes that he'd told me over the years, but I couldn't think of any. Not a one. Nothing. I realised that I'd never heard him say anything, except that a couple of years in the army would do them good, anybody, everybody; skinheads, bikers, hippies, the unemployed, gays, me, anyone, basically, who was different in any way, or who disagreed with him.

He was still gripping my hand. He swallowed hard and looked into the distance. I watched as he mulled something over. He seemed to settle an internal debate, then looked back at me.

'Your dad didn't take to the army, son—'

'Didn't take to it how?'

'It's not for everyone—'

'What happened?

'There was a lot of horseplay—'

'Horseplay?'

'Tomfoolery. In the training camps—'

'What do you mean by tomfoolery?'

'You know, high jinks—'

'Bullying?'

'You might call it that, yes. Most men can take it—'

'But he couldn't?'

'No. No, he couldn't—'

'What happened? What did he do?' My mind was racing. Had he deserted? Gone AWOL? Had some sort of breakdown?

He still had my hand in his. He held it tighter, gripped my elbow with his other hand and looked me in the eye.

'He tried to take his own life, son.'

* * *

I didn't know how to feel. I knew I should probably have been upset, angry, too, but I wasn't. Instead I felt a strange calm.

The taxi driver appeared again in the doorway. Les glanced up at him. 'Sorry, lad. Go and do your other fare, and come back for me. I'll pay the extra, don't worry.'

Les got another thumbs up and the driver disappeared again.

Les looked at me. 'Are you alright, son?'

I nodded. 'How did he do it?'

'Are you sure you want to know?'

I nodded again. 'I'm sure.'

'He tried to hang himself. In the latrines.'

I bowed my head. I was still perfectly calm, but tears began to fall, like rain from a clear sky, into my lap.

'He couldn't even get that right,' I said.

'Bloody chain snapped,' he said, and smiled. 'Lucky for you, eh?'

I tried to smile back. 'I suppose,' I said. 'Did he get done?'

'Done? How do you mean?'

I dragged my forearm across my eyes. 'I thought getting depressed and trying to kill yourself was a crime,' I said. 'You know, back in the good old days.'

'Oh, yes. Yes, it was,' he said. 'But it was an embarrassment to the military. It was common, and cast a rather dark cloud, so they denied it ever happened, and conscripts who tried to commit suicide weren't prosecuted. Some they owned up to, the ones they couldn't hide, but most were recorded as accidental deaths. The rest of us were even told not to mention any suicides in our letters home.'

'So what happened to him? Afterwards, I mean.'

'I expect he'll have been sent to a sanatorium, a convalescent home somewhere, Kent, maybe, or the east coast. I don't really know.'

He let go of my hand and put his on my shoulder.

'I don't want to harp on, but you need to believe me when I say that Archie knew nothing of this until last week. I didn't think I was telling tales out of school. I assumed he'd already know, but it turns out Frank had never seen fit to tell your mother. She's always believed he was in Malaya, or Singapore.'

'Maybe she knew but—'

'No. Her and Archie have no secrets. Until now, anyway. Me and my big trap. I've been kicking myself since. He's as straight as a die is our Archie. He can't stand the thought of knowing something like that and keeping it from your mother. It doesn't sit right. I told him. "If Frank didn't tell her," I said, "then why should you?" He saw sense in the end. Sleeping dogs and all that.'

'So why was it in your speech?'

'It was just me having my own private … well, I'm sorry. About the remark. It was crass, but it was never going to be read out.'

The notes were still in my hand. I held them out, and he took the damp sheets and put them in his pocket.

'I thought all along, since he said you were Frank's son, that you ought to be told,' he said. 'I believe a man deserves to know where he's from, if you get my meaning, for better or worse, so that he can … so that he can keep an eye on himself and, well, you know … see where he might be going wrong, and make any … any adjustments.' He stood and started to fasten his coat. 'For that reason, if no other, I'm glad we had this chat.'

'Me too,' I said. 'I think.'

He looked at me. 'Yes, well, I just hope I don't come to regret it.'

'You won't,' I said.

'You know, I should probably say that, Archie and myself … our father … well, let's just say that national service was a godsend for the two of us.'

The taxi driver appeared again in the doorway, looked at his watch, and gave Les a quizzical look.

'I'll be with you right now, young man.'

He started to follow the driver out through the door, then turned back to me.

'I enjoyed my time in the army, son. I would have made a career of it had I not made other plans, but I never did agree with national service. Nobody should be forced into the army. It was a distraction for the career soldiers, too, and the officers, you know, side-lined from their proper duties. They resented it, and they took it out on the poor buggers who didn't want to be there. If they saw a weakness, they worked on it.' He paused, briefly, seemed to be collecting his thoughts. 'No,' he said, finally. 'What happened at Oswestry had no bearing on how I felt about Frank Woods. Like I said earlier, I just didn't like him, that's all. I know I'm telling you nothing you didn't already know, but he was an arrogant sod, your father. Always playing the big I am.'

EPILOGUE

Thursday 6th of November 1986

There'd been a storm in the night that delayed the dawn and when first light finally arrived the rain was still teeming. It seemed to be set for the long-term and I'd resigned myself to a cheerless day, indoors at Primrose Terrace, nursing a hangover and trying to make sense of my newfound knowledge.

Something had come back to me during the night, something my father said one day a long time ago, about Archie, and his brother being called Lesley and it being a girl's name, and him not being able to hack it in the army.

I hadn't thought anything of it at the time; I hadn't even met Archie then, never mind his brother, but now I'd met him I had no doubt that Les was telling the truth about my father, that he *had* tried to take his own life, that it was *him* who couldn't take the military life, and that he'd been deflecting, all those years ago, when he said what he said about Les.

I just believed him, instinctively, every word. For all his faults, Les came across as a genuine bloke – a gobshite, yes, but a genuine, no-nonsense gobshite.

I'd been mulling it over for most of the night, listening to the thunder and the rain, watching the lightning flashes beyond the curtains, and as I mulled, the anger and the upset finally came, and I wept quietly, thinking about what had happened all those years ago at Oswestry, the effect it had had on the rest of his life, and on our family, and my frustration that, with him gone, there was no way of ever putting things right.

I left Jan snoring softly in the dark and got up and went to the kitchen. I took painkillers and made a coffee and went to the living-room and opened the curtains. I sat at the table in the front window and stared at the rain streaming down the glass.

I'd been torturing myself for another hour when Jan appeared in the doorway. Her hair was all over the place and she'd slept in her make-up. She looked like a peroxide Siouxsie Sue. She tied the belt of her dressing gown, folded her arms, and yawned massively as she shuffled towards me in her huge, fluffy slippers, effortlessly comical, as always, no matter what the circumstances.

I opened my arms as she turned and sat on my lap. She pulled my head into her chest.

'You ok? she asked.

'I'm alright,' I said. 'Do you remember what I told you?'

She pulled my head away gently by the hair, leaned back and looked me in the eye.

'Of course I do,' she replied. 'I wasn't drunk.'

I burst out laughing.

'I wasn't,' she scoffed. 'Unlike someone I could mention.'

I settled my head back on her chest and we held each other for a long time and listened to the rain.

'Do you believe him?' she asked, eventually. 'Les? The stuff he said?'

'Oh yeah, definitely,' I replied. 'I've been thinking about it all night and it all makes sense somehow. I don't know, it just does.'

I picked up the skins and the baccy from the table but Jan

took them off me.

'I'll roll you one,' she said, and moved to the adjacent chair and started sticking the papers together.

'I've tried to imagine it,' I said. 'You know, being forced to join the army as soon as you turn eighteen. Plucked from your life and thrown in with a bunch of total strangers for eighteen-months, half of them fucking head-cases, and those in charge worse still. Eighteen,' I said, again, incredulous. 'When I think what I was doing at eighteen.'

Jan pulled a face and rolled her eyes. 'You and Lenny were probably shagging little miss posh.'

More laughter. 'No,' I said, 'that was later.'

She finished rolling the spliff and turned it around and put it in my mouth.

'You don't mind that I told you about all that stuff with April, do you?' I asked.

'Course not,' she replied, 'I love it that we don't have any secrets. It's healthy as long as I'm allowed to mention it now and then.'

'You are. It doesn't bother me at all,' I replied. 'And you're funny.'

She sparked the lighter and helped me light the spliff.

'How come you don't bring up *my* past escapades? she asked.

'It never crosses my mind.'

I had a few draws on the spliff and held it out but she raised her palm.

'Not for me, ta,' she said.

'You sure?' I asked.

'Positive,' she replied.

I shrugged, carried on.

'Anyway,' I said. 'This national service business. At eighteen me and Lenny were kids, out looking for birds' nests most of the time, smoking a bit of weed, going to the reserve, going to gigs. I'd just passed my test and got my first car … I can't imagine it. Some people enjoyed national service. Les said him and Archie loved it, said they were glad to get away from home. I'm not sure I wouldn't have ended up like my Dad. Les said he was bullied, my Dad, I mean. It's hard to imagine your dad being picked on … adult bullies … fucking hell.'

'But they weren't adults, were they, not really.'

'The fucking officers were.'

'Yeah, well, they've no excuse, but the *conscripts* I'm talking about. A lot of eighteen year olds these days are still at school or at college.'

The rain had stopped and the window was steamed up. I leaned across and cleared it with my forearm. A blue tit flitted from the feeder above the window and was immediately replaced by a great tit. We watched it feed.

'Didn't he succeed in the end, anyway?' I said.

'How do you mean?'

'My Dad. Didn't he succeed? In the long-run?'

'I'm not with you.'

'Well, you know, tries to commit suicide when he's eighteen, fucks it up, and spends the next thirty-five years finishing the job. Every cigarette, every pint, every whisky, every rum chaser, every fucking scowl, every outburst, a lifetime of negativity, anger, bitterness. Wasn't he was just playing the long game?'

'I'm not sure it's what he intended—'

'I know, I know that, I'm not saying it was a conscious thing, but … well, you know, I doubt you ever get over something like that, especially at that age. I think from that day till the day he died, he was just killing time.'

'I don't know about that, but I do know it's good to hear you call him your dad. It's better than what you used to call him. I never liked that.'

We fell silent again for a while. I finished the spliff, put it out and sat and stared out of the window.

'Are you going to tell your Mum?' Jan asked.

'No, am I fuck. I can't tell her.'

'You said last night you were going to, that's all.'

'I didn't, did I? Fucking hell, I must have been pissed. No, I mustn't ever tell her. Give me a fucking slap if I ever say that again. That's Archie's call, not mine.' I shuddered and put my hand over my face. 'Fucking hell,' I said. 'What a tool.'

Jan stood and stretched. I felt her hand, warm on the back of my neck. 'Come on,' she said. 'You go and get a quick shower and I'll make us some breakfast. I know you're itching to see what Rod's done to the footpath.'

* * *

We finished breakfast and sat talking for an hour or more and it was almost two o'clock when I hung my binoculars around my neck and left the house. The day had gradually faired and now, back-lit by the late-autumn sun, the sky had the look of molten lead.

For the past couple of weeks the lane had been out of bounds, blocked off at both ends by heavy vehicles, and I'd had to listen from afar to the sound of chainsaws and watch smoke drift across the sand quarry and birch wood and taint the horizon, as the job of widening the lane between Hawksheads House and Yelland was completed.

This was the day of reckoning, and I'd been dreading it. I'd been using the footpath for as long as I could remember.

The undergrowth and shrubs that lined the edges were rich in wildlife – bees and butterflies, shrews, voles and stoats – and a wide variety of birds built their nests there.

Rod had promised to do as little damage as possible, but I couldn't see how he could achieve his aims without complete devastation.

I walked past the Post Office, down the ginnel, and made my way to the bottom lane, to the dead end where it becomes the car park for the Eagle and Child.

Across the park a raucous gang of rooks and jackdaws was seeing off a buzzard, its broad wings beating laboriously as it struggled to gain height in the cool air.

The buzzard soon gave up and managed an ungainly landing in a low tree branch. The corvids gave it a victory fly-by then veered off towards the churchyard, mocking as they went, with their harsh caws and metallic chacking.

I entered the lane by the first of the new kissing-gates outside the Eagle and Child.

I stopped under the railway bridge for a few seconds, shouted as loud as my lingering hangover would allow – 'JOHN!' I shouted. 'JAN! LENNY!' spitting the sounds so as not to interfere with the reverberations, and I counted, just like we used to. Six echoes, like aural skimming-stones.

I emerged from under the bridge and followed the lane towards Hawksheads Wood. Even from this distance I could smell charcoal, and as I got close to the point where the lane had previously narrowed to a footpath my heart was in my mouth.

At first, I was pleasantly surprised. The right-hand side had barely been touched. In fact, it hardly looked any different. A little bit tidier, yes, trimmed back here and there, and I could see the wall in places, which hadn't been the case before, but he seemed to have preserved most of the plant life.

But I knew not to get my hopes up – he was turning it from a footpath about a metre wide, to something that could accommodate a small lorry – so as I neared the sharp left turn up ahead I prepared myself for a shock.

Sure enough, the other side had been completely cleared. Everything had been ripped out and burned, and I found myself face to face with the original dry-stone wall, the one I'd always known must be there – there had to be something between that mountain-range of brambles and the field – but had never seen.

I stood, stock-still, and stared. Where, a few months ago, there'd been an enormous expanse of rosebay willow-herb, a proliferation of spindly pink pagodas stretching as far as the eye could see, now there was nothing. The brambles and nettles, bracken, foxgloves, dog-roses, elder, the buddleia, were all completely gone. All that remained was the handful of hawthorn and blackthorn bushes that grew closest to the wall.

After the clearance, the ground had been bulldozed to remove all the roots, and I could see shiny patches of limestone where the teeth of the digger had scraped the bedrock. There was a strong smell of earth and sap.

I walked on.

A hundred yards further along, a stretch of the 'new' wall, maybe thirty-feet long, bellied slightly outwards and the lane was wider. Here were the remains of the fire, the scorched earth, where a huge amount of trees, bushes, and undergrowth, and no doubt a large number of small animals, had been burned alive.

I stood for a long while by this miniature wasteland. There

was total silence. Nothing stirred, no birds, no mammals, not even an insect. I imagined this was the kind of silence that followed a nuclear explosion.

The warmth was still rising from the ground. I was sure I could feel it on my face. I looked ahead, beyond ground zero, at the newly-revealed wall stretching all the way to the kissing-gate by Hawksheads House.

I walked on.

I was taken by the wonderful array of lichens, the subtle splashes of colour – mustards, rusty-reds, pale blues and greens, some almost turquoise or aquamarine, that covered large sections of the wall.

A shrew squeaked close-by. I heard geese overhead, looked up to see two large, overlapping skeins travelling south.

I walked on.

A charm of goldfinches, twenty or thirty strong, hung in the air above the lane, twittered noisily for a few moments, then moved on across the field.

I walked on.

A weasel, its head thrown back, pranced like a tiny dressage-horse across the lane, a slow worm hanging limply from its jaws.

Small groups of starlings passed overhead on their way to join the enormous murmuration that would soon be performing a natural miracle over the reedbeds of the reserve for the lucky few there to see it.

I walked on.

Thirty-yards and the lane entered the woods. Squirrels seemed to be everywhere; on the path, the wall, in the trees and in the leaf-litter, busily preparing for winter.

A nuthatch prised a grub from the loose bark of a nearby ash, its restless whit-whit … whit … whit-whit-whit, resonating through the cool air.

A family of Jays scrarked in the distance.

A treecreeper landed low on the trunk of a silver birch and spiralled its way up to eye-level before dropping to the base of the next and starting again.

Behind me, a bullfinch piped insipidly. I turned and glimpsed two white rumps disappearing between the tree trunks.

A green woodpecker yaffled somewhere deep in the woods.

I heard the call of a hawfinch, just once, a few puny notes, like distant feedback, and I stood and scanned the high canopy for a minute, looking in vain for the elusive bird whose bill can crack cherry stones.

I walked on.

Through the kissing-gate. Four vans were parked on the car park; electricians, plumbers, plasterers, and I could hear distant voices coming from the courtyard.

I carried on to the gatehouse and went inside. I'd finished the commission and it was still on the easel. I'd told Roz it wasn't quite ready yet – I didn't want her to collect it until the plants had gone.

The final crop was a week from harvest. Soon I'd be able to start my new venture. I raised the lights one last time, quickly updated the journal, and set off back along the lane, retracing my steps past Hawksheads House, through the last of the kissing-gates and into the sand quarry.

In the quarry-bottom, the pool was hidden by a screen of tall grasses and iris leaves. A few gorse bushes had managed to sink their roots in the sandy earth and render the old Ford Anglia totally invisible behind their spiky green branches and yellow winter flowers.

I crossed the weighbridge and entered the office. The remains of the blackbird nest were on the floor, and on the windowsill the faint outline of a circle where it had been. I remembered the twins' laughter, the nest flying over my head, the chicks chirping helplessly on the rough ground. I could still picture the glee on the twin's face as he trod them into the dust, and recall the anger I felt, anger the likes of which I have never felt since.

The sky had cleared and the sun was low in the sky when I circled the quarry and made my way to the top of the sand cliff. I took up my favourite position, legs hanging over the edge, and looked at the pond, and the patches of rusting blue roof, barely visible now behind the surrounding reedbed.

The sky was darkening and there was a chill in the air. I put my hands in my armpits and shivered. I thought again about the wedding and my encounter with Les Beech.

How I wished I could talk to him now, my Dad. As I sat I began to remember things, things I'd long forgotten, the good times hiding behind the bad.

I remembered infants' school, him watching me play football and me holding his hair as I rode home on his shoulders.

I remembered wobbling along on my first bike, looking around to see that he'd let go and I was riding free, and him rubbing the pain from my grazed knee.

I remembered playing on the beach, fairground rides, going round and round on the cups and saucers and the carousel, crying because I was too young for the ghost train, and him ruffling my hair.

I remembered going to the pictures, the three of us, to see Greyfriars Bobby, The Incredible Journey, Flipper.

I didn't cry – there was no sobbing, no bawling or

convulsions – but I did shed tears, silent, long-overdue tears full of nostalgia and regret, that left me feeling liberated, cleansed, somehow, and I smiled as they rolled freely down my cheeks.

* * *

The low cloud had begun to clear and the watery sun was low in the sky when I heard them, just a couple at first, their high-pitched chi-zik, chi-zik calls, like static left over from the storm.

I looked but was blinded by the sky's silver glow. I closed my eyes, squeezed them shut, opened them again and raised my hand to shield them from the glare of the horizon, and when my vision returned, there they were, a dozen or more, tottering about on the sandy surface, tails wagging, calling constantly as they searched for the day's last morsels.

More were arriving by the minute, in pairs and small groups, like monochrome rags carried on the wind and dropped twittering to the ground to mingle with the growing throng.

Soon there were a hundred birds, a hundred and fifty, two hundred birds, two hundred tails see-sawing, and they continued to arrive, in ever-growing numbers, until the ground in front of the pond seemed to undulate.

I'd seen a pied wagtail roost before – the trees around the Bright Lights Library had been a favourite site for a few years, but only to maybe a hundred birds, attracted by the street lights and the extra one or two degrees of warmth in the town – but I'd never seen anything like this, and by the time the last few stragglers had arrived there must have been upwards of a thousand birds gathered on that small patch of land.

There was still a half hour until dark, and I watched them

for a while, but an ominous bank of black cloud was looming behind me and the threat of more heavy rain was growing. I didn't fancy getting soaked so I stood, sending the wagtails into the air like a cloud, their wingbeats like the riffle of pages, until they all dropped back to earth and were silent.

I started for home, skirting the quarry between the cliff and the gorse, and walked through the gate onto the lane. I passed the field where, all those years ago, having outrun the pursuing demons, I'd stopped to catch my breath. I remembered that night like it was yesterday, the unwelcome acid trip, poor Ibby and Clare, the madman.

I thought about Lenny, about April and the end of the frolics, and I thought about all that he'd been through since then. I hoped he'd call sometime soon, and had no doubt that he would, eventually. We'd be friends again, one day soon.

I thought about my new venture, too. I was champing at the bit, couldn't wait to get started, but all of that would have to wait – another story for another day. Right now I had bigger things to think about.

Earlier, when Jan had turned down the spliff, it was a first, and it got me thinking. I couldn't remember her having a smoke when we got back from the pub the night before, either. On top of that Jan normally drank vodka and orange, but all her drinks in the pub had been clear. I'd assumed she was drinking vodka and tonic, her second choice.

'I wasn't drunk,' she'd said this morning.

Another first.

And so it was that I set off for home with a spring in my step and the hangover long gone. The first thing I was going to do when I got home was book a table for two, in a quiet corner of the best restaurant in the Bright Lights, somewhere nice and cosy for Jan to spring her surprise.

I crossed the bottom lane and walked past the Eagle and Child and on towards the church. To my left, the sun sat low on the horizon, and straight ahead, revealed by the retreating black cloud, a perfect double-rainbow bathed the roofs of Primrose Terrace in a soft, spectral light.

THE END

Acknowledgements

To my wife, Patkinson, thank you for your unwavering faith in me, your belief in Wagtail, and your canny narrative suggestions; to Jake Hughes and Will Taylor, your contributions since 2019 – when I decided to finish what I'd started in 2006 – have been priceless.

And to the following people, your support and encouragement certainly helped get Wagtail over the line;

Sue Cottiss, Paul Edmondson, Gill Hughes, David Johnson, Reg Spanner, Jill Taylor, Ste Tyson, and Rachael Usher (for your patience with an ageing technophobe).

And to the late, great Al Marsland. Picking your brains was an absolute pleasure, my friend.

No professional proof-readers were inconvenienced in the production of this work. Any and all typos factual and timeline errors are entirely my own.

Ian Atkinson, Ulverston, December 2023

About the Author

Ian Atkinson was born in Morecambe, Lancashire in 1957. He left school with no qualifications aged 15 to take up an apprenticeship in engineering. Over the years his love of writing saw him enrol on creative writing courses at colleges around the country, wherever he happened to be working. Wagtail began in 2006 as a daily exercise – 500 words a day – and after a couple of months Part One was completed as a stand-alone short story. In 2020, with the onset of Covid 19, Ian returned to it and Wagtail was completed in August 2021.

Wagtail is the first in a series of novels and short-stories, all set in the Bright Lights, a name used by Ian's late mother, Noreen, to describe any town big enough to have a night club.

Ian lives with his wife Pat in Ulverston, Cumbria.

Printed in Dunstable, United Kingdom

74858148R00234